GHOST SINGER

GHOST
A NOVEL
SINGER

ANNA LEE WALTERS

UNIVERSITY OF NEW MEXICO PRESS
Albuquerque

ALSO BY ANNA LEE WALTERS:
The Sacred: Ways of Knowledge, Sources of Life
The Sun Is Not Merciful
The Spirit of Native America
Talking Indian: Reflections on Survival and Writing
Neon Pow Wow: New Native American Voices of the Southwest

Library of Congress Cataloging-in-Publication Data
Walters, Anna Lee, 1946–
  Ghost singer: a novel / by Anna Lee Walters.
  p.   cm.
  ISBN 0-8263-1545-3 (pbk.)
    1. Indians of North America—Fiction. I. Title.
PS3573.A472284G46   1994   94-5229
813´.54—dc20   CIP

Designed by Linda Mae Tratechaud

Although the Smithsonian Institution is a real place with collections of Native American artifacts, references to it in this book, including its collections and employees, are fictional. Any resemblance of characters to actual persons, living or dead, is purely coincidental.

Dedicated to all students who have ever attended
Navajo Community College . . .

CAST OF CHARACTERS

In order of appearance

RED LADY (b. 1809) daughter of White Sheep, great-grandmother to Jonnie Navajo, wife of Tall Navajo, mother of Tall Navajo's Son and twin daughters

WHITE SHEEP (b. 1751) father of Red Lady

TALL NAVAJO (b. 1800) great-grandfather to Jonnie Navajo, husband of Red Lady, father of Tall Navajo's Son and twin daughters

TALL NAVAJO'S SON (b. 1822) son of Red Lady and Tall Navajo, grandfather to Jonnie Navajo

DAVID DRAKE historian; brother of Jean Wurly

JEAN WURLY museum personnel, Washington, D.C.

NASBAH NAVAJO granddaughter of Jonnie Navajo

GEORGE DAYLIGHT AND RUSSELL TALLMAN tribal officials visiting Washington, D.C.

LECLAIR WILLIAMS deceased; friend of Wilbur and Anna Snake

JONNIE NAVAJO (b. 1889) son of Hosteen Diné, grandfather to Willie Begay and Nasbah Navajo

HOSTEEN DINÉ son of Tall Navajo's Son, father of Jonnie Navajo

HOSTEEN NEZ (b. 1862) brother of Hosteen Diné

WILLIE BEGAY grandson of Jonnie Navajo, cousin-brother to Nasbah Navajo

ROSA (b. 1868) mother of Anita (b. 1900)

MARIA (b. 1829) daughter of Red Lady, one of twins

GEOFFREY NEWSOME museum personnel, Washington, D.C.

DONALD EVANS museum personnel, Washington, D.C.

WILBUR AND ANNA SNAKE medicine people from Oklahoma

JUNIOR SNAKE AND ERLEEN son and daughter-in-law of Wilbur and Anna Snake

BETH WILLIAMS friend of Rosa

ELAINE MINTOR friend of Donald Evans

Come dress, my gallant souls,
a standing in a row
Kit Carson — he is waiting to march
against the foe.
At night we march to Moqui
o'er lofty hills of snow,
To meet and crush the savage foe
bold Johnny Navajo,
Johnny Navajo! O Johnny Navajo!

(New Mexican Volunteers Marching Song, 1863)

PREFACE

BEAUTIFUL MOUNTAIN
NAVAJO COUNTRY

A lone woman followed six goats into the aspen trees. A large white dog also followed them, ahead of the woman. The goats plodded over the trail, through the thousands of slender, white-barked trees rising up the highest part of the mountain.

As far as the woman could see, the aspens were thick. The goats disappeared into the trees. The forest of white trunks stretched upward, and far above her, silver-green leaves rustled in new summer. Beneath the waving leaves, she thought she heard something else, a muffled noise. A voice?

She stopped momentarily to look around. Her head tilted to hear any small or unusual sound that the trees muffled. Her body tensed, and she strained to hear. Her eyes and stance were on guard as she studied the rustling, silver-green forest. The afternoon sky was not fully visible. It existed in floating patches of blue amid the waving leaves overhead. The goats, knowing well the trail back to their corral, moved out of sight. Gnats flew around the woman's hair and ears, and she brushed at them through the cool air. The forest was dark and definitely cold in some places, although pools of filtered sunlight drifted down through the maze of trees. The woman took a few tenuous steps on the goat trail, cautious and tense over the possibility that strangers might be near. Her feet stopped beside a young spreading fern.

Red Lady was excruciatingly thin and much younger than she looked. Her woven black dress hung loosely over her shoulders and small frame, and was belted at the waist with a rope. Her hair was gathered at the back of her neck. It was quite long, but had been folded several times and wrapped with white yarn. The hem of her black dress ended just below her knees. Buckskin wound down and around her legs to the hard-sole moccasins she wore. The dress had faded in places to a spotty brown. Except for a thin border, a terraced design woven in an uneven orange-brown dye along the hem of the dress, Red Lady was undecorated.

The chirping of birds was all she heard. No other sound mingled with the leaves rustling above. Nor were there any unusual signs of strangers nearby. She let out a long sigh. The tenseness escaped from her small body with the sigh, and at once her face grew more youthful. She walked on, following the goat trail that led deep through the aspen forest. She walked for nearly a mile before she came to White Sheep's camp.

Six men rode six mules. One of them led four more animals by long, worn, leather straps. Three of the men were very fair. The darkest of the others looked like a mixed blood and was possibly part Indian himself. At this moment the men were silent as their mules began the ascent up the mountain. They had been riding in a southwesterly direction since dawn, straight for the mountainside and the Navajo camps hidden there. Now and then one of the group lifted his eyes from the sandy landscape to the green aspens on the side of the mountain a few miles ahead, an elevation a few hundred feet higher than the level on which they rode.

In the afternoon, the men dismounted to eat cold meat and tortillas under a lone cottonwood tree. They were quiet in this alien desert and now carefully studied one another. Two were middle-aged, and short and bloated by overweight. They looked alike and were actually brothers a year apart in age. They had separated themselves from the others, who sat and lay around the dry wash, nervously eyeing the surrounding terrain.

In the other group were three very fair-skinned men who talked to each other in low tones as they chewed the dry, rolled tortillas. They were also brothers, and very young, possibly approaching their twenties. The odd man in the group had black, shoulder-length hair, black eyes, and a mustache. He wore moccasins, but was otherwise dressed the same as the other men.

After the men ate, they stood and rubbed their backs and buttocks before climbing onto the mules again. The man with the mustache led his mule to the front of the group. He lifted his hand and pointed up the mountain to the grove of aspens. "Not too much longer," he said. The men behind him intently surveyed the aspen forest far above them. Then the small caravan of slave-hunters climbed onto their mules to continue their journey. Their destination was now very close. Three of them, the dark man and the aging brothers, had been here before, had been here several times before. They knew exactly where they were going.

Red Lady approached the clearing on the other side of the aspen grove. The goats were in the corral. She didn't bother to lift and place the logs that would confine them. They wandered about the rest of the day.

Camp consisted of the goat corral and a summer shelter. The shelter had a roof and four walls of aspen logs that ran up and down. The walls were entirely covered with oak boughs. In the east wall was the entrance.

Red Lady entered. The breezy shelter held spots of bright light and darker shadow. At the south end of the shelter, an old man sat on goatskins. He held a squirming a child about a year old. The child, a girl, wore a large, loose shirt. Not far from the old man, a cradleboard rested in a pool of sunlight, leaning against a log beam that supported the shelter's walls. Another child identical to the one squirming in his arms peered out of the cradleboard at the old man. When Red Lady entered, the child in the cradleboard looked at her and smiled. Red Lady went to the old man and took the child from his arms. The old man pushed himself up and went outside.

In the center of the shelter was a fireplace built of mud and sandstone. Red Lady carried the wriggling baby to the fireplace and stirred the charcoal. She built a small fire and poured water, carried from the lake beyond the aspens, into the blackened pot sitting in the ashes, and made a mush of corn meal and water. She fed this to the child she still held. When the child was full, she laid her down on goatskins. The baby promptly closed her eyes and slept. Then Red Lady unlaced the second child from the cradleboard, fed it the mush, and laid it down beside the other one. As soon as the second baby closed her eyes, Red Lady went outside and looked around. The old man was not in sight.

A narrow footpath led to a sunken sweathouse nearly five hundred feet away. The sweathouse was nearly invisible to the sharpest eye. The old man sat just behind it on the trunk of a fallen aspen. He brushed at large black ants crawling from one end of the decaying tree to the other. At his side sat a boy about thirteen or fourteen years old. The old man and the boy were laughing. The youth looked at Red Lady as she approached.

"My mother," the boy asked, "how long will it be before my father returns?" The boy bore a striking resemblance to the woman. His long hair was tied in the same fashion as hers. Under loose-fitting trousers, his body was very lean, his face gaunt. He wore no shirt. His shoulders were broad, but the bones under the skin were clearly discernible. He stood the same height as his mother.

The woman answered, "Soon. Soon. He should have come back from *Tséyi* by now. Maybe today or tomorrow." She looked off toward the shelter and then toward the trail the boy's father had taken to visit his relatives when he'd left her alone with the boy and the old man, who was Red Lady's father. Although the boy's father was overdue, the woman kept her face clear of the thoughts that had been creeping through her mind.

"We will go check the corn," she said to her son. "The babies are asleep," she said to the old man.

As Red Lady and her son disappeared into the aspens, the old man rose, brushed the ants off himself, and went to gather mountain tobacco. He was dressed like his grandson, except that he wore a faded shirt.

He gathered tobacco for a few minutes, then remembering the babies, he walked leisurely toward the shelter. Camp was quiet and the day was very pleasant. Goats nibbled at tender vegetation sprouting around the corral, but they stopped to watch the old man go into the shelter. The baby girls slept soundly. The old man shook out two goatskins, spread them beside the babies, and lay down too. His long white hair, tied in the back, was loose, and the knot holding his hair together hung beneath his shoulders. He pulled his hair to one side so he could lie flat on his back. He closed his eyes and in a few minutes snored loudly.

Red Lady and her son walked down to their cornfield. It was in a clearing beside the spruce and aspen forest at a lower level on the mountainside. It took several minutes to walk the distance. As they came out of the thick aspen grove where their camp was located, the aspens thinned and spruce trees were dominant. From a nearby overlook they could see the mountainside and the earth lying below them in pastel stripes. The earth's edge stretched upward to meet the sky. They decided to go to the overlook.

They saw jagged rock several miles away, which protruded from the earth in many places and rose to heights of several hundred feet. They saw "the winged rock" and "the speckled rock." Beyond these landmarks were faint mountains in the northeast still covered with snow, and one of these was Big Sheep Mountain, *Dibé Nitsaa*, the people's sacred mountain of the north. Due north of the overlook were other mountains of their enemies, the Utes. They'd been enemies since the days before the people came to this place—Beautiful Mountain, as they called it.

Standing together, the woman and the boy surveyed the mesas in the distance and the base of the mountain below. They stood quietly as they had learned to do, listening for distant voices and studying each level of the mountainside meticulously. The scene was quiet and peaceful, without a hint of a stranger in sight. After they had stood at the overlook for a few minutes, Red Lady motioned for her son to follow, and they went on to the cornfield.

Tiny green leaves had sprouted in the rich, black lava soil, and now lifted off the ground. However, the woman was unable to think of corn. Her mind was on the boy's father, *Diné Nez* (Tall Navajo). Surely he should have returned by now.

The woman and the boy opened the ditches to divert water from a spring to the rows of corn. Rain usually came to the mountain every day, but when it was sparse, the woman, the boy, and Diné Nez watered the corn from the spring where water seeped out of the mountainside. When the last plant had water trickling around it, they closed the ditches with crude hoes, and started for camp.

Approaching the camp shelter, they found two visitors waiting, although there were three horses tied along the edge of the aspen grove. The visitors were a young man and an old man. The older man was called Thin Man, and the younger, Thin Man's Son. When Red Lady and the boy entered the shelter, the visitors greeted them and then continued to talk to Red Lady's father, White Sheep. They explained that they'd come after White Sheep so that he might sing over another of Thin Man's sons, who was very ill. White Sheep agreed to go with them.

Then Red Lady listened reluctantly as the visitors told of fearful strangers in the land. Thin Man spoke of a raid that had been made on a family near Wild Horse Canyon, which was a little distance north below the mountain. Red Lady looked thoughtfully at her children—the boy, called Tall Navajo's Son, and her infant twin daughters.

Thin Man added that in the Wild Horse Canyon raid, women had been left alone by their families and were stolen. An old woman and another in middle age were killed. A very young girl, about eight or nine, was carried off by the strangers. But along with the girl were her own two young aunts. This had occurred less than a month before.

And in *Tséyi*, it had happened again, but several families had suffered. A young boy, a toddler, was carried away with a married woman and her three children. The little boy and the woman were from different families. The toddler had been caught quite easily when he wandered off from the camp by himself. He was captured first. Later, the young boy's father and two other men caught up with the slave-hunters at the place where the woman and her children were captured. In the melee that broke out when the slave-hunters made their escape, the toddler's father and the woman's old mother were killed. The Navajos had managed to wound one of the enemies, but not seriously. There were three slave-hunters besides the wounded one. The woman with her old mother had been alone with the children. One of the woman's children was not even weaned. This, too, had occurred a little more than a month ago.

Red Lady refused to hear any more. She moved toward the door. The infants were awake and they crawled toward her. At the shelter entrance she paused. Thin Man's words rang in her ears. One of her babies was at her feet. She stooped over to pick up the baby and went outside.

Two days had passed, and dawn was near. A fire glowed in the shelter. Red Lady, Tall Navajo's Son, and White Sheep were awake. The babies slept under goatskins while Red Lady prepared the morning meal. Her son and the old man sat close to the fire, the orange flames coloring their faces. Tall Navajo's Son was restless and uneasy. He had not slept well. He had been pacing back and forth between the fire and the shelter entrance since early morning while his mother and grandfather still slept. The wood popped in the fireplace, and Tall Navajo's Son jumped at each popping sound. His mother noticed his uneasiness as soon as she awoke, as did White Sheep.

Finally, Tall Navajo's Son could not contain himself any longer and fled into the forest. It was still dark when he left. Several minutes passed, but he did not return.

He ran in the direction of the slowing rising sun, trying to clear his mind. He had dreamed a terrible, frightening thing. He would run from it if he could, but he was too intrigued by its meaning. He wanted to be alone, to think. His father had not returned. . . .

He found himself near the cornfield. He recognized two or three birds from their screams as he approached the cornfield clearing. A woodpecker flew over him. First, he looked at the corn, and then he went down to the lookout where he and his mother were two days earlier. By then the sun was a hand high over the curving horizon. The morning was cool and the mountains in the north were distant, although they appeared to be much closer than they actually were.

He did not mistake the sound of gunshots. One. Two. They were heard easily from where he was. The gunshots cracked from the direction of White Sheep's camp.

Tall Navajo's Son ran as fast as he could back to camp. It took only several minutes, but it took too long. He was sweaty, and his chest heaved. As he approached, he heard departing voices, perhaps three male speakers, and hooves breaking through the forest. The voices faded. Then very clearly he heard a baby cry, a dog growl, and the goats bleat over the baby's cry. Far off in the distance he recognized his mother's scream. She warned her unseen son, "Run, son, run! Get away!" But he couldn't tell exactly where her voice was in the aspen trees. Then Red Lady's screams stopped. The forest was silent. A noisy woodpecker was the only presence.

Camp was deadly quiet. The goats did not bleat, but two of them looked at Tall Navajo's Son curiously. He did not see all the goats and wondered why the slave-hunters hadn't taken them too. He had heard of slave-hunters taking sheep and goats whenever it was possible. He stood between the corral and the shelter.

Faint sounds came to his ears. They did not come from the goats. He entered the shelter. It was empty. The fire still glowed dully. Tall Navajo's Son strained to listen again. "Grandfather," he said very softly. The unidentified sounds came again. Tall Navajo's Son thought of the sweathouse.

On the path to the sweathouse, one of the missing goats met him. Then, just into the thick of the forest, he found White Sheep lying face-up on the ground. Gnats buzzed around him and large black ants crawled on him. Blood covered his face and body.

He felt White Sheep's body. Two places were torn open, one just under White Sheep's rib cage, and one above his right hip. Tall Navajo's Son wiped some of the blood off White Sheep. Then he gently lifted the old man's head to cradle it in his hands. He turned White Sheep's head from side to side. That was when he saw that White Sheep's left ear was entirely gone, along with part of his right.

Blood continued to ooze into Tall Navajo's Son's hands. He pulled one of them from underneath and let the warm blood trickle onto the ground. With his other, he lifted White Sheep's head completely off the ground. More blood dripped from the back of it. Tall Navajo's Son then understood; the slave-hunters had tried to take some of the old man's hair, as well as his ears.

Tall Navajo's Son cradled the old man in his arms for a long time. When the boy finally gave up hope and it seemed that death was certain, he laid the old man down. But then White Sheep opened his eyes and managed to turn to his grandson. In a hoarse whisper, White Sheep said, "Get the baby."

The boy was stunned. "What?" he asked.

White Sheep again whispered. "Get the baby. . . . I hid her in the sweathouse, under a black goatskin. . . ."

I

WASHINGTON, D.C.

AT 4:45 P.M. David Drake turned off the microfilm reader-printer. He slipped the microfilm reel carefully back into its box and took it to the archivist who had helped him for the last four days. By now the two had put aside some of the stiff formality of their new relationship, although not much.

"Dr. Withers," David said as he handed the microfilm reel to him, "I'll be returning in the morning about ten. If you'd be so kind as to keep this on your desk, I'll just pick it up here."

Withers replied, "No problem." Then he quickly turned his attention to another researcher behind David Drake.

David returned to the table with the reader-printer and collected his note pads, along with a half dozen pencils. At the door, the security guard, now familiar with the gangly Drake, pulled out David's leather briefcase from a dozen identical ones placed upright on a long shelf behind the security desk.

David picked a key from several dangling on a chain and unlocked his briefcase. When it opened, he placed his pencils and note pads inside and snapped the case shut again.

His summer jacket hung on a coat rack to the left of the security guard. David pulled the jacket off the hanger and draped it over his arm. Carrying his briefcase and jacket, he went out the door into the hallway to the elevator.

As he waited for the descending elevator, he checked his gold watch. In five minutes it would be five o'clock. He would probably be late. Jean would be angry. She had seemed on edge ever since his arrival on Sunday. Today was Thursday.

He walked at a brisk pace to his hotel in a light summer rain. He had chosen this particular hotel because it was the closest to the National Archives Building where he would be working. The walk there took about ten minutes. When he saw the four lanes of traffic all moving frantically in the same direction, he was glad that he was walking. The afternoon traffic moved in the opposite direction from the way it flowed in the morning.

Jean. He'd called her from the airport as soon as he'd stepped off the plane on Sunday evening. She'd said, "Dave? You're here already?" She'd acted unprepared for his arrival, although he'd written two weeks earlier telling her of his upcoming visit. He'd even followed that with a phone call, leaving a message at her office when he'd learned that she was out. David knew Jean's moods, and the tone of her voice on the phone Sunday had left him wondering if she were angry or pouting at him for dropping into D.C. like this. But he had come to work; a visit with Jean was incidental. Nevertheless, he felt that he had a right to call her. After all, she was his older sister.

On Tuesday, Jean had come to the National Archives Building, searching for him among the filing cabinets and wire screen partitions. He was struck by her strange appearance. Jean, the always-slightly-stout girl that he knew, had changed dramatically. She was actually skinny. Always pretty and conscious of her appearance in the past, she had come to see him this time without a trace of make-up. Her skin was sallow and blotchy. Her eyes were the same blue he remembered, but they were different, too, puffy and tired looking. Her shoulder-length brown hair was dirty and pushed carelessly behind her ears. He wondered how long it had been since she had combed her hair or changed her clothes. Her appearance was not at all in keeping with the Jean he knew. It was both appalling and instinctively disturbing.

Jean had forced a bland smile and embraced David loosely with her skinny arms. "Davie," she'd said over and over, "Davie." Not much else was said. He'd tried to talk to her, but their conversation was awkward.

"How are you?" he asked.

Jean answered, "Davie. I'm fine. As you can see." Then she turned quickly away to avoid his penetrating gaze.

With her back to him she asked, "How's Jill? The kids?"

Only now did David realize he had spent most of that visit talking to Jean's back. "Jill's great. We can't stop the kids from growing." He laughed, genuinely.

Jean ignored his good humor. "What brings you here?"

"My work," he answered, "endless research. I'm working on an Indian history."

She nodded her head. "Indian?" she asked. "American Indian, as if I don't already know?"

"American," he repeated.

She turned and faced him then, saying, "I guessed. This obsession you have with Indians will kill you someday, Davie." She had not been teasing.

David remembered trying a smile. "You once shared that 'obsession' with me when we were kids. Remember?"

"Davie. . .," she said.

David's smile faded. "Enough about me. I haven't heard from you since your divorce, Jean. That was over a year ago."

"Davie," she'd said. "The divorce was. . . . Well, it was the hardest thing I've ever done. I wanted time to get myself together. Do you understand?"

David remembered her sitting opposite him at the long table in the research room. They'd been alone. In the course of their conversation, she stared vacantly away from David, past David, and through him.

At one point she closed her eyes and said in a mumble, "Davie, I need time. I'll get it together. Time. That's all, Davie. Remember when we were kids, Davie? Playing cowboys and Indians all the time? Davie always wanted me to be the cowboy. Davie? Davie. . . ."

Her sentences had broken in places. When she'd opened her eyes, there was surprise at being where she was. She'd realized David was staring at her, and turned her back to him again.

David said, "Jean, there's something wrong. Is it only the divorce?"

Jean looked directly into his eyes, the only time that entire day. She just said, "Davie, Davie."

Then, explaining that she was expecting Canadian visitors at her office, Jean left abruptly.

David was unsure how to proceed with her, whether to ask to visit her before he left Friday night, or to simply show up on her doorstep one evening and surprise her. As it turned out, Jean said to him just before she left, "Davie, meet me Thursday evening at six. I'll call to tell you where. I have a secret, Davie. Just like when we were kids and told each other our innermost secrets. You're going to love this," she'd said with a gleam in her eyes. It was the only time that she had resembled her old self.

"A secret?" he'd asked. "About what?"

Although perspiration had dotted Jean's forehead, her hand had been clammy and cold as she'd patted her brother's arm. A shrill laugh—on the verge of hysteria, David thought—had come from her. "Indians!" she'd whispered and hurried away.

David's walk from the National Archives Building to his hotel took thirteen minutes. The room was a depressing place on the fifth floor, with a view overlooking rooftops of other buildings. With the rain outside, the room looked worse than ever. When he took the room on Sunday, he'd promised himself that he would not be here longer than necessary.

He threw his jacket over the nearest chair and picked up the telephone to call Jill in Albuquerque. She agreed to pick him up at the Albuquerque Sunport on Friday night about eleven.

David and Jill talked a few minutes about his progress on his research project, and about their children. Then he told her that he was meeting Jean at a local restaurant, carefully neglecting to mention his and Jean's conversation earlier in the week. They said good-bye, and David hung up the phone.

Taking a clean pullover shirt from a dresser drawer, David unbuttoned his damp, white, short-sleeved dress shirt. He changed into a pair of faded jeans and scuffed hiking boots. He hoped the restaurant Jean had chosen would seat him dressed like this, and he gambled on his knowledge of Jean.

He left for the restaurant at a quarter to six. He hadn't been there before. Jean had chosen the place because it was the midpoint between their working places, the Natural History Building of the Smithsonian Institution and the National Archives Building. She had called his hotel room on Wednesday and left a message at the front desk. It had irritated him somehow that she had chosen to call when she knew he would not be there. It had also irritated him that she had chosen a restaurant as the meeting place, neutral ground so to speak. It seemed to him to say, "don't get too close." He'd been thinking about Jean's personal life a great deal in the last couple of days.

He was intrigued by her secret, though, he admitted to himself. Perhaps it had something to do with her present appearance and state of mind. Jean and her secrets.

The restaurant sat on a corner of a three-way intersection. When David entered, he explained that he had reservations for two and was shown to a small, round table in one corner of the room. He was relieved to note that there was a hodgepodge of people in the restaurant dressed in a variety of styles, from the casual, careless dresser such as himself, to a much more sophisticated crowd.

David ordered iced tea and waited for Jean. She arrived late, much too late, to David's annoyance. It was about 6:20 when she charged into the dining room, looking as if someone had been chasing her.

She looked worse than she had on Tuesday. She may even have been wearing the same clothes she'd worn then. Dark circles shadowed the area under her eyes and her eyelids were definitely puffy. Jean's incredible appearance pushed away David's annoyance, and he stood and embraced her in spite of himself, and in spite of Jean's reluctance to let him touch her. She firmly pushed him away.

"Sit down, Jean," David said and she sank into the cushiony chair on the other side of the table. They made small talk until their orders were taken. When the waiter carried away the laminated menus, Jean could wait no longer and anxiously asked David, "Are you ready?"

"Your secret," David asked with a hint of a smile.

Jean nodded. The hair tucked behind her right ear came loose. "David," she said, "what I am about to tell you will make you think that I'm crazy." She lowered her voice and kept her gaze fixed on David's salad fork.

"It's been happening over a period of three years now, Davie," she said. "You've visited my office before?"

David nodded and tried to visualize her office in his mind. It was well over two years since he'd last been there. Things were better then. Jean had been happily married. . . .

"So, what's the secret?" he asked.

"Davie, there are Indians there!" Her whisper was high-pitched, and her forehead gleamed with perspiration. The restaurant was cold. David had switched to coffee after his glass of iced tea.

"Jean, what are you saying?" he asked, confused. "I don't understand."

Jean's whisper came again, more urgently. "David, I can't explain it any more than that, but there *are Indians there. I've seen them. They don't look like they're from today. Davie, they're ghosts!*"

David watched Jean very carefully. Her eyes were too bright and she kept them focused on the salad fork at David's left hand. David didn't say anything, prompting Jean to look up into his eyes for a split second.

5

She took a deep breath and went on. "The first time this happened was in the winter three years ago. I got to my office very early in the morning. The only other person there besides me was a security officer. The halls and the offices were still dark.

"That morning, standing in the hall, was a dark figure who appeared to be waiting for me. Davie, he was very tall, lean, and he was an Indian. There's no mistake about it. He was nearly naked, Davie, except that there was a long piece of cloth or something trailing after him, on the floor."

"What did you do?" David asked.

"I screamed for the security officer, I was so scared. The security officer came and checked through the empty building, but found nothing out of the ordinary.

"A few months after that, I went to another office to pick up a manuscript I was planning to proofread. This was in the afternoon. Between the usual crowd of visitors and our own staff, the halls were crowded. And in the crowd, I saw three distinct figures unlike the others.

"Davie, there were three old gentlemen in the crowd, wearing suits in the style of the late 1800s. I call them that, though they were Indians, I'd say from the turn of the century. They had a distinguished look about them. One of them had very white hair, worn in long braids. He wore plain moccasins. I saw the footwear clearly, though I don't know why. I noticed that in particular. Another of them had what may have been a blanket draped over his shoulders, and he carried something else which I didn't recognize. The third wore a strange fur hat with ornaments dangling from it in places. They walked down the main hall, mixed in with the usual tourist crowd, but I noticed these three men immediately. Again, they seemed to be aware of me, like the first time I saw the naked man. I approached the crowd to speak with them, but by then they were no longer there. That's when I realized that they weren't real."

On that note, the waiter appeared, carrying a tray. He served Jean first, and then David.

As Jean ravenously ate her shrimp cocktail, she said, "There's one more thing, David. Someone else saw those three men that day. I wasn't the only one."

"Who was that?" David asked.

"I really can't tell you because I don't know his name. There was a young man, a tourist, I think, who sat on one of the benches in that part of the museum. When I realized what I was seeing, I moved out of the crowd and sat down on one of those benches. Next to me was this young man. He said to me, 'they're gone'. When I asked 'who?' he looked annoyed and got up and left. Davie, he was an Indian, too. Not one of those from the Southwest, though. But still, he was an Indian, a real one. And he *knew*, Davie."

David countered everything that Jean had said with a comment about her appetite. "How long has it been since you've eaten a decent meal?"

Jean looked at him impatiently and said, "Davie, I have too many other things to do than to worry about decent meals."

"Go on with what you were telling me," David said when he saw that Jean was glaring at him. The suggestion seemed to work, and Jean's attention returned to her food and her secret.

"About two years ago, I began to see things, people, ghosts, whatever they are, almost on a regular, though not daily, basis. By then, they didn't frighten me anymore. They simply drifted by me.

"I made a mistake, then, Davie. I told Dennis. He didn't believe any of it, wouldn't allow me to talk about it. Davie, this was one of the reasons for our divorce. Dennis thought I was going crazy."

Jean was quiet for a time as she ate. Then she said, "I didn't really mind seeing these things. In fact, you might say that I've learned from these experiences. I wasn't frightened after the first two experiences. That is, until recently. *Before*, these incidences didn't disturb me or frighten me, and I didn't feel threatened by them in any way. But just lately, I find that I'm frightened by one or two of these Indians I keep seeing."

Jean became sullen.

David studied his food and carefully chose his words. Finally, he said to her, "Jean, why not come home with me—for a visit? Jill and the kids would be so happy to see you."

Jean put her coffee down, picked up her purse, and said, "Excuse me, Davie, I have to go to the ladies' room."

She left the table. She did not come back.

David sat there for twenty minutes, finally asking someone to go into the ladies' room to see if Jean was okay. But Jean had gone.

David paid the tab and walked slowly back to his hotel. There, he called Jill and told her everything, stating frankly that he was worried about

Jean's mental state. Would she mind if he brought Jean home with him? Jill said she'd be happy to have Jean come to Albuquerque for a visit.

David stayed up late that night, organizing research notes and thinking about Jean. When he got into bed, it was 1:20 in the morning. Yet, he couldn't sleep. He tossed and turned. The last time he looked at the clock, it was nearly three.

2

WASHINGTON, D.C.

AUGUST 1968

THE next morning, David realized he had overslept when he felt the sun shining directly on his face. He looked at the clock. It was well after ten. He couldn't believe it. This was his last research day and he had planned to put in as much time as possible before catching his evening flight. He dressed quickly, grabbed his briefcase, and went to the coffee shop on the first floor of the hotel. He gulped down a warm cup of coffee, a bowl of cold cereal, and then practically ran to the National Archives Building.

Dr. Withers waited for him, a bit impatiently. As soon as David came in the door, Withers handed him a piece of paper. There was a telephone number written on it, with the words "PLEASE CALL."

David went out to the hall and asked the first security guard he saw about finding a phone. The guard led him to a row of telephone booths.

David called the number, gave his name and explained that he was returning a phone call. The woman on the other end of the line said hesitantly, "Dr. Drake, you don't know me, but my name is Lucinda Washington. Jean told me that you were here in D.C. this week, and in fact, you spoke to me on the phone when you were arranging your trip out here. That's how I knew where to find you.

"Dr. Drake, I'm sorry to tell you that your sister died this morning in an accident. I'm sorry to have to be the one to tell you this." The woman's voice had a heavy accent.

David was shocked. He was quiet for awhile. The woman spoke. "Dr. Drake, are you all right? Please answer me, Dr. Drake."

David asked softly, "What happened? What happened to Jean?"

"Well, sir," Lucinda Washington replied, "we really don't have all the details. It was what might be called a freak accident. You see, sir, she fell down a flight of stairs. Dr. Drake, I worked very closely with Jean, and I liked her very much. I can't tell you how sorry I am."

3

NAVAJO RESERVATION

IT was the longest day of the Northern Navajo Fair. People began to line Route 666 at the south side of Shiprock, New Mexico, about six that morning. For the tiny community, there had been heavy traffic all night. The line of spectators forming for the parade extended eastward past the junction that led to Cortez, Colorado, and toward Farmington, New Mexico. By nine, pickup trucks and cars lined both side of the two-lane highway. And the columns of people on both sides of the road stretched into a couple of miles.

The parade was scheduled to begin at ten, but it had never actually started right on time in the last ten years. Vendors circulated through the crowd, selling helium-filled balloons, soft drinks, monkeys on sticks, and a variety of other things to the spectators.

The spectators were, for the most part, Indians, mainly Navajos. The older Navajos, both men and women, were carefully dressed. The women wore flared sateen skirts and velvet blouses, while the men wore jeans and cowboy or velveteen shirts. Turquoise and silver were abundantly displayed in their hair, on their ears, on their wrists and fingers, and in their belts and heavy necklaces. The elders even wore moccasins with silver buttons. They were the most picturesque group here, the most formidable for all their fragile bones and numerous years. They were the memorable ones in the thousands gathered together.

The Navajo youths were faceless, looking much like young people anywhere in the United States. Of course, there were a few exceptions.

Among the Navajos were a few Pueblo Indians—distinguishable from the Navajos by their hair style and clothing. There were also representatives from other tribes, who, like the few Anglos there, were lost among the dominant Navajos.

The smell of coffee and a variety of foods filled the air. The odors wafted from the west side of the highway, where crude, roughly-hewn concession stands held Navajo vendors catering to the familiar Navajo

appetites. A cool breeze carried the smell of food to the line of spectators, causing people from the roadside lines to cross back and forth to
the stands for a cup of coffee or something to fill their stomachs.

Already, a thin cloud of dust hung over the people. As the day grew,
the dust would overpower them. In this town and on the reservation in
general, only the main roads, of which there were too few, were paved.
Other roadways were sand and clay, which lifted in a fine silt under heavy
use. This, like other things, was part of reservation life.

Finally, the parade began. It noisily and slowly made its way from east
to west and then south. There were seventy-seven floats, all accompanied
by deafening music and built to resemble a variety of things, including
hogans (Navajo homes), oil derricks, mesas, landmarks such as Shiprock
or Window Rock, schoolhouses, and over seventy other shapes and forms.
Between the floats were bands from the reservation high schools, with
Navajo majorettes, tribal officials in elegant cars, and numerous "princesses" of Indian clubs and other organizations, sitting either on top of a
bright blanket on the hood of a car or on horseback.

The seventh in the line of princesses was a petite teen-age girl. She
wore a black woven dress, an ancient dress that was faded in places to a
spotty brown. The dress had been skillfully repaired in several places.
The hem was calf-length on the girl. About knee length ran an orange-
brown terraced design the width of the dress on both front and back. The
girl wore moccasins, and her legs were wrapped in white buckskin to her
knees. Around her waist was a new, wide sash belt interwoven in red,
green, and white, and over the sash was a thin metal belt made of shiny
silver links centered with turquoise nuggets. Several strands of turquoise
chunks hung around the girl's neck, and her wrists were adorned with a
number of silver bracelets.

The girl waved first right and then left. She didn't actually smile, but
merely acknowledged the people's presence around her.

She had soft, deep-set, black eyes. In startling contrast, her hair was a
deep, rich, mahogany brown. It was tied in the Navajo hairstyle, and a
trail of long, white yarn hung down the girl's back. She wore no make-up.
Long turquoise earrings framed her face, as did a high, sparkling, silver
crown resting on her forehead and red-brown hair. A large ribbon-like
banner was draped over her right shoulder and down under her left arm
proclaiming RED POINT INDIAN CLUB in gold letters.

The girl sat on the hood of a new 1968 sedan. Signs were tacked on both sides of the car. The letters said NASBAH NAVAJO, PRINCESS 1968, RED POINT, ARIZONA. From the loudspeakers resting on the roof of the car came a recording of a Navajo chant.

Nasbah Navajo scanned the crowd. She was aware of an Anglo woman who had been following the car for the last half mile. The woman easily kept pace with the moving vehicle. Actually, the car crept along and came to a halt several times in the course of the parade. Just when and where the woman had begun to follow, Nasbah did not know, but she had become aware of her on the bridge. Nasbah did not turn directly to the woman but watched her out of the corner of her eye. Yes, she was definitely following. The woman's clothing, a smudge of pink and yellow, moved through the crowd.

"Nasbah!" someone yelled. Nasbah turned to the sound of her name and discovered several relatives waving and laughing. She returned a broad smile.

The parade neared the end. The floats were all turning off the main highway onto a dirt side road. The dust was thicker at this end of town. The driver of Nasbah's car followed the floats onto the side road, but drove farther back and away from the other vehicles. The car stopped. Nasbah climbed down off the hood, took the blanket, folded it, and put it inside the car. She slammed the car door shut as three girls came running up to her. They were the same girls who had called her name earlier in the parade. "Nasbah," one of them said, "let's go to the carnival."

Nasbah agreed, but first turned back to the driver's side of the car. She spoke quietly to the driver for a few minutes, accepted the money that he gave her, and then hurried to meet the other girls.

Nasbah saw the Anglo woman approach from the corner of her eye. She didn't actually see the woman, but recognized the colors she wore. Now that the woman was getting closer, Nasbah could really see her. She was a middle-aged woman with graying hair. The woman spoke. "Honey, could I speak to you for a minute?" The three girls with Nasbah stepped back and waited.

"Me?" Nasbah asked, though she already knew whom the woman meant. Nasbah didn't move.

"Why, yes," the woman said with a pleasant smile. "You may not have noticed, but I've been following you for awhile now." The woman's face was dotted with perspiration, and she wiped it away with a tissue. The woman looked at Nasbah's dress. Nasbah didn't know if the woman expected a response or not. She didn't offer one.

"I'm a collector," the woman said, looking into Nasbah's deep-set eyes. She wondered if Nasbah understood what a collector was. "I collect rugs," she continued. "I'm very interested in your dress. It appears to be very old. I thought you might be interested in selling me the dress."

Nasbah watched the woman touch the dress and check the repaired places on it. Then the woman's fingers traced the orange-brown terraced design, studying it carefully.

The woman said, "You know, I was right. This dress is very old. Did you know that?" She smiled sweetly at Nasbah. Then she said, "I would be willing to pay one thousand dollars for this dress, honey."

The woman searched her purse for something. She pulled out a card and said, "Honey, my name is on this card. I'm staying in Farmington at this place. Talk over my offer with your parents, and if they're interested in selling the dress, come and see me. But do it soon. I must go back to Sedona tomorrow."

Nasbah accepted the card. She said, "The dress belongs to me."

The woman answered, "Well, honey, whoever owns the dress has a very valuable item there."

The woman walked away, and the three girls ran to Nasbah. "One thousand dollars!" they said. At that moment, the car on which Nasbah had ridden honked. It had not moved yet.

Nasbah ran back to the car. This time she did not go to the driver's side. She opened the back door and got inside.

The driver was a man, Nasbah's father. Sitting beside him was a woman in a red velveteen dress. She had Nasbah's deep-set eyes. In the back seat was an old man who might have stepped out of another time. His long hair was white, and it was wrapped in white yarn. He wore long turquoise earrings and a purple velveteen shirt that had silver buttons around the collar and rows of quarters and dimes down the sleeves. He sat very straight.

"What did she want?" the old man asked Nasbah in the Navajo language.

Nasbah answered, "The dress. It's the same every time I wear it. The white people want to buy the dress."

13

"How much?" the old man asked.

"A thousand dollars," Nasbah said in Navajo.

The old man shook his head from side to side. "They are offering more now. Whatever is offered will never be enough."

Nasbah got out of the car and went to the three girls who were waiting for her. The people in the car were going to stay where they were until the traffic cleared.

The old man in the back of the car was content to sit and watch everyone through the glass.

4

OKLAHOMA CITY, OKLAHOMA
FEBRUARY 1969

RUSSELL Tallman walked into the building beneath the sign that said
WILL ROGERS WORLD AIRPORT. Carrying two well-used bags and a briefcase, he stood in line before the TWA desk for awhile. When his ticket
and baggage were checked, he proceeded to the gate where his plane
would leave. Once there, he removed his heavy western-cut gray jacket
and threw it on one of the seats. He did not remove his black cowboy
hat, though. From his back pants pocket, he pulled out a rolled-up *Time*
magazine and sat down in the seat next to his jacket. He glanced at his
watch. Boarding time was in another forty minutes.

The area was nearly empty. Besides Russell, there were three other
people. Through the glass sidewalls, a jet could be seen in the distance,
soaring into the sky. It was gray and overcast outside, making the drab
landscape seem more colorless than usual. The scene was deceptive. Everything looked peaceful and calm outside, but Russell knew the wind
was starting to pick up. It depressed him.

"Ho, Russ," someone said beside him.

Russell looked up. "George! George Daylight!" he exclaimed with a
broad smile. He stood, extended a hand, and said, "Damn, guy! Long
time no see. . . . Where have you been keeping yourself?"

George Daylight was a smaller man than Russell, with a ready smile
and a sense of humor. He carried a small bag and wore a jacket made
from a Pendleton blanket.

He answered Russell, "Ah, hell, man, I've been everywhere since the last
time I saw you. Purty near two years since then, ain't it? I came down here to
the city a week ago to see one of my ex-wives. I was supposed to stay just a
day or two but I was here the whole damned week. Them women just won't
leave me alone. Must be my sex appeal," he said with a grin.

Daylight sat down beside Russell and lit a cigarette. He turned more
serious. "Russ," he said, "I'm on my way to D.C. I done went and got
myself elected a tribal official two years ago. Can you believe that?"

Russell smiled. "Hey, man, me too. I'm going to D.C., too."

"Yeah?" George said. "I heard that you were out that-a-way some time ago. What you doing out there? You living out there now, or what?"

Russell nodded. "Yeah, sort of like that. I've been out there a year, with six months to go. Working, studying, researching, you know."

The waiting area began to fill.

"Yeah?" George said. "That reminds me, been meaning to ask you something if our paths crossed. I hear tell they's some spooky things happening over yonder where you're doing your research. That right?"

"Where'd you hear that?" Russell asked.

"Well, I heard something from Junior Snake long time ago. Seems that his daddy, Wilbur, and a whole bunch of others went up to D.C. years back. Claim they seen something. Claim they know something."

Russell listened to George carefully. Outside, the wind threw things past the windows. The sky grew darker.

"Well?" George asked. Russell looked at him. Sitting next to George was a woman. She looked as if she too expected an answer from Russell. When she realized this, she quickly put her head down.

Russell motioned to George that the woman was listening. Then he said, "Hell, George, you know how these things go. Talk, that's all there is to it. Just plain talk."

George nodded, understanding what Russell was saying. Then both men became quiet and watched the crowd swell until all the seats in the area were occupied.

Later, after George and Russell had settled into their seats on the plane and were well into the flight, George asked Russell again, "What's going on over there, Russ? Junior Snake said things used to happen around there, people dying all the time, stuff like that. . . ."

Russell looked out the window but couldn't see anything except clouds. "Aw, hell, man, I don't know," he sighed.

George accepted that. He puffed on a cigarette, then put it out when the "No Smoking" sign flashed on. The flight became bumpy, and the pilot explained to the passengers that the plane was passing through some turbulent spots, but not to be alarmed.

George said, "The story goes that close to thirty years ago, Wilbur Snake, Simon Littlefoot, LeClair Williams, and about four others went over to D.C. Those three are the only ones I know for sure that went. The others, I don't know. Think they all passed on by now, though. Have you heard about old LeClair yet? He died. Yep, but that's another story. Wait a minute, seems like Wilbur took Anna. She was in purty good health then. She's getting old, too, now, must be near eighty. She's older than Wilbur, you know, by a couple of years. Her and Wilbur been together since they was kids. Shoot, Wilbur said him and Anna got married when he was just under seventeen."

"What happened?" Russell asked. "What happened in D.C.?"

"Oh, yeah, D.C." George answered and lit another cigarette. "The group, Wilbur, Simon, LeClair, and the others, got the royal treatment there. Ain't sure exactly why they went out there—went by train—but they saw D.C. from one side to the other.

"Now you know how Wilbur is. How he can catch a scent of something? Junior Snake said that Wilbur told the group that something big and powerful done had a hold of that place."

"Did he see anything?" Russell asked.

George puffed again and nodded. "Said they's people there. Lots of them."

"Who are they?" Russell asked.

"Junior says it's hard to say. Wilbur told him they's too many. One thing for sure—it ain't just one kind of people—er, one tribe. They Indian, sure enough. Wilbur says they's people there from tribes we ain't even heard of. Shoot, Russ, Wilbur claimed it'd be like wrestling the devil trying to sort it all out.

"And that ain't all, Russell. Wilbur said back then that this here thing's going to grow like one big tornado—damn near has to, he said."

Russell looked at him. "What are you saying, George?" he asked.

"Aw, hell, Russell. You know damn well what I'm saying. Things are going to turn mean over there. Russ, ol' buddy, you better get your brown buns outta there." George was dead serious.

The stewardess came by with a round of black coffee for the two men. George drank his loudly before saying, "Junior Snake thinks a lot of people might already be dead from this. Poor things, their families probably think it's caused from heart attacks and other things that appear to be natural. No telling how long it's been going on now. But, then, in a way, too, it's their own fault—in a way they contributed to it.

"How do you mean?" Russell asked.

"Come on, Tallman, you *know* that. They were there—*in* it," George

17

said, leafing through a flight magazine he had pulled out of the pouch in the seatback in front of him. He flipped the pages until he came to an article on New Mexico, the Albuquerque and Santa Fe areas. He skimmed the article and among the colorful photographs of the Indians in the area was one of an old silver-haired Navajo man. He wore a purple velveteen shirt with dimes sprinkled on the collar and down the sleeves, and he posed beneath a clear turquoise sky. The caption beneath the photograph read "Jonnie Navajo, a well-known Navajo Chanter. The sixteen-million acre Navajo Reservation is a four-hour drive from Albuquerque."

Russell was quiet, considering George's words. "What exactly did Wilbur see? I need to know, George," he said.

George studied the photo in the magazine. "You know," he said, "I think I know the guy in this picture. Met him somewhere in Utah, or maybe in Arizona, a few years back."

Russell took the magazine away from George, looked quickly at the photo, and said impatiently, "George, what exactly did Wilbur see?"

"Okay, okay. Let me think, . . ." George answered. "Maybe you should go see old Wilbur Snake, if it's so important to you. His hearing's going, though. You're going to have to shout at him.

"Now if my mind is working right, this is the way it goes. Wilbur and LeClair got called on by some researchers, you know, white people, to help them out, look at old photographs of Indians and other stuff. Shoot, LeClair loved to show off what little he knew, and Wilbur went along to kind of keep LeClair out of trouble, keep him from talking too much, telling too much. . . . Understand?"

Russell nodded.

"From the minute they stepped into that building, to the time they left it, old Wilbur—he shore was uneasy. He'd never been there before, hadn't known that it even existed. But the place felt bad. Well, LeClair and Wilbur traipsed from one office to another, and while they did, Wilbur tried to get a handle on where this power was coming from. Couldn't get close to it on the first visit.

"The second time around, Wilbur let LeClair answer all the questions by hisself. And Wilbur kind of wandered around the place. They let him do that. Guess they figured he was a harmless son-of-a-gun.

"In the main hall, Wilbur sat down and watched the tourist crowd move in and out. Wilbur then heard a song—he thought it was a song, maybe it wasn't. Wilbur said it was a 'crying song'—maybe he meant a 'mourning song.' The song was low, very soft, and pitifully sad. Wilbur listened to it for a minute or two, and he saw that no one else heard it but him. He began to hum the tune. The melody stayed with him. You know, Russ, I think he still knows it.

"Anyway, he caught hisself thinking 'bout that tune all day. It was an Indian song, but it was one he'd never heard around our part of the country. LeClair took all day answering questions. He really showed off. 'Bout evening time, they were done with LeClair and had some food brought in before taking Wilbur and LeClair back to their hotel. LeClair and Wilbur then had some time to theirselves. The building had cleared out purty much and just those few people in that office were around.

"Well, while LeClair and Wilbur were alone, Wilbur caught hisself singing the song that had been on his mind most of the day. It happened then. Before they knew it, a man was in the room with them. He looked as real as you and me, but his appearance was different. Wilbur told Junior that the man was stark naked, but there was something wrapped around one of his ankles, and it dragged on the floor. Wilbur said that when the man first appeared, the look on his face was of rage—pure hateful and mean. Wilbur said he pretended not to see the figure, the same way LeClair did. Then Wilbur turned to LeClair and told him that a song had been on his mind the whole damned day. He said he had to sing it so the song would let him go. And Wilbur did try to sing it just the way he'd heard it. That spirit man walked around Wilbur and LeClair while Wilbur sang. Wilbur closed his eyes when he sang, but LeClair took care to watch the figure indirectly, out the sides of his eyes, and with another part of hisself. When Wilbur finished singing and opened his eyes, the man was gone. LeClair said to Wilbur, 'that's his own song'. Wilbur told LeClair that he already knew that.

"That evening, when Wilbur and LeClair had been fed and were ready to fall asleep from gorging theirselves so much, the people who fed them began to collect Wilbur's and LeClair's belongings. Their visit to D.C. was just before spring, so they had heavy coats, gloves, and other things to carry out or wear. Well, on top of Wilbur's coat lay a tiny buckskin bag. It was old and kind of dirty. One bead hung on the bag's strings. Thinking that this little bag belonged to Wilbur, they brought it to him along with his other things. Wilbur looked at it curiously, and left it on top of the desk where LeClair had sat all day.

"Well, lo and behold, that night, when Wilbur was undressing, in his pocket was that same little bag. He thought 'bout the meaning of it for a while, and when he couldn't figger it out, well, he just climbed into bed and went on to sleep.

"Next morning, he opened the bag—it was just a little thing—and inside it was a bear claw.

"Later, Wilbur took it back and put it in the same place where he'd left it earlier. Same thing happened again. That night the bag was in Wilbur's pocket.

"The group stayed in D.C. for five days. LeClair got hisself invited back to answer more questions. Wilbur, too, I guess, because he went along with LeClair when those people questioned him and wrote down every little thing LeClair said. So that's what happened the first time Wilbur went over there.

"Wilbur ended up going back with LeClair several times over a four-year period. At the end of it, Wilbur said he was beginning to understand. He said there were many people there, but four figures kind of overshadowed the others. In fact, I guess the reason the two quit going back to D.C. was not because the researchers lost interest in them or what LeClair was saying. The whole mess kind of lay heavy on Wilbur. He told LeClair that enough was enough, and strangely, LeClair agreed. I say that because I knowed how LeClair loved to be the center of attention.

"But I guess LeClair just agreed, quick-like-that, with Wilbur, no argument from him at all."

Russell listened carefully. He asked, "Who did the bag belong to?"

"I s'pose it belonged to the man whose song Wilbur had sung. Anyway, that was Wilbur's thought. About ten years ago, Junior and his wife, Erleen, went out to D.C. on tribal business. Course Erleen just had to go over there where you're doing research now to see the place Wilbur had talked about. Junior introduced hisself to the official there and dropped his daddy's name. It turned out that one of the people who had worked with LeClair and Wilbur as a young man was still around there—you know, Russ, what they say 'bout bureaucrats—and he very generously offered to show Junior and Erleen the collections that Wilbur and LeClair had worked with.

"At the time Junior was there, those research people had just come through a bad time. Seems that one of their staff had just committed suicide, and the whole office talk centered on that. Junior didn't think nothin' of it at the time—but later learned that suicide was a purty frequent happening there. He made the connection between that and the spirit people that Wilbur'd seen there. Evidently, no one—the white people—knew 'bout these spirit people, or if they did, they kept it purty quiet. Wilbur told Junior that he doubted anyone there knew anything about the spirit people, their senses were too damned plugged up! Now, does that answer all your questions?" George looked at Russell.

He answered, "All except one. Why? Why is this happening?"

George was annoyed. He said, "Damn, Russ, you been gone too long. Starting to think like them. What the hell kind of question is that? *Why? Why is this happening?* You sound like you're just going to sit down and work this out till all the answers come up clean and simple. It don't matter! *What matters is that people—spirit people—are there.* You going to question or doubt that? You going to question or doubt Wilbur Snake? Now, I asked you earlier, ain't some spooky kinds of things been going on over there, lately? I heard talk. . . . Heard it from that Navajo man, what's his name—Begay? You work with him, ain't that right?"

Russell wasn't too surprised. He looked out the window again and closed his mouth to keep from asking more of his own questions.

George didn't push for an answer. He just leafed through his magazine and waited.

Finally Russell said, "It's true, George, something's going on. I saw something myself—three old men who were walking the halls of the Natural History Building, arm-in-arm, looking just as if they owned the place. That Wurly woman—she died a few months back—she saw them too. I didn't know who she was then, but I went out of my way to find out her name—she was there too. She tried to act like she didn't *see*, but she did. Didn't do her no good to deny it, didn't help her any, as far as I can tell. I don't understand any of what's happening." That was all he said about it for the rest of the flight.

In D.C. Russell and George parted, Russell for Virginia and George for Maryland. By that time George was back to his old self. He shook Russell's hand and said with a straight face, "Russ, my heart soars like an eagle to have seen you again."

Russell grinned and hit George on the back as he walked away.

5

NAVAJO RESERVATION

THE earth was damp from a light intermittent rain that had begun about midmorning. It was now mid-afternoon, and the sky was still covered with blue-gray clouds that blew over the aspen forest surrounding the summer camp.

A hogan had sat here in virtually the same spot for eight or nine generations, although periodically it had been entirely dismantled and rebuilt, or sections of it had been repaired. It now sat a hundred feet north or so from the place where the very first one, a forked-sticked hogan, had been built nearly two centuries earlier. At that time, the hogan had been just at the edge of the forest in a narrow valley between two peaks on the highest part of Beautiful Mountain. Now the hogan was padlocked and badly in need of repair. The roof threatened to collapse. Next to it was a summer shelter made of aspen logs. It was thoroughly covered with green aspen boughs except at the entrance, which was on the east side.

Inside, at the south end of the shelter, was a bed with the mattress frame resting on pine-log sections. A square piece of tarp attached to the roof beams overhead kept the blowing rain off the bed. On the same end of the shelter, a piece of canvas about five feet wide had been stretched between the structural beams and aspen boughs to give further protection. In front of this canvas wall, two logs about four feet in length were suspended from the roof by wires. Sheepskins and neatly folded blankets hung over the log. On the northeast side of the shelter was a fireplace built of sandstone and mud. A fire had burned all day to keep the old man and the old woman warm. Between the bed and the fireplace stood a shaky table. Pine-log sections beneath it served as chairs. Wooden crates nailed securely to the west side of the shelter behind the table held household items, pots and pans, and foodstuff. Just to the right of the crate shelves was a large loom about six feet in height and nearly five feet wide. Cotton cloth was draped over the loom, front and back, to protect a partially completed rug from dust and rain.

The old woman sat at the table on one of the log sections, carding black wool. She was seventy-three years old, dressed in several skirts and a faded dark blue blouse patched with green cloth on the bodice and elbows. Her shoes were old and worn, tied only at the top eyelets. Despite her age, her face was smooth under her white hair. Her intelligent eyes held a trace of a smile.

The old man sat on the bed. He was dressed in black pants and a red woolen shirt that was the upper half of his long johns. He, too, was in his seventies, a year or so older than the woman. At least, that's what the two old people thought. They had figured it out, based on a long chain of events in the lives of their older family members. He was the same man in the photograph that George Daylight had pointed out to Russell Tallman. He was the same man who had been in the car with Nasbah Navajo.

The photograph in the flight magazine had been taken some years earlier, when the old man was closer to sixty than eighty, and that same image of him had appeared continually in books and magazines since then. On the day it had been taken, he'd been escorted some three hundred miles to Santa Fe to be involved in a historical pageant and celebration there. He'd spent the night alone in an elegant home not far from the Plaza. The next day, with due pomp and ceremony on the part of his Anglo host and hostess, he had again been escorted back to the reservation—actually, to this place—Beautiful Mountain.

He had made the trip to Santa Fe back then not so much for those people as for himself. Santa Fe, called *Yoo'tó* in Navajo, represented many things to him and to his people, and there was an unsatisfied curiosity about events and things long past. So he'd spent his quick tour of Santa Fe carefully inspecting the Plaza, the Palace of the Governors, and the Fort Marcy area. The trip had not resolved anything for him. On the contrary, it had raised more questions and thoughts. When he'd left Santa Fe, he'd been quiet and uncommunicative. His driver and interpreter had left him alone, and all the way back to Beautiful Mountain, his mind replayed stories that his uncle, *Hosteen Nez*, had told him.

Jonnie Navajo's hair was whiter now than it was in the photograph, and there were two or three more furrows on his forehead and face, but otherwise he looked much the same. Also now, on occasion, he wore a pair of black-rimmed magnifying glasses to help him do the close work of weaving horsehair into a number of skilled patterns for belts and hat bands. He spent entire days doing this, enjoying the rare times that allowed it, because at other times his days were spent caring for his sheep, goats, and other livestock. Even now as he sat, his fingers wove strands of black and white horsehair back and forth, patiently and surely.

Rain dripped rhythmically in a soft mist while the old woman carded wool and the old man wove horsehair. When the fire burned down to embers, the woman stirred the charcoal and added kindling with a couple of logs.

A car was coming through the forest. The man heard it as did the woman, but he continued to work the horsehair, and she resumed carding wool. Soon a brown pickup truck drove out of the trees, with two people in it, bouncing up and down.

At last the pickup came to a stop. The windshield wipers also stopped. The driver was a Navajo, but the passenger was not. The old man quickly surmised this with one glance up and over his glasses, and then went back to his work. The two men in the pickup sat inside momentarily, talking between themselves.

Finally, the door of the truck opened. The driver, wearing a light jacket, made a dash for the shelter, as did his passenger. The summer shelter was cozy.

The Navajo visitor went up to the old man and said, "Hello, Grandfather" in Navajo. He extended a hand. The old man took off his glasses and looked into the face of the visitor. Then he smiled broadly and took the younger man's hand and pulled him close as he embraced him for what seemed like a long time. This embarrassed the white man, a tall, lanky figure, who stuffed his hands into his jacket pockets and cleared his throat to remind the other two men of his presence.

Then, speaking in Navajo, the younger man said, "I've brought this white man with me. His name is David Drake." He turned to the white man and said in English, "Shake his hand. Shake my grandfather's hand." Drake did as he was told, rather awkwardly.

The woman put aside the black wool and embraced her grandson. She smiled pleasantly at Drake, and shook his hand.

"Willie," Drake said to the younger Navajo, "I'm not very knowledgeable about Navajo courtesies. Tell me if I do something wrong."

Willie didn't answer, but turned to the old man and spoke to him in Navajo. Drake could only guess about the subjects they might be discussing. They completely ignored him.

Slowly the sky cleared, and rays of light settled on the summer shelter and dried the pickup. After about forty-five minutes, Willie and the old man's discussion turned to Drake. The old man's eyes turned to the white man.

Willie said to Drake, "I'll tell him the purpose of our visit now." Drake nodded.

"Grandfather," Willie said in Navajo, "I brought this white man up here to see you because he asked me to do this for him. He is writing a history of the People and he wants you to tell him if his ideas are right. He got most of them in books and old papers. He would like to work with you if you have some time. He says he will pay fifty dollars a day for your time."

The old man studied the ground, not responding. The woman put a pot of coffee beside the fire, and the aroma of fresh coffee soon filled the shelter. She made herself busy, hovering over the fire and laying flat round pieces of dough on a grill fashioned from coat hangers. Charcoal burned under the grill, and to the side of the coffee pot was a cast iron skillet with a lid. The contents of the skillet sizzled.

Willie went on explaining David Drake's project. "The work doesn't require you to travel or anything like that, Grandfather. I will bring him up here at different stages in his work, or he could come up by himself, when an interpreter is here—maybe when Nasbah is around."

Still there was no response from the old man. He kept his eyes off Willie and David. Willie wanted to give the old man time to think about the offer. He began to tell him about his own work in Washington, D.C. "I'll be returning to *Washingdoon* in a week. I'm going to summer school in Georgetown," he said.

The old man looked up and nodded.

"But as soon as summer school is over, I'll be back," Willie continued. "David won't be ready for my or Nasbah's services until August at the earliest. While I'm going to school, I'm going to do some research on the Navajo Tribe, the People. You know, Grandfather, in *Washingdoon* there are buildings filled with records on us—on the People. I plan to read everything I can get my hands on."

The old man asked him, "There are papers over there that talk about the People?"

Willie laughed and nodded. He said, "Boxes of them. Boxes and boxes of them."

"What are those people in *Washingdoon* going to do with them?" the old man asked, completely serious.

The question was the last one Willie expected. He shrugged, laughed, and ignored it. The old man saw that Willie wasn't going to answer him.

"Perhaps they have papers on *Hosteen Nez*, then? Or *Hosteen Diné*, my father? If *Washingdoon* keeps papers on the People, perhaps they have written something about Tall Navajo's Son, my paternal grandfather. Maybe even Tall Navajo himself?" He looked hopefully at Willie.

Willie shook his head no. "I haven't come across any of them, Grandfather."

The old man sighed and looked out of the shelter.

Willie added, "But that doesn't mean there aren't records of them. It just means that I haven't found any yet. I'm going to search for them. I promise you that if any records are there on them, I'll find them.

"David also works with records, but he mostly works with those in New Mexico. Just like in *Washingdoon*, there are many papers on the People, the Navajos, in Santa Fe."

This sparked the old man's interest. His eyes gleamed and he looked hard at Drake.

The woman had finished cooking. She cleaned the table and put down the coffee, bread, and the skillet, which held fried potatoes. To those items, she added fresh green chilies.

The four people ate while the old woman told them a story about her grandfather who had come to Beautiful Mountain years before she was born. Her point in telling the story, she said, was to make all of them wonder whether or not this was written down somewhere in *Washingdoon*. It seemed to her that someone would have wanted to remember it, and the white people, being a people committed to paper, would most likely have written all this down.

Willie said, "My Grandmother, I haven't read that story anywhere, but I agree with you that it is worth remembering."

The old man turned to Drake and asked a question. Willie translated, "What do you know about the People? My grandfather wants to know what you know about the People, and he means the Navajos."

David said, "I have always had an interest in Indians, since I was a little boy. I've studied about them since then. I'm from back East. We used to have some Indians out there—not as many as out here. They're almost gone out there." Willie translated this into Navajo.

"Where'd they go?" the old man asked. Willie translated, "He wants to know where they've gone to, those Indians in the East—what did you do with them?" Willie's face held the beginning of a smile, but the old man's face did not.

Drake responded with a smile too. "Well, . . ." he said. He laughed and then frowned.

"Never mind," Willie said, "he has another question. He wants to know how soon you want to start work."

"Does that mean he's consented to work with me?" David asked.

Willie answered, "Only on a temporary basis. If it doesn't work out, he'll suggest someone else to you who would be more suitable than he."

Drake was pleased. He said, "On the second weekend of August, I will return. Will you come with me?" he asked Willie, who nodded and repeated this information to the old man.

The sky was blue now and the ground was drying out. Drake was in no hurry to leave the mountain, and neither was Willie. They had driven from Albuquerque that day, and planned to make the return trip the same night.

David got up and told Willie, "I'm going to sleep in the pickup for awhile. You visit with your grandfather. We'll leave before dark." He went out to the truck, took a blanket from the cab, and spread it out in the pickup bed. Then he climbed into the back of the truck.

The old man watched Drake and asked, "Is he ill? To be so young and to sleep in the daytime?"

Willie answered. "I don't really know. He says he sometimes does not sleep. Grandfather, this white man has had some trouble lately. He told me about it.

"He had a sister who worked in *Washingdoon*. She died recently. He was there when it happened. But there seems to be some question about how she died. She fell. Not from a great height, though. And she was alone when she died.

"He thinks that it might have been suicide, Grandfather. He says that he had visited her that week, and she wasn't acting normal. She told him that she had seen people who were not alive."

The old man listened and wove horsehair at the same time. His eyes looked up at Willie over his glasses and he asked, "This woman saw people who were not alive?"

27

Willie nodded yes. "At least she *said* that is what she saw," he corrected himself.

The old man continued to weave.

Willie went on. "David feels that his sister might have been losing her mind. He thinks that is the only thing that would make her do such a thing. Her death has done something to him. He can't sleep and he has lost weight."

The old man asked, "Why doesn't he do something about this situation?"

Willie laughed, "White people are different from us, Grandfather. You know it, I know it. Anyway, Grandfather, there have been other deaths where his sister died."

"*He didn't believe his own sister?*" the old man asked incredulously. Willie was preparing to answer when the old man asked, "This didn't happen any place near you in *Washingdoon*, did it?"

Willie was quiet. The old man stopped weaving and asked, "Is *Washingdoon* filled with crazy people?" Willie didn't answer and didn't dare smile.

"What else do they have over there besides paper that has to do with the People?" he asked when Willie did not respond.

This Willie could answer. "Well, Grandfather, they have a lot of things. Not just of the People, but of other tribes, too. Old photographs, records of people singing and talking, and they have some clothes, dresses, shirts, moccasins, shields, gourd rattles, and medicine bundles."

On the last item, the old man stopped what he was doing and poised his hand in the air. "They have medicine bundles?" he wanted to know.

Willie nodded.

"What do they do with them?"

"Well, nothing, Grandfather. They don't do anything with them. They just keep them," Willie answered.

"Why?" the old man asked.

"I don't know," answered Willie. "You see, Grandfather, these are not the People's medicine bundles. They do not belong to the Navajos."

"Well, who do they belong to?" the old man asked.

"Other Indian tribes. I don't know really. I've seen some of them. They're all mixed up. Things inside have become separated. I don't know if the bundles are all in one piece."

Willie's grandfather asked, "These other tribes do not mind? They know their bundles are over there?"

Willie answered, "Maybe they know about it, maybe they don't." Willie was remembering something he had seen in *Washingdoon*. A far-away look was in his eyes.

The old man's questions ended. He went back to weaving the horse-hair. When he didn't say anything more, Willie got up and went to the woman, who was now weaving the rug.

It was large, nearly the full size of the loom, woven predominantly in black, but with stripes of browns and reds throughout. The woman beat down a new layer of yarn with a weaving comb.

"Did you have a hard time driving up the mountain in the rain?" she asked.

"No, it was dry most of the way. The rain is only at the top of the mountain," Willie answered, and visited with her for awhile. Then he walked to the pickup truck where David slept. He didn't want to wake him, so he walked around the summer camp.

Most of the goats and all the sheep were penned in a corral. One or two goats were outside the corral, standing on their back legs, nibbling at tree boughs. The sheep dogs were laying around the corral, watching Willie curiously. One of the dogs growled at him.

Willie decided to walk up one of the peaks. It had been awhile since he'd been up here, herding sheep for the old man, summers back. He was gone for nearly two hours; the sun was low when he returned. David sat in the back of the pickup.

"Shall we go?" Willie asked. David nodded.

The old woman had a pot of coffee on the table. "Have some coffee before you go," she suggested. Willie poured himself a cup, and David entered. The old man watched David. When David had a cup of coffee in his hand, the old man rose, tapped David on the arm, and indicated to him that David should follow. Davie carried his coffee and followed the old man. Willie put his coffee cup down and followed too.

The three walked for a few minutes, with David sipping his coffee on the way. It was nearly evening. One or two stars were visible in the summer sky. "Where are we going?" David asked Willie, who merely shrugged in response.

The old man led them to a place deep in the aspen forest. Coming to a fallen tree trunk, he sat down and looked over the area. It was cold here—not cool, but cold. Tree leaves glittered; the white aspen barks lit the forest.

David looked questioningly at Willie, who shrugged again. Willie sat down beside the old man, and David realized that he should sit too, and he did, placing his coffee cup on the trunk.

For a few minutes, there was no conversation. The old man was pensive.

"What is it?" Willie asked his grandfather.

"It happened here," the old man said. "I was told that it happened here. Right over there." He pointed among the trees. The forest was thick. Young trees stood all around them.

Willie was quiet, waiting. David was puzzled.

"The sweathouse was back there," the old man continued, pointing in another direction.

"What's this about?" David asked.

"Sh. . . ." Willie quieted him.

"Tall Navajo's Son was here when it happened, with White Sheep and the woman Red Lady. Strangers came and stole Red Lady with one of her children. Here is where it happened." The old man spoke quickly and tersely. "The strangers were stealing the People in those days. They scalped the old man White Sheep, who was Red Lady's father, and the strangers took his ears. In Santa Fe, a bounty was paid for a pair of Navajo ears, about twenty dollars, although I don't know how it was known for certain that these ears came from the People."

"They scalped White Sheep, Grandfather?" Willie asked.

The old man spit and said, "Tried to."

"Did the strangers kill the others, the ones they did not capture?" Willie asked.

"My paternal grandfather, Tall Navajo's Son, escaped because he was not in camp at the time. However, he returned in time to hear the strangers run away with his mother, Red Lady, and one of his sisters. Red Lady had baby girls, twins. One of these little girls was stolen with Red Lady."

"Why didn't he go after them?" Willie asked.

"Eventually he did. But he was young, maybe thirteen. And for the moment, there was White Sheep to look after, and the child that White Sheep saved by hiding it in the sweathouse." Willie's grandfather quieted as Willie began to translate all of this for David.

"I don't get it," David said. "Why is he telling us all this?"

Willie frowned for a moment and answered, "This is a part of the history of the People. Weren't you going to write a history of the People? From their side?"

David agreed, trying to understand.

For a long time, Willie and the old man discussed something, occasionally looking at David. The evening was darkening. Then the old man led the way back to the summer shelter where a fire glowed in the early dark.

Willie and David climbed into the pickup and began the long trek down the mountain. As they drove along the mountain forest road, David said, "I'm sorry if I annoyed you back there."

Willie laughed. "I'm sorry that it showed. Forget it. There is something else that I must tell you now. The old man, my Grandfather, wants something from you."

"Yeah?" David asked uncomfortably.

"Yeah," Willie answered. "He wants you to find out what happened to the child, the little girl who was stolen."

"What?" David asked incredulously.

Willie nodded. "Tall Navajo and Tall Navajo's Son found Red Lady three years after she'd been stolen. In Taos. But they never did find the child. The old man is curious about this, that's all. He says you work with papers in Santa Fe. He says that you can find out about the missing child."

David laughed. "That request is impossible! It's taken me several years to write and do my own research. When did all this happen? If I'm expected to track down a missing girl, I need to know when it all happened. How long has this child been missing?"

Willie kept his eyes on the road and answered, "About one hundred years ago, maybe one hundred fifty years. I'd say in a span of one hundred to one hundred fifty years."

"What?" David asked. "A hundred and fifty years ago? How am I supposed to accomplish this? Where am I supposed to begin looking?"

Willie smiled. "You're the researcher."

David fell silent for a couple of hours. Outside of Gallup, New Mexico, when he'd traded places with Willie and taken over the driving, he said, "Those were turbulent times for the Navajos. A century ago was perhaps the worst time of all for them. They were being pursued by everyone, including slave-hunters and the military.

Willie replied, "It was called 'the fearing time' by the People. You probably know that already."

Then David said, "Willie, I think your grandfather expects too much of me, but I'll do what I can. No promises, though. How old was the child when she was taken?"

Willie answered, "She was about a year old."

David continued, "You introduced your grandfather to me simply as your grandfather, and all these months we've referred to him as your grandfather. He does have a name, doesn't he?"

Willie laughed. "His name is Navajo. Jonnie Navajo. He's close to eighty. He's my deceased mother's father."

6

LAS VEGAS, NEW MEXICO

ROSA Lopez sat in a rocking chair, staring out one of the long narrow windows to the mountains west of Las Vegas. Everything outside was a thick green, although the sky was filled with dusty summer rain.

She was frail, now, as thin as the wood in the frame of the rocking chair, as limp as the dainty handkerchief she kept in the pocket of her dressing gown. It was a long, dark gown with white lace around the neck and at her wrists. Her feet were covered in the same color. A crocheted coverlet lay across her lap.

The room was massive, dwarfing her against the afternoon haze pouring through the wispy, ivory curtains. A large, soft, maroon rug covered most of the floor area, and dark, heavy, polished pieces of furniture filled the room. The bed was under the long, skinny windows.

She had been sitting where she was for perhaps two hours, staring out the window, and waiting. Death was certain now, as certain as the light spray of rain on the window panes. After nearly one hundred years of living, Rosa didn't mind it too much.

She began to undo the bun that held her hair. Her movements were painstakingly deliberate. Her hair was white, as white as the lace around her neck. Lifting a heavy brush from the dressing table, Rosa slowly began to brush out her long hair.

Finally, she put the brush down and stared at her hands. They were brown and wrinkled. She picked up the heavy hand mirror and hesitantly peeked into it. Her face was ancient. The black eyes gazed into the mirror for a long time, and then she put the mirror down.

Rosa hadn't said much in the last eight years, only the few words that were necessary in day-to-day life. She had spent much of that time in thought, reflecting on her long life, her three children, and her two husbands. At times she could not completely remember all of her life. These gaps did not alarm her, though, because sooner or later everything came back to her. Today was one of those days when her memory was crystal clear. She ached from remembering almost everything.

She hadn't thought of Taos for a long time. Today the image of Taos Pueblo loomed up before her. How could she remember after so long? Nearly eighty years. She'd been a lithesome eighteen-year-old, and the Taos man who became her husband had been nearly thirty. She could feel the strength of him even now, the firm muscles in his arms and back. He wore long braids. What was his name? She couldn't remember. She should remember his name!

Rosa winced. How could she forget? Her teary eyes found the mountains outside the window again. Raindrops slid down the window panes.

His name was on the time of her tongue. There were two children, Maria and Domingo. She remembered the weight of them in her belly, the odor of milk on them. The girl was born shortly after the marriage, within a year or two. The boy came later, perhaps four years.

Those children had lived past middle age. The girl had died at the age of sixty. What year was that? 1949? 1948? The boy had died more recently, as an old man. Rosa always remembered him as a boy, a dear boy. She'd outlived both of her first two children. A hundred years! Rosa had had a hundred years. It was more than enough.

The face of her first husband darted across Rosa's mind again. His eyes were a light liquid brown, and he had a crooked smile. What was his name?

Rosa had actually lived in the Pueblo for a brief time, maybe five years, with her husband and children. Then he was killed on the eastern plains in circumstances she never fully comprehended. Her children stayed in the Pueblo and she went to Española after that, to work for a family there. Sitting in the hard rocking chair now, Rosa could feel the two warm children in her arms as she prepared to leave them in Taos with her husband's family. They had not cried out when she'd left. They'd waved.

Rosa was lonely then. It seemed that for must of her life, Rosa had been lonely. As a child, she had grown up in the care of several families, all of whom had shown her tender kindness and charity. But something had always been missing. In the void, Rosa had often been lonely.

She knew nothing about her own mother and father. None of the families in whose temporary care she'd lived had discussed her parents with her, although at times the faces of her foster families held inscrutable expressions when they looked at her. But then they were careful to smile very brightly at her, and Rosa's own doubts would vanish.

Maria was the only constant in her early life, the Indian woman Maria.

Rosa never knew what tribe Maria belonged to, and Maria never volunteered this information. It was funny that Rosa hadn't spoken to Maria for sixty years, and yet at the same time there wasn't a day that went by that Maria wasn't there in her memory. Even in these last few years, when the memory lapses became serious, Maria stayed secure somewhere inside Rosa's head and heart.

Maria was strange, enigmatic, to Rosa, and their relationship, though somehow bound together forever, was undefinable. Even now Rosa wasn't sure what she felt for Maria. Maria, with her dark eyes and long, black hair in the earliest memories. Maria must have been in her early forties then. Later, Maria's hair was as white as Rosa's was now.

Rosa lifted the heavy mirror again and looked at herself. Yes, Maria *did* look like this. The white hair *and the eyes too?* Rosa put the mirror down.

In Rosa's first memory of Maria, when Rosa was about five or six, the two had been running. It was dark, and Rosa ran after Maria as if life itself depended on it. As Rosa ran, she called Maria by another name. What was it? Maria, a night shadow, had turned and lifted the child, Rosa, and carried her. Rosa bounced in Maria's arms. Maria smelled of food and smoke. Had she been cooking? Why had they been running?

Maria had always been near, close by to Rosa. Rosa saw that now. When Rosa had lived with different foster families, Maria had been a distant, shadowy figure who had followed Rosa everywhere.

This vivid recall was suddenly overpowering and exhausting to Rosa. It was also threatening somehow. She leaned her head back and rested it on the high frame of the chair.

A voice came from the kitchen. Rosa looked over her shoulder to see Anita put a tea kettle on the stove. Rosa studied her. Anita had once been a handsome woman. In her sixties now, Anita was still a striking woman, despite being a little overweight.

"Anita," Rosa called. "Anita."

The woman in the kitchen came to Rosa.

"I was thinking of Maria," Rosa said in Spanish, her voice not very strong.

Anita sat down on the bed. She wore a surprised look on her face. "Maria?" she asked. "The Maria from Taos Pueblo? We haven't seen her for a long time."

"No, Anita," Rosa answered, "that is another Maria, your half-sister, a younger one. I've never told you about the older one, the other Maria. She died just before you were born, in the same year. You were born in 1900, no?"

Anita nodded.

Rosa continued. "Maria was about 65 when she died. Your father, Santiago, knew her though."

"Who was this Maria, Mama?" Anita asked curiously. Rosa didn't look well.

"I really don't know, Anita. But now I think that she was somebody important to me," Rosa whispered, her voice cracking.

"You said you had no family, Mama. No mother, no father. You yourself have often said that." Anita carefully watched Rosa, whose face was drained of color. Alarmed, she asked Rosa more softly, "You want to talk about Maria?"

A tear rolled down Rosa's face. Anita wanted to hold Rosa but did not.

"Anita, Maria was an Indian woman." Rosa wiped the solitary tear from her face.

"Yes?" Anita asked expectantly.

"The first person I have a memory of is Maria. All my life, the first half of my life, Maria was there, not close, but always apart from me. When I was a child we were in Taos together, then later Española, and then Santa Fe. She was always there. Even after Santiago and I came to Las Vegas, Maria followed us."

"What happened to her, Mama?" Anita asked.

"I don't know. I don't know anything about her except that she spent her life alone. To the day she died, she was alone. She was not lucky like me to have found a man like Santiago, your father. And so late in life. I was over thirty. After Taos, I thought my life was ruined. . . ." Rosa smiled a girl-like smile.

"Santiago was good for me. And then I had you—when I was an old woman too! Life should not be spent alone. I think Maria's was. There was a sadness about her.

"The day that Maria died, she walked to our first little house in the early dawn. She was old then. Santiago built that house for me, Anita. It still stands. Maria came into the house, appearing to be very tired, and carrying corn meal, which she had ground the day before. She set the meal on the table and then sat down beside Santiago.

" 'Rosa,' Maria said, 'After today, you will not see me again'."

"Maria spoke to Santiago and me about her life then. She did not often do this. Her life had been long and very hard, but Maria said she had lived the best she could. She also said that sometimes she had been lonely, very lonely, but somehow she had survived it."

Rosa stopped here, picked up the mirror again, and gazed at herself. Anita was frightened at Rosa's weak appearance.

"Mama," Anita said, "let's eat. You haven't eaten all day." When Rosa did not object, Anita went into the kitchen, poured tea and cut a melon in two. She returned carrying a tray to Rosa, who was still studying herself in the mirror.

Anita served Rosa, placing the saucer and teacup on the dressing table. Then she sat down again and said, "Mama, Maria is gone. Don't think about her."

Rosa looked up at Anita and then at the melon and the cup of tea. She drank the tea, and then said heavily, "On that last day, Maria told me a truth and a lie."

"What was it?" Anita asked.

"Maria said that she was there on the day that I was born. She said that my mama died in childbirth, and Maria said that she then promised to look after me. She promised this to my mother. Maria said that I did not scream when I entered this world, but my mother wept, she said." Rosa quieted.

"And your father? Did Maria tell you about this man?" Anita asked.

Rosa said no. She picked up the hand mirror again and looked into it.

"Mama, what lie did Maria tell you?" Anita asked. "Was it about your mother? Who was your mother, Mama?"

Rosa held the mirror on her lap. Her eyes brimmed with tears.

"Come here," she told Anita.

Anita went to Rosa, who held up the mirror and told Anita to look inside. Rosa bent and looked in the mirror. The only thing she saw was her own face and Rosa's.

"Anita," Rosa said, *"that is Maria* in there. She is older than Maria lived to be, but it is Maria."

"What are you saying, Mama?" Anita gasped.

"Maria was my mother, Anita," Rosa said tearfully. "I didn't know it until today, until this afternoon sometime."

"Why?" asked Anita. "Why didn't she tell you, Mama?"

"I don't know," Rosa said, as tears flowed freely down her face. "Go away, Anita, for a little while, please. I must be alone. This is a shock to me somehow, though there is really no reason to be surprised. No reason at all."

Anita hugged Rosa and then disappeared into another part of the house.

Rosa sat the rest of the day alone, with Anita peeking in on her from time to time. Most of Rosa's thoughts were of Maria. Maria cooking. Maria praying. Maria seldom laughing.

Toward dusk, Anita entered the room. Rosa watched her turn on the lights and pull the bed covers down. Then Anita gently lifted Rosa and guided her toward the bathroom, and then to the bed. When Anita had helped Rosa change to a nightgown and put her under the covers, Anita sat down on the bed beside Rosa. She took Rosa's hand in her own. She did not intrude on Rosa's thoughts, but looked into Rosa's eyes for a long time.

Rosa asked one question. "Why didn't Maria tell me, Anita?"

Anita patted Rosa's hand and let it go. She left the room.

Outside the narrow windows, the rain stopped. Night came. For awhile, Rosa's memories kept her awake. She tried to remember her Taos husband's name. But try as she might, his name escaped her. Then, once more, she saw his brown eyes staring into hers. His eyes were hypnotic, lulling her to sleep. In this peaceful state, she remembered his name. Manuel. She smiled. Then about two hours later, Rosa died quietly, in her sleep.

7

WASHINGTON, D.C.

THE tourist crowd was heavy behind the Natural History Building, and the day was muggy, making breathing seem more of a chore. The sky was more gray than blue, although by Washington standards it was a clear day.

Geoffrey Newsome had a headache. It was one of those that pounded when he looked down to make notes on the five-by-seven index cards, or when he gulped his coffee. That morning, he drank a lot of it. It was now near twelve.

He'd arrived at his office late, about 9:30. The headache had been with him since dawn, and it hung on through most of the morning. He left the office about eleven, walked around the building, and bought a breakfast sandwich from a vendor set up behind the Natural History Building. Then he lay down on the grass momentarily, spread eagle, under a tree. That seemed to ease the throbbing that ran down the back of his skull to his shoulders. After a few minutes, when the crowd increased as the noon hour approached, he returned to his office.

On the long work table in front of him were hundreds of prehistoric North America pots—pots in fragments and pots in different stages of reconstruction. At one end of the table were several examples of finished, reconstructed pottery that included bowls, vases, and cylinders. All the pottery was from the Southwest, virtually all of it from the four corner states of Utah, Colorado, New Mexico, and Arizona. Most of the pottery had been dated between A.D. 1200 and 1300. All the pieces had been made by Indian people hundreds of years ago.

Some of the pots were black-and-white ware, but there was an assortment of other types mixed in. It was Geoffrey's job to sort out the pieces. He'd been at this for weeks, and it would probably take several more weeks to complete. He sat down at the table and began to glue pottery fragments together.

When Geoffrey had chosen this field, he'd genuinely loved the work. In his younger years, it was truly his passion in life, and he'd sacrificed marriage and children in order to pursue this life on his terms alone. Now, Geoffrey was forty-eight and alone in the world, but being alone had never bothered him in his entire life.

Geoffrey had discovered a long time ago that he did not really need people, didn't want clinging vines tugging at him. He could live without them, had done without them since he'd left home for school at the age of about seventeen. He'd never regretted choosing the single life—until the last few days.

Lately, he'd experienced an unspoken apprehension or anxiety about his work. This apprehension was directly related to where he was, physically. His work space, and office, was the cluttered attic of the Natural History Building of the Smithsonian Institution. He worked alone most of the time, except when he taught students or museum trainees the art of pottery reconstruction or preservation and reconstruction techniques and methods.

As Geoffrey reconstructed the 500-year-old pot in front of him, he occasionally glanced uneasily around the office. A few minutes later, Geoffrey was visited by one of his colleagues, Donald Evans, who was the closest thing to a best friend that Geoffrey had ever had. Their friendship had developed over a four-year period in which the two had shared these cramped quarters, sorting out fragments of history together, and making the pieces fit into something they both understood. After Donald's visit, Geoffrey walked him down the narrow staircase outside the attic. The staircase was the only connection between the top floor and the attic, and was the only entrance to Geoffrey's office.

Donald annoyed Geoffrey by pausing to point down the stairs to the place where Jean Wurly had been discovered stretched out on the narrow stair and floor space.

"I can't understand how she did it," Donald wondered aloud. "How could it have happened?"

Geoffrey wouldn't take this. "That damned woman," he said. "What was she doing up here? She had absolutely no business up here at all!"

After Donald had left for an afternoon of endless meetings, Geoffrey settled down at the table among the potsherds, still fuming over the Wurly woman.

He could not concentrate. In fact, he had had trouble concentrating for several days now. He poured a cup of coffee out of the not-too-clean percolator. Several minutes later, he discovered that he must have been daydreaming, because reconstruction of the pot had not progressed any further and several empty paper cups sat before him. He had poured those cups of coffee, hadn't he?

The headache still pounded. To make it worse, the cluttered office space seemed to be closing in on him. The office had never seemed small to him, ever. Though there were no windows in the high walls, he had never objected in the slightest. Geoffrey had conceded to himself last night and early this morning, and only in his most private thoughts, that something unexplainable about the work space had surfaced lately and made him uncomfortable. Just when he had become aware of this he was not certain, but it had happened very recently, within the last month.

Geoffrey ignored his uneasiness and the pounding in his skull, and turned again to the pottery fragments. He told himself that sooner or later he would feel better, that more fresh air was probably all he needed. From the table he selected several black-and-white sherds that were similar, with painted designs of lizards, and which conceivably could have come from the same pot. These he moved to another smaller work table where other reconstructed pots sat in boxes of sand.

The silence, the emptiness of the room, the alienation from the rest of the building played on Geoffrey. He looked toward his small radio. One morning five or six weeks ago, he had discovered it smashed into bits. It looked as if someone had taken a heavy object and simply dropped it on the radio. The clock in the radio was ruined too. The hands pointed at ten. Geoffrey couldn't understand it. What could have happened? Geoffrey replaced the radio within days, but the new one was defective. At times the volume worked, and at other times the radio shut itself off. Consequently, Geoffrey left the radio on all the time and sometimes it played unexpectedly. He now looked at the radio wishing for companionship to come out of it.

These last few weeks, Geoffrey had become increasingly conscious of the fact that he was alone in the room over eighty percent of the time. He'd become aware of his own intake of air, in gulps, his breathing patterns, the sound of sherds as they dropped on the table, and his footsteps on the wooden floor.

Now the door at the bottom of the stairs sounded as if it had opened. Geoffrey waited for footsteps to climb the stairs. However, no one came.

The door to his office at the top of the stairs was open. He looked in that direction and remembered Jean Wurly. He pictured her in his mind, an intense, frowsy woman he'd never liked. Had she come up here before? Why?

This idea was new to him. The thought that someone he did not know very well and whom he disliked intensely could come and enter *his* space and violate his territory, without his approval or knowledge, angered him.

Perhaps she had been up here before. He looked around the attic. In addition to the long work tables that filled the center of the southern half of the room, shelves ran along both east and west walls from floor to ceiling on the north side of the room. Large wooden cabinets stood between the shelving there. The north wall itself had no shelving or other attachments to it. Boxes and trunks were stacked along it, behind the wooden cabinets.

Maybe Wurly had gone through the attic collection. Maybe she had even taken something. But why?

Geoffrey got up from the table and walked into the narrow aisle between the east wall shelves and the cabinets. The items on the east shelves—metates, manos, and stone hammers—were in order. In fact a thick layer of dust had settled on everything. Geoffrey breathed a little easier.

Then he walked to the other aisle, the west wall of shelves that held baskets and dolls. Again, nothing had been touched. Geoffrey told himself that everything back here was due a good cleaning.

Dust was harder to see on the wooden cabinets in the center of the room. The cabinets were back to back and the drawers faced each wall of shelves. In one cabinet there were two rows of twelve shallow drawers facing the west wall. Geoffrey decided to inspect them. One by one, he went through each drawer.

He started at the bottom. The drawer slid out easily. A piece of tissue paper covered the contents. An unfamiliar odor drifted up from the drawer. Pulling away the tissue paper, Geoffrey noted that the drawer space was filled with five necklaces. Three of them were made of bear claws and one was elk's teeth. The fifth was a necklace of twenty human fingers, the nails on the fingers blue-tinged. Geoffrey had seen the necklace many times. On occasion he'd playfully put the necklace on. He was the kind of man who did that, and he did it now. The necklace lay on his plaid shirt, the fingers pressed against him.

He could not really tell if the items in the drawers had been disturbed. He replaced the necklace, then the tissue paper, and opened the next drawer.

Only in two drawers did it look as if there were empty spaces where something might have been removed. Later, he would come back to these two and confirm the contents by his inventory records. Now, he moved to the other cabinet and stood in the aisle running between the east shelves and that cabinet. These drawers, which also faced the east shelves, were deeper than those in the first cabinet. Here also were two rows of drawers, but each row contained only ten drawers. On this side, too, he started at the bottom. The drawer slid out smoothly. Brown paper lay over the contents. Geoffrey removed this.

Seven human skulls sat in a circular arrangement. There were several other items among the skulls, but as far as Geoffrey could remember, everything was as it should be.

The next drawer held shields, small circular shields of hide. This drawer released an overpowering odor that almost made Geoffrey retch. The odor was unusual—it was not foul-smelling, but in some other sense it was totally offensive. The odor was new. Geoffrey had not noticed it before today. He recognized it, but could not identify it at the moment. What was it? He turned away from the drawer and inhaled deeply, then turned once more to the drawer, to quickly count the shields. Eight were there. He closed the drawer swiftly and got up and ran to his open office door to gulp the fresher air there. What was that odor?

The radio blared loudly, unexpectedly, behind him. Geoffrey jumped two inches off the floor in surprise, and, feeling foolish, turned the volume on the radio down and went back to inspecting the drawers. The rest of the inspection was without incident. When he finished, he returned to the two drawers in the first cabinet that might have had items removed from them. He read the information giving coded numbers on the outside of the first drawer and then pulled a corresponding book out of a gray metal filing cabinet.

The items in the drawer were all from the southwestern United States, and something *was* missing. It was a full scalp, with the ears attached.

Geoffrey tried to visualize this missing piece. It had been over a year since he had had reason to pull it out of the drawer.

The scalp, he remembered, was dry human flesh, coated with a perpetual layer of oil. The ears were shriveled, and the gray hair attached to the scalp was coarse and stubby. Geoffrey had tugged at the hair, intrigued by the scalp's resilience to his touch, his rough and careless handling, as well as its resistance to time. It showed no signs of obliteration from existence, as many items in this room were prone to show after exposure to time, the deadly air, and the environment.

The last time he had showed the scalp was to a group of American Indians, who had raised their eyebrows at it and refused to handle it as Geoffrey did. That was last summer, possibly June. In fact, Geoffrey had always kind of thought that Wurly had had something to do with that group barging in up here, looking into business that had nothing to do with them.

Perhaps the scalp was simply misplaced, but how could he have been that careless? All the items up here in the cabinets were kept separate from the other Indian collections downstairs because of their highly controversial nature—controversial mainly to American Indians; other groups were more educated and tolerant. Still, Geoffrey agreed, keeping quiet about the existence of the collection was probably best.

He went on to investigate the second drawer where he once more read the information on the outside of the drawer and pulled out another book that matched the coded numbers there. As Geoffrey read, his face took on a perplexed expression. Missing here was a cloth sack that held the bones and skull of an infant. The bones were from the southeastern United States, taken from looted Indian ruins about 1860. Geoffrey was going to catch hell if these two items were really gone!

He had to think about this carefully. He settled in his swivel chair among the potsherds. Sooner or later, he'd have to report the fact that these items were missing. Could it be that the Wurly woman had taken them? Why? He looked at his watch. It was nearly three.

A few minutes later, Geoffrey was outside the building, walking briskly in the direction of the Washington Monument. He wasn't going anywhere in particular, he was simply moving. He had to move. He had to think.

If the Wurly woman hadn't taken the missing items, who had? For what purpose? To sell? Geoffrey quickly disregarded the last question. All the staff were professional people. Still, there was a black market for such items.

As Geoffrey walked, he became absorbed into the tourist flow. The odor of people hit him hard and fast, bringing him abruptly out of his reverie. That same odor of living, breathing people had been in the attic! It had flown up out of the cabinet drawer. But that was completely impossible! Geoffrey felt nauseated. He fought his way out of the crowd and collapsed on the lawn in front of the monument.

Was he imagining things? He lay there looking up at the top of the white monument and the gray sky, considering the possibility. Nearly three weeks ago, he had imagined that he had heard something move behind the cabinets, along the empty north wall. Nothing had been there, of course, when he'd examined the room. The only items back there were trunks and boxes that held an assortment of various tribes' medicine bundles and a couple of other things. Yet, about a half a dozen times recently, while working on the sherds, he did feel that someone had tapped him on the arm or shoulder. Although it had momentarily unnerved him, each time he'd handled it in a rational way. The last incident, however, had been the most unnerving.

Geoffrey had been carefully piecing together a large black-and-white bowl, a beautiful specimen of extinct Indian culture. He'd been standing, leaning over the nearly completed bowl and filling in the missing pieces. Suddenly he'd felt as if he'd been roughly shoved from behind. He'd lost his balance and fallen forward on the bowl, breaking it into four large pieces and upsetting other pots on the table. Geoffrey had been the only person in the attic at the time. Somehow, he'd decided, he must have lost his balance. That was the only logical explanation.

Children ran around Geoffrey now as he lay in the grass. Tourists around him spoke in English or other languages.

Geoffrey then found himself thinking of home, a small beach town in Delaware. He hadn't thought of home since he'd left it. There was no one there, really. He had no parents, no other family. For the first time in his life, he missed not having these people. He closed his eyes. When he opened them again, he saw five American Indians in the crowd of visitors and tourists surrounding him. Among the five was George Daylight, whom Geoffrey had met several times. The last time he had spoken with George was last summer when Geoffrey had shown the missing scalp, along with other items, to the group of American Indians.

Geoffrey hadn't liked Daylight at first sight. Their relationship deteriorated from there. Geoffrey thought Daylight was both arrogant and ignorant. Daylight had questioned (perhaps "challenged" would be a better word) Geoffrey too often on the Indian collection in Geoffrey's care. The confrontation in the attic last summer had been the last straw.

Daylight now spoke to his little group, switching alternately from English to a tribal tongue. He was dressed in a manner that left no doubt that he was an American Indian. Geoffrey was thoroughly disgusted by Daylight's appearance and presence.

Daylight had seen Geoffrey Newsome sprawled on the ground as soon as his group had come out of the monument. In his tribal language, he'd made a condescending comment about this man on the ground. The group, which consisted of an older woman and three men, looked curiously at Geoffrey, and deciding to trust George's opinion, walked carefully around Geoffrey, ignoring him as much as possible.

Geoffrey sat up, brushed the grass off his clothes, and reluctantly decided to return to his office. He wondered if he could get back without being seen by Daylight. He casually looked in the opposite direction from George Daylight and strolled away.

Geoffrey took his time and tried to enjoy what was left of the afternoon. His headache was gone, but in its place was a buzzing or humming inside his head. His vision was becoming distorted by white dots of light that flashed before him. Perhaps a cool drink would help. A sidewalk vendor stood beneath a red and white umbrella and sold fruit juices and soft drinks to the crowd. Geoffrey made his way to the vendor and bought a bottle of grapefruit juice. The vendor opened the bottle and handed it to Geoffrey.

At that moment, the humming inside Geoffrey's head blocked out all other sounds, and he lost all vision as dots of flashing light danced around him.

He did not feel himself fall. He later remembered only that his eyes closed. A couple of minutes later he became conscious. His hand still held part of his broken grapefruit juice bottle. A circle of people stood over him, carefully watching. The first person he saw was George Daylight. Geoffrey frowned.

Daylight simply asked, "Are you okay?"

Geoffrey found his voice. "I'm fine. I've never fainted before."

No one offered to help him get to his feet except the older Indian woman in Daylight's group. She put out a hand to pull him up, but Geoffrey wouldn't take it. The woman stepped back. He sat up and pulled himself to his feet as the circle of spectators cleared.

"I'll go to my office now. I'm all right," Geoffrey said to Daylight.

George didn't say a word. He just watched Geoffrey. This made Geoffrey angry. George could make Geoffrey angry as easily as that. He asked George, "Well, is there anything wrong with that?"

Daylight answered, "You tell us."

Geoffrey turned angrily away and stomped off.

The older woman with George Daylight asked, "What'sa matter with him?"

"He's caught up in a whirlwind he don't understand, Auntie," George answered. "I feel kind of sorry for the poor thing."

"Oh," the woman answered as if she understood perfectly. Then she asked, "When do we get to see some tribal people, George? I'm tired of looking at all these ol' buildings and statues. They ain't no good."

George answered, "Come on, Auntie. We're going back to the hotel. We've nearly walked your feet off."

Instead of returning to his office, Geoffrey went directly to his Volkswagen parked behind the Natural History Building. He drove out of the parking lot and entered the four lanes of one-way traffic. In about a half an hour, he was inside his own apartment building.

Geoffrey was not usually an orderly man. His apartment, although clean, reflected this. He ignored the clutter to take care of the humming in his head. He located the aspirin bottle under some towels in the bathroom, took three tablets, and lay down on the bed.

In a couple of hours Geoffrey woke to an even more intense humming in his brain. Again he took three more aspirin. The room was extremely warm, too warm for comfort. It felt as if hot, humid air was entering the apartment. Maybe he'd left a window or the sliding terrace door open. No, he couldn't have. The room had been cool and the air conditioner had been blowing cold air when he'd come home. He would have noticed an open window earlier, wouldn't he?

Geoffrey checked the windows and found them all closed and locked. Then he went to the sliding door. The drapes were drawn over it. He felt beneath the drapes. The sliding door *was* open. He opened the drapes, slid the screen door aside, and stepped out onto the cement floor of the terrace. It was early evening. He gazed down at the nearest freeway and the roofs of several other apartment buildings. He was on the thirteenth floor.

The hammering in his head did not cease. In fact, Geoffrey was a little dizzy.

He looked around the terrace. He seldom came out here. There was a lounge chair off to the side with a small iron table near it, and a white, cloth sack on the table. He turned around, went back inside, closed the sliding door, pulled the drapes shut, and began to undress. None of the lights were on in the apartment and all the drapes were closed, but the apartment was illuminated in a pale glow that filtered through the drapes.

Geoffrey lay down, fulling expecting to be asleep in less than five minutes. But as he closed his eyes, his thoughts returned to the terrace. There was something about it. What was it? The lounge chair had been there for over a year, the table had been carried out only a few months ago. The sack was taken out when? The *sack*? There had never been any sack out there. It looked familiar, though. He'd seen it somewhere. It looked like something from the museum. The *museum*?

Geoffrey jumped up quickly and swayed, nearly losing his balance. He retraced his steps to the terrace, opened the drapes and slid both the glass and screen doors aside. He sat on the lounge chair and stared. Yes, the sack was on the table. It looked innocent enough, but Geoffrey felt a terrible dread.

He pulled the string on the cloth material and untied the sack. He looked inside, but he already knew what was there. The sack contained the bones and skull of an infant, the same ones missing from one of the cabinet drawers in the attic of the museum.

What was this doing here in Geoffrey's apartment? Geoffrey sat on the lounge chair and once more tried to think, but with the steady buzzing in his head, he was unable to concentrate. Holding the sack of tiny bones, not knowing how they'd arrived there, Geoffrey felt an unknown fear wash over him.

8

WILLIE Begay jumped off the bus and headed toward his apartment. The exterior of the building was a bright blue-green, and the interior hallway was painted a bizarre red. He climbed the stairs leading to his door. This place depressed him. He felt closed in here. The walls, the city, the miles of freeway all combined to strangle him. There were no open spaces to which he was accustomed and needed. He could not breathe here. He gasped for air and wide, open spaces. He was glad he would be going home soon, in ten days to be exact. He was counting the days, marking them off his calendar each morning.

His apartment was stale and musty. Reaching for the air conditioner, he turned the cold air on full blast. The air conditioner was old and noisy, but it did circulate the air. Willie wondered if people here ever opened windows to allow fresh air inside. Everywhere he went, the buildings were cooled and heated automatically. No, they probably didn't open their windows. The outside air was often too bad to breathe.

Willie went into his bedroom to change his damp western-style shirt. The humidity was another thing he could do without; he preferred the dry weather of Arizona and New Mexico. He poured a glass of ice water and spilled it on the cheap, red carpet, which was desperately in need of cleaning, and turned on the television set. He had some reading to complete, but the sound of another person in the room appealed to him. Then he remembered that he had some tapes that were in Navajo. That was even better. He lugged out the bulky reel-to-reel recorder and set it up on the coffee table. The tapes were on the top shelf of the bedroom closet. He went to get them.

The man on the tape was Willie's grandfather, his maternal grandfather. Jonnie Navajo. On the tape Jonnie Navajo sang a Navajo protection song. Willie sang along with the tape, and the voice of his grandfather soothed him.

Willie had not been well. He'd had severe headaches the last few months in D.C. He guessed that the headaches were probably caused by the stifling heat. But there were other problems, too. He also had dizzy spells, or vertigo, off and on the past few days. His stay in D.C. was becoming a nightmare, combatting illness and strange people. And now strange things were happening, too.

Eight days ago, Willie had been involved in an incident that numbed his senses. He'd been preparing a research paper for a class at the university and had secured access to the Navajo collection held by the Natural History Museum of the Smithsonian Institution. Several items of Navajo manufacture and origin had been carefully placed before him, of which he took notes from the accession cards that matched each particular item. Then he'd come across a small, innocent looking bundle wrapped in white tissue paper. Before reading the accompanying card, Willie had clumsily pulled away the tissue to discover that beneath the tissue paper the item was wrapped in an oily white cloth. He'd undone the tight knots on the cloth and opened it. A peculiar odor had drifted up from the cloth. Willie had dropped the cloth and the item when he saw what he held. It was a complete scalp, with gray hair and both ears attached to it! Willie was stunned. It was the last thing he expected to find here, the last thing he expected to be brought to him! He was clearly shaken. After he recovered from his shock, he located the card for the bundle and read the words "NAVAJO SCALP." That was the only information given, except to say that the item had been bought just before the turn of the century by a well-known photographer passing through the Southwest on a photographic excursion.

Willie felt sick from this. For the rest of the visit to the museum, Willie sat and stared at this grotesque thing, somehow powerless to turn away from it. He didn't want to touch it and unconsciously rubbed his hands on his jeans. A layer of oil from the scalp stayed on his fingers. Eventually the assistant curator came and took away everything on the table. The curator was not at all affected by the scalp, expressing only mild surprise that it was among the items provided to Willie. However, the curator did say with some confusion that such artifacts were not accessible to the average researcher. Willie let him rewrap the scalp in the piece of cloth and once more in the white tissue. The numbness of this incident stayed with Willie the rest of that day. He could feel the numbness of it in him now, too. He looked at his hands and rubbed them on his jeans.

Jonnie Navajo's voice sang the fourth stanza of the song. Willie's body came out of the numbness a little as he heard his grandfather sing of beauty before him, beauty behind him, beauty above him, beauty below him, and beauty all around. There was a blank space of about five minutes before the next song. Willie lay on the couch and waited for the next one to begin.

The doorbell rang. He wondered how long it had been ringing. Willie opened the door. Russell Tallman and George Daylight stood out in the hall. Russell carried a paper sack.

"Yatahey," said George. He put out a hand and vigorously shook Willie's hand.

Willie answered, "*Ya'tééh*. How long have you been here? I didn't hear you. The air conditioner is so loud, and I had the tape recorder on too. Come in."

George led the way. He took the chair in front of the television set and pulled off his beat-up, pointed-toe cowboy boots. He had on one gray sock and one white, and still wore his cowboy hat. "Damn, it's hot outside," he said as he sank into the chair.

Russell walked directly to the kitchen and set the paper sack on the table. He pulled out a six pack of beer and a large white package. "What's in the package?" Willie wanted to know.

Russell answered, "Lox. Food."

Willie watched him unwrap the paper. "Fish?" Willie asked, "fish?"

"Lox. I've acquired a taste for it," Russell nodded.

"But it's fish!" Willie said.

Russell looked offended.

George yelled above the air conditioner. "Russ, don't you remember nothing? Navajos ain't fish-eaters. Ain't that right, Willie? You guys don't go for no fish, do you? You know that, Russell. What the hell's the matter with you, hauling fish over here?"

Willie said, "Well, you guys go ahead with your meal. I've already eaten anyway. What are you doing way over here?"

Russell took off his cowboy hat and set it on top of the refrigerator. He said, "Since today's Sunday, we decided to come on over and visit you. I caught a bus to George's place yesterday morning and we rented a car. We were tired of just sitting around on weekends, so we drove up to Gettysburg to have a look-see. We thought about coming over and getting you then, but didn't get around to it til now."

Willie answered, "Don't worry about it. I couldn't have gone yesterday. I didn't feel well. In the afternoon I went to a movie at the shopping center a couple of blocks from here. Today, I went and had myself a real meal. Just got back a few minutes ago."

"Want a can of beer?" George asked Willie.

"I don't think so, George. My stomach has been real sensitive lately," Willie answered. "That's why I thought a good meal would help me out. I guess I haven't been eating well. I've lost maybe six pounds in the last two weeks."

"Suit yourself, Will," George said. He looked at the tape recorder and asked, "What have you got there?"

Willie turned on the recorder. "I was listening to some songs from home. When I get lonesome or start to feel like I need to be around the People for awhile, I just push the button and sooner or later I start to feel better."

"I know what you mean," George agreed.

The three men listened to Jonnie Navajo sing until the tape ended. The venetian blinds were closed, and the room was dark and now very comfortable.

George put his feet up on the coffee table and drained his first can of beer. Russell stretched out on the couch, while Willie lay on a blanket that covered the filthy carpeting.

"Click that off for me, will you, George?" Willie asked.

George turned off the machine and sat back down in his chair. "What are those songs about?" George asked.

"Protection, mostly," answered Willie.

Russell said, "I know a protection song," and he began to sing it. George opened another can of beer and Willie motioned George to bring him one too.

When Russell had finished singing, Willie said, "That's a good song. What kind is it? I mean, what tribe does it come from? I don't even know what tribe you are, Russell."

George answered, "Ol' Russ is a little bit of a half dozen tribes. He's part Kiowa, part Caddo, part Pawnee, part Comanche, and what else, Russ?"

"Cheyenne," Russell put in.

"I always tell Russ that's why he's got two minds about everything. You know, he couldn't make up his mind really hasty if his life depended on it. Pawnees and Cheyennes tried to wipe each other off the face of the earth, and practically all the other tribes he is fought one another too. Seems like half the time Russ is fighting a constant battle within hisself just trying to answer or decide one thing. I tell him it's 'cause all the blood got mixed up like that. Russ might go insane from it one of these days, if he ain't a little crazy already," George said.

Russell grinned but made no comment.

"Now me," George said, "I'm Creek and Cherokee. I'm the real thing, the real Cherokee, none of this imitation stuff."

Willie was surprised. "All this time I thought you were from a Northern Plains tribe."

"Lots of people think that," George said. "I married up with those people. One wife from Montana, one from North Dakota, a couple from Oklahoma. One of Russell's cousins was one of my wives. Heck, I even married a white woman for awhile. Can't help myself. Those purty little things just wrap me around their fingers."

Willie smiled and slowly drank his beer, trying to gauge how his stomach was going to respond to the stuff flowing into it. He said, "What does the song mean, Russ, the one you just sang? It's a lonesome song, isn't it?"

"I suppose," Russell said. "It's a song that says you're lost, far from home, far from family, and you want to find the way back. In the song you call upon some unseen force or power to take you home, because you can't find the way, the path, alone."

Willie nodded. He did not feel well. The image of Russell swayed in front of him twice, but still his vision wasn't as bad as it had been yesterday.

"You alright?" George asked.

Willie nodded again and tried to get up. He wanted to make it to the bathroom. If he didn't, everything he had eaten today was going to be on the floor. His stomach churned. George stared at him, and George swayed, although Willie knew that George was sitting.

"Hey, man," George said, "if you feel bad, just lie down. Don't try to move around for a minute or two."

Willie took the advice and stretched out on the dirty rug.

George put Willie's beer can on the kitchen table, saying, "No more beer, Willie, til we see what we got here."

Russell sat up and said to Willie, "Man, I thought you were going to

53

take care of this the last time I saw you at the university. When was that? Didn't you go to the doctor?"

Willie said, "It's nothing. I'm going to be all right. Didn't see any reason to pay a medicine man right now. I'm low on money, and they're hard to locate around here." He grinned, although he didn't feel much like it.

"Well, I'll admit you do look a little better now than the last time I saw you. You could barely sit still then. Looked like you were going to fall over any minute," Russell said. "Better take a chance on a white medicine man, Willie. I'm serious. Right now, you look like hell."

George was quiet as Willie pulled himself up to go to the bathroom. When Willie had closed the door, George asked, "How long has he been like this? He shore enough does look like hell."

"Beats me," Russell answered, and carried the lox from the kitchen table to the coffee table. "Taste this," he said to George. "It's pretty good."

George broke off a piece.

"It is really true that Navajos don't eat fish?" Russell asked.

"Hell, I don't know. Ain't no expert on them. I just heard it somewhere, or read it, or somebody told me. Probably some do these days."

The door to the bathroom opened, and Willie stepped out.

"Is it true that Navajos don't eat fish, Willie? Damn, I didn't know that. Didn't mean anything bringing lox. Next time I'll bring a pizza," Russell said with a smile.

Willie didn't respond.

George said, "We gonna educate Russ, Will. You can teach him about Navajos, I'll teach him how to get women. Poor thing, right now no woman wants him. But when I get through with him, he's gonna have to send them away. Know how I'm gonna do it? Indian style. Gonna teach him about love medicine," George laughed.

Willie was frozen where he was. He put his hands over his ears and began to yell in Navajo. His voice was deep, loud, and strong.

Both Russell and George looked up in surprise at the same time. Willie moaned, and his legs gave out beneath him. He fell backward against the bathroom door. Russell and George looked at one another. Russell said, "What the hell? . . ."

He went to Willie, who was now in tears, sobbing hysterically, and talking in Navajo. He fell on his knees. His eyes were open, wild and red.

Russell said, "Hey, man, what's going on? Are you hurt?"

Willie looked at him, but Russell couldn't tell if Willie really saw him. Willie continued to talk in Navajo as he tried to get up. His legs would not support him. Russell tried to pull Willie up.

"Speak in English," Russell said. But Willie continued to speak in Navajo, sobbing and pointing randomly around the room.

"Will, speak English," Russell said sharply to Willie. Russell's words somehow connected to Willie, who responded, "My legs won't move. See that?" He pointed. There was nothing in the direction that Willie pointed.

Even as Willie spoke, he leaned forward and began to crawl across the room, with a speed and force that surprised Russell. Russell followed him a little way and then looked at George, who was watching the whole thing from his chair. "What the hell?" Russell asked again.

Willie headed straight for a wall, giving no indication that he knew it was there. Both George and Russell made a mad dash for him before he hit it, but they were too late. Willie rammed the wall with such force that one of the pictures on the wall tilted at an angle. He did not appear to be hurt, but turned in another direction and headed for the kitchen table, talking rapidly in Navajo between his tears and sobs. He rammed the metal legs of the table, and toppled over one of the dinette chairs.

"He's gonna hurt hisself," George said. "We're gonna have to get a hold of him and pin him down."

"See that?" Willie pointed.

"What's he talking about?" George asked.

"I don't know," Russell said.

George managed to grab Willie by one of his arms and turn him on his back, but Willie was unnaturally strong. He struck out at George. "Damn near got me," George said. "We'll have to tie him down."

"What?" Russell said in disbelief.

"Find something, Russell. Now. Now, damn it!" George yelled.

Russell looked in Willie's bedroom. There was nothing with which to tie Willie. Maybe a belt or a tie would do. He opened the closet door and saw two ties hanging over a hook in the back of the closet. Russell grabbed both ties and hurried back to George.

George sat on top of Willie, whose arms and legs were thrashing up and down around George. George still wore his cowboy hat, although it sat too far to one side. George grabbed the hat, set it straight, and pushed it down hard while he held one of Willie's arms down with a knee.

Russell grabbed Willie's free arm and wrapped one of the ties around that wrist while George yelled, "Roll him over on his stomach!"

Both Russell and George pushed him over. Willie resisted with a strength that neither knew he had. "Damn," George said as Russell pulled Willie's other arm behind his back and tied both wrists.

Willie tried to lift himself up onto his knees, but was unsuccessful. He continued to sputter in Navajo.

"What the hell happened to him?" Russell asked. "What are we going to do with him? Is he going to be all right?"

George answered, "Russell, this is a fine time to talk up a storm! Any other time you never have much to say. I don't know what the answers are. I ain't no goddamn expert!"

They both stood over Willie, trying to decide what to do with him. "Let's put him in the bedroom, on the bed," George finally said.

Russell picked Willie up and dragged him to the bedroom. They untied his wrists, but his arms shot out and hit George in the stomach. He tried to get up.

Russell said, "Looks like we're going to have to keep him tied, George."

George nodded, rolled Willie on his stomach, and retied his wrists behind his back. Willie continued to mumble in Navajo.

Russell and George went back into the living room. Russell ate and had another can of beer. George watched Russell and occasionally glanced toward the bedroom where Willie lay, muttering loudly to himself. When Russell finished his meal and the can of beer, he washed his face and hands in the bathroom. He'd had time to think. As he came out, he said, "George, ol' buddy, we got ourselves a hell of a thing on our hands."

George nodded.

"You know what this here is, don't you?" Russell's voice boomed across the room.

George nodded.

"Well, what are you going to do about it?" Russell asked.

George looked at Russell and grinned, "Me?"

"All right, you and me, then," Russell conceded.

"Don't know," George said, "I. . . ."

Russell cut him off. "You ain't no goddamn expert, I know," he said.

"Sit down, Russell. Let's think this one over," George answered.

After several minutes of staring at each other and the walls, George asked, "Willie ain't got no family out here?"

"Not that I know of," Russell answered.

"Well, that settles it, then, Russ. We're gonna have to help him out," George said decisively.

"What?" Russell asked. "We don't know anything about Navajos!"

George nodded. "True, true. But, Russell, it can't be too different from what your people and my people know. Besides, poor thing, who else here in D.C. is gonna help?"

"Alright! Alright! I'm with you. What'll we do? I've got some cedar at home. Maybe we should *smoke* him? This place, too," Russell said, indicating the apartment.

"Good boy," George said, pleased. "But wait, maybe Willie has some cedar right here. Go check through his things."

Russell quickly rummaged through Willie's few possessions while Willie watched him without recognition. He returned to George empty-handed.

"You're gonna have to get your cedar, Russell. Your place is closer than mine," George said.

"Alright," Russell agreed. "I should be back here within a couple of hours. Are you sure you can handle him?"

"No problem," George answered, "but hurry back!"

Russell was gone nearly three hours. In that time, George paced the floor while Willie attempted to free himself and George struggled with him. It was evening when Russell returned.

"Damn, man," he said when George let him inside. "I got a ticket. I was going the wrong way on a one-way street."

"That doesn't matter," George said. "Did you bring the cedar?"

Russell nodded but said at the same time, "The hell it doesn't! Damn near got myself killed. How is he?"

"Just the same," George said. "Keeps talking in Navajo. I answered him in Creek and we got along fine."

Russell handed him a pouch of cedar sprigs and a large beaded and feathered fan. George took them into the kitchen. He turned on one of the electric burners and set a frying pan on the burner.

Russell went into the bedroom. Willie was still speaking to some unseen presence, his finger pointed stiffly, though his hands were firmly bound.

A few minutes later, George entered the room carrying the frying pan. Smoke drifted up out of it, and the scent of cedar filled the room. He and Russell turned Willie over, forcing him to sit as George fanned the smoke over him. Then they laid him down again on his stomach.

George carried the pan into all the rooms, including the bathroom, until the apartment smelled of cedar smoke throughout.

When this was done, George and Russell went into the other room. George again claimed the chair in front of the television set, and Russell stretched out on the couch.

They waited the remainder of the evening without turning on the lights in the darkening room. Only once did either of them speak.

Russell asked, "Know what?"

George answered, "What?"

"That whole damned place needs to be smoked. It's crying for it," Russell answered.

George nodded without asking which place Russell meant.

About nine o'clock that night, Willie returned to normal. Russell had untied him sometime after seven, when Willie had quieted and appeared to be asleep. George then fell asleep in the chair, his feet on the coffee table, and Russell snored on the couch.

Willie shook George awake. He was embarrassed about the whole thing, although he seemed to remember nothing.

"Man, I'm sorry," Willie said. "I must have fallen asleep on you guys. The only thing I remember is trying to make it to the bathroom. I felt awful."

"Are you okay now?" George asked, and Willie nodded. "Well, you don't mind if Russ and I sleep over tonight, do you? It's late, and we ain't too good on the freeways yet, keep getting lost."

"Naw," Willie said. "Glad to have some company."

Russell woke about seven the next morning. Apparently Willie had been up for some time by then. He entered the apartment carrying a white paper sack. "Bought some coffee and donuts down the street," Willie said. "I usually don't eat a big breakfast myself."

Russell groaned and went into the bathroom. In the kitchen, George ducked his head under the cold water faucet.

They drank coffee and chewed on the donuts. George asked, "How long you been sick, Will?"

"Not too long," he answered. "It's been bad only a few days. I'm going home in nine days. I plan to get some help then."

"Good, good," George said. "Best thing to do is to go home, fix things up. Understand?"

Willie nodded his head in agreement and finished off the coffee.

As they parted in the parking lot, Russell looked at Willie. "You going to be alright?"

Again Willie nodded. George and Russell looked doubtfully at each other and drove away.

9

NAVAJO RESERVATION

NASBAH had a small rectangular loom and was now midway through her fourth rug. She was improving. The design on this rug was more centered and more uniform than on any of the three earlier rugs. All in all, she was fairly satisfied with this one. She looked over to her grandmother—her teacher—who was also weaving beside her. For the first time in her life, Nasbah wondered about this skill.

"Grandmother," she asked, "who wove the first rug?"

Nasbah's paternal grandmother kept weaving but answered, "It was probably Spider Woman. She brought weaving to the People."

The answer satisfied Nasbah temporarily, and she put aside the weaving comb and gray yarn. She got up off the ground, off the sheepskin on which she sat, and walked around the summer shelter. It was approaching the warmest part of the day, although it did not ever get hot up here on the mountain summit. Her grandfather would bring in the sheep and goats soon. Realizing this, Nasbah stirred the fire and started a new blaze. She rinsed out the enamel coffee pot and filled it with water, sprinkling coffee grounds on top. Next, she peeled potatoes, slicing them into cubes, and added a carrot. Last of all she sliced some squash, and put everything into an enamel pot with a lid. She set the pot beside the fire. The dough for the bread was already made. All she needed to do was to lay the flat pieces of dough on the grill and turn them over when the time was right. She was hungry. She had had only coffee that morning, with a tortilla.

She sat down beside her grandmother. "When did you learn to weave?" she asked.

Her grandmother smiled. "It's been so long ago, I don't think I remember. Maybe when I was twelve years, maybe earlier, maybe later. Old Lady Mexican taught me. She was my mother's aunt."

Nasbah went back to her own weaving. It was funny that she only now had thoughts about serious things, things she had taken for granted all these years. In school the past spring, Nasbah had found herself questioning many aspects of her life. She had then concluded that she did not know very much, and had never made it her business to learn certain things. The little she did know, she'd decided, was entirely inadequate now.

Her grandfather, Jonnie Navajo, was returning with the sheep. She could hear the sheep dogs and the bells dangling on the goats.

She set the table, spread some charcoal beneath the crude grill, and began to make bread. By the time Jonnie Navajo had penned the sheep and goats in the corral and rested a few minutes, the midday meal was ready. They ate leisurely.

When the table was clear and the old man had settled down to his horsehair weaving for awhile, Nasbah approached him.

"Grandfather," she said, "I've been wanting to ask you something since early spring. I read something in school about the People. I was wondering, where did the People come from?"

The old man momentarily stopped his weaving and looked over his glasses at Nasbah, a pleased gleam in his eyes. He had waited a long time for her question. He was ready for it. He said, "The People were created by Changing Woman. It was she who made the People."

"But, Grandfather," Nasbah said, "the books don't say that. They say something else."

The old man nodded. "I have heard that," he answered. "It doesn't matter. I was told that the People came from Changing Woman. This was told to me by *Hosteen Nez*, my father's brother. My father, *Hosteen Diné*, probably would have told me this himself if he hadn't died first. But I was very young when that happened, and I probably could not have made sense of anything at that age. Later, in my teens, *Hosteen Nez* felt sorry for me and took me in his care. He told me these things."

Nasbah was quiet and went back to her weaving. From across the shelter, she finally asked, "And who told this to *Hosteen Nez*, Grandfather?"

The old man frowned. Was there doubt in her voice? He answered, "The father of *Hosteen Diné* and *Hosteen Nez* was a man named Tall Navajo's Son. Not only did he give this information, he also passed on two ceremonies to *Hosteen Nez*."

"Did you know this man, Grandfather, Tall Navajo's Son?" Nasbah asked.

The old man answered, "He was alive when I was born, although he was old and blind. They tell me that he held me on his knee, though I don't remember anything of it."

Jonnie Navajo was quiet for awhile and then added, "Tall Navajo's Son married a girl from the south side of Beautiful Mountain when he was just about twenty. This woman was the mother of *Hosteen Diné* and *Hosteen Nez*. She was about sixteen when she had her first child, my father."

"Who were Tall Navajo's Son's parents? Did he have any brothers or sisters?" Nasbah was curious now.

"Ah," answered Jonnie Navajo. "His mother was called Red Lady, and his father, of course, was Tall Navajo. He had one brother who died before the child reached a year old, and two sister, twins, much younger than he. It is said that they lived here." He waved his hand around the shelter.

"You mean right here?" Nasbah asked in amazement.

"Well, not exactly right here, but in this area, yes," her grandfather answered.

"Tall Navajo's Son was reared by his mother and father, and his maternal grandfather, until the age of about thirteen, or maybe fourteen. Then a great change came into his life, so said *Hosteen Nez*."

"Where was Red Lady from? Who were her mother and father?" Nasbah asked.

"I don't know who her mother was, but White Sheep was her father. It seems that he, White Sheep, went by two or three names," the old man answered.

"You said that something happened?" Nasbah reminded her grandfather.

He nodded. "It was a time of great unrest. Life was uncertain. It happened in early summer, around here. Red Lady was stolen, along with her infant girl, her daughter, one of the twins."

"What?" Nasbah asked. She put aside her weaving tools and went to Jonnie Navajo.

"It is so," he said. "Some men came and carried away Red Lady and the infant."

"Were they Utes?" Nasbah asked.

Jonnie Navajo sighed. "No, Mexicans, probably, but it is not certain."

"How did this happen, Grandfather?" Nasbah asked.

Jonnie Navajo put aside the horsehair strands, took off his glasses, and looked intently at his granddaughter. "The men came at dawn," he said. "Only Red Lady was here with her twin daughters and White Sheep. Tall Navajo's Son was in the vicinity but was not actually here. He arrived in time to hear his mother scream a warning to him that he should hide."

Nasbah swallowed hard and asked, "Why didn't White Sheep help her?"

"In a way he did," answered the old man. "He hid one of the baby girls under a black goatskin in the sweathouse before the raiders realized there were two babies. But White Sheep had been partly scalped, and they cut off his ears, too. Tall Navajo's Son found him lying in a pool of his own blood with other minor wounds."

"Why were his ears cut off, Grandfather?" Nasbah asked.

"Money," Jonnie Navajo answered. "A bounty was paid for Navajo ears in those days."

"What?" Nasbah asked, appalled at what she heard. "Is this true?"

The old man nodded.

Nasbah was overwhelmed by all this information. She glanced from her grandfather to her grandmother, who had also stopped weaving and stared off into the aspen trees.

"Then what we were told in school is partly true," Nasbah finally said. "The People were slaves. Did they also hold slaves in turn?"

Jonnie Navajo nodded, "Yes, this is true. Red Lady was a slave for over three years. She was held successively by two families. Tall Navajo scoured the country in search of her. News came back quickly to Tall Navajo's Son that the slave-raiders were moving east. On this mountain, they attempted one more raid, and took a young man, perhaps fourteen years old. Tall Navajo returned the same day, and with his son, began to track the slave-raiders. About five days later, they came across the young man who had been taken from the mountain. He had escaped. He told Tall Navajo that he thought the slave-raiders were going to Be´eldiildahsinil (Albuquerque).

"At that time, I suppose Tall Navajo was very close to catching the slave-raiders, but somehow they slipped away. All in all, it took three years to track down Red Lady. All the information Tall Navajo used to determine her whereabouts came from our people who had escaped captivity. There weren't many. It took years. He was rewarded, but many of the People who lost family members to these raiders were not so lucky. He found Red Lady north of Yoo'tó (Santa Fe), just south of To´holnii (the Pueblo of Taos). He purchased her from the family who held her. They were of mixed Pueblo and Spanish blood. He paid two hundred and fifty dollars for Red Lady and brought her back here. But she was different somehow. The three years of absence had changed her, aged her beyond years.

"She told him that she had often tried to escape. At least twice she was nearly successful, but being unfamiliar with the terrain, she became lost and eventually was recaptured. She gave up hope of ever returning to the People."

"And what about the baby, Grandfather?" Nasbah asked.

"The baby was never recovered. Red Lady said she was allowed to keep the baby until it was fully weaned. In Taos, when both Red Lady and the baby were sold, the family that took Red Lady either did not have enough money to purchase the child too or they did not want it. The baby went to another family. Red Lady said that this broke her heart.

"She tried to keep track of the baby, who was named Maria by the first family who had held both Red Lady and the child. That family lived on the far east side of the Taos mountains. Red Lady and the child were taken that far, probably because it was known that their family was likely to come looking for them. The farther away they were taken, the less chance there was of their family locating them. This worked too. Tall Navajo himself thought Red Lady was in the area of *Be'eldiildahsinil* or in the towns south of there. Quite by accident did he realize that she might have been taken north toward Colorado. When he changed his ideas on where she might be and began to question people returning from that area, Red Lady was located about a year later. When Tall Navajo rescued Red Lady, he and his son attempted to find the baby and purchase her too, but they had no luck. The baby had already been taken from Red Lady at least two years before. For several years after, Red Lady and Tall Navajo questioned freed Navajo slaves who had returned to our people about the baby, Maria. But no one could say where she was. When Red Lady was an old woman she was still asking people who had intermarried with Pueblo people in that area where her child might be. Maria was lost forever."

"And what about the other baby, Grandfather? The other twin?" Nasbah asked.

"She died when she was about forty at Fort Sumner, where the People were held in captivity. This happened a few days before the People were allowed to return to their own country. This was about 1868, after the People had been there nearly four years. I was told that the other baby grew to be a sickly woman, not at all strong. She was always ill.

"At Fort Sumner, life was black, it was so bad. The People were prisoners of war for four years, living in holes in the ground and eating spoiled food. But even before that, several hundred died en route there, and at that time, perhaps one-half of the tribal members were held as slaves in New Mexico alone. This woman, of course, knew that she had a sister somewhere, whom she hoped was alive and free, someone who looked exactly like her. She called her missing sister 'the lost one.'

"There were more slaves in Colorado and Utah, too. Anyway, there was much illness at that black place, and her husband died there, too, although I think he was shot by the soldiers.

"Therefore, Tall Navajo's Daughter did not return to this place, Beautiful Mountain, nor did her husband who was from *Tséyi*. But their children were luckier. They had three daughters who ranged in age from about nineteen to twelve. The middle one died on the return trip to Navajoland, somewhere east of Albuquerque, but the other two survived.

"When the youngest daughter was fifteen or sixteen, she married a Mexican man who was raised as a Navajo. That's what I was told. The Navajos even adopted him into one of the clans. I did not know him, though I have heard a lot about him. He thought he was Navajo," Jonnie Navajo chuckled.

Nasbah said, "That's a sad story, Grandfather. So much death, so much suffering. All for what?"

Jonnie Navajo nodded and said, "My story came from *Hosteen Nez*. He taught me a lot after *Hosteen Diné* died. I even took one of my ceremonies from him."

All this information exhausted Nasbah. She wanted to mull over these new facts. As she looked toward the hills, her grandfather said, "Nasbah, see that peak? You have herded sheep there countless times. Just below it is where the old man, Tall Navajo, is buried, in the cliff, in the rocks. *Hosteen Nez* said that somewhere near that place his father, Tall Navajo's Son, is also buried. Red Lady is between us and the peak. My father, *Hosteen Diné*, is buried near 'the winged rock' (Shiprock), as is my mother. *Hosteen Nez* lies under the rocky section in the aspen grove. Some day you may know exactly where. The rest of our people are scattered out over this mountain. They make up the mountain."

The old woman spoke. "Red Lady's dress. . . ."

Jonnie Navajo nodded and said, "You have Red Lady's dress. In Taos, Red Lady had to wear the clothes of the white people. When she put on their clothes, she took off her dress, folded it, and set it aside, thinking that she would never wear it again. It was the only thing she carried back

65

to Beautiful Mountain when Tall Navajo brought her back. She wore the clothes of the whites even then.

"Her other little girl waited here all during Red Lady's absence. When Red Lady came back home, the child was three years older, and had been cared for by Tall Navajo's kin.

"Red Lady only touched the child on her return and was then separated from the family again until a ceremony was given for her. When this was done, Red Lady could go to her child again."

"Why did Red Lady need a ceremony, Grandfather?" Nasbah asked. "Was she ill?"

Jonnie Navajo nodded. "Red Lady had been with strange, alien people— the enemy. The ceremony was to cleanse her from them.

"In the ceremony, she took off their clothes and put on different ones which were given to her. That dress you have now, she set aside for her daughter. Her only daughter then, as things eventually turned out. Tall Navajo's Daughter was much smaller than Red Lady—she was tiny and sickly, as I told you earlier. The dress was much too big, and so Tall Navajo's Daughter later gave the dress to a daughter of *Hosteen Diné*. After that, your old grandmother over there took the dress, for you."

Nasbah's grandmother was weaving again.

"This old woman told you all this before, when you were about six or seven, but your mind was probably not ready to hold all this or to understand it," Jonnie Navajo said.

"The dress is old, it has value, but its worth is not in money. Do you agree?"

Nasbah nodded.

Jonnie Navajo continued, "This old woman and this old man will not always be here. . . ."

Nasbah put an arm around him. He went back to his horsehair weaving, and Nasbah's grandmother left the shelter for awhile. Rather timidly, Nasbah asked, "Where was White Sheep buried after he was scalped and his ears cut off, Grandfather?"

Jonnie Navajo answered, "Did I say he died? Yes, eventually he did and was buried in a secret location, but he did not die here on this mountain. He did not die at the hands of those slave-raiders."

"You mean he survived?" Nasbah asked in disbelief.

Jonnie Navajo nodded and answered, "White Sheep was not an ordinary man."

10

WASHINGTON, D.C.

AUGUST 1969

GEOFFREY Newsome circled the terrace area of his thirteenth floor apartment. It was dusk, and Geoffrey was not himself. He climbed up on the metal rail that encircled the terrace protruding from the side of the building. He wore swimming trunks and nothing else. He poised himself on the rail and saw the green swimming pool sparkling thirteen stories below him under carefully placed lights. Other smaller lights raced on the freeways and around his building. As Geoffrey stood there, his hand touching the side of the building for temporary support, a black man and woman from the next apartment stepped out onto their terrace, which was on the same level as Geoffrey's. They were approximately forty feet away. The light from inside their apartment flooded the terrace behind the couple.

Geoffrey saw them before they could catch a glimpse of him. In fact, they didn't see or hear him at all. He acted quickly. He jumped.

II

TULSA, OKLAHOMA
AUGUST 1969

RUSSELL planned to drive out to Wilbur Snake's homestead as soon as he could. He borrowed his sister's ancient Ford and left her house about six that morning. No sense in waiting til the sun got high. Already he could barely breathe in the heavy morning humidity. He just hoped old Wilbur would be at home. These old folks had to be caught early before they disappeared into town or the hills or the fields or wherever they scattered to.

Russell drove with all the car windows down and tried to remember how to get to Wilbur's place.

Wilbur was kind of a legend in his own time. Although he was actually a member of the Ioway tribe, he was known to all tribes in Kansas and Oklahoma and had been nicknamed "Uncle Wilbur" by most everyone he met, including elders. His fame came from an ability to communicate with unseen forces through prayer, meditation, and other means. Wherever he went, Wilbur Snake was a man to be reckoned with. Perhaps, too, this status grew out of a little fear of him.

Russell hadn't seen Wilbur in about six years. Actually, Russell was related to Wilbur through Anna. She was Pawnee and was Russell's grandmother in a complicated relationship.

Russell arrived in the town of Pawnee about 8:30. He stopped at the cafe on Main Street for a cup of coffee and a donut, dripping with sugar.

There were a half dozen people in the cafe—the waitress, the cook, two old Indian women, and a white man sitting with a young Indian man. When the waitress, a young Indian girl, brought Russell's coffee, he asked her, "You from Pawnee?"

She nodded.

"Does old Wilbur Snake still live out by the lake?" he asked.

"Yep," she answered. "But Uncle Wilbur ain't out there now. He went over to White Eagle for some doings there."

"Damn," Russell said. It meant he'd have to drive another hour or so and still might miss Wilbur. The waitress left Russell with his breakfast, but returned in a few minutes.

"You looking for Uncle Wilbur?" she asked with a smile. "What do you want to see him about? Is it important?"

Russell didn't answer. He'd had enough of these kinds of questions in D.C.

"Look," the waitress spoke again. "Aunt Anna is over at the hospital right now. She could probably tell you when Uncle Wilbur will be back."

"Thanks," Russell said, and the waitress left.

Russell went to the hospital and found Anna Snake sitting alone in the lobby. She looked toward Russell but didn't recognize him.

Russell went over and sat down in one of the cushiony chairs on either side of her.

"*Ucca*," he said, using the Pawnee term for grandmother. She turned and looked at him carefully and said with a cheery smile, "Are you one of my grandchildrens?"

Russell nodded.

"Well, which one are you, Sonny?" she asked.

"I'm Russell Tallman, Myrtle Black Bear's son," Russell answered.

Anna Snake laughed. "Oh, my, I'm getting too old. I can't tell who's my grandchildrens anymore. How's Myrtle, Sonny? Is she still living over in Cheyenne country?"

It was Russell's turn to laugh. "Yeah, Grandma. She's fine, she's well."

Anna said, "Junior and Erleen are here, too. Do you know them, Sonny? They're here, too. Erleen just came to drop some things off for a sister of hers who's here in the hospital. We just came in from Ponca City. Junior lives up there now. Do you know Junior, Sonny?"

"Yeah, I know Junior," Russell said. "But, Grandma, I really came to visit the old man."

Anna asked, "You mean Wilbur?"

Russell nodded.

"Well, Sonny" she said, "Wilbur ain't home right now. But he'll be back this afternoon. Some folks came after him and carried him up to White Eagle. They're done with him now, though, and they're carrying him back this afternoon. Sonny, you come for supper 'bout sundown, and Old Man's gonna be there. We out at the house by the lake. You know where it's at?"

Russell said, "Okay, Grandma. I'll be there." He stood to leave.

Behind him he heard someone bellow. "Russell Black Bear Tallman, if you ain't a sight for sore eyes!"

It was Junior Snake with Erleen. Junior was a giant of a man. He made Russell feel like a dwarf, and Russell was six feet without shoes. Junior came over, hugged Russell, and lifted him two inches off the ground. Erleen shook Russell's hand. She had red hair and didn't look Indian at all, but she was.

Russell said, "Look, Junior, I'm going to see Old Man this evening. If you ain't doing nothing, why don't you come over, too. I'd like to visit with you some."

"I don't know about that," Junior said. "We brought mama back and was going to leave her at the house and go on to Erleen's folks. It depends on what time we start to head back toward Ponca. Anyway, it's good to see you again. I'll try to make it in tonight."

Russell left the hospital. It was only ten, and he had the whole day to spare. He thought that he would drive into Oklahoma City and be there by 1:00. He wanted to work at the Historical Society building for awhile anyway, researching family history, a favorite pastime of his. He counted his money, and decided he had enough for gas over there and back, with still enough to make the return trip to Tulsa. He'd be back about sundown.

Russell left Oklahoma City about 5:30, heading north. His thoughts were occupied with Willie Begay back in D.C. Willie was supposed to have returned to Arizona in the third week of August, but for some unexplained reason, he'd stayed longer. In fact, he was still there. He'd called Russell one evening last week, three days before Russell had flown back here. From the conversation, Russell knew that Willie wouldn't return to Arizona until mid-September. Willie said simply that something had come up and he would stay where he was for three more weeks. This bothered Russell, but he figured that Willie knew what was best for himself.

George Daylight took this news less calmly. He told Russell that Willie was pushing his luck, and that he would check in on him in Russell's absence.

George's stay in D.C. wouldn't end until October. After his initial trip in March to set up a project to research his tribes' relocation to Oklahoma, the tribes had sent him back in May. They were preparing their own series of publications on the five civilized tribes. Russell, however, doubted that George would keep his promise to look in on Willie because George had recently acquired a new girlfriend, a student at Georgetown University and a member of the Abenaki tribe. Heck, Russell thought, neither he nor George even knew if there was a tribal government set up for that tribe. Russell found it hard to believe that she was Indian. She didn't know anything about herself, or any other Indian people, for that matter, and she frankly didn't care about her own ignorance. Nevertheless, George was hooked, again.

The evening drive from Oklahoma City was pleasant, and as Russell drove through the grassy hill country, he found himself anxious to return here from D.C. as soon as he could. North of Pawnee, Russell found the dirt road that led to Wilbur Snake's house by the lake.

Anna sat outside in a heavy, metal chair. There were five other chairs like that there. Russell drove up and parked his car a few feet in front of her.

"Sonny," she said, "I heered your car maybe three miles away. Wilbur went down to the creek a couple of hours ago. He went to fish. Says they's too many people over at the lake, so he fishes in the creek. He's going to be back pretty soon."

Russell looked in the direction of the creek. Wilbur was walking toward them through the high grass, carrying a cane fishing pole over his shoulder.

Russell sat in one of the chairs beside Anna. "Grandma," he said, "you and Old Man ever get lonesome out here?"

"No, Sonny," she said. "What's lonesome? This place is here. It's home. I stay out here alone lots of times—Wilbur, too, sometimes. But they carry Wilbur away all the time. It's alright, though, I don't mind it.

"Aw, when you're young, like you, Sonny, there's lonesome. When you get as old as us, lonesome don't do no good. We cry. Lonesome causes it, but tears don't do no good, don't help nothing. We pitiful, Sonny, cry all the time—maybe we lonesome, maybe we hurt. Life too hard, Sonny. It's hard on us, sometimes kind of whips us down, but we have to take it. When you get my age, nothing ain't any clearer, but us old peoples made it this far—live a long time, have childrens, grandchildrens, great-grandchildrens," Anna said as she watched Wilbur approach. Besides the fishing pole, Russell could now see that Wilbur also carried a string of fish and a coffee can.

Russell was shocked at how old Wilbur seemed to have grown since the last time he'd seen him. His hair had gone entirely white and he was as thin as a rail. A white wire hung out of his right ear. Russell felt a sense of loss when he saw Wilbur this way, but when Wilbur walked up to him and shook his hand, Russell saw that Wilbur's eyes were the same sharp brown ones that he remembered. Russell felt better.

"So you Myrtle Black Bear's little boy, huh?" Wilbur asked. He studied Russell minutely, from his long, brown hair tied in a pony tail to his boots. Wilbur sat down beside Russell.

"What'd you catch?" Russell asked, looking toward the stringer of fish now hanging on a nail at the corner of the house.

"Couple of cats, and three perch. I ran out of worms. Worms down by the edge of the creek is at least a foot long," Wilbur said as he leaned toward Russell.

Anna got up, took the stringer of fish off the nail, and came back to Russell. "Sonny," she said, "you going to have to talk up to Old Man, now. They stuck wires in his ear to help him listen, but you going to have to do your part." The weight of the fish pulled her to one side.

Then she turned to Wilbur and said, "Old Man, Sonny don't want to talk about no fish. I'm thinking he came round for something else. You talk nice to Sonny now 'cause he's Myrtle Black Bear's little boy. I'll be fixing supper. Sonny's going to stay and eat with us."

Then Anna turned toward the road and said loudly, "A car's coming down the road, Old Man. I'll fry up the fish. Have to be sure Sonny has enough to eat. But Old Man, you have to clean 'em. Sonny, you going to sleep with us? Or, are you going home tonight? It's getting late. Where did you come from anyway?"

"Tulsa," Russell answered. "I might stay overnight, though, if you got room. And, Grandma, I brought some groceries." He went to his car, and took out a grocery bag. "It ain't much, Grandma, but flour, coffee, and some sweets."

He carried the groceries inside the house. When he returned, Anna was saying to Wilbur, "Sonny can put up the cot out here." Then she turned to Russell and said, "Me and Old Man sleeps outside, Sonny." She went inside the house.

In a minute she carried out a pan of water, and in her apron pocket, a pair of pliers and two knives. Russell got up to help with the water pan that caused her to totter a little. Wilbur began to clean the fish skillfully and quickly.

The car Anna had heard could now be seen in the evening sunset, but it was difficult to make out the shape and color of it.

Anna hollered from inside the house. "Sonny, that'll be Junior. I know the sound of his car. My ears is growing stronger now cause I have to hear for Old Man, too."

Wilbur interrupted. "Where you been, Sonny?" Wilbur asked. "Ain't seen you since you and Junior stole LeClair's watermelons and he chased you outta his fields. That was you, ain't it?"

"Yeah, that was me alright," Russell said. "I've been away at school mostly."

Junior Snake's car was now parked beside Russell's car. It was several years newer than Russell's.

"Nice looking car you got there," Russell said.

Junior slapped the hood of the car, and answered, "Yeah, me and Erleen owe the devil for the rest of our lives on it." He wore a straw hat.

"Where's Erleen?" Russell asked.

"She's over to her folks. Her mom's putting together quilts, and Erleen thought she'd just stay overnight there and help out.

"What you doing, Daddy?" Junior asked. He saw the fish, picked up the other knife, and cleaned one.

"Mama, these here fish are ready for the frying pan," he yelled to Anna. Junior dunked all the fish in the pan, picked up the pliers and the two knives, and carried everything into the house. When he returned a few minutes later, his hair was combed and he appeared to have washed the entire upper half of his body. He smelled like baby powder, and Russell could see the white spots of powder around his damp neck.

Junior said to Russell, " 'Member that time you and I took old LeClair's melons out of his fields? He was madder than hell."

Russell said, "I heard LeClair went on. That right?"

Junior said, "Daddy can tell you 'bout that, he was there. Daddy?"

"LeClair felt it coming on. He didn't mind too much. LeClair was like that these last years. Never minded things too much. Was sorta relieved, I think. We waited for it. I kept him some company, that's all."

"What happened?" asked Russell.

"Ain't much happened," Wilbur said. "LeClair went to sleep, didn't wake up."

"You miss him?" Russell asked Wilbur.

"Haven't had a lot of time on my hands to miss him. But saw him a couple of times since then. LeClair ain't hurting none, he's alright," Wilbur said matter-of-factly.

"Where'd you see him?" Russell asked.

"Saw him once in my dreams and another time out in his fields. LeClair's alright. He ain't hurting none," Wilbur repeated.

"Old LeClair was a character and a half," Junior said. "Sometimes I wish he was here."

Wilbur answered, "He is."

That ended the subject of LeClair temporarily. Wilbur got up from the chair and said, "Fish on my hands." He went inside the house.

While Wilbur was inside, Junior Snake said in a low, serious voice, "What you want to talk to Daddy about, Black Bear?"

Russell laughed. "No one's called me that in years."

Wilbur could be heard talking to Anna inside the house.

"Junior," Russell answered, "I came to talk to him about his trip to Washington years back."

"Which one was that? Daddy's been out there a lot of times," Junior said.

"Well, actually, it was the first trip, I think," Russell answered. "He went out there with a delegation. LeClair went, Simon Littlefoot, and some others. Know which trip I mean?"

Wilbur stepped outside.

"Daddy," Junior said, " 'member those trips you took to Washington, D.C., years back?"

Wilbur settled into a metal chair and looked at Russell.

"I've been in Washington for several months, now," Russell began. "My main office is over in the BIA Building, but at the same time I spend a lot of time at the National Archives and the Smithsonian's Natural History Building.

"George Daylight is in D.C. right now, too, on a six-month program sponsored and paid for by his tribes. You 'member George, used to be married to Florene?"

"Yeah," Junior said. "I think I'm beginning to understand." He turned to Wilbur and said loudly, "Daddy, Russell's living in Washington, D.C. now."

"I heered," Wilbur said, staring at the ground and pursing his lips at the same time.

Both Russell and Junior waited for Wilbur to speak. He appeared to be considering something. His eyes were thoughtful.

Russell wasn't too sure that Wilbur was going to say anything about

Washington after all. He decided to try to explain a little more. "Old Man," he said, "I'm here on behalf of myself and George. I'm trying to watch out for us—don't want us to get hurt out there. The reason I'm thinking that someone is going to get hurt is this: a lot of people kill themselves there."

Wilbur stared at him. Russell felt like Wilbur could see right through him.

Wilbur spat and said, "Some peoples carried me to a doings once—just over the state line, in Kansas. They held the doings in someone's pasture. Lotsa peoples was there. These was medicine peoples, Sonny—come together to show each other just what they could do. They was powerful, see?

"These mans, these womans, they stand in line, face each other, Sonny. They shoot poison, it's medicine, see? They shoot it at one another. They spit it. This poison, this medicine, it flies over through the air, to wherever it s'posed to go. Sonny, those peoples took whatever was threw at them, was spit at them. It's poison, see? Didn't hurt anyone of 'em. *You think it was nothing?*

"Well, let me tell you. . . . Horses stand behind a line of people. Horses graze in the pasture. The medicine, the poison, it flies to one of the horses, goes to a horse whenever a medicine person sidesteps this stuff. Right away, a horse keels over. By the time this whole show is over, well, Sonny, half the horses in the pasture is dead! But the medicine peoples, they okay," Wilbur said, hitting his thigh with a rolled fist for emphasis.

Russell was quiet, and Junior, too.

Wilbur looked at Russell and asked, "Sonny, you git what I said?"

"No," answered Russell truthfully.

"Well," Wilbur said, "I guess it's kind of hard to git. Best way to git at the meaning of it is just to tell you flat out. Stay outta it. It can't be understood. You'll git hurt. No ifs, ands, or buts 'bout it, you'll git hurt. You going to keel over like one of those horses if you git in the way!"

Russell didn't quite know how to take this. He had known when he'd come here that Wilbur could refuse to talk to him, but he'd rejected this possibility. He cleared his throat and chose his words very carefully. "Old Man," he said, "I've seen certain things in Washington. Once, in one building, I saw three of our people in broad daylight who I know were not really there. They were not of our time. They were spirit people. I've heard things, too. There have been three deaths, by suicide the white people claim, in the last eighteen months.

"At this very moment, George Daylight is keeping an eye on one of our buddies who is slowly coming apart—he's Indian, Old Man. Navajo Indian. This thing is reaching out and grabbing at us."

Wilbur nodded. "Well, that's what you should expect. George knows better too—he knows how things stand. He was brought up better than this. His old Creek peoples taught him, I know they did. George better come on back, right away!"

"He plans to, Old Man, as soon as his program is finished," Russell answered. "I have to go back to Washington, too, in three days. I made this trip especially to see you, to ask for help. Me and George, we've gone to school. We've had years and years of school. Don't do no good now, though. We don't know nothing. Old Man, please."

Wilbur studied the ground. He spat beside his right shoe. "Sonny," he said, "the first thing to learn is there ain't nothing to do 'bout the whole thing. Accept it. It's bigger than anyone dreams.

"Sonny, I was at Washington, too. Long time ago. Seven of us from different tribes went up there the first time. They was me and Anna, LeClair, Simon, Horton Watson, and Bert and Winnie Willie. I seen what you up against, and you ain't no match for it. Don't take it personal, but it's bigger than you.

"Those three who you saw, well, Sonny, I know them, too. They want something that belongs to them. I'd say give it to them, but it beats me just what it is. I thought on it. Didn't come up with nothing, though. Best thing to do is for you boys to pack up and come on home. This thing ain't going away, ain't going nowhere. Spirit peoples don't know time, don't care nothing 'bout clocks. Yep, Sonny, they going to stay right where they are."

"Can't someone take this away?" Russell asked.

"Could if it were just one thing and we knew how come it got there. But, Sonny, they's too many peoples there—can't fight 'em. 'Sides, Sonny, those peoples have claims there. They's a reason for this, though it's hard to see," Wilbur answered.

"But people have died, Old Man!" Russell said passionately.

Wilbur spat again. "Don't talk to an old man about dying, Sonny. It's like trying to teach a fish to swim.

"They's two choices here. Stay there at that place in Washington and have your brains rattled, or git out and put aside dying for a little while longer."

Russell looked downward. He was quiet.

"Don't like what you hear, Sonny?" Wilbur asked. "It's the only way. I'm telling you the truth, ain't no other way. Now I'm going to help you out a little here tonight, 'cause you Myrtle Black Bear's little boy and she loves all her childrens. I'll say this. In this place where you saw those three peoples is a giant man. He's naked, Sonny. He's crazy, too. But his craziness ain't his own doing. Someone or something made him that way. Still, this one ain't to be trusted. When he's around, Sonny, leave right away! His heart is all black.

"There's something else, too. It's at the top of the building. I ain't never seen it with the eye, but I felt and smelt it. Go 'round this thing, not through it.

"That's all I can say now. They's other things that might help, but it's too late for them now. It's a hard lifetime of learning.

"Sonny, you know how things is in this world. They's some good things, they's some bad. Everything comes out even. Don't put more hold in one over the other, they's the same size, the same thing. They big, Sonny. We're puny things next to them. A lot of things is bigger'n us. Step back and look at them sometimes."

At that moment Anna appeared at the door. "Let's eat," she said.

Wilbur looked at Russell. "Sonny, think on it tonight. Now, let's eat." He led the way into a large kitchen.

Junior showed Russell where the bathroom was. Everyone was seated around the table when Russell came out.

"Anna, say a word of thanks for the meal on the table," Wilbur said.

Anna nodded, closed her eyes, and said, "Creator, Old Man wants me to say thanks. Thank you, Creator, for looking down on us and picking us up when we fall. Keep us on our feet and watch out for Junior and Sonny. There's a craziness loose in the world. Don't let it touch 'em. Amen."

She smiled brightly at Russell from across the table. "Sonny, I made iced tea, fish, corn, and fried tomatoes. Eat it, Sonny."

Junior, Russell, Wilbur, and Anna laughed and visited throughout the meal. It was dark when Anna and Junior cleared the table and the four went outside to sleep.

Junior set up two cots beside the cars, away from Wilbur and Anna. Just before Russell closed his eyes, Junior said in a low voice, "Black Bear, don't hold this against Old Man. He knows what he's doing." There was no apology in his voice for Wilbur's earlier words to Russell, only a matter-of-fact acceptance of it.

Russell yawned and agreed, "He's right, Junior. I can feel it."

12

ALBUQUERQUE, NEW MEXICO

AUGUST 1969

DAVID Drake sat before his typewriter trying to organize his thoughts. He had three stacks of papers that dealt with different periods of Navajo history.

He had reluctantly started the initial research on the Navajo slave period that spanned nearly two centuries in documented history. He only included this aspect of Navajo history at the insistence of Willie Begay and Willie's grandfather. Since then, he'd come to realize that no historian had given it serious treatment, and the few references to it by historians were casual and doubtful, skipping over it carelessly.

Jonnie Navajo's story of the stolen child and Red Lady did intrigue him, though. He also knew that he had practically no chance of discovering what had happened to the child. In the few documents available—correspondence and military reports—that described taking prisoners or captives, the information was too scanty and generalized to be really helpful. Often, specific places where captives had been taken were not mentioned at all, or were given Spanish names that did not correspond to Navajo ones. On occasion, the slave-raiders did not really know exactly where a raid had taken place, and only guessed at approximate locations.

David searched through the scanty records available to him for the 1800-1850 period, and discovered nothing to coincide with the incident that Jonnie Navajo had described to him. Perhaps the old man was wrong about the time. Could he have made up the entire story? No, David thought, that was very unlikely. Besides, these oral stories were usually fairly accurate when researched. Therefore he had to conclude that the men who had taken Red Lady and the child were a private expedition. Those groups were notorious for operating randomly and were the worst to trace. David frowned. He had acquired a hopeless task.

He now attempted to compose a short advertisement, which he would forward to history magazines, newspapers, and other publications in the hopes of receiving some responses. He admitted to himself that it was a last ditch effort, a desperate reach into the past. He typed for a few minutes, and pulled out the sheet of paper. It read "RESEARCHER/HISTORIAN WISHES TO CONTACT DESCENDANTS OF NAVAJO/SPANISH SLAVES IN NEW MEXICO AND COLORADO." At the bottom of the page, he put his mailing address. He crumpled the paper, threw it down, and stepped on it. He was in a miserable mood.

Willie Begay had sent him a postcard saying he wouldn't be available to help with David's project until late September, if then. Willie had suggested that David contact Nasbah and ask for her help in translating from English to Navajo if David needed help before Willie returned. Willie had added Nasbah's address.

This change in plans would set David back in his target completion date for his manuscript.

He picked up the sheet of paper on the floor and brushed off his footprint. He figured he might as well send it out, for whatever it was worth.

13

WASHINGTON, D.C.

WILLIE Begay was at home alone. He did not feel well. He'd lost more weight and nothing stayed in his stomach. Today he was going to a doctor. He had an appointment at eleven, but planned on visiting George before then. George expected him.

Willie caught the metro bus outside his apartment about 7:45. The bus carried the usual assortment of people, who all studied Willie as he got on and then totally ignored him for the rest of the ride. About forty minutes later, he jumped off the bus a block from the Smithsonian.

George sat at a table littered with papers and books, completely absorbed in his reading. His cowboy hat sat on top of the books. When Willie tapped George on the shoulder, George jumped a foot high.

"What's the matter?" Willie asked in a low voice, trying not to disturb other researchers in the room.

"I'm so damned edgy, Willie, I don't know what's getting into me," George answered. "How you been?" He looked Willie over.

Willie answered, "I'm still kicking, but I'm on my way to a white medicine man just to be sure."

"That's the best thing," George assured Willie, and explained his surprise at Willie's presence.

"You know, when you came in, I was reading these unpublished manuscripts that were left here by writers decades ago. I guess they've been lying here all this time. It's a hell of a thing, the ideas they had 'bout 'red Indians.' It's enough to scare the crap out of you. What's even more spooky is that people acted on these ideas, made decisions based on them, decisions that still affect us guys. Willie, you and me's lucky even to be sitting around here at all."

Willie nodded, "I know what you mean. You'd never guess what I came across the other day—a scalp! A Navajo scalp, the entire head of hair with the ears, too. To find that thing here!"

George said, "Yeah? But it ain't too surprising. There's a savagery here alright, no doubt 'bout it. It's always been here. We perpetuate it. Willie, right now, it's probably over in Saigon. They're probably taking ears and scalps over there. And then there's a more subtle touch. . . .

"Know what I seen here the other day?" George asked in a whisper. "There's a mummified body of a prehistoric Indian woman upstairs—must be six hundred years old. Poor thing, the pitiful woman is all dried up. Well, the guy who stole her from a cave out in Colorado said that *he* found the woman *grotesque*, Willie, '*grotesque*.' That was *his description of her*. He also made fun of the size of the woman's breasts. They're huge alright, but my point is this: the insolent fart who dug her out of her cave and had the nerve to stuff her into the trunk of his car and then *sell* her for a handsome profit—it's all here in these hand-written notes—then says he *finds her grotesque!* This is savagery, Willie. First-class savagery. His act, his mind, his existence scares the shit out of me. *This is what we're up against!*"

Willie leaned back in the chair. He felt light-headed. Someone came into the room, a tall naked Indian man. Willie was startled. He looked around to see who else saw this man. No one did, not even George, who thumbed through the manuscript on his desk.

The Indian was a giant of a man, standing almost seven feet tall. As he advanced through the unknowing people at work in the room, each step he took around the tables emphasized his size and power towering over everyone there. His wide shoulders, upper arms, and thighs were solid and firm, but not overly muscular. Despite his height and size, the man was not clumsy or uncoordinated. Even in his obvious rage, he carried himself elegantly, much like an animal in the wild. Willie could feel the man's anger, see the rage in his strange and tormented eyes. His long hair, hanging well below his waist, flew around his square face when he moved quickly, ready to pounce on his foe. The man lifted both his arms over his head and said something, *howled* something. His right hand curled into a fist, which hammered down on the nearest table. Willie heard it and saw the man scream angrily, but Willie was a lone witness. Then the man looked at Willie for a second and the scowl on his face disappeared. He motioned at Willie. The man pointed at several people in the room and indicated that he wanted them out! Willie understood.

In a logical part of his brain, Willie knew that the man could not be there, but then again, he'd seen the most extraordinary things in D.C.

He'd once seen a naked white women on the bus wearing only pasties and a G-string under a black taffeta cape. Her skin was the color of a water-logged cigarette and her eyes were empty of life when they met Willie's. She might have been dead, too. Everyone had looked at her twice as she climbed aboard the bus, her stacked heels clicking on the bus floor, and then like all the other passengers, she ceased to exist for the rest of the ride.

He'd also seen a naked black woman fall, or *jump*, from a third-floor apartment window to the sidewalk below. Her body had bounced, buoy-antly, on a gold canvas awning that cast shade and tattered elegance on a sidewalk cafe where "beautiful" people wined and dined. Then she'd rolled, ever so slowly, down the taut canvas, her dark glistening blue-black body still buoyant and alive even then, and, in the next second, it was heavy and still against a shattering and splitting of long-stemmed crystal glass-ware. Yes, there was strangeness here.

The naked Indian man faded. Willie frowned and looked at the floor. His eyes now played tricks on him. The light areas around him reversed out and became dark, while the human figures in the room became darker shadows or vestiges of themselves. George was the only one who kept a semblance of himself. George was looking at Willie. George's eyes blinked and he said, "Willie, are you okay?" The voice became tangled in the darkness around him and was disassociated with George, whose mouth opened and closed. Willie himself tried to speak, to respond to the voice he heard in the darkness. His tongue curled and tied itself in his mouth. He tried again to answer the voice. It was George's voice, Willie told himself. Finally, Willie's tongue flapped free. He could feel it moving stonily and heavily in his mouth. But words were forgotten. Willie panicked.

"George," Willie managed. His own voice sounded alien—was it really his own? "George, I need help. Something's wrong," Willie stammered hoarsely. "I'm lost." Maybe he was screaming. Willie realized that the figures, the dark vestiges in the room, had turned toward him. They wore no expressions on their faces. Only their eyes were clear little lights. They looked like demons. Their terrible eyes lit the room and hurt Willie like stinging cactus needles when they looked at him. He covered his eyes with his hands to shut out the demons. He leaned over on the table, threatening to collapse.

What was George doing? Willie uncovered his eyes. George moved toward Willie, slowly and awkwardly, as thick and powerful as a bear.

Willie had seen a small bear once in the mountains of Arizona, near Jonnie Navajo's summer home. What was George doing? Should Willie trust him? He heard other voices drifting nearby in the room. The demons with the stinging eyes circled Willie.

George said something, but his voice was out of range—other voices drowned out George's.

"George," Willie tried to say. His tongue stuck to the roof of his mouth again. Then George was in front of Willie. George's face was distorted. His mouth moved, but his eyes were so strange—perhaps frightened? Angry? Had the demons frightened George? George looked so funny like that. Willie tried to laugh, but the laughter died somewhere in his mind.

Someone pulled him. Was it George? No, George was gone, out of sight. Only demons were here. They were *touching* him. Willie hated it. He hurt, burned, where they touched him. Willie tried to cry, but his eyes were dry, too dry for tears. He pushed the demons away from him, flinging his arms like helicopter propellers. It worked. He was stronger than they were.

Out in the darkness he heard George somewhere. The demons stepped back and then George was there. Good old George. Willie was so happy to see him. He tried to tell him, but only gurgling sounds came from deep in his throat.

George's mouth moved again. He came close to Willie and put a muscular arm under Willie's arm. Willie could barely hear George.

"Hey, man," George said. "Let's get the hell out of here. Can you hear me?" George looked curiously at Willie, who tried to nod.

George put on his hat and steered Willie. He heard George's voice. "Damn, man, you're heavy for a guy who can't hold anything in his stomach. Can you make it? You gonna be alright?" He guided Willie out of the room.

The darkness lifted around Willie, but his legs wobbled. George kept him moving. He unbuttoned Willie's shirt and loosened his belt. People stared at them. One tall man raised his eyebrows and said very loudly, "Queers!"

"What's going on here?" asked a uniformed security guard at the entrance of the area. He looked at Willie and asked, "Is he drunk?"

George asked, "Can you call us a cab? He's sick."

The security officer, a little man with green eyes, said sarcastically, "Well, I don't know. . . . We don't usually offer cab service, you know."

"It's an emergency," George said.

While the security officer used the phone behind him, George asked Willie, "Where is that white medicine man? What's his address?"

Willie pulled a white card from his Western-style shirt pocket, which was fastened with pearl snaps.

George and Willie arrived at the doctor's office about twenty minutes later. Willie was actually fifteen minutes early for his appointment.

Willie still was not himself. In the cab he'd been quiet but disoriented, asking George twice where they were and where they were going. George did not call this disorientation to Willie's attention. Out of the cab, George had to support Willie all the way into the building.

The receptionist, a young black woman with a tiny waist, took one look at Willie and motioned to George, indicating that he should take Willie into another room where he could lay down. Once there, George filled out the necessary forms for Willie, who was dazed and weak. George also answered the receptionist's questions. When George asked Willie about those parts of his life that required answers on the form, Willie merely looked at George without recognition or knowledge of what George had asked. George wrote what he could and left it at that.

The doctor, an older woman with graying hair at the temples, entered the room a few minutes later. George explained the nature of Willie's problem, since Willie now seemed unable to handle this simple task. He told the doctor about Willie's recent moments of uncoordination, his blackouts, and his headaches, but he did not really go into details or specifics of the incidents Willie had experienced. Then George left Willie alone with the doctor.

George was anxious. What was he supposed to do with Willie now? It would help if Russell was here. Russell was supposed to have returned yesterday, but as far as George knew, he was still in Oklahoma.

About thirty minutes later, the doctor emerged from a back room and asked for Mr. Daylight. George went to her. Willie was stretched out on an examining table. Willie's eyes were closed, and he snored softly.

The doctor turned to George and asked, "Do I understand correctly that Mr. Begay has no family here?" She spoke with a New York accent and mispronounced Begay.

George nodded. He took off his hat and held it in his hand. "How is he, Doc?" George asked.

The woman answered, "He really should be in a hospital, Mr. Daylight. He needs to have some tests run on him."

"Well, whatever you think is best, Doc," George said firmly, but with a frown at the same time. "When will this happen?"

"I'll try to arrange his admittance for tomorrow morning. If it's not possible then, for one reason or another, then as soon as it's feasible. Two or three days at the latest. I've given him a light sedative for now. He needs a lot of rest and he may need help," she answered.

It was George's turn to speak. "Alright, Doc, I understand. I'll see to it that Willie gets to the hospital. Just name the place and the time."

She turned to leave the room and said, "I'll make the arrangements. Please wait here. It shouldn't be too long, and Mr. Begay can get a little much-needed rest. He's near exhaustion."

George stayed in the room with Willie for about forty-five minutes. In that time, he stared at Willie off and on, paced the floor, and thought. Willie didn't move once.

Finally, the doctor returned. She handed George a piece of paper with several forms attached to it. "Be here next Wednesday morning at 7:30. Mr. Begay should not eat for twelve hours prior to this."

As she spoke to George, she shook Willie. He opened his eyes and looked at her, puzzled. Then recognition came. He apologized, "Sorry, I fell asleep." He looked at George and said, "Thanks for hanging around, George."

The doctor interrupted, "Mr. Begay, I've made arrangements for you to enter the hospital on Wednesday morning for some tests."

Willie looked questioningly at George. The doctor saw the look and tried to soften what she had said. "There's no reason to be alarmed. This is just a precaution, and the tests really are necessary."

Willie looked at George again, expecting a comment from him. George looked at the doctor and she nodded to George, who said, "Hell, yeah, Willie, it's just a precaution, to make sure it ain't nothing serious."

"Well, I'm going home—to Arizona—in a few days," Willie said. "Can't this wait until then?"

The doctor shook her had no. "That isn't really advisable. It would be better to undergo the tests here and now, to find out what the problem is immediately. Then, treatment may be done in Arizona or here, whichever you prefer or whichever is more feasible."

She took the paper and forms from George's hand and gave them to Willie. "The time of your admittance to the hospital is written here, along with other information and instructions, which should be followed to the letter prior to hospital admittance. Attached to that are forms that require your signature. Now, if you'll excuse me, I have other patients to attend."

George and Willie left the room. Willie settled the matter of his billing while George checked the bus schedule. The bus they needed was due in fifteen minutes.

When Willie came outside, George was sitting on a bench waiting for the bus. Willie said to him, "I'm going to go back to my apartment. I'm okay now, a little sleepy, but I feel better."

George answered, "You sure you gonna get there alright?"

Willie assured George that he would.

George asked, "What about Wednesday? You gonna check yourself into that there hospital?"

Willie nodded.

George grinned and said, "Alright, Will. I'll take another bus then. Heck, me and Russell will drop in on you at the hospital, if he's back."

George waited with Willie until Willie's bus pulled up. As the bus stopped and let off a half dozen people, Willie turned to George and said, "I have a cousin who you should contact if it becomes necessary. Her name is Nasbah, Nasbah Navajo, and this is her address and a phone number where you can reach her. I'll try to call her myself when the tests are done." He handed George an envelope bearing the doctor's office address in the left-hand corner.

George was puzzled. "What's this for?" he asked.

Willie answered, "Just in case—you know."

After Willie had gotten on the bus, George read the back of the envelope. "Arizona," he said.

When George returned to the research room, it was early afternoon. Russell sat in George's chair.

"When'd you get back?" he asked Russell.

"This morning. Heard there was a problem here earlier. Willie?" he asked, pushing George's books aside.

"Yeah," George answered. "He's going into the hospital on Wednesday morning for tests."

"Hmmm," Russell said, "sounds serious. What do you think?"

"Don't know," George answered. "Ain't no goddamned expert, but it does appear that he ain't well, Russell, and he ain't getting no better. Let's go get a pastrami sandwich or something to chew on. I haven't eaten all day."

At the delicatessen Russell told George about his trip back to Oklahoma and of Wilbur Snake's advice to simply pack up and head home. "Wilbur's getting on in years," Russell said. "It seems like the wind could just blow him away. He's much smaller than I remember, shorter, thinner, and weaker. Time sure flies, don't it, George? It just blows us poor people away."

George finished his sandwich. "Don't be fooled, Russ, 'bout Wilbur Snake. He's strong, as strong as the wind. Shoot, Russ, Wilbur is the wind. His looks and size don't make no difference, either. Maybe he shrunk a little, but so what—he ain't any less for it. The fact is, Russ, Wilbur is stronger than you and me put together. If he put a mind to it, he could blow us away. So, you see, he is the wind. But you know, Russ, about Wilbur's suggestion, came to that same conclusion myself. Hell, this place gets to you. . . . Scrambles your brains.

"The first time I was here in D.C., I saw something over in that building. I was just in town for a few hours, but on that trip I played tourist and went over to the Natural History Building. Well, that's where I saw them, Russell. You know, ghosts, spirits . . . call them by any name you can think of. I should have knowed then that I was in over my head. Actually, I did know it, but thought that they couldn't touch me. I was smarter than ghosts and the poor bastards here.

"Now, old what's-his-name, Newsome, is dead, too. Suicide, I heard. Poor arrogant son of a bitch. The thing is, it could have been me just as well, or you, Russell.

"I've been doing some serious thinking on this since you've been away. I plan to leave here, Russell, sooner than I expected. I don't mind it much, saw a few things, did a few things, but now it's time to just go on back home and admit to myself that they's a whole lot of things bigger'n me. Besides, I'll be traveling back and forth to D.C. as long as I stay a tribal official. Ain't no loss, really. I can tie up loose ends in a few days."

"What about that new girlfriend of yours? I thought she done had you hooked and was reeling you in," Russell challenged him with a grin.

George smiled, too, and said, "She ain't right for me, Russ. Hell, she can't even make fried bread or dance. I guess both of us don't have to know how to do them things. If it came to it, I s'pose that I could cook and dance for the both of us. But, I ain't right for her either. She wants a castle in a town like D.C., and shiny cars. Heck, Russ, a castle is the last thing on my mind. I need a tepee, something I can carry around with me. It's all I need, really. Besides, I already have wives. Even the white one makes damned good fried bread, and she can dance with the best of them. I got children, too, Russ. Three of them. Did you know that? Old George Daylight is a daddy."

George turned more serious. "I've been giving some thought to this. The old timers say that there comes a time in a man's life that he begins to have sense. He thinks and acts in one coordinated motion. They say this don't come to a young man, generally, but one who's ahead few years. I kind of think that time has come for me, Russell. Damn, I must be getting old. Can't believe that George Daylight just said what he did."

Russell slapped George on the back and said, "Do what you have to do, George. How soon you going to head on back home? What about Willie?"

"Well, right off, I'd say I'll try to leave by the end of next week," he said, stroking his chin. "Come on, Russell," he added, "let's get some change. We've got a phone call to make."

Russell gave George all his change and asked, "Where are we calling?"

"Arizona," George answered.

14

WASHINGTON, D.C.

DONALD Evans forced himself to go up to the attic, to Geoffrey Newsome's old office, to work. He inherited the location by virtue of the fact that he had shared it with Geoffrey off and on through the last six years. Sooner or later, it was likely that Donald would have to share it again with someone else because extra working space in the crowded building was a rare commodity. Donald didn't mind that. He actually welcomed the company.

It had been nearly two weeks since Geoffrey's death, and Donald had avoided the office in that time, working with museum trainees in other parts of the building, until there were no more excuses for not entering the space and settling down to work, alone.

He sat in Geoffrey's swivel chair and surveyed his surroundings. Several used paper cups littered the room. Pottery sherds were still scattered across the long table from end to end. The door that led down the narrow staircase was open, held by a doorstop under it, and Donald noticed something about it that he had not seen before.

A very large hand print in a quiet, subtle color had been pressed onto the outside of the door that was painted in an off-white enamel. The hand print was centered on the door and pressed in a light tan earth color, a third of the way down the door. The color was probably the reason Donald hadn't noticed it when he'd entered the room, and the dark stairway hadn't helped to make it clearer. Under this lighting, the hand print was more visible. Donald walked to the door, looked at the hand print carefully, and touched it. The hand print had a rough texture and probably wasn't paint, Donald decided. It looked like clay but did not flake off under his examination. Donald placed his own hand over the hand print and found that his hand was considerably smaller. Suddenly the radio blared out unexpectedly and Donald jumped. It played momentarily and then stopped. Donald went back to the chair and settled down.

Since he was now the keeper of the collection stored here, Donald was planning to reacquaint himself with the contents of the room. He would start at the north side of the room after he'd gone through the files. But first he had to finish his quarterly report to his supervisor on his activities in the last three months and on the status of several projects that had been assigned to him.

Several hours later, about 4:00 P.M., Donald completed the scan of Geoffrey's files, accession cards, and notes. What he found amazed him. Though he had worked with Geoffrey for years up here, Donald had never known the private nature of the collection under Geoffrey's care. Now that he did know, he decided that a complete inventory was in order. He would do that as soon as possible, perhaps next week. He did not want to be responsible for any irregularities that might have occurred up to Geoffrey's death. He had no reason to suspect irregularities or inconsistencies in the records and collection, though, because Geoffrey had always been a stickler on institution policies, however casual and careless he might have been in his personal life.

Donald walked to the shelves on the northern half of the room. He had seen all the artifacts on the shelves many times before. They didn't interest him. What did prod his curiosity were the items in the cabinet drawers. One by one, he opened each cabinet drawer and quickly studied the contents. He did not touch anything. In several drawers were skulls and various parts of the human body. These parts of the body were not always easy for Donald to identify, but after he studied them for a few minutes, recognition and comprehension eventually came to him. After about half an hour, he pushed the last cabinet drawer shut and closed his eyes as he leaned against the cabinet. He wasn't sure what to think.

Donald now recalled that Geoffrey had tended to be defensive about this collection. That defensiveness sometimes caused Geoffrey to be over-protective about what was here. Eventually Geoffrey had tried to exercise strict control over who gained access to the collection and who did not. He'd tried to rule with an iron hand here in the attic. Donald now understood why.

Donald had always considered himself a rational, reasoning human being, and he prided himself on possessing these characteristics. But even possessing these qualities, Donald wasn't sure what to think now about the collection. He moved into the walking space behind the cabinets. On the floor were boxes and large trunks. He pulled a large heavy cardboard box out into the aisle and opened it.

Laying across the top of the open box was a faded, red flannel cloth. Donald pulled at the cloth, uncovering the contents. When he saw what was inside, he grimaced. A mummified child was tucked into the box in a sitting position. Donald touched the dry, little body and tried to remove the flannel cloth entirely, but the flannel was firmly wrapped around the bottom half of the body.

The boy was possibly thirteen or fourteen when he'd died. Parts of his skin had deteriorated, and his facial bones showed through the remaining transparent flesh. Despite this, his face was remarkably preserved. His eyelashes were thick and dark, and his black hair was matted in places. Donald covered the boy again and closed the box.

The trunk was padlocked. Donald went to search Geoffrey's desk for the key. He could not find it in the desk, but saw a ring of keys on a hook beside the filing cabinet. He tried each key. Finally, one slipped into the lock.

The trunk was very old, and the interior structure was falling apart. Pieces of brittle, colored paper stuck on his fingers. A broadcloth blanket lay right on top, and eagle feathers were attached to it in certain places. There were several brown paper sacks stuffed with an assortment of things. Donald wouldn't go through these things now. It was nearly five. But he did open the largest paper sack and unrolled a long war-bonnet with perhaps two hundred eagle feathers. The bonnet would have trailed on the ground when worn.

Donald was awed by the bonnet, although he was not particularly into Indians, their culture or history. American Indians were curiosities to him, people who should have become extinct by all the rules of the game. He lifted the bonnet to his nose and inhaled. Even now it smelled of a man. Donald rolled the war bonnet into a bundle again. He decided to go through this trunk tomorrow. He pushed the sack back into the trunk more forcefully that he'd intended, and another sack opened, spilling its holdings.

The sack contained strings of human ears, although it took Donald a while to recognize the dried shriveled objects. There were three strings of ears that were each about four yards long. The strings held at least two hundred pairs of ears, in all sizes and shapes. Some ears were not whole.

Donald put the strings of ears back into the sack but couldn't make everything fit as neatly in the trunk as before. Finally, he pulled out the sack holding the ears and put it on top of Geoffrey's desk, now his desk. Then he left the attic for the day, not at all sorry to leave.

The next morning Donald entered the office a little after eight. Today he'd brought dish detergent, a can of coffee, and a plastic sack filled with colored sponges. He carried the percolator down the stairs and returned a few minutes later with a sparkling pot filled with water. He added the coffee and plugged in the percolator. Then he left the room again to fill a pan with water. Donald recalled that this inconvenience had always annoyed Geoffrey. He had had to go downstairs to get water as it was needed. Donald was beginning to understand that annoyance. When Donald returned with the pan of water, he squeezed detergent into it and scrubbed the area around the coffee pot and the top of Geoffrey's old desk. He pushed the sack on the desk top back and forth until he was satisfied that the desk top was clean.

Donald sat down at the desk and dumped the sack upside down. With his left hand, he fingered the strings of ears. They were dry and leathery. With his right hand, he poured himself a cup of coffee and put the cup down on the desk top.

Donald tried to remember whether or not he'd seen any information on the strings of ears in the files or elsewhere. No, he didn't think so. He sipped his coffee, concluding that the ears were Indian. They had to be. Everything up here was created by Indians or had come from them.

Donald once more picked up the key ring and carried his coffee to the northern half of the room again, to the trunk. He opened it for the second time and set aside the blanket and the bonnet of eagle feathers. The first sack he opened this morning contained several parts of animals— the foreleg of a deer with the hoof attached, eagle claws, and other items. Donald laid this sack on the floor beside the trunk and took another one. The second sack contained exquisite tiny animal fetishes carved in turquoise, black jet, or semiprecious stones. Donald was puzzled. The fetishes came from the Southwest, a long way from the place where the bonnet and blanket originated. He carefully laid the sack of fetishes next to the other sack.

The next things he discovered were several slabs of red pipestone slate in varying shapes. There were depressions in the slates. Donald set these aside.

There was a lot of jewelry made of shells by the southeastern mound-builders, with ornate figures in mica. Besides these items, the trunk held sandals and large carved shells that depicted men rowing boats. Again, Donald recognized most of these as representative of the mysterious mound-building Indians.

At the very bottom of the trunk was a faded pink envelope. Donald opened it and found a sheet of paper with a message written in longhand. The message read simply:

D.—

Get what you can for this Indian stuff. It should be worth something in $. Try a museum first.

The blanket and bonnet were my granddaddy's. He said they belonged to Crazy Horse himself. Claimed he traded two horses for them, from the fellow who originally came by these things. Don't ask me how.

I don't know what the red stones are, but they came outta a woman's grave in Nebraska. Those people are extinct. I doubt the stones are worth much, because no one knows what they are.

I do know the little animals and the jewelry are of some value.

We dug up the jewelry near the Oklahoma/Louisiana line ourselves. We had a lot more of this stuff, but our kids often played with these and broke a lot of them. Had to throw most of the broken stuff in the trash. I bought the little carvings from a pot-hunter in Arizona years ago.

Daddy ran across the ears in New Mexico and won them in a poker game about 1890. They're Indian ears all right. They won't be of much use to anyone, except to someone who may want to hang them on a trophy mantle—a conversation piece for sure.

Guess that's about it. I sure could use the $ if you could sell all this junk. It's been in the attic for years.

—*John*

Donald reread the note. He surmised that these items had not been cataloged yet. He repacked the trunk and locked it once more.

Other boxes waited to be examined, but Donald didn't feel up to it. He didn't want to know what was inside them just yet. He went back to the desk. He'd forgotten to repack the sack with the ears. He took the strings of ears and hung them in coils on the key-ring nail. One string reached down to the floor. He would put them away later. There was no hurry.

The door leading down the narrow staircase was wide open. Did Donald's eyes deceive him or was there now another hand print on the door? He went to inspect it. Yes, there *was* a second hand print just to the right of the first, placed an inch or so lower. It was more smudged. It looked as if someone had slammed a hand against the door. Donald frowned.

15

LAS VEGAS, NEW MEXICO

SEPTEMBER 1969

ANITA stood before the white cross and the fresh new mound on the sand and crossed herself. The cemetery now held seven graves. Anita's mother, Rosa Lopez, was the last person carried out to it.

Anita looked around. The cemetery was extremely isolated. Crumbling adobe walls of a long abandoned mission building were a hundred feet away outside the wrought iron fence that surrounded the graves. Thick walls lifted out of other mounds of dirt and ruins. Anita had heard that the mission was abandoned about two hundred years ago, partially because of fear of Comanche Indians who roamed the area at will. There were no trees here except the remains of four fruit trees that still stood in one straight line just beside one of the back mission walls. There was only space here, a lot of space between the slanting turquoise sky and the dry, waterless land dotted with chamisa and cactus. Still, the location was very beautiful, the empty space timeless and haunting. The land was alive, bright with vivid color that pulsated around Anita.

She decided to have her late lunch before driving the forty miles to Las Vegas. She went to her car, a large heavy sedan that was only about five years old. She opened the car door and dug out her sack with a store-bought sandwich, an orange, and a red drink in a white plastic container. She carried these to a large flat boulder under one of the fruit trees and settled down there.

The day was warm and gusty. It was hotter here than at Rosa's house, now Anita's house, below the mountains.

Anita had been very busy the last three days, much more so than she'd expected. She had driven herself to Taos. She had gone alone. It was important somehow that she go alone. She didn't know what she sought there, and she didn't know what she might find.

Three days ago, Anita had packed a small bag, gotten into her car, driven first to Santa Fe, then to Española, and on up the winding mountain road to Taos. She had arrived in the late afternoon and checked into a motel. Anita had never in her entire life spent a single night in a hotel or motel, but on that night she did. After she had unpacked her car, she drove northward to Taos Pueblo. The Pueblo smelled of smoke, food, and ancient, enduring life.

Anita parked her car in the area reserved for visitors and headed for the plaza area. She had been here only once before in her life, when she was a very young woman, with her mother, Rosa. It was cool this evening, the oncoming winter a promise in the wind. Anita pulled her gray sweater tightly around herself.

At the entrance to the Pueblo, where most visitors and tourists were monitored, a young Taos woman looked at Anita and said without batting an eye, "If you're Indian, you don't have to pay for your visit here." Anita experienced momentary confusion and nodded, but she didn't know what to do. There were several people in line behind her. The young woman looked once more at Anita and said, "Well, go ahead."

Anita entered the plaza. There were many tourists, carrying the usual tourist gear. Several people snapped photos of the Pueblo. The Taos people sold pottery and other items around the plaza. Anita walked to the bank of the stream flowing through the middle of the Pueblo and sat down beside the water, facing north.

Now that she was in Taos Pueblo, she realized that she didn't really know *why*. She was there on instinct more than anything else. The Pueblo looked the same, the people remained the same. The Pueblo was as high as four stories in some places, and there were two or three people sitting out on the roof of the first level of houses. The tourists were like racing ants moving rapidly in one direction and then another. Several came out of the doors of two of the houses.

Coming down the bank of the stream toward Anita was a Taos man. He was lean and wore long, thin braids laced with the color red. He used a cane, skillfully pushing rocks out of the way with it. Anita watched him for awhile and then forgot about him.

She tried to remember everything that Rosa had ever said about Taos. Why hadn't she listened better?

Rosa had come to Taos Pueblo as a young woman, a child, really. She was perhaps seventeen or eighteen and was married to a Taos man. They had lived here in this place. They'd had children, children who would have looked much like these Taos people. Anita closed her eyes as she thought hard. What else had Rosa said?

Anita opened her eyes. The Taos man stood beside her. Why hadn't she heard him? He looked down at her. He wore a dark blue shirt, brown trousers, and moccasins. Anita guessed that he was older than she was, though his hair was still dark. His skin was a rich walnut brown, and his eyes were a lighter shade of brown with a hint of green in them. The eye color startled Anita and she looked quickly away.

He poked her arm gently with the top of his cane. He spoke to her in his language. Anita did not respond. Then he spoke to her in Spanish and she looked at the cane. Then in English, he asked, "Who do you want? Who are you here to see?"

Again Anita did not respond. She watched the tourists.

The man sat down beside her. He stretched out his right leg in front of him.

"Tourista," he said. "You are not tourista. You might be Indian. You look like Indian."

Anita looked at his moccasins. The man said, "I trade for this shoe. It's Cheyenne shoe. You're not Cheyenne or you would know Cheyenne shoe."

Anita shifted her body away from him. Her back then faced him.

He was quiet for awhile, then said, "I eat at my sister's house. That is her house there." He pointed to one of the doors of the Pueblo.

Anita did not look up.

The man got up by himself and said, "My sister like tourista. Sometime, she feed tourista." He walked away, his cane making no sound on the earth. Five minutes later, Anita saw him go inside.

Anita sat for a few minutes watching the tourists and feeling deeply unsettled. She wasn't one of them, she wasn't one of the Taos people. Where did she fit? She was old. Now she was lost. Her footing had slipped when Rosa had revealed old truths and old lies.

Rosa's death had not caused this confusion, and it was not what Rosa had said on that last day. No, it was what Rosa *hadn't said* all those years.

Anita sighed and decided to go back to the motel. Whatever she had come after in the Pueblo was not here. Before she left, though, she would buy a little token in remembrance of Rosa's short life here.

Anita visited two vendors before deciding on a tiny clay vase. Just as she took the bills out of her purse to pay the Taos woman, someone put a hand on her shoulder. She turned and saw the Taos man who had talked with her at the water. He and Anita were the only two at the vendor's table. Dusk was drifting into the Pueblo.

The Taos man spoke to the vendor in their language. Then the woman turned to Anita and said, "You didn't say that."

Anita looked puzzled. The woman spoke again. "I give discounts to Indians. We're poor people. You didn't tell me that you were Indian."

Anita looked at the Taos man who kept his eyes on the woman vendor, and said in English, "Cheyenne. She is Cheyenne."

Anita handed the bills to the woman, who returned one. Then the Taos man said to Anita, "I told my sister about the Cheyenne woman. She wants to feed a Cheyenne who came a long way to see the Taos people."

Anita was not amused. She frowned, but let herself be led away by the man. His cane was between Anita and him. As they walked, she blurted out, "I'm not Cheyenne!" Her words had a heavy Spanish accent and were spoken rapidly.

He didn't respond, but kept on walking. Finally, Anita asked, "Do you really have a sister at all?"

On that note, the Taos man stopped, leaned on his cane, and looked back at her. He turned his head from side to side and then went on.

A lamp on the table was the first thing that Anita saw when they entered the house. Then the man spoke to someone sitting in a dark corner. She rose, took Anita's hand, and motioned for Anita to sit on one of the chairs at the table. Anita sat down beside the Taos man, while his sister carried in food and coffee. Anita ate quietly. When she was done, the Taos man asked again, "Why are you here?"

Anita answered, "You invited me."

He shook his head no again, and then Anita understood.

"My mother was once married here. To a Taos man," Anita said. "It happened a long time ago."

"Then you are from this place?" he asked. His eyes looked more green in this light.

"No," Anita answered, "that man was not my father. That man died somewhere east of the mountains here. In the flat country, before I was born."

"Your mother is Indian?" he asked.

"Yes, she was, but she didn't know that until the day she died. She thought she was Spanish," Anita answered.

The Taos man squinted at Anita. His eyes were brown again. He asked, "And you?"

Anita looked away and said, "My father was Spanish."

The man's sister entered the room again and poured Anita another cup of coffee.

Anita felt that what she had said was inadequate. She added, "I was hoping to learn something more about my mother. This is why I came up here."

The man stared at the lamp. His face was highlighted by the flickering flame, his eyes clear and bright green. "What did you find?" he asked.

"Nothing," Anita answered.

The man spoke again. "The *tourista* come looking for Indian. Looking for Indian. . . ." he said.

Anita thought she heard a note of finality. She rose to leave, and he took his cane out of a corner and walked with her.

She said, "Thank your sister for the meal."

Anita and the man walked to her car. It was dark, and stars hung over the Pueblo. She could hear the gurgling stream.

Anita got in the car and backed out of the parking area. She rolled down the windows to say goodbye to the man but he was already gone. She drove back to the motel and went to sleep.

Early the next day Anita began to drive to the home of a family whom Rosa had often mentioned in the course of Anita's life. It took nearly three hours to drive over the mountain roads until the landscape changed. The mountains were on the west side of Anita, falling farther behind as she drove eastward. Ahead of her now were only occasional low buttes and mesas and the rolling plains of northeastern New Mexico.

Near the main road where a large sign pointed to Colorado, Oklahoma, and Texas, Anita turned onto a gravel road. She had also been here before, perhaps a half a dozen times with Rosa. Anita remembered that there was always an element of mystery surrounding this family. The last time Rosa and Anita had come out here was sixteen years ago. Anita had driven Rosa, after Rosa had made her promise not to ever mention the trip.

Back then, when they'd driven up to the white, wood frame house, only a woman had been home. The woman was plain, with brown hair and blue eyes. She was thin and nearly the same age as Anita. She had come running out of the house, taken one look at Rosa who was inside the car with Anita, and opened the door and pulled Rosa out of the car, laughing and crying at the same time. Rosa had taken all of this calmly, with a tender bashful smile. And Rosa had hugged this strange woman. Rosa had held her in her arms a long time.

Anita had waited outside on the porch while Rosa and the woman had laughed inside for nearly an hour. Then Rosa had come out of the house and they'd gone home.

Now, Anita approached that same white house. She wished she knew the woman's name. No, she didn't know that, but she knew that this woman was a member of the family that Rosa occasionally described, and kept firmly distant and apart from Anita.

The house might be empty now, though, possibly deserted. Anita stopped the car and sighed. It did look empty. There were no cars around. This had never occurred to her—that she could make this trip for nothing. What to do now?

A curtain in one of the windows moved. Then the front door opened. A woman in a housedress came out and stood there.

Anita quickly brushed her hair, opened the car door, and got out. The weather was very mild—not too warm or too cool. The woman waited.

"Hello," the woman called.

Anita walked up the steps to the porch. This woman was the same one who had pulled Rosa out of the car. Anita was relieved to find her still here.

"Hello," Anita answered. She studied the woman for a few seconds. Then she said, "I never knew your name."

The sandy-haired woman had aged. There were deep little lines that laced around her blue eyes, which now stared at Anita.

The woman answered, "I'm Beth Williams. Are you looking for someone out here? People get lost off the main road. Who do you want to see?"

Anita kept looking at the woman and answered, "You." Then she laughed, "I'm sorry. I'm so happy to see you. I'm so happy that you are still here."

The woman didn't answer. She frowned.

Anita said, "Mama died."

The woman still didn't answer.

"Rosa died. You know, Rosa?" Anita said and waited.

Then the woman understood. She said, "Are you Anita?"

Anita nodded.

The woman put an arm around Anita. She said, "Rosa died? My Rosa died?" The woman's eyes glistened.

Anita let the woman lead her into the house, into a large, square room with a high ceiling.

"When did this happen?" the woman asked.

Anita told her. When she was done, the woman slumped back into the leather chair and looked at the ceiling.

Beth said, "I had a feeling. . . . I'm sorry to hear about this. Thank you for coming all the way out here to tell me. You did come from Las Vegas, didn't you?"

Anita nodded again but added, "That isn't really why I came out here. I came for another reason."

The woman waited. The color of her eyes darkened to a deep blue. A slight frown crossed her forehead.

"Yes?" she asked.

Anita said rapidly, "Beth Williams, will you please tell me about my mother?"

Beth looked at Anita for awhile and then asked if Anita would like some lemonade. Beth left the room momentarily and returned carrying a pitcher of iced lemonade. She poured two glasses.

"What do you want to know?" Beth asked.

"How did you get to know my mother? Why didn't she ever allow me to talk about you and your family?" Anita didn't mean to be impolite. She hoped she wasn't.

Beth nodded and answered, "Well, Anita, I knew Rosa for a long time. She took care of me for a couple of months after I was born as a favor to my parents. My older brothers and my sister were actually delivered by Rosa and another woman. I'd say Rosa was about thirty when my oldest brother was born. That was about 1901. I have three brothers and one sister, and I was the youngest. There's a span of nine years between the oldest brother and myself. By the time I was born in 1910, Rosa had had you. You must have been about nine or ten then. In fact, Rosa told me you were about one year old when she delivered my brother. She came all the way from Las Vegas to be with my mother at these times. We are not so far apart in age, you and me, Anita. Anyway, after her marriage to Santiago, Rosa of course preferred to stay in Las Vegas with him. She was so happy then. Eventually, she left our family, but returned off and on throughout her life.

"Before that, Rosa stayed with my grandparents at different times in her life, from the time she was born, about 1868, until Santiago took her away to Las Vegas. So for a period of about thirty years, even during her life and marriage in Taos, my grandparents' place was Rosa's other home. After her first husband died, Rosa returned to my grandparents from Taos for a couple of months. I suppose she was lonely then, and at that time, she shared my mother's room. My mother was just a young girl. She knew better than anyone else of Rosa's hard life, spent in foster homes up to the time of her marriage. Rosa shared a lot of her experiences with my mother, maybe because my mother was younger than she was. She talked to my mother a lot. And my mother loved Rosa dearly, although Rosa was actually about sixteen years older. I think my mother saw Rosa as the older sister she never had because she was an only child." Beth stopped talking and drank some more lemonade.

"I have always thought of Rosa in the same way that I have thought of my mother. You may not know this, but as a child I called Rosa 'Mama' too. My mother died when I was about ten, and I always kind of thought of Rosa like that, even though she was older than my mother. Really, Rosa was the only motherly figure that I ever knew after my mother was gone."

Anita wasn't sure what question to ask next. She had so many of them. Finally she said, "Did you know Maria?"

Beth's eyes darkened again and she nodded. "She died before I was born. But I know of Maria, yes."

"Please tell me who Maria was," Anita said.

"Who did Rosa say she was?" Beth asked cautiously.

"Her mother," Anita said. "That was the last thing she said before she died. She said that she didn't know it until that day, that afternoon. Is that true? Was Maria her mother?"

Beth looked at Anita and then away.

"It is true, no?" Anita asked.

Beth nodded.

Anita said, "Say it then. Say that Maria was Rosa's mother. That my mother was Maria's flesh and blood."

Beth answered, "Yes, Anita, it's true. Rosa was one of Maria's children. My grandmother, Delores, always said that one day Rosa would know. I guess there's no point in keeping it a secret anymore. Maria is gone, Rosa is gone. They can't be hurt anymore."

Anita got up and walked around the room and then turned and asked, "What was the secret? That Maria was an Indian?"

Beth stood and tried to gauge Anita's reaction to what she was going to say. "Anita," she began, "this is a long story. My mother's mother, Grandmother Delores, was half Spanish. When she was twenty, she married an American, from Missouri. They had one child, who was my mother. She was born in 1884, and Maria was the midwife at my mother's birth. This was a year or two before Maria left my family for good, when she decided to move to Taos. Maria was probably in her fifties then. It took that long for her to break away completely. By then, of course, Maria had grown children of her own. My Grandmother Delores was in her twenties when she had my mother.

"My mother died at a young age, nearly thirty-six. When I was almost ten, just before my mother died, she told me that Rosa's mother, Maria, had died some twenty years earlier, and that Maria was actually a Navajo Indian who had been brought from that country long ago to New Mexico along with Maria's mother. I don't know if it was true, but it was said that Maria was brought here as a baby. And I don't know who Maria's mother was or what happened to her.

"My Grandmother Delores had told my mother that Maria came to *her* family, *her* grandfather actually, when Maria was about six or seven. He more or less adopted Maria into the family, but this happened about twenty years before my Grandmother Delores was born, about 1840, I believe. Grandmother Delores's grandfather was Spanish." Beth stopped talking.

Anita was sitting again. "How did your Grandmother Delores's family happen to become involved with Maria?" she asked.

Beth looked at the floor and answered, "Well, Anita, I wouldn't tell this to anyone but you. You deserve to know the truth. My great-great-grandfather was a Christian man and he sincerely felt that Maria was not being treated well by the foster family who had her in their keeping. As a child, Maria was often in poor health."

"Yes?" Anita responded.

"Well, he adopted Maria, Anita. She was both a servant and a member of the family. Before that, she was what was called an Indian slave. My great-great-grandfather purchased her freedom. She lived in his home most of her youth," Beth said slowly.

Anita's mouth dropped open.

Beth held up a hand and said, "It happened in those days, Anita. That's all I can say about it. It happened in those days. It seemed that Maria had been separated from her real mother for a couple of years by then. Maria had been sold two or three times by the time she came to know great-great-grandfather's family. It wasn't all bad, Anita. She became one of the family and was dearly loved by everyone."

Anita didn't know what to say. When everything that Beth had said finally sank in, she asked, "Where did this happen? Where did Maria come to your family?"

"Near Taos," answered Beth, "by Cimarron. You know the area?"

Anita answered no and asked, "And what about my mother, what about her? Why didn't Maria tell her this?"

"Anita!" Beth said. "How could she tell her that? *Maria herself didn't know the whole story.* She knew only that she was a foster child. There were many like Maria—Indian servants. In those days, the Indian servants seldom returned to their own families, or people, for one reason or another. They didn't even know for certain to what people they actually belonged, because they had lived with foster families since infancy or early childhood. Maria was one of these. She didn't know for sure that she was Navajo. *We don't even know that now.* When she grew up, it was too late to do anything about her situation, even if she'd been told then."

"Was she ever told?" Anita asked sadly.

"I don't know," Beth said. "Grandmother Delores said she had heard that Maria claimed to be Indian a couple of times, but then when Maria was questioned about the Indian people to which she belonged and couldn't answer, she quieted and didn't pursue her claim. Grandmother's father thought that eventually Maria would forget about it, though Maria hadn't by the time my Grandmother Delores was born."

Anita asked, "You said that Maria had other children?"

Beth smiled. "When Maria was about eighteen, a marriage was arranged for her. My great-grandfather's family, Grandmother Delores's family, had a large ranch then near Cimarron. There were perhaps five people to help run the ranch and house. Maria's future husband was one of these."

"Were those people bought, too?" Anita asked.

Beth winced and answered, "Well, yes and no. Some were hired help and then a couple were Indian slaves. One of these men was a Navajo, and grandmother's family thought that he and Maria would make a good match. For about five years, Maria and her husband lived in a cabin not too far from the main house."

"They had children?" Anita asked.

Beth said, "Yes, they had children. Two of them, two little boys. One day, Maria came to the big house that great-grandfather's family lived in and told them that her Navajo husband had decided to go back to his country. Just like that. He'd left the previous night and taken his two children with him. Evidently he had tried to persuade Maria to go with him, but she refused, fearing that she would not be accepted in his country if it turned out that she was *not* a Navajo. That happened about 1850, I think—over a hundred years ago." Beth sighed.

"Who was my mother's father?" Anita asked.

"That I don't really know. I don't think my mother or grandmother ever knew either. It happened many years after her Navajo husband had left. Maria's stomach began to grow, and then Rosa was born. Maria was well over thirty, perhaps close to forty then.

"But by then, she had come to her own terms with life. She gave the child, Rosa, up to great-grandfather to place in a foster home. But Maria didn't really relinquish all of Rosa because she followed Rosa everywhere. She really did love Rosa, you see."

Anita closed her eyes. Her mother, Rosa, never knew.

"When Rosa's first child, a girl, was born in Taos Pueblo, Maria was there. Rosa's baby was christened Maria, too. Rosa never knew how much that meant to old Maria, I heard.

"When Rosa was about twenty-two, she had a son. I think she said that was her age then. Again, Maria was there to deliver the boy, Domingo. You knew the boy and girl?" Beth asked.

"Not really," Anita said. "I met both of them twice, once when I was a teenager, and we went to Taos to visit them. Later, they came to Las Vegas. I don't know where they are now. We weren't close."

"They died," Beth said. "Rosa told me about the girl, Maria, the last time she was here. The child died in 1949. Rosa wept when she told me. I heard that the boy, Domingo, died in '66. Rosa once said that she felt like she had led three separate lives—the one in Taos with her first husband, the one with my family, and the one with you and your father."

"Where did she meet my father?" Anita asked.

"Española, I think," Beth said. "I've never been there. Never been to Santa Fe either. Can you imagine that? The only place I've been to is Las Vegas to visit Rosa. Anyway, Santiago married Rosa about six years after her first husband died. She was staying with old Maria at the time. I heard this from Rosa."

"Why did Mama want to keep these visits to your family quiet?" Anita asked.

"I don't know, really, except that she did worry that someone might harm you. I sensed that she was ashamed of her being an orphan, and the mystery and the stigma surrounding it. The secrets were for your benefit, and for herself, too. She worked hard to provide you with a good life. In a sense, old Maria did, too. Have you ever known real poverty or hunger?" Beth asked.

Anita admitted that that was true. She had not known those two things. Her father and her mother had been well off. With both parents' deaths, Anita might be considered a wealthy woman. The wealth came from the land, her father's land.

Anita stood and said, "Thank you very much," and then she turned to leave. Beth rose with her and on the porch she said, "Anita, what I have told you is written down. It's in my great-grandfathers's and Grandmother Delores's handwriting. My great-grandfather wasn't the best speller around, but he could write a little. . . . He and Grandmother Delores even wrote some of it in Spanish. We have an old family Bible, and all this is there in the Bible if you'd like to read it for yourself."

Anita shook her head no and walked to her car. She drove back over the mountains to Taos, and spent the second night there. The next day she drove slowly back to Las Vegas, stopping in Española for awhile and in Santa Fe.

The trip had led her here, to this isolated cemetery, staring at Rosa's grave. Anita had chosen this site because Rosa had mentioned several times that she would like to be buried here. Anita could not say now how many times she'd heard Rosa say it. Anita's father, Santiago, had heard it, too, because he'd said the same thing—that he wished to be buried here—but that was after Rosa had been so adamant about the location of her final resting place. In the long run, Santiago was brought out here before Rosa.

Now Rosa was beside Santiago. The other graves inside the fence were much older.

Anita gathered the remains of her lunch and took everything back to her car. Then she opened the trunk and took some plastic flowers that she had bought in Española to stick in Rosa's and Santiago's graves. She went back inside the fence again and pushed the wire stems deep into the sandy soil. Then she read the other markers on the graves. She knew no only else here.

As she drove away from the wrought-iron fence she noticed that not all the graves were inside the area. Two more were on the far side of the thick adobe walls. One was very old. Its cross was broken, but the other was more recent, though it was also older than those inside the fence. It, too, had a sandstone cross, much smaller than the one on the other grave. Purple, plastic flowers, broken and faded, lay bent on the site. Plastic petals lay scattered on the ground and had faded to white.

Anita stopped the car and walked through the ruined adobe mission. She stepped out of the ruins to stand beside the grave with the disintegrating plastic flowers. Carved in the center of the sandstone cross was the name "MARIA." Below that were the words: *"Born? - Died 1900."* Just below that the face of a woman with long braids had been carved into the sandstone.

Anita looked up from Maria's grave, through the crumbling walls, to Rosa's grave, about eighty feet away. Why was Maria buried apart from everyone else, Anita wondered. Her eyes shone. The sun was too bright. The pulsating colors of the day were too radiant. They made her eyes blink and brim with tears.

16

NAVAJO RESERVATION

THE trading post was situated amid the sagebrush and greasewood at the end of a long, bumpy ride. It was the only building in sight for a few miles in any direction, and there were five mobile homes behind it. Several miles to the north stood Beautiful Mountain.

Nasbah arrived at the trading post about ten minutes late for her job as a cashier. The position was a temporary one. In January, she would attend the University of New Mexico.

The morning was clear and crisp. Customers were already parked outside waiting for the trading post to open. As she parked the pickup truck beside the building, two more pickups with fat cattle in the stock racks drove up beside her. It was going to be a busy day.

Inside, Nasbah prepared for the first morning customers. Two other women worked with her. As the trading post owner opened the front doors, customers streamed in to make early morning purchases or to trade or to sell livestock and other goods to the owner. Nasbah read her daily work assignment, which the owner was in the habit of posting for all employees. Because the trading post provided a variety of services to its customers, Nasbah found herself involved in many sometimes unrelated work assignments in a week's time. These tasks involved writing letters for those who didn't know how to write, assisting customers in making a major purchase, such as a car, a tractor, or livestock, and arranging credit in the reservation border towns for qualified people. At the bottom of the sheet was a note that Nasbah should see the owner.

She went to the cubicle at the back of the store where the owner or his wife usually sat and maintained all the books. The owner's wife, a blonde woman with a ready smile, was there now.

"Good morning, Nasbah," the blonde woman said.

Nasbah nodded and said, "There's a note to see Elton. Do you know what it's about?"

"Oh, yes," the woman answered. "I did something stupid. There was a phone call for you a few days ago, and I neglected to tell you. I'm sorry, but the call came during the lunch hour while you were unavailable. I asked if the person wanted to leave a message, but the answer was no."

"Well, thanks anyway for letting me know. I suppose it wasn't too important or I would have been called again," Nasbah said.

The blonde woman added, "The call was from Washington, D.C."

Nasbah nodded and went back to her cash register. One of the women working with Nasbah sorted mail into boxes just beside the door.

She said, "Nasbah, you have a lot of mail today."

Nasbah answered, "Probably bills," as she rang up the purchases for an elderly woman who was the first in a line of several people.

The day was busier than usual due to the arrival of monthly social security checks for several of the trading post customers. Nasbah peeled an orange for lunch, stuffed her own and Jonnie Navajo's mail into her jacket pocket, and went back to work. About four, the blonde woman came and told Nasbah that she could leave early because Nasbah had worked through lunch. The woman was laughing with Nasbah's co-workers as Nasbah got her jacket and left.

About a half an hour later, Nasbah drove up to Jonnie Navajo's house. Only a couple of dogs were in sight, staying close to the sheep corral. All the sheep were there. The old man had to be nearby. Nasbah unlocked the front door and went inside. The large three-room house was dark and quiet. She opened the curtains in each room and turned on a transistor radio. The disc jockey spoke in Navajo.

After changing her clothes, Nasbah filled the kitchen stove with wood. In a few minutes the fire warmed the house, and she prepared the evening meal. When that was done, she went outside to carry wood to the box inside the house. Then she put on a sweater and sat on a folding aluminum chair outside the house to wait for the return of the old man and woman.

To the south, Beautiful Mountain had changed colors. It was now bright yellow and gold in places. In mid-August it had become too cold up there at night for the old man and woman, and they had moved back down the mountain. Nasbah had loaded up her pickup with cooking utensils, bedding, and a few articles of clothing for her grandmother and had driven slowly down the steep and treacherous road that led to this side of the mountain.

The old man had not ridden down the mountain. He'd walked with his herd of some eighty sheep and goats. He'd started for this house at the first ray of dawn and had arrived at sunset. The sheep bleated his arrival several minutes before Nasbah and the old woman actually saw him. Nasbah smiled at the recollection of this, because for the rest of that evening her grandfather had bemoaned the fact that it had taken him so long to walk down the mountain at this time of his life.

The old man topped the hill southeast of the house now. The horse he rode trotted after three others running in the direction of the corral. Nasbah rose to help the old man. One of the horses turned north toward Nasbah, and she headed it back in the direction of the corral as the old man followed the other two to the gate. The third entered the corral, and the old man got off the horse to help Nasbah lift the posts that closed the corral securely. He walked back to the house, and Nasbah rode the horse to the front door. She left the reins loose and went inside the house.

The old man was lighting half a dozen lamps, which lit the dark places of the house.

"Where is my grandmother?" Nasbah asked him.

He washed himself in an enamel basin and Nasbah set the table. "She will return after dark," he answered. "She is visiting her older sister right now. The daughter of that sister came for her this afternoon. She will bring her home tonight."

The old man ate ravenously, and when he was done, he went outside to unsaddle the horse. Nasbah ate more slowly and separated the mail for the old man and herself. She looked out the window and saw her grandfather at the sheep corral north of the house. It was dusk and the evening was very cool.

She put wood in the stove in the big front room of the house, although she did not light it. That could wait until tonight sometime. Then Nasbah cleared the table by lamplight and washed the dishes in water that she and the old man had carried from the well in barrels in the pickup truck two days earlier.

The old man came back into the house and took off his heavy shirt and shoes. He wore a white undershirt. Nasbah brought his mail to him and read two letters aloud to him before tossing a colorful brochure into the stove. Then she opened her own mail, and one by one tossed each envelope with its contents into the fire, too. The last letter bore a return address in Washington, D.C.

They heard a vehicle outside. The old man got up from the table and lifted a curtain at the window. All he could see were two yellow headlights crawling toward the house.

"It's probably your grandmother," he said to Nasbah, and sat down again.

Nasbah opened the letter. She unfolded the five-by-seven sheet of paper and scanned the message, frowning as she read. Then she folded the paper and slipped it back into the envelope.

The vehicle came to a stop outside, and the motor was turned off. Nasbah and the old man expected the old woman to come in. When after a few minutes she didn't, the old man went to put on his shoes and shirt. A minute or two later, there was a knock on the door.

Nasbah opened the door. In the door frame stood a young man and a young woman, perhaps in their thirties. The woman had a child who was laced into a cradleboard. They entered the large front room and, after gently shaking Nasbah's hand, took a seat on a very old couch pushed against a wall.

The man said, "It's a long way from Kayenta. Is my grandfather here?"

Nasbah answered that Jonnie Navajo was home.

He came out of the kitchen and stared at the man and woman momentarily. The woman held the cradleboard on her lap. The lamp light softened the features of the visitors. He did not know these people.

Jonnie Navajo walked to them, extended a hand to each, and then sat on the floor, leaning his back against a suitcase on which blankets were stacked. For a few minutes, the room was quiet and motionless, except for the baby sounds and movements on that side of the room.

Then the young man began to talk about their trip here. The woman listened without interrupting him; she kept her eyes on the floor or on her child.

"Ah," said the young man. "We drove a long way. We came from north of Kayenta." He took off his felt hat and brushed his fingers through his hair and then laid the hat next to him.

He said to Jonnie Navajo, "This is a beautiful area. We've never been here before. We could have been here earlier, but we got lost and went to the wrong house. Three times," he laughed.

Then the man finally introduced himself, his wife, and the baby. He said, "I'm from the family of Long Whiskers. He was a member of the Black Sheep Clan, and was my paternal grandfather. Maybe you have heard of him?"

The old man answered, "Yes, it's possible that I have heard of him."

"On the other side, my mother's family comes from near Shiprock. They are the Redhouse Clan."

The old man thought about this information for a minute and nodded.

The young man continued. "Grandfather, I have come to ask you whether or not you could sing over us, my family and me. We have been having some problems, and my mother told me that we should visit you. What we would like you to do is perform a Protection Way."

Jonnie Navajo was quiet a minute before he asked, "These problems you have been experiencing, what are they?"

At this time, the woman looked at Jonnie Navajo and said, "Grandfather, I'm thinking that perhaps someone has bad wishes for us. It may have something to do with what has been happening to us. The baby has been ill. There are unknown people coming near our hogan at odd hours. This thing worries me."

"Yes," added the man, "this is true. We have gone to see a stargazer. He has helped us. The next thing we must do is have a Protection Prayer—soon."

"This can be done," Jonnie Navajo said. "But what did the stargazer say to you?"

The woman spoke. "The stargazer said that a few days ago, while I was outside the hogan weaving and this man here was out with the sheep, that someone came and made the baby ill. The baby is fine now, but earlier we nearly lost her."

The young man nodded as the woman finished speaking.

Nasbah left the room and put two flat irons on the wood stove to heat. Then she unfolded an ironing board and began to iron shirts for the old man. The voices in the next room could easily be heard. Her grandfather agreed to do the ceremony. They were now discussing when he might do it.

Nasbah wondered if her grandfather ever tired of this. Sometimes people came for him every week. When he was younger, he was gone more often.

In the next room, the couple was leaving. The door closed, and she could hear her grandfather taking off his shoes as soon as the visitors went outside. In a few minutes, he entered the room where Nasbah ironed his shirts. He went to the calendar and picked up the pencil that was tied to it with a string. Nasbah asked, "What day?" He told her the date, three days away, and Nasbah took the pencil from him and put an X through that date.

"Where?" she asked. "Kayentá?"

He nodded and she wrote that in under the X.

"The man's name?" she asked. Her grandfather handed her a piece of paper with the man's name, Jimmy Tom, scrawled across it. Nasbah added this information on the calendar.

The month of September was filled with a half a dozen X's. She looked back through other months, flipping the pages up, and each month had its quota of X's.

The old man poured himself a cup of coffee and put two teaspoons of sugar in it, stirring twice. He sat down at the table and faced Nasbah to drink his sweet coffee.

"Willie's ill, Grandfather," she said. "He's ill in *Washingdoon*." She continued, "I got a letter from some man. I don't know him. But he said that Willie wasn't feeling too well and was in the hospital."

The old man thought about this and finally said, "Willie should come home."

"Yes," Nasbah said, "that is what he wants to do as soon as they let him out."

"What kind of sickness does he have?" the old man asked.

"I guess they don't know," Nasbah said, hanging a pressed shirt on a doorknob. "It must be serious, though, or this man would not have written." Nasbah started another shirt.

For several minutes the room was quiet. The only sounds were the old man swallowing his coffee and Nasbah setting the iron down on the quilted board.

Nasbah asked, "Grandfather, what if Willie can't come home on his own?"

"We'll have to go get him then," Jonnie Navajo said. "Someone must go—perhaps it will be you."

"How will I go? *Washingdoon* is a long way, all the way to the big water. We have no money. Perhaps his aunt can help, though I doubt it.

She barely has enough money to take care of herself. Perhaps we can sell some of Willie's cattle if necessary. I will have to talk with him first on that. Maybe he is already recovered from this illness," she said.

"That could be so," her grandfather nodded. "We will wait."

The matter settled, Nasbah asked another question. "Grandfather, from whom did you learn how to do the protection ceremony?"

The old man answered, "From my uncle, *Hosteen Nez*.

"These things that are done today among the people—where they are willfully harming one another—were originally done under other conditions," he said. "In the old days, they had a place.

"At that time, the people had enemies, who were other tribes, or other alien people. It was acceptable then to create turmoil and ill wishes for those strangers. Under those circumstances of war, sorcery was used against the enemy. Now, in these times, the people are using it against their own kind, sometimes their own families. This is because of the time in which we live."

"Does this sorcery really work against others, Grandfather? I mean, does it work against other races?" Nasbah asked.

The old man nodded. "It is possible. I have heard stories about this.

"A long time ago, it was used on occasion against the white strangers. It was said that there was a warfare between the People and these strangers, and the People decided to give it a try against the strangers. They called in a great medicine man to do the ceremony.

"The strangers were camped in Navajo country. The medicine man asked for specific things he would need to accomplish this thing. He labored that night on this ceremony, and toward dawn said that the task was done. All that need be done then was to wait and see what the result would be.

"The People's spies watched from hidden places around the strangers' camp. At dawn, the strangers carried a stretcher through camp and brought out the leader of that party. The man was completely covered with a blanket. He was dead."

Nasbah continued to iron. She traded a cool iron for a hot one. She answered, "I suppose other tribes have this, too. I suppose they have ceremonies to use against others, too."

"It is possible," her grandfather answered. "People have learned to protect themselves in whatever way they can."

"I suppose that nowadays there aren't too many people who could do what that medicine man did to the strangers?" Nasbah asked.

The old man didn't answer.

Nasbah asked, "Who was the man who performed that ceremony, Grandfather?"

Nasbah's grandfather mumbled something. Nasbah couldn't make it out.

She asked again, "Who was the man who performed that ceremony, Grandfather?"

This time he answered clearly. "White Sheep," he said. "White Sheep did the ceremony."

Nasbah put the iron on the stove and walked to the table, where she sat across from her grandfather. The lamplight flickered and she raised the wick a fraction of an inch. The flame steadied.

She asked, "Is this the same White Sheep who was up on the mountain? The one who saved the twin child?"

Jonnie Navajo nodded. "There were a handful of men like him during his lifetime. I told you before that he was not an ordinary man. He knew ceremonies such as this, some of which are gone today. They are not practiced anymore."

"How old was he when he did this thing, Grandfather?" Nasbah asked.

"That is hard to say," he answered. "But he was very old. This thing occurred after he had lost his daughter, after they had stolen her. So you see that he recovered from his own wounds sufficiently to accomplish such a thing."

Another vehicle came toward the house. "That will be your grandmother," the old man said.

A car door slammed, and soon the old woman came into the house carrying a sack. This she handed to Nasbah and hung her jacket on the wall. The sack was filled with food.

For a few minutes, the three discussed the old woman's visit to her older sister's hogan, and then the old man and woman prepared to go to sleep on the floor in the next room. It was about eight o'clock.

A couple of hours later, Nasbah found herself thinking of Willie. With his illness on her mind, she climbed into bed to sleep.

Early the next day at the trading post, Nasbah was called to the cubicle at the back of the store. The blonde woman handed Nasbah the phone. "It's from Washington, D.C.," the woman whispered. Nasbah spoke into the phone and heard Willie's voice in response.

"Nasbah?" he asked. "I guess you received a letter from a George Daylight?"

"Yes," she answered.

Willie said, "I'm still not feeling well. The doctor wants to run more tests."

"What's wrong?" asked Nasbah.

"Would you give a message to my grandfather?" Willie said in response. "Tell him that I think I have the same sickness the white woman had—the sister of David Drake. I told Grandfather about this woman. You remember David Drake? We're supposed to work for him as interpreters for our grandfather. Drake is the writer doing the Navajo history. Has he contacted you yet?" Willie asked, his voice fading in and out over the miles of telephone lines.

"Yes, yes, I remember the man, but he has not contacted me," answered Nasbah.

"Well, that doesn't matter right now," Willie said.

Nasbah asked, "Where are you?"

"I'm in the hospital," he said. "I've been here two days. Ask what my grandfather thinks about all this. I'll try to call again tomorrow."

"Yes, yes," answered Nasbah, and hung up the phone.

The rest of the day went slowly, and finally Nasbah went home. Again, the house was empty. The sheep were penned in the corral.

About dusk, Nasbah's grandfather and grandmother came home. They came in a neighbor's pickup truck. While Nasbah served them their evening meal, they shared the day's news. The old man and woman talked about grazing rights for their livestock and the new regulations for owners of livestock that they had learned about earlier that day. Then it was Nasbah's turn to speak.

She said, "Willie called me at the trading post this morning. He said to tell you that he thinks he has the same sickness as the white woman he told you about."

Her grandfather thought about that a minute and nodded.

"What sickness is that, Grandfather?" Nasbah asked.

Jonnie Navajo answered as he ate. "Willie told me of a white woman in *Washingdoon* who had taken her own life. Well, it is not known for certain that she did so, but this is what most people thought. He said that before her death, she had been seeing things, such as people who were not alive."

The remainder of the meal was eaten in silence. Finally Nasbah asked, "What is the meaning of this?"

"It means that Willie is not well," her grandfather sighed.

"Willie wanted to know what you think about this, Grandfather," Nasbah said.

The old man went into the other room and lay down on the floor. He did not answer Nasbah that night.

Early the next morning, as Nasbah prepared breakfast, her grandfather said, "Tell Willie that we will have to sell three or four of his cattle if he is unable to come back within a week. Tell Willie that I have never seen *Washingdoon*. You will go with me. Ask him how we should go about getting there and tell him that we shall see him soon, after the ceremony at Kayenta is concluded."

17

OKLAHOMA CITY, OKLAHOMA

WILBUR Snake held Anna's hand as they attempted to cross the street. The traffic raced in front of them, refusing to stop to allow the two old people to venture into the crosswalk, although it was clearly marked with white lines.

Anna wore a cotton print dress, and black shoes with thick stacked heels, "old lady's shoes," Junior called them. The hem of her dress hung about four inches below her knees. She wore a black scarf tied around the top of her head; it fashioned a cap, and her long white braids fell out of this. Everything she wore dwarfed her frame. Even her large handbag seemed too heavy for the diminutive woman.

Wilbur didn't appear much stronger as the two figures stood before the state building with columnar architecture and the imposing oil derricks rising out of the landscape. Wilbur wore dark blue cowboy-cut trousers, a short-sleeved white cotton shirt, and cowboy boots. Anna had made his beaded belt for him. He had stuck the feathers in his hat himself.

Finally, one of the cars braked, and the traffic in the other three lanes followed suit. Wilbur pulled Anna across the street, her tiny feet in no hurry at all. The cars began to honk, and Wilbur reached to his hearing aid to shut out the noise.

"Oh my gosh," Anna said, "maybe there's a fire somewhere."

On the other side of the street, a wide walk led up to the historical building. Anna and Wilbur stood in front of the building a second and Anna said, "Wilbur, shall we sit outside for a while?"

He evidently didn't hear, and looked at Anna. She pointed to a cement slab beside the walk and then at Wilbur and herself. He nodded.

The cement was cool under her fingers. Anna put her purse down and sat beside it. Wilbur sat down, too, adjusted his hearing aid, and enjoyed the view. The sky was hazy blue and filled with clouds. There was minimum humidity.

"Purty day," Anna said.

Wilbur nodded and said, "Long time ago, some mans—some womans—they like to sing on a day like this. It causes them to sing."

"What do they sing, Wilbur?" Anna asked, looking at him.

Wilbur began to sing. "Hey-ya-ya-hey. . . ." His voice was small but firm under the vast sky. It floated loosely up in front of the carved, ornate buildings and the sounds of traffic on the freeway.

As Wilbur sang, a few people came out of the building and down the steps. They looked curiously at Wilbur, who continued to sing. Anna smiled and said to them, "He singing. He likes to sing."

The people moved on.

The glass doors at the top of the steps opened again, and Junior stuck his head outside. "Mama! Daddy!" he said. "You all coming in?"

Anna hollered, "It's all right, Junior. You and Erleen go ahead. I can't breathe in there."

Junior nodded and closed the door.

Wilbur stopped singing and looked toward the door.

Anna said, "Wilbur, old man, you sure we're doing right? You think we ought to go back again? You old, Wilbur. I'm older, older'n you. Sometimes when peoples get old, their minds kind of gets away from them. We still got our right minds, Wilbur?"

He nodded. "You're right, Anna. We old. But sometimes when peoples get old as us—some things don't matter no more. Nothing to be afraid of no more."

"All right, Wilbur," she said. "We're bound to go over yonder. Bound to see how far things is come," Anna said. She looked up at the sky and the clouds moving rapidly overhead. "It's purty," she said. "This day is too purty, Old Man. I can feel those clouds on me. I can feel every little bitty thing. What's that mean?"

Then she said softly, "Old Man, don't it seem like Junior cares for old peoples? Look at how he's been taking us to town all these times, and now he's taking us back there—Washton, D.C. For the ride, Junior says. Going to take us for a long ride. Wilbur, when was the last time we was in Washton, D.C.?"

Wilbur counted on his fingers. "Together? Together, just about twenty-eight years ago. Last time I was out there was maybe eighteen years ago. Me and LeClair went."

Anna said, "Maybe LeClair wants to go to Washton, D.C. again with us. You should of asked him, Wilbur."

Wilbur looked off toward an oil derrick and said, "Anna, LeClair went on. How many times do I have to keep telling you? He's dead."

Anna smiled. "Oh, my, it's true. I keep forgetting. It's not my fault, Wilbur. LeClair might have gone on all right, but they's a part of him that's still hanging on to us. I can feel him right here. You? You feel him, Wilbur?"

Wilbur nodded.

He and Anna sat outside the building for perhaps half an hour, and then Junior and Erleen came out.

"Well, Daddy," Junior said, "we're ready. I guess we can load up the car again and head on out east. Me and Erleen figure that we'll drive slow, do some sight-seeing along the way, and be in Washington in just about three days."

"Mama, Daddy," Erleen said, "are you hungry? We can get a bite to eat before we leave the city if you want."

"Some lemon pie would taste good," Wilbur said, "but that's all for me. Old men don't hold a lot of food." Anna nodded in agreement.

Junior said, "You all wait here and I'll bring the car up and pick you up."

He drove the car to the crosswalk, and his three passengers climbed in. Wilbur and Anna sat in the back seat. It was filled with pillows, Pendleton blankets, a small bundle that Wilbur usually carried with him everywhere, and a drum. There was a gourd rattle above the back seat.

After Junior entered the eastbound lane on the freeway, he said loudly to Wilbur, "Daddy, Russell Tallman is going to let us stay at his place for two days. I talked to him last night. Heck, two nights is enough. That's all the time we need, really. Two days should do it. I'm sure glad me and Erleen could take this vacation now."

"Who's that we going to sleep with, Junior?" Anna asked.

"You know, Mama, that's the man who came to visit Daddy not too long ago, Myrtle Black Bear's boy."

"Oh, my, you mean Sonny?" Anna asked. "That's good. It's good to have relatives and family in a strange country."

Erleen smiled out the window to her right. Junior looked out the window to the left, and he smiled too.

Wilbur picked up the gourd rattle. He shook it a couple of times and began to sing an ancient song as the car raced down the freeway.

At that very moment, George Daylight stepped off the plane at the Oklahoma City Airport. He breathed a sigh of relief. He was glad he was home.

18

WASHINGTON, D.C.

DONALD Evans sat alone in the attic, sorting paperwork. He was annoyed with the place, with the increasing hand prints on the door. There were several now, superimposed on one another in a different substance, an oily base that rubbed off under Donald's fingers. As soon as Donald had entered the room this morning, he'd taken a cloth coated with scouring powder and wiped the door roughly. Streaks stayed on the door over the two hand prints in clay. He sat down at the desk and began to answer old correspondence.

He wished that he had not come in today, or yesterday, or the day before. Things had changed too drastically with Geoffrey's sudden death. Donald was no longer the light-hearted person he was before moving here.

Behind him the radio suddenly blared, but only static drifted out of the speaker. Donald turned off the radio and unplugged the cord from the wall outlet.

He didn't like his job anymore. He didn't like being here. The room was too small, there were no windows, and he had to go downstairs for water and to use the bathroom. Sometimes this place produced a strange, acrid odor, too. Donald broke his pencil in half. He let out a long breath.

His thoughts were not on correspondence, but on George Daylight. Donald now remembered that Geoffrey had really despised George. Donald, on the other hand, found him curious. The way that George saw things sometimes bordered on superstition. His existence at all—a practicing heathen who endowed each life form with a personification of his own mind—in a fast-paced society that hurled itself toward high tech and outer space was wryly amusing to Donald. He couldn't help but chuckle at George and his kind, and Donald meant no harm. His observations were impersonal assessments, much like a report on earth from another planet.

The last thing Donald wanted was involvement with George's kind.

Not for the same reasons that Geoffrey held against George. Donald was more realistic than that. George's kind was already overextended—they were on borrowed time anyway. It was simply an accident that such simple heathen types had made it this far—all the way to the twentieth century. That's why Donald wasn't particularly into Indians or any ethnic groups. By all odds, sooner or later, all the groups would be sucked up into one big vacuum. Consequently, Donald couldn't, and wouldn't, encourage ethnic plurality and diversity. It was a waste of time, but more important, it was unrealistic to his way of thinking. He couldn't condone such indulgence.

But that damn George Daylight had showed up here a few days ago. Donald chewed on his pencil and looked toward the door where George had entered and said, "Hey, Evans, how's it going? I'd like to visit with you a couple of minutes if you can spare the time."

Donald had a lot of time, too much on his hands up here lately. He nodded and George entered, saying, "Haven't been up here for months. Newsome showed us around last time."

George scanned the room. Everything was in the same place.

"What's on your mind?" Donald asked, pulling up a chair for George.

George sat, took off his hat, and looked intently at Donald. "Heck," he said, "they's a lot on my mind, and that's what brought me here. You ever hear of spirit people?"

Donald smiled, careful to hold his laughter inside. This query was exactly what Donald would have expected from George. Should he humor him? Donald didn't know his own patience. He answered, "Ghosts? Is that what you're talking about? Everybody knows what ghosts are. Did you come up here to talk to me about ghosts? If that's the purpose of this visit, George, you're wasting both my time and yours. Ghosts aren't my field of study. That's more your line—from what Geoffrey told me. He said you and he really argued over the subject of ghosts. Is that true? If you ask me, the question of ghosts is a moot issues to this collection up here, though. That's why you're here, isn't it?"

George poured himself a cup of coffee and let a minute pass before answering. "It's true we argued somewhat. I can't say for certain if ghosts was the root of it, though. Don't matter. I guess I did step on his toes. Hell, I admit I jumped up and down on them, stomped all over them, I suppose."

"Well, Geoffrey was indeed possessive," Donald answered. "This collection was his baby. . . ."

"That right?" answered George. "I guess it's my fault then that we got started off on the wrong foot. From the minute we met, well, heck, sparks just flew."

Donald did not answer.

After a minute, George plunged into his reason for being here. "I'd like to throw some ideas at you, Evans, see how they hit you. Stop me anywhere along the way if you want something clarified, or have a question, or simply want to disagree."

Donald nodded, certain that he understood George's motive for being here.

"Been doing some thinking and studying on an idea that keeps running through my mind. Let me backtrack first and explain something to you, so that we're both starting off at the same place, so to speak. This here collection in the attic is Indian, that right? Comes from different Indian people?"

Donald nodded again.

"So far, so good," George said. "Now, then, Indian people have some very opinionated ideas about items they produce, items they own."

Donald smiled. He was ready. "The items in this collection," he said, "are no longer the possession of any Indian people. They haven't been in their possession for some time. When items such as these are created and become separated from the original maker, well, that separation was a distinct possibility before the item was created. It would be rather naive to think otherwise. Therefore, George, these items cannot still be considered Indian possessions, though there's no doubt that they were created by Indians or came from them. American Indians aren't the only group to have raised this question, and the amount of American Indian materials housed in museums is certainly substantial by now. So even I admit that I can understand why the question of ownership keeps arising."

"Let me go a little further," George answered, unperturbed. "The extent of feeling, or cultural belief, of a particular tribal person, or tribal group, creating a religious or sacred item goes beyond *possession* or *ownership* of it. In a sense, such a thing cannot be *owned*. Do you understand?"

Donald nodded his head, though he wore a deep frown.

"*Ownership* in tribal context implies several things, and not necessarily possession of an item. To *own* it, one must be able to make use of it, and that implies that one is aware of the purpose for which it was created and has the means, the information, or the knowledge to use it as it was intended." George stopped speaking.

Donald responded. "George, the fact is that these items are *here*. Another fact is that many Indian people no longer want to be reminded that they ever created items such as these. This legacy is an embarrassment to them. With education and acculturation, they've wisely chosen to put all this hocus-pocus behind them. You'd do well to follow that example, George!" Donald waved his hand around the room and casually added, "These objects and items stored up here are from dead cultures, George, dead! When will you people wake up to this realization? There's no point in trying to revive the dead. Life can't be breathed into these things."

George's face remained blank, although the color of his pupils lit for an instant. He answered, "I'm gonna have to argue with you on that last point, Evans. It'll have to be later, though. I'll get to it. Right now, I want to pick up with my thought where I left off a minute ago.

"Granted, not all Indians care about what's housed here. And not all of them know exactly what's here either, just as the majority of the American people don't know. But a good many Indian people have been informed of what's here and they are very concerned.

"This concern revolves around the role of the caretaker of these items. Yes, the items are *here*. You claim *ownership*, by however means the items came to be here. Though this aspect ain't under discussion now, we both know that even *how* the items came to be here, through legal or illegal acquisition, might also be another issue. But this aside, the items are here. Now, how to take care of them? Is simply 'storing' and 'fumigating' them enough? For the moment, *you* are the caretaker—hell, American society don't even know what it has here! Not even the Board of Directors, or Trustees, or whoever governs the operation of this here place is the caretaker. It's possible that not even they know for certain what's in their possession. It's you, Evans, you're the caretaker! You're also the only one who really knows for certain what's up here!"

Donald's face was red.

George's tone softened a little. "Now, I ain't saying that you ain't the person for the job. What I'm saying is maybe the time has come to rethink this whole process of buying Indian artifacts and materials for collections like this, along with the *need* for a collection like this at all. Who does it benefit—American society? Indian people? American society don't even pretend to know what all these objects here are by name or use, and maybe that knowledge wouldn't change the situation much. And the collection sure as hell don't benefit Indian people none. How does it claim to do that?

"This collection is going to be a sore spot between groups of people as long as it exists. You already know that, and had better accept the fact that it will stay that way until there is an attempt to understand what Indian people are saying about this, but more importantly, *why* they say it."

Donald pushed his chair closer to George and looked him in the eye. "George," he said, "this isn't getting us anywhere. All your arguments aren't going to change anything. Nothing will change, not our policy on accepting or purchasing Indian material, nothing! You are not going to make any difference, not one iota!"

George was not in the least surprised. He blinked his eyes, stood, and stretched. "That's what I thought," he said. "Yep, that's just what I thought."

He walked slowly around the attic in a clockwise direction, his eyes sweeping the shelves, the cabinets, the corners of the room. Then he turned and looked at Donald and asked, "You ain't seen him yet, huh? Is that why you're so damned sure of yourself?"

"What are you talking about?" Donald asked, losing all remaining patience.

George stood still and raised a hand to quiet Donald. He sniffed the air and made a face. Then he walked to the door, looked down the stairway, and came back to Donald again.

"Evans," he said, "the first time I came up here a few years back, I learned something. I want to pass it on to you now. Might be worth something to you later, not in money, but it might be worth your life. The first time I walked into this room, I felt the spirit people here, in the drawers, in the cabinets, in the corners of the room. Don't get me wrong, Evans, these ain't ghosts. Now let me elaborate on this some. It might not be what you want to hear, though, an educated man like you. But I have to make a throw at it.

"A while ago, you said that all these things in this room were from dead cultures. I think that you also meant that everything up here is also dead. . . .

"Well, that's where we're like day and night, Evans. The cultures who created these items ain't dead simply because you're blind to them and deem them so! These cultures manifest themselves differently now, that's all, though the word 'differently' might be a poor choice. *The people who created these things exist*—they're still here! Whether or not they have recollection of the items here being a part of their cultural inventory don't change that fact. The fact that these items are now in your possession don't change it either.

"More than likely, the people who created these items can still recognize most of what's here, would be able to describe the purpose of each, and quite possibly may even have similar items among their respective groups today. It's why the issue of the caretaker role is the crux of the question.

"These things here are quite *extraordinary*, wouldn't you say? That quality alone separates them from the rest of the Indian collections in this building. They were *made* that way. They were *created to be extraordinary*. Like a child that is molded, groomed, and taught to become a particular kind of person, so were these items made, with that single-mindedness of purpose. You might say that is their 'power,' though a man like you might object to the use of the word. Also like people, these creations have characteristics and a nature. As long as these articles exist, these characteristics, this nature, and their power are embodied in that creation.

"Even you have been filled with wonder and astonishment when you've come across some of the items up here. Even you have been touched by the extraordinary nature and quality of some items here, which transcend language and a particular culture. Look closer at them, Evans. They have impressions on them—marks of their creators—fingerprints, hand prints, or the odor of the person to whom they belonged. These human marks and odors have persisted over centuries, as fresh today as three hundred years ago. Doesn't that tell you anything?"

Donald scowled and said, "I think we should consider this conversation ended, George. I don't like the direction it's taking."

"Well, I did say that it might offend an educated man like you," George smiled.

Donald raised his voice. "Don't play dumb with me, George. You're not the hayseed hick you pretend to be! I've watched you slip in and out of that disguise."

George wiped the smile from his face and looked into his empty coffee cup. He stood and lifted his hat and briefcase before speaking. "Evans," he said, "any day now you're bound to see a naked Indian man come into this room and give you hell. I ain't seen him myself so I can't rightly describe him to you, except to say that he's a mighty tall fellow, and he's ornery."

Donald's eyes were round. "Are you threatening me, George?"

George sighed and shook his head. "This man is what *you* call a 'ghost', Evans. Since you don't believe in them, though, you ain't got no worry, right? They's others besides him, but it appears that he's the one that's gotta be whipped. He may have had something to do with the Wurly woman's death, and maybe even Newsome's. Who knows how many others?"

Donald stood. "You know something about these deaths? Have you gone to the proper authorities?"

George smiled again. "I don't know if I've gone to the proper authorities. I came to you."

"What?" asked Donald. "Are you saying these deaths are related to this collection? That's impossible!"

"Is it?" George asked. "Just how many suicides and other unexplained deaths have occurred in this building, or to staff people working here, in the last forty years, since the collection has been here?"

"You have no basis for this insinuation," Donald yelled. "You're proceeding on hocus-pocus!"

George raised a hand. "Now, Evans, just simmer down! I came here today to throw some ideas at you and to see how they hit you. You threw them back. Of course, none of what I've said to you can be proven. You're the kind of man who has to have things proven or shown to him in black and white."

George walked around Donald's desk, his eyes on the coiled strings of human ears hanging on the nail above it. He asked, "Are those ears?"

Donald nodded, and George shook his head incredulously. "Indian ears, I suppose?"

Donald nodded again. "I suppose."

George's frown disappeared then. His eyes gleamed mischievously as he asked, "Where's the rest of those people?"

Donald's thoughts were on George's earlier comments. "What?" he asked. George pointed at the ears. "Where's the rest of those people?"

"Never thought about that," admitted Donald, looking differently at the ears now.

"You should think about that, Evans. Those people are still probably mad as hell," George said with a blank face. He left with a wave at Donald. Donald didn't know if the remark was supposed to be funny.

Several days later, staring at the coils of ears still hanging on the mail, Donald was aware of a growing odor around him. Was it coming from the stairway? He closed the door for a moment, but that did not help. He opened the door again. Static blared from the radio. He went back to the table where the radio sat. It was quiet. His hand felt for the cord of the radio and he pulled it on top of the table. The radio was unplugged.

Donald sank into the swivel chair and put his face in his hands. He heard the door at the bottom of the stairway open and close. Someone was climbing the stairs. Donald was relieved. He welcomed a visitor, even George Daylight. Now the visitor was at the top of the stairs. Donald waited. Nothing happened. No one entered the room. Donald sat expectantly for a few seconds and then went to the stairs. No one was there. He rubbed his forehead, returned to his desk, and picked up a pencil. The unanswered correspondence waited. He drafted a letter, then put a sheet of paper into his portable typewriter that was sitting on a metal stand and began to type.

Over the clicking of the typewriter keys, he heard the door at the bottom of the stairway open and close again. Someone climbed the stairs. The stairway creaked. Trying to ignore the footsteps, Donald continued typing. At the top of the stairs the footsteps stopped. Donald brushed his fingers through his hair and put his face into his hands.

A rustling noise came from the north side of the room. Donald sat up straight, determined to ignore this. He deliberately kept his eyes on the words he typed, his fingers pecked slowly at the keys. The rustling noise moved to the other end of the room, and a feeling of motion or movement passed by him. He stopped typing and sat attentively, listening for another sound and studying the room. When nothing else happened, he went back to his work.

After several minutes had passed and Donald had completed two letters and answered several memoranda, he felt an unusual sensation. Someone was in the room with him. Donald could feel the presence of a living, breathing person. He knew it was a person, and the certainty of this knowledge startled him. George Daylight had really gotten to him. Now, Donald was once again angry at George, and at himself. He closed his eyes and held his face in his hands.

When he opened his eyes again, he saw it—the ghost. The man was a true giant, but graceful as he dashed around the room. He was naked, his body taut and firm. Around his left ankle was a piece of cloth or hide about three feet long. It slid over the wooden floor. The giant's long hair sailed behind him. Donald could not see the giant's face as the man's hands explored first one shelf and then another. Moving from shelf to shelf, from cabinet to cabinet, the man became more frantic, more desperate. He finally hit a cabinet door with a giant fist, but the blow made no sound. Donald felt a stir of motion in the corner where the man stood.

Donald was totally mesmerized. He still held a pencil in midair and, realizing this, dropped it on the desk. It made a small sound as it hit the desk and rolled a couple of times.

The giant turned on Donald.

His face was black in places. Paint? But it was his strange eyes that would stay with Donald for many days. They were the eyes of burning hate, and Donald felt himself wilt in their glare.

The giant approached Donald. His steps were slow but forceful, and the cloth on his ankle slid after him. He soon towered over Donald. The giant picked up the pencil and threw it across the room. Then, in one motion, he wiped Donald's desk clean. Everything scattered to the floor.

He walked slowly around Donald's desk while Donald scooted his swivel chair backward and tried to move the typewriter stand. The wheels squeaked over the wooden boards. The giant did not stop but continued toward Donald. He could have reached Donald in an arm's length, but made no effort to do this. This puzzled Donald even as he found himself backed against the wall. There was no place to go.

Then, the giant slowly and calmly reached over and picked Donald up by his arms. Donald felt himself being lifted upward a few feet and then dropped. He tried to brace himself for the fall, but was not entirely successful. Again, the giant came forward, picked Donald up off the floor, and threw him down. This time Donald felt the impact.

He was near mental collapse. This could not be happening. For the third time, the giant came at him and momentarily raised him to eye level. The giant's face was determined and angry as he lifted Donald and then threw him. The table with the reconstructed pots shook as Donald fell against it. And then as suddenly as the man had appeared, he was gone. The stir of movement in the room settled. Donald sat on the floor, touching his body to see if it was whole. He was not hurt, but his nerves were ripped to shreds. He held out a hand. It shook. When he could hold his hand still, Donald pulled himself off the floor. His legs were not steady yet, though. He held onto the edge of his desk and pulled the swivel chair to him.

For several hours, Donald sat there, not seeing, not feeling anything. When he finally got up to go outside, it was evening. Most of the other staff had left. Donald locked his door at the top of the stairs and, feeling very old and very tired, went down the stairway and out the rambling, deserted building.

19

NAVAJO RESERVATION

THE ceremony performed by the old man for Jimmy Tom's family was brief and took place just north of Kayenta in the area of Monument Valley. Jimmy Tom had picked up the old man on the previous evening and was now returning him this morning to the foot of Beautiful Mountain. It would be nearly a three-hour drive, one way, to Jonnie Navajo's home at the base of Beautiful Mountain. Just Jimmy Tom and the old man were making the trip. Jonnie Navajo sat beside Jimmy Tom, surveying the valley in the bright morning light. The old man wore black sunglasses, and the glare of the sun bounced off his silver and turquoise hat band whenever he was jogged forward by the rough dirt road. As they drove through the red and dark purple mesas and buttes of Monument Valley, Jimmy Tom pointed out the location of his relatives' homes and certain landmarks that he knew about and thought might interest the old man.

Jimmy Tom said, "Between those mesas is where the People hid for months during Kit Carson's campaign against them." The mesas he identified were to the north and extended into Utah. The longest of them was about two miles wide. Behind the mesas, the mountains of Utah rose, giant and pale blue.

The old man looked toward the mesas and nodded.

"As it turned out, the People hid in that area for about three years, until the rest of the People returned from *Hweldi*," Jimmy Tom added.

"So your ancestors did not go to *Hweldi*?" the old man asked.

"A few did, yes—those who were caught out in the open spaces. But the others were luckier, I suppose. They were at camps in the mountains of Utah or up on the mesas, and they were spared the suffering the rest of the People had to endure at that time. In the period that most of the People were gone away from Navajoland, the People here who escaped actually experienced a little prosperity. Later, when the rest of the People were granted the right to return to this country and had each been issued a few sheep by the government to help start their lives once more—well, these people who had been hiding out all during that time had thriving herds of sheep and goats. Their poorer relatives, those returning from *Hweldi*, had to make an immediate choice to either eat the few sheep and goats given to them or to try to increase their livestock. As you know, the People were in such poor condition that many of them ate their livestock right away. Then, these others who had escaped shared their livestock with their poorer relatives."

"Yes, I've heard about that," the old man answered. "There were others who escaped besides those in this valley, but they were far to the west, beyond Grand Canyon and slave-hunters. I don't think they fared as well as this group, though, because eventually some turned to other tribes for help. I think there was much to be feared at the time, but the slave traders may have been the worst. Because of this, some of our people went so far as to seek out the right white officials—when they were lucky enough to locate them—in order to surrender themselves. Then, these people who surrendered were escorted to *Hweldi*, too. I have heard that they transported the People to *Hweldi* in groups of one thousand to two thousand, and that soldiers escorted the groups. I understand that many of those soldiers had no compassion for our people. It is said that hundreds of us died en route to *Hweldi*—no doubt when the soldiers shot some of us, as they actually did do. The soldiers may have considered these shootings a service to their government and our people, too, because this act of treachery, or mercy—depending on how it was viewed—would have saved their government some time and expense. And as for our people, the soldiers probably figured that our time was short anyway. It may be that *Hweldi* was designed to shorten our time—the People's time—upon the earth."

"Yes," agreed Jimmy Tom. "I have heard stories from other elders concerning the hardships and indignities they underwent at *Hweldi*. I understand that the People lived in holes in the ground and that many people died there.

"One old man, called *Tsékooh*, said that his family was caught starving in a canyon near Chinle in the winter; snow was on the ground. Actually, his family surrendered themselves when the soldiers came among them and called to the People to come out and give themselves up. He said that the soldiers carried food and showed this to the Navajos, who had been surviving on berries, seeds, and small game. That is what enticed his family to surrender themselves, and like thousands of other Navajos, they were then led to *Hweldi*. He claimed that some of the wealthier Navajos took some of their own livestock to *Hweldi*, where these families then had to protect their livestock, not only from their own people, but also from the Apaches, the soldiers, and other marauding Indians.

"I myself do not know if our people were ever wealthy in the way the white people describe. They have another way of thinking about wealth. Anyway, that old man said that at the time of *Hweldi*, it seemed that the whole world had come against the People. I understand that the Navajos tried to carry on at *Hweldi* as they had done here in this land, that they tried to live by their ancient philosophy, but it was difficult to do. Everything was against it. It seemed that their very survival was threatened there. Everything was against them. I was told that they planted corn for three years in a row, but that it was destroyed for one reason or another. It seemed that the water itself had turned against the People, for it was hardly drinkable and made the People ill. I guess with those hardships, and then having to familiarize themselves with the new food that they had not experienced before, and having also to defend themselves against the soldiers and other Indians who came at will among the captive Navajos there, the time must certainly have seemed very bleak to them."

Jonnie Navajo's dark glasses hid his eyes as he answered. "It's true that death was always prevalent there." As an afterthought, he added, "I, myself, have seen this place called *Hweldi*."

Jimmy Tom looked at the old man. "You've gone back there?" he asked.

The old man nodded. "Some years back. The place is somehow deceiving to see now. It is silent, empty, and barren. Yet in my mind it seems that there is an echo of the voices of our people.

"Now it is like a park that the white tourists come to visit. I do not know how many of our people visit there. Like I said, not too much of us is there to be viewed, though we know in our hearts and minds that we left a great deal there—many of our people. I don't know where they put our people when they died there. I asked, but no one in the park seemed to know. That is very strange, too, because there is a nearby town that honors a white outlaw, a bandit, I'm told. The town does not want to forget about this man. It seems that more is known about the bandit, that young outlaw, than about *Hweldi* in that town. I suppose there is a reason for this, though.

"When I visited one of the museums in the town, it displayed some skulls, which they charge tourists to see. I did not know that that was what we were paying to see and would not have entered that place if I had known in advance. You know that it is not the practice of our people to preserve human bones for this purpose. We are taught that all people should be allowed to return to the earth and the elements. But it was possible to see the bones there for the price of admission, a dollar or two. Nevertheless, I went into this place and was surprised to see that in a small box, under glass, were some Navajo skulls. It is doubtful that the owners of this museum knew that these were Navajo skulls—skulls of our people—but I knew it, and of course, the other Navajos with me, we knew it immediately! We recognized our people by the flattened back of the skill made by cradleboards. The skulls had holes, bullet holes, between the eyes. So that is how I paid to see Navajo skulls with bullet holes between the eyes, which I really did not wish to see at all. I suppose, though, that this experience did serve a purpose. It confirmed for me what the elders always knew."

"Who was the outlaw, Grandfather?" Jimmy Tom asked. "Was it Jesse James? Billy the Kid?"

Jonnie Navajo answered, "It doesn't matter. All those outlaws are the same."

The old man was quiet for awhile. Both men were lost in their own thoughts. Finally, the old man said, "I wonder what would have happened to those people who escaped if the others had not returned. . . . If the prisoners at *Hweldi* had been forced to go to another country, to Wide Plains, as the officials in *Washingdoon* were considering at the time?"

Jimmy Tom answered, "I don't know. I haven't thought about that. *Halgai Hateel*, Oklahoma, or Wide Plains. I think that would have been as bad as *Hweldi*. I have heard about other tribes, about what happened to them when they were relocated there. They died. In their minds, they died. Sure, all in all the people survived or lived, but at great sacrifice to their original homelands, to their ceremonies, and to their people and other things. Have you been there, too, to Oklahoma?"

Jonnie Navajo nodded. The chunks of turquoise at his earlobes swung back and forth with the jerky motion of the pickup truck. "On several occasions."

"What is it like?" asked Jimmy Tom. "I've never been there, but I have heard that the land is very flat, that there is water in the air much of the time, and that in the summer, it is very hot."

Again Jonnie Navajo nodded. "Some of the land looks much like *Hweldi*, but as you go farther east, the land is very green in the warm weather. Many sheep could be fed there." Taking a long, hard look at the thirsty land spread out before him, he continued, "There are some Navajos there—in Oklahoma—not many, but a few who are married into those tribes. They don't raise sheep, though.

"It seems to me that this—Navajoland—is where the People belong. My uncle told me of the beginning of our people, of the Five Worlds that were created, and of our four sacred mountains by which we are protected in this world. He told me that this place was created for us by the Holy People, so it seems appropriate that we were allowed to return to this place after *Hweldi*."

The two men had come to the outskirts of a tiny town. Their pickup truck passed a few buildings and came to a halt outside of a trading post. Here Jimmy Tom got out of the truck and returned in a few minutes with two bottles of colored drinks. He handed the red one to the older man.

Later, riding down a narrow highway that wound around volcanic peaks and sheer mesas, the men saw the mountains of Colorado pushing up the horizon. They continued their discussion.

"There is a song for that mountain," Jonnie Navajo said, indicating the sacred mountain of the north. "Do you know it?"

Jimmy Tom admitted that he did not.

Jonnie Navajo began to chant in a sing-song voice with which Jimmy Tom was well acquainted. All the medicine men sang that way. In his mind, as Jimmy Tom listened, he could not tell exactly where the old man's own voice separated from all the voices of other medicine men he had heard in the course of his lifetime. Yes, they all sang as one. The melded voices drifted down to him through time. That voice was one of the few things that was clear to Jimmy Tom about the past of the People. It somehow connected him to the earlier worlds and to the Holy People. Jimmy Tom could feel the old man's voice tug at him and gently pull him away into a more ethereal place and time.

The mountain of the north that Jimmy Tom now studied in the distance, and all the sacred mountains, had been made out of sacred soil brought from a lower world by the Holy People. The northern mountain had been fastened to the earth with a rainbow and was then decorated with various plants, animals, and birds. Each mountain had been similarly created.

That was why the mountain was beautiful to him now, shining with a spot of snow in the distance. And the promise of the sacred mountains to him and the old man, to all the People, was that they were symbolic peaks that stood to clearly mark their world in the past and the future.

The old man sang for several minutes all the stanzas of the song. His voice had a hypnotic effect on Jimmy Tom, and even himself. Before their eyes, the two man could see the mountains being formed in front of them. They were oblivious to time, to the asphalt highway, and to the traffic on the narrow road. The present time and place were secondary to the song.

When the song ended and the two men had been abruptly jerked back to today, Jimmy Tom asked, "Grandfather, I have heard that there are others—not Navajos—who have sacred mountains too."

The old man agreed. "Yes, there are other tribes who share this idea. I think that is all right, because we all have been among each other for some time now. Who really knows for sure how long? The elders explained this to us years ago. We have met certain people more than once in our existence as Navajos. We can see through our clans that it must be so. These clans were created when new people joined with us, the Navajos. After so many years now, it seems that we have forgotten just how many other tribes or people have joined us." The comment made Jimmy Tom recall what he had heard about his own clan and its origin.

"How many clans are there now?" he asked.

"I am not certain," the old man replied, "but some of the earlier ones have become extinct, and I have heard that today there are over one hundred clans."

The travelers could see "the winged rock" by now, an imposing silhouette on the horizon to the south, although it was several miles away.

Along the unfenced roadside, a lone Navajo woman sat on horseback, herding many sheep. She was accompanied by two large dogs that crouched beside the road and darted furiously after Jimmy Tom's pickup truck, barking and growling at the truck as it slowed to allow the sheep to cross the highway. When the pickup resumed its speed, Jimmy Tom said, "Grandfather, there is something I have been confused about. Who were the four original clans? There is some disagreement, I have heard."

"There is no disagreement," the old man answered. "All the stories are right, no matter who the four clans were."

Jimmy Tom nodded while the older man continued. "It seems that today we have come to a confusing time. Years ago, in the time of my uncle *Hosteen Nez*, we Navajos were more sure about ourselves. We were given information about the twins, Monster Slayer and Born-for-Water, and Changing Woman. We had ceremonies to ensure that our bodies and minds worked together in harmony instead of against each other, and for the most part we followed the advice given to us on how to live, how to think of our Mother Earth and Father Sky, and how we should address one another in a system of kinship.

"Now we hear other things about ourselves from outsiders. Some of us are prone to accept this new information more quickly than we accept older information that has been around for years, and which was given to us by our relatives. We have tested the older knowledge countless times through ceremonies and songs, and it has worked for us time and again. This new information must also be tested, it must be tried. That is all I can say about the situation."

Jimmy Tom accepted what the old man said. In answer, he said, "I think the same way as you do. I think school has something to do with it. I went to school myself for a couple of years. But I was older, and I guess that's why they put me through so fast—before I became a grandfather." He laughed. "But it has been my experience that what is taught in school is not consistent with what we learn in the hogan. Sometimes it seems that these two things work against each other, much like what you described today with our minds and bodies. This makes it hard on us, especially on our little ones. It seems like we are told that we can choose one source of knowledge or the other, but we are discouraged from having both, because it seems that the two don't go together. Some day we are going to have to do something about this."

"Yes," Jonnie Navajo answered. "That's right. One is not more important than the other. I myself have nothing against school. The young people are going to need it. In my time we had to herd sheep every morning. If we did not give our full attention to this task, we would not be here today. But now things are a little different. I still have my sheep and I am an old man. If I were a child today, perhaps I would think differently. A great deal depends on our relatives, what they teach us. If we are willing to pay the cost for what we learn from them, then there is much to be gained.

"I learned my ceremonies from my uncle, *Hosteen Nez*, and from another elder called *Bich´ah Lizhinii*. It seems that my relatives got together when I was merely a child and decided that in order for me to be useful to myself and others, I should learn something about the Holy People. So they set me on this path that I am traveling now. I didn't have a choice in the matter. I suppose that I could have been lazy about the whole thing and could have been stubborn and pulled away from this idea, but for some reason I discovered that I learned in spite of myself, my youthfulness, and my childish ways.

"Then my relatives saw to it that I was carried over to these elders, and I sat up countless winter nights learning these ancient things. To me, this way of life is important. Its value, with the old men, has nourished me for nearly sixty years.

"These prayers and rituals for good health and long life have a place in our lives even today—especially today—they have value. At one time, we Navajos recognized that everything was holy. Long, long ago, there were songs for everything, from horses or livestock to the hogan. I myself have been taught that the hogan is holy because it shelters the family, and our children are conceived and raised in its shadows.

"Unlike you, Grandson, I never had an education—a white man's education—though I do not particularly feel that I have been deprived of anything. I was raised in the old way, rising at dawn and running when the sun reached a certain point on the horizon. I was taught to roll in the snow in winter and to splash in ice water at the same time. I still recall the tastes of certain berries and seeds that our people were accustomed to eating until recently, before there were trading posts and soda pop.

"And as a child, I received good treatment. Like most of our people, my mother believed that scolding and yelling at children only made the children unruly and everyone involved irritable. Therefore, she made it a point to try to reason with me and to explain certain things to me—the Holy People and my relatives, for example. So I tried not to misbehave in my youth, and shame this woman or my relatives.

"That is how I came into possession of my ceremonies and songs. They serve a purpose yet, and we live by their holiness. It is through them that we realize the sacredness of things, such as fire, the colors of the day, and our own bodies. And I have since learned that everything is holy."

The two man were now turning east on the final stretch of road to Jonnie Navajo's home.

There, Nasbah was packing luggage for herself and her grandfather. She had spoken with Willie earlier. Nasbah and her grandfather would stay at Willie's apartment in Virginia. She was packing for a seven-day stay, although she doubted that they would actually be there that long.

She had already made reservations with the airline and, at Willie's suggestion, had also called David Drake in Albuquerque to arrange a meeting with him on the way to D.C. Drake had invited her and the old man to stay overnight in his home, and Nasbah had accepted the invitation. Their flight left Albuquerque at 10:30 the next morning. She and her grandfather planned to be in Albuquerque by six this evening.

Nasbah's grandmother was now weaving in the hogan. When Nasbah had finished packing, she joined the old lady for awhile, waiting for her grandfather to return.

The old woman had run out of white yarn, and was spinning more onto a spindle. "Are you ready?" the old lady asked. Nasbah nodded and said, "Grandmother, don't you want to go to *Washingdoon* too?"

The old lady flashed a radiant smile. "Me? Why should I want to go there?" Nasbah grinned too and said, "The white people like to travel all the time—to Europe, *Washingdoon*, Mexico."

The old lady smiled again. "I don't know where those places are. I only know where our four sacred mountains are. And I am *Diné* (Navajo). It is better that I stay where I am for now. That is why I have grandchildren—to do the talking on behalf of the elders, and the traveling to places like *Washingdoon*. That is, providing that my grandchildren are good representatives for us." She gave Nasbah an appraising look.

Jonnie Navajo had by now turned his thoughts toward Willie in far-off *Washingdoon*. The old man really didn't know what to expect there. From past experience in his travels, he tried not to expect anything but to just observe things and people as he encountered them. He pursed his lips thoughtfully.

Jimmy Tom sensed that he had lost the old man's attention as the two approached the old man's home.

"Ah," Jimmy Tom said, "it's a long way . . . from there to here."

The old man nodded. He gazed out the window, mentally marking his location within the four sacred mountains, within Navajoland.

"I suppose that you were worried about your sheep this morning?" Jimmy Tom said. "My other grandfathers are always concerned about their sheep."

Jonnie Navajo agreed but said, "They'll be cared for. As for me, I am leaving this place for a few days."

"Oh?" asked Jimmy Tom.

"Yes," answered the old man. "I will travel out of Navajoland to *Washingdoon.*"

Jimmy Tom raised his eyebrows. "When?" he asked.

"Tomorrow. Today I will go as far as *Be´eldiildahsinil.*"

Jimmy Tom's pickup truck raised a red trail of dust that could be seen by Nasbah through the doors of the old man's hogan. When the pickup turned toward the hogan, she went to make the final preparations for the journey to D.C.

20

MEMPHIS, TENNESSEE

JUNIOR had been puzzled by his father's behavior ever since they'd left Oklahoma City. Wilbur's attention was elsewhere, and had been for the last day or so. Whenever Junior or Erleen spoke to him, he did not respond, and didn't even seem to notice that he was being addressed. Either Wilbur simply didn't hear or had tuned everything out. It was possible that Wilbur's hearing loss had gotten worse, but overnight? Furthermore, when Wilbur's face was turned in Junior's direction, Junior was aware that Wilbur's eyes were brightly glazed. Even now Junior could see Wilbur in the rear view mirror. And Wilbur's eyes, although wide open, were blank and unseeing.

Junior and Erleen had made several sightseeing stops in Arkansas and Tennessee. Thus far, they had asked both Anna and Wilbur to join them. Anna did, but Wilbur was usually not interested, although he was polite in his refusal. He either waited inside the car or sat on the nearest curb, alongside the car. When he did join the other three, he was unimpressed by the sites. Finally, Junior asked, "Daddy, are you lonesome?"

"Maybe," Wilbur answered.

Anna, for her part, showed no concern or alarm over Wilbur. How many times had she seen Wilbur like this? She tried to remember all the times, but couldn't be exactly sure—perhaps eleven or twelve times in their life together. She didn't really trust her memory, though. It wasn't too keen anymore. After all, she had been absent-minded about LeClair. . . .

It had been a long time since Wilbur had acted like this, and she knew from experience that he could do this at will. What he did was kind of voluntarily break with the everyday world and slip into another consciousness, a different state of awareness. Once long ago he had told her that there was more than one world of existence and experience, but not in those exact words. She tried to remember now what he had said as she stared out the car window. She nodded to herself, remembering his words. "Anna, the world is pretty damn big, and it's likely they's more to it, even big as it is. Not only that, it's got an edge to it that ain't too clear either, but sometimes peoples stands on the brink of it, where everyday things don't matter none. In fact that brink, that edge, it's everywhere. Right here on the edge you can reach out and feel something else you can't get a hold of in this everyday world, some other thing that don't have no end to it."

Anna looked at Wilbur now. His face was turned toward the window. The last time he had done this—slipped away—was perhaps ten or twelve years ago. At that time, LeClair had gone with him. LeClair could do that, too. If LeClair were around now, maybe she could talk to LeClair about this. But everyone said LeClair was dead, and Anna had seen him too at the funeral. He did look deader than a doornail then. She quickly touched her hand to her forehead, regretting her last thought, and looked ashamed. It was so disrespectful to LeClair.

She sighed. It was just that she, now in her seventies, seemed to view life differently than she had at eighteen. For one thing, she was more convinced than ever that people didn't die for nothing. There was a purpose to it, to being born, to living, and then to dying. She herself had seen people *after* their deaths on several occasions. But many of the Oklahoma tribal people often found that to be a normal experience. From this, Anna discovered that these people who had passed on didn't look any worse for having gone into the next world. On the contrary, they looked to be in one piece, whole and okay, as far as Anna could tell. Shoot, some looked better in death than they had in life—no pain, no suffering.

Like Anna's people around her, she was taught not to be fearful, or ashamed, of these experiences of seeing deceased people. Actually, Anna smiled, according to her people's way of thinking, something would have been wrong with her if she didn't see beyond this world. It would mean that her senses didn't work, and that she, in a way, was handicapped by her own lack of sensitivity. And on each occasion of seeing someone who had recently passed away, Anna had learned a fraction more about living and dying. She now wondered whether during each of these experiences, she had then been on the brink of another world, as Wilbur had described it. Nonetheless, the continual appearance and presence of people who had gone on had consistently reaffirmed for her and other tribal people that there was something more to existence—beyond death. The tribes knew it all along. Even in their burial ceremonies, this was a prime consideration in how the deceased were buried and treated.

With LeClair, for example, Anna could not see an end to him, his existence. She'd been over to LeClair's burial mound and looked at it a time or two since LeClair had gone on, but his death was not that cut and dried. He was still around. Yet, Anna knew that Wilbur was annoyed with her constant forgetfulness about LeClair being absent from the people now, although Wilbur tried not to show his annoyance. Anna smiled. That was another thing about old age. People became more tolerant and forgiving with each other.

Anyway, it was in the fall a few years back, when Junior must have been in his twenties, that Wilbur and LeClair went glassy-eyed and became uncommunicative. Anna left them alone and went about her daily chores around the house, pretty much minding her own business. At nightfall, she'd left the two men in each other's company, sitting outside, unspeaking but perhaps not really unseeing. They'd stayed that way for perhaps four days, taking hardly a bite to eat and a little water. In that time, Wilbur must have dropped eight pounds. LeClair could hardly stand to lose any weight at all because he was rail-thin, but his flesh relaxed a little more around his old bones anyway, and Anna worried a little when the pounds melted off his bony frame.

Although Junior had been around then and on earlier occasions when Wilbur was like this, he had yet to notice any difference in Wilbur's behavior. Until today, Anna wrote it off to his youthfulness. She had never doubted Junior's goodness or his love for her or Wilbur, but she had to admit that Junior wasn't too quick about catching onto his father's unique abilities. Sure, Junior knew a little something about what Wilbur did for the people, but not really firsthand. Anna stared at the back of Junior's head, his longish hair tucked into his collar in places.

Now she was relieved to see that Junior had finally become aware that something was eating at Wilbur these last few days. Junior had never showed evidence that he had inherited Wilbur's ability. He was close to being forty now, but none of Wilbur's doings in the past forty years had rubbed off on him, it seemed. Anna sighed. Junior was her only living son, and she and Wilbur loved him dearly.

Anna didn't realize that a tear had rolled out of her eye until Wilbur's finger reached over and wiped it off. He was back in this world again, momentarily. "What is it?" he asked.

Anna answered, "It ain't nothing. I was just thinking about some little boy who came and went—how many years ago?"

Wilbur looked carefully at her. He indicated that he didn't hear, pointing to the wire in his ear. Anna guessed that he had the volume turned down or off.

Wilbur asked again, "Huh?"

Anna spoke loudly into his ear. "Wilbur, how long ago did we have that little baby boy who died?"

Wilbur looked at Junior a moment and said, "Maybe forty-seven years ago?"

Anna shook her head. "Um-hum, um-huh."

"How come you ask?" Wilbur said.

"Ain't no reason," Anna said, "just counting time. . . ."

Wilbur nodded. "Nice little boy. Black hair and little round eyes. . . ."

"Um-hum, um-huh," Anna said, pleased. "You remember it, the boy?"

Wilbur nodded and turned away.

Junior listened to Anna's and Wilbur's conversation. At least Wilbur was talking now, he thought.

"What little boy was that, Mama?" Junior asked.

"Ours," Anna said. "Me and Wilbur's."

Junior quieted. He had heard about that child before, not too often, but more than once. Junior wondered what it would have been like to have had a real brother when he was growing up. He had had plenty of cousins, though, and it was nearly the same as having real brothers and sisters. That was how Anna came to have so many grandchildren.

Anna turned her attention back to Wilbur's preoccupation of the moment. Actually, if the truth be known, his was a lifetime preoccupation with the extraordinary in life. And she knew that he himself didn't choose it this way. People like him never chose it. Something always chose them. He was a tribal man. He'd lived a long time, and come face to face with the extraordinary so many times. He couldn't turn it off as he turned off the hearing aid. The only way he could will certain things to end, and then he could not will them to stop, was to cease living. Nobody knew better than Wilbur that death wasn't an end to everything. So Wilbur's dealings with the extraordinary were a fact of life. There was no way around it.

It was now near dusk, and the lights of Memphis began to turn themselves on along the road. Junior pulled the car out of the line of traffic and parked in front of a big motel. "I guess we'll stay here overnight. It's as good a place as any, and I think Daddy might be kind of tired." Erleen looked over the seat at Wilbur with a concerned expression on her face.

When Junior disappeared into the motel office, Anna said to Erleen, "It's all right, honey. He's thinking. Old man Wilbur Snake is thinking. Old mans got lots to think about." Wilbur didn't even notice Erleen or Anna.

Later that evening, after Junior took the family out to eat and everyone settled down for the night, Wilbur excused himself and said he wanted to go sit outside awhile. Anna got up to go with him, but Wilbur said, "Now, Anna, you stay here. You don't have to baby sit this old man." Anna let him go.

Junior took this opportunity to go and sit on the bed beside Anna. He asked, "Mama, something bothering Daddy?"

Anna looked in Junior's eyes. He was so large and yet so gentle with her and Wilbur. She said, "Know what, Junior? You as soft as a cotton boll." She smiled brightly and took Junior's big hand in her tiny one. Then she said, "Don't mind Wilbur. He's alright. He ain't sick. Sometimes that old man acts like this. I know what it is, but it ain't for me to tell."

Junior said, "Mama, I'm worried about him. He don't seem to be all there lately. He's not thinking right. He sick?"

Anna shook her head no. "That old man's all right. I know it." She continued, "What's on that old man's mind? Junior, it's cause of the way things is, between peoples and time."

"What are you talking about, Mama?" Junior asked with a frown.

"Lots of things, Son. I'm talking about lots of things. I'm talking about how long me and Wilbur been together. I'm older than he is, I always was. I'm talking about LeClair, Wilbur's kin. They was childhood together. Then, they was old age together, too, after that."

Junior studied Anna's tiny hand as he tried to figure out what she meant. He looked at Erleen, who shrugged her shoulders, also at a loss for meaning.

"One time, when you was a baby, Junior, you hurt yourself pretty bad. You was dying, Son. Little by little, you was going to die. I saw it. Everybody saw it. Junior's going to die, everybody said. Not Wilbur, though. He already lost one baby. He couldn't stand around waiting for it to happen. He wanted to fight for it. That's how it all began. Wilbur picked up your pitiful, broken, little body and carried it over yonder to LeClair's folk, and over there, those folk began to put everything back together. Now look at you, Son. No one would ever know." Anna's eyes were thoughtful on Junior.

She continued, "Back then, we don't hardly have any white doctors. Have to count on our own, but my old folks claimed ours was good as any. You think so, Junior?"

"I don't know, Mama," he answered. His thoughts still lingered on the story Anna had just told him. He'd never known that about himself.

Anna looked from him to Erleen. "Time was when our people didn't go to just anybody for healing like today. We have to know, was so-and-so a good man? Did he whip his kids? Did he lie to his family or the people? Did he cheat or steal? Everyone said back then that those things show. I think it's true. When our medicine people ain't good to each other and their family, well, it's bound to show up in some way. Wilbur's a good man, Junior. He don't lie, cheat, or steal. We poor, Junior. Us peoples is poor, no money. It's all right, though. Our people like Wilbur. He's a good man, he can do things for us, help us out."

"Mama, what are you trying to say?" Junior asked, completely without comprehension.

Anna eyed him firmly for a few seconds. "You don't get it, do you, Junior? You don't get it one little bit?" she asked.

Junior shook his head no.

"Well, I'll clear it up for you, Junior. Wilbur is getting ready for Washton, D.C.!"

Junior stared at her.

"Washton, D.C. always took a lot outta him. He's making sure that it don't take all he's got!"

Anna could see that Junior was beginning to understand. He slowly shook his head. Erleen, too, understood.

Junior went to the window and pulled back a drape to try to find Wilbur out in the darkness. He couldn't see anything, so he opened the door and walked out to the car. Wilbur sat in the terraced rock garden, his figure hardly discernible in the shadows. Junior walked back to the motel room.

"Nothing ain't going to happen in D.C., Mama," Junior said. "What's Daddy putting himself through this for? D.C. ain't important to us, Mama.

We're just going to do a little sightseeing. We don't even have to go over to that place where everything's been happening."

Anna said, "Wilbur ain't that way, Junior. He don't see it like that. He sees something else, always has. He seen what's there. It's not good over there at Washton, D.C. Even I know it, and I don't know much. But I been there, too, don't forget that, and I'm old, but I ain't blind—yet."

Erleen came forward then and asked, "What's there, Mama? What's so terrible about that place?"

"It ain't bad for us, honey," Anna said, "if we don't stay too long, and if we see the light about the way things really is."

"But if people are killing themselves, . . ." Erleen whispered.

"Shh," Anna said. "They doing that to themselves because they scaring themselves. The bad thing here is nothing don't change in Washton. Wilbur's right, though, it ain't Snake business. Best thing to do is stay outta it, 'cause Wilbur's getting too old. I'm older than him. And you young ones don't know the old ways anymore. . . ." She sighed. "Anyway, that's the only thing wrong with Wilbur. He's taking care of hisself is all."

Junior shoved both hands in his pockets. "What do you mean, 'those people are scaring themselves'?" he asked.

Anna pulled herself off the bed and went over to Junior. "It don't have to happen the way it's been going. Our folks see spirit peoples all the time, we know them. Peoples don't have to run around like chickens with their heads cut off about it. We cross the paths of spirit peoples all the time. We have to because lotsa peoples have lived and then went on since the world began. That's how come our folks told us how to treat them, so we won't go crazy when we run across them."

Junior sank down into one of the chairs around the tiny circular table in the room. "I guess you're right on that, Mama," he said. "But I still can't help but feel sorry for those people who keep on dying over there."

Anna sat down in the next chair and said, "That's because you as soft as a cotton boll, Junior. But that's good, ain't bad. You care for peoples is all."

Erleen added, "Me too, Mama. I'm like Junior. I feel the same way."

Anna nodded. "Um-hum, you just like Junior, Erleen. Spirit peoples ain't the whole thing, though. More to it. Long time ago, when me and Wilbur was kids, our old folks showed and told us a thing or two. Well, anyway, Childrens, one thing they claim was that all peoples has some kind of power, each people has it to hisself. Even if a people don't know it, they still has it. This power is how come we live. The thing is that this power ain't all ours to us alone—lots of things got it. We all in it together. We can't pull away from it and the other things that got it, too. We tied up together. Now me and Wilbur is old, but even old age don't take away the power. Maybe dying don't take it away either, is what me and Wilbur's been thinking. Some old peoples thinks like this."

Erleen was taking pins out of her red hair. She pulled out a hairbrush and asked, "Mama, do you think spirit people have that power yet?"

Anna looked thoughtful. "Well," she said, "spirit peoples is around. No doubt about it."

Erleen had another thought. She said, "Mama, can spirit people hurt us?"

Anna smiled and answered, "My old folks always say if some peoples going to hurt us, it's going to be them peoples who's alive. I think so too. The main thing is not to scare ourself. That old man Wilbur knows about scaring ourself."

Junior said, "Thought Daddy said one of those spirit people he saw over in D.C. was dangerous. He said that one was mean and hateful."

Anna looked at him and said, "Now you talking about something else, Son. LeClair and your daddy had some ideas about him. I don't remember all of them, but you could ask Wilbur sometime. It's late now and I'm old, older than Wilbur. Old peoples have to sleep sometimes or young peoples think us old peoples don't know what we're doing. Old peoples always have to show their minds ain't snapped."

Junior said, "All right, Mama. Me and Erleen will be next door if you or Daddy need us."

Anna stood up and put her arms around Junior. The top of her head came just below his chest. "Junior," she said, "the best way to act around spirit peoples is the same way we act around live peoples. Don't steal from them. Don't lie to them. They might be related to you.

"Some peoples say it don't matter what we do to them 'cause the dead's dead and dead people don't amount to much after that. They say it's okay to take their things from them. But our people call *that* stealing, plain and simple—it's stealing from the dead. It's shameful and bound to stir trouble. No matter if other peoples say that the living can do anything against the dead, way deep down inside of us, we going to know what we did. Maybe we lied about them or stole from them. Then, Son, we might become crazy, and that kind of craziness is going to make us more foolish peoples than ever. I don't want me and Wilbur, or my grandchildrens, crazy like that. 'Cause that will make us all sick then, that's how these things is."

Anna tried to squeeze Junior's waist and then let him go. Junior and Erleen left for the next room, but before he went inside, Junior stood beside his car and watched Wilbur. Junior was suddenly aware of the fact that Wilbur had grown considerably smaller than Junior remembered him as a teenager. Junior finally went inside the next room and climbed into bed with Erleen, but about midnight he woke, restless and jumpy. He looked outside again, and Wilbur had not moved at all.

The next morning, when Junior went to Anna's and Wilbur's room, Wilbur was seated at the little table, sipping strong black coffee from a paper cup. "Did you sleep well, Daddy?" Junior asked. "Where'd you get that coffee?"

Wilbur pointed to the motel office and said, "Visited that young man over there. He's from down near Tahlequah, Junior. Says he's part Indian, too. Coffee's sure strong."

"Did you sleep, Daddy?" Junior asked again.

Wilbur nodded.

A few hours later, the Snakes had left Memphis behind. Erleen read a movie magazine and Anna dozed. Wilbur was wide awake. The car wound through the Smoky Mountains. Junior pulled off the road at an overlook with a picnic table.

"Sure is pretty here, Daddy," he said as he got out of the car. "Want to stretch your legs?"

Wilbur got out of the car with Anna and Erleen. As Erleen took photographs of the autumn ridge nearby, Wilbur wandered into the bushes of oak leaves. Anna sat down on one side of the table. Junior climbed onto the table and stretched out on it.

Several minutes later, Wilbur had not returned. "Daddy," Junior called, "let's get back on the road." But Wilbur didn't respond. When several minutes more passed and Wilbur still was nowhere to be seen, Junior went to look for him.

He found Wilbur sitting under a tree, leaning against the trunk. His eyes were closed and his breathing was raspy. Junior reached for Wilbur's hand. It was limp and heavy. He shook Wilbur's shoulder, but Wilbur did not wake. Junior realized something was wrong. He picked up the old man as if he were a child and carried him back to the picnic table, where he laid him gently down.

By now Junior was alarmed. Anna was quiet and thoughtful. Junior thought about taking Wilbur to the nearest clinic or hospital.

Anna said, "Let's just wait here awhile, Junior, and see what happens. We ain't in no hurry. Wilbur's alright. We can stay with him right here."

Erleen looked doubtful, but Junior reluctantly agreed. After about two hours, Wilbur woke up in good spirits, looking completely refreshed. Anna smiled brightly at Wilbur as he stared at her from the top of the table. "Pretty day, Wilbur," she said. "You ought to see it. Some peoples like to sing on days like this one here."

"What happened to you, Daddy?" Junior asked.

"Nothing," Wilbur answered. "Sometimes old mans get worn out. It was the air that done it to me. It's sure sweet up here."

After making certain that Wilbur had recovered fully, Junior again started the car and helped Wilbur inside. After that, Wilbur became his old self again. He sang and teased Junior about being as soft as a cotton boll.

21

LOS ANGELES, CALIFORNIA
OCTOBER 1969

ANITA woke feeling particularly displaced this morning. The Los Angeles suburb which had been her home for the last week represented no more to her than a temporary refuge, an overnight stop, although she now possessed a home here. This recent acquisition had come as quite a surprise to her, but after reviewing the circumstances of it, she decided that it was not illogical.

Anita's maiden aunt, her sole surviving relative on her father's side as far as Anita knew and as the court had determined, had willed this elegant rambling house to Anita. The woman's death had preceded the court hearing by about three weeks.

Actually, Anita hadn't known the woman. They had hardly any contact with one another at all and had met only twice, years before when Anita's father had still been alive. The aunt had been kind of a mirror image of her father, Anita recalled. Both brother and sister were the same height, same build, and had the same coloring, with night-black hair and thick-lashed hazel eyes. It was all that Anita could remember.

She felt guilty now. What had she done to deserve this big, beautiful old house? Should she sell it? She would think about that for awhile before she did anything rash. She stared at a large portrait of her aunt in her more youthful days. The painting hung under an arched wall. Yes, she felt guilty about getting this house. The sooner she left here, the better.

She packed her bags in one of the guest rooms across the hall from her aunt's portrait. The woman's eyes in the portrait stayed on Anita as she carried clothing from the closet to the bed.

As Anita finished packing her belongings, she was startled by the housekeeper, who entered the room behind her and asked, "Can I help you, Ms. Mondragon?"

Anita said no, and turned to find a tray with tea and toast. The housekeeper was gone. Anita sat down on one of the velvet armchairs and ate her breakfast. She had lost weight over the last few weeks, along with her interest in eating. When the tea was gone, she looked at the clock and found that it was nearly 8:00. Her plane was scheduled to leave at 9:30. In a couple of hours, she would be in Albuquerque. From there she had to drive to Las Vegas, which was about two hours away. She breathed a sigh of relief. At home she could relax. Everything would be familiar. This place, even this beautiful house, was getting on her nerves somewhat. She just wanted to go home and mull over everything that had happened to her recently.

Again the housekeeper appeared in the doorway. "Are you ready, Ms. Mondragon? We really should leave for the airport within the next thirty minutes because it will take us at least that long to drive over there."

The housekeeper was a round-faced woman with a crooked smile that covered her face as she spoke.

"Yes, thank you, Elvira. I'm ready." Anita picked up two pieces of luggage, and Elvira grabbed two more.

On the tedious drive to the airport, Anita was quiet, nearly sullen. She ignored the endless stream of homes and fast-food places along the freeway. Elvira tried to draw Anita out in the first ten minutes by pointing out local landmarks and sites, but when Anita failed to respond, Elvira quieted and left Anita to her own thoughts.

Anita frowned unconsciously. What was happening to her? She seemed to have stopped all feeling. Her body and mind failed to react to what she saw, heard, and tasted. What was left in place of these senses was an overall feeling of emptiness. She felt as if she were floating through time at this moment, failing to make contact with the world around her. But the odd thing about this was that Anita didn't even feel inclined to reach out, to break beyond this fog of alienation. Perhaps this malaise was due to her age. All these years, she had never felt old. Even now she wasn't sure that she felt old. She felt more tired than anything. How did it feel to be old?

Rosa probably could have told her, could have confirmed what old age felt like. But Rosa wasn't here anymore, and in her last years wasn't prone to speak that often. Her advanced age was never a topic of discussion between the two, wasn't something to be spoken about, but was a heavy burden Rosa carried. Had Rosa ever felt this way? Detached from the world and set adrift by a chain of events?

When Anita came back to reality, Elvira was edging her way into a narrow parking space. Anita gathered her things together and got out of the car. She went around the car to unload her luggage. Elvira looked at her strangely and said, "Your luggage is already at the door. We unloaded it before we parked." Anita didn't remember that. She followed Elvira. Sure enough, outside one set of glass doors were four familiar pieces of luggage. She and Elvira each took two pieces and went inside the automated doors.

Elvira kept Anita company through the long process of waiting in line, checking baggage, and even walked her as far as she could, to the gate where Anita's plane would depart. Finally, Elvira said good-bye and retraced her steps to the parking lot. Elvira's figure could be seen disappearing into the crowd.

This area was full and noisy. A man nearby puffed on a cigarette and read a Los Angeles newspaper. There were hardly enough chairs to accommodate the number of people here. Several young people, teenagers, sat on the floor, their feet clad in sandals and their long hair uncombed. Anita chose the only empty chair nearest her. Children shared the seats beside her. Two of the children were screaming at one another, while the mother tried to quiet them.

As Anita studied the crowd, she once again had no reaction, no sense of being part of it. There were no surprises, no emotions, no feelings inside of her, nothing toward the group or the screaming children beside her—no annoyance, no compassion for the mother. Nothing.

She decided to knit and pulled the knitting needles out of her white bag. She held them a minute and then returned them to the bag. In place of them, she pulled out a magazine and began to thumb through the pages.

The mother with the screaming children had switched places with the little ones and was now seated beside Anita. The woman said to Anita, "I hope they don't disturb you. They're not feeling well. But it's not serious. I hope their crying doesn't bother you."

"No," Anita said. She went back to her magazine, but the young mother wanted to talk. "We're going back to Oklahoma City, all of us." She waved her hand to include all the children there. "Came out here on a bus; we've never been on a plane before. Thought it might be fun." The woman smiled widely. She had a slow drawl, which Anita had never heard until now. "You been on a plane before?" the woman asked.

"Yes," Anita nodded. She didn't want the woman to continue the conversation. She shifted her position away from the mother, who was now lifting one of the smaller children into her lap. The mother didn't notice that Anita had shifted away from her. "Where are you going?" she asked.

Anita sighed. "New Mexico."

The plane was now loading its passengers, to Anita's relief. She gathered her purse and her white bag and jacket, and went to stand in line.

On the plane, she found herself seated next to the same young woman, whose children were in the row of seats behind them. The woman smiled broadly and said to Anita, "I sure am glad I got to sit next to you. I feel like I know you already. My name is Mary Lou."

Anita looked out the window on her right. This was going to be a long flight. She wasn't in any mood to talk or to listen. It required too much effort, too much thought. The young mother beside her was still talking and smiling. Anita stopped listening, though she was now looking directly at the woman. The young woman was plain. She could have been pretty. Her mouth was large, and her complexion clear and white. But her eyes were her best asset. They were wide and gray. Anita looked away from her.

Anita did not have children of her own. Looking at this talkative gray-eyed woman now, Anita longed for her own child. Never in all her life had the longing been so acute as it was at this moment. She felt it like a piercing little stab in her belly. Why hadn't she had children? It had been so long since she had asked herself that question. She sorted through her memories.

She'd been pregnant once, when she was about twenty. Or maybe it was a thousand years ago. Mary Lou was still talking, her mouth forming words which Anna pushed away. Anita had never been pregnant after that. She'd never had to deal with children if she didn't want to. In a sense, the choice had been hers.

Rosa had wanted Anita's child perhaps more than Anita had. When Anita's man had left with "that" woman, Anita's anger toward him transferred to the child she carried. *That* woman. She hadn't thought of *her* in decades. She had forced herself not to.

Yes, Rosa had looked forward to the baby, Anita admitted again with a heavy sigh. Rosa had bought pieces of cloth for baby clothes, for the baby who never came.

Anita might have caused the miscarriage with her own wrecked mind, with the stress and pain of finding that he had gone, fled. The humiliation afterward. . . . Anita never understood why he had betrayed her. Eventually, she assumed responsibility for all of it. She surmised that it was caused by some defect in her. She was not pretty enough, or smart enough, or was inadequate in other ways.

She always wondered how she had ended up with him in the first place. He was so handsome. He had flashing emerald eyes and pearly teeth, and a ready smile that enticed all the females around, old and young alike. Oh, he was smooth as silk, all right.

Mary Lou was pulling down the table in front of Anita. "You do want something to drink, don't you?" The stewardess was standing beside Mary Lou.

"Tea," Anita answered. Had the plane left the runway already? Anita looked outside. Streams of clouds lay under the plane. The stewardess handed Anita a snack in a cellophane wrapper.

"You been thinking hard about something," Mary Lou said. "You didn't even hear my kids scream when we took off. Scared the youngest one half to death, I guess. Hope it don't do him any harm. I have to admit I was just a little nervous about it myself. I guess you got to admit that the things people do today is just amazing, flying and such."

Anita drank her tea while Mary Lou continued to talk. "My grandmother used to get the same look in her eyes when she talked about something that happened before my time."

Anita looked at Mary Lou blankly. Mary Lou said, "You got it. Like you're a thousand miles away. What you thinking about anyway?"

The question annoyed Anita, and she thought that Mary Lou's behavior was the height of rudeness, the obvious mark of someone who had not been taught proper manners. But Mary Lou smiled disarmingly and obviously didn't realize her error.

Anita said, "It's not important. For some reason, I just thought of someone I once knew, someone who was very close to me a long, long time ago."

"It's a man, ain't it? I'll just bet it's a man," Mary Lou said. Her eyes twinkled.

Anita looked out the window again. "Yes, Mary Lou," she said, "it's a man."

"Hey, are you Mexican?" Mary Lou asked. "You talk kind of fast. I like the way you said my name. I ain't never heard it like that before."

Again, Anita was annoyed by the woman's manners.

"Spanish," Anita said.

"Yeah," Mary Lou said, "you're from New Mexico, that's right."

Anita was tiring of this conversation. She wanted to end it. She sat back in the seat and manipulated it so the back dropped to an angle. She closed her eyes. I'm glad I don't have children, she thought. Maybe they might have turned out like Mary Lou. Such manners!

Then she smiled in her faked sleep. Rosa would never have let that happen to Anita's children. Rosa's patience with children had been remarkable. But Anita couldn't say the same thing about herself. After *him*, her choice had been to keep children at arm's length—she had never let them get too close, boys and girls.

She had never known what sex her own child had been. She had not thought of its appearance until this moment. Perhaps if it had been a boy, he would have favored his father, the man with emerald eyes and light skin. Or maybe the boy would have looked like her. She was darker than he was and her hair was darker, too. If the child had been a girl, perhaps the little thing would have looked like Rosa, or maybe she would have had some green in her eyes.

These thoughts were pointless, Anita knew. But that gray-eyed Mary Lou would ask more questions if Anita took out her crochet needles or magazine.

It was Rosa who tended to Anita when the infant was lost in Anita's sixth month. Anita didn't know how she felt then either. At this memory Anita's eyes opened for a second. Yes, it was coming back to her now. Anita hadn't known whether to be happy or sad then. All she knew was that she didn't have to care for anyone from then on, children and men inclusive, if she didn't want to. And she didn't either. She'd kept her word, and other peoples' children at arm's length, as she did with all men. Soon this group grew to include everyone around her. She'd become a recluse.

Once, Rosa tried to warn Anita that such action might be harmful. And Rosa had also encouraged another marriage for Anita, with a man who was nearly the exact opposite of Anita's first husband. Anita was insulted by the man's appearance, though. He was dark, aging, and there was nothing physically attractive about him that Anita could see. Rosa told Anita to look beneath his appearance and try to substitute something else.

He was a widower, a kind and just man. But Anita refused him as she'd refused others after him. Before she knew it, Anita was in her forties.

Rosa was Anita's closest friend. Anita found it hard to get close to anyone, to let down her walls and allow anyone near. Rosa's other children knew, instinctively perhaps, how Anita felt about them. It wasn't personal. Anita pushed everyone away.

When she was in her fifties, when Rosa retreated to one end of the house, Anita began to miss her child, the infant who had never seen the light of day. Anita even forgave it for reminding her of *him*, that man who'd traded her for another woman so long ago.

By accident, she'd met *him* on the streets of Santa Fe, several years later. And she didn't recognize him on first sight. He was a face in the crowd. Eventually, they recognized one another about the same time. He'd nodded to her, and she'd looked hard at him and then turned away. That was it. That was all. He'd looked different. He wasn't as handsome as she'd remembered, and his pearly teeth were then a dull gray. During that experience, too, Anita hadn't felt anything—no hate, no love, no pain, no joy. She was empty.

Later, Rosa held her hand as Anita described the incident. "He's the same man that lived here for a few months. But, Mama, he's a stranger, too."

Again, Mary Lou was shaking Anita. "The stewardess is collecting trays." Anita handed Mary Lou the tray with the teacup and the snack still wrapped in cellophane.

"Hey, do you mind if I keep this for my children?" Mary Lou asked Anita, and took the package before handing the tray to the stewardess.

Mary Lou was holding her youngest child on her lap. The child had wide blue-gray eyes, which looked at Anita with curiosity.

Anita sat back in the seat again and closed her eyes.

In a sense, Anita had come to envy Rosa's other children, particularly the girl, Maria. Maria had several children. Some were Indian, and two were Spanish and Indian. Even Rosa's boy had children.

Anita felt exhausted now. She wanted to sleep. She hadn't slept well last night, waking to the portrait of her aunt several times throughout the night. She could hear Mary Lou talking to the child on her lap, telling the little boy not to touch or wake the lady in the next seat. The little boy asked, "Does the lady like kids?" All the little boy's *l*'s sounded like *w*'s.

Mary Lou answered, "I don't know, Honeypot, but I sure do."

22

ALBUQUERQUE, NEW MEXICO

OCTOBER 1969

THE view of the Sandia Mountains from David Drake's home was spectacular this morning. The very peak of the mountain itself could be seen, and the jagged blue-gray rocks, the crevices in the mountainside, were in sharp focus.

Jonnie Navajo sat at the wrought iron table with the glass top, a coffee cup in hand. Nasbah sat facing him.

He had risen at the first light that crept into the bedroom where he'd spent the night. When the dawn spread out into the sky, he left the bedroom, a child's room, and went outside to greet the new day. In the cool morning, he felt better, more familiar and at ease with these surroundings than he felt inside the house. He then walked outside the fence that surrounded Drake's house and climbed two little hills before coming upon a broken metate lying in the wash beside a few stunted piñon trees. He turned around and went back to Drake's house. The old man waited another hour before Drake rose and made some coffee, much too strong for the old man's taste.

Drake was speaking to him now. "As I told you last night, I wish there was another approach to this issue of Indian slavery. The records are entirely inadequate." Drake looked at Nasbah to see if she understood. She translated rapidly for the old man. He didn't respond.

"I am grateful, however," Drake continued, "that we were able to make a start on my history project last night."

Nasbah nodded and said, "Well, it was Willie's idea to go ahead with it. He didn't want to be the cause of any delay in your work."

"You're an excellent translator, Nasbah," Drake said. "Obviously, you have done this quite often."

"Since I was a little girl in school, my grandfather has often had need of my help, though he knows some English and Spanish," Nasbah agreed.

"Aw, yes," Drake said. "I'm particularly glad that he's consented to work with me, as I told Willie. I need the input of someone exactly like him, that is, someone who can provide information on the ceremonial aspect of Navajo history. What I intend to find out is how the two intertwined, or how ceremony affected the chain of events that has occurred since the Navajos met the 'Americans' over a century ago. Perhaps the religious ideas of the Navajos had no impact at all upon the chain of events in the course of Navajo-white relations, but if not, I'll satisfy myself that I have at least tried to explore this."

"What did he say?" Jonnie Navajo asked.

Nasbah translated, and the old man looked blankly at David Drake. The old man made a comment that Nasbah didn't translate to English. Drake's family could be heard rising in another part of the house.

"For instance," Drake said, "while the Navajos were incarcerated at Fort Sumner, it would be expected that some aspect of their ceremonial life continued there, but government documents don't support this. It appears that if ceremonies were held there, they had absolutely no effect on the daily life there or on what happened between the people and the federal government later."

Nasbah repeated this to her grandfather. The old man let out a long breath and said to Nasbah, "What is this? What does he mean? *He is going to write our history?!*"

Jonnie Navajo continued. "I have heard certain things about *Hweldi* and ceremonies there. Some people say that no blessing ceremonies were held there, because *Hweldi* is not within the borders of the four sacred mountains, and that these ceremonies should only be practiced here. Yet, I have also heard others say that certain ceremonies were indeed practiced, but these were not Blessing Way. There seems to be some question about it. Today, as you know, Granddaughter, our people live scattered out, even beyond the four sacred mountains, and yes, the *haataalii* are carried outside the four sacred mountains to help our people as they request it. Now, I can't help but feel that this information will be useless to this man. I don't know if he is capable of understanding it."

At that point, Drake's wife entered the kitchen and began to prepare breakfast. Drake helped her for a few minutes while Nasbah and her grandfather talked. He wanted to know how long it would be before they caught their plane. Nasbah said a couple of hours. He was looking forward to it.

When Drake rejoined them, Nasbah said, "My grandfather has asked whether or not you have found anything about the missing child, the one who was stolen from Beautiful Mountain."

Drake dreaded the question. He shook his head from side to side, no. "I've found a few accounts of slave raids, yes," Drake said. "Actually, several did take place on Beautiful Mountain, though in the Spanish accounts it is called by another name. What I've found is interesting enough. It just isn't what we're looking for. There's a really curious account of one raid, which describes how the Navajos took refuge on a high mesa. According to the description, the people tricked the slave-raiders into going into a particularly narrow canyon and then showered them with boulders. Again, another account states that the Navajos pushed some slave-raiders off a high cliff or forced them to jump off sheer drops of a thousand feet or more."

Nasbah translated this for the old man, who nodded his head. He answered and drew something on the table.

Nasbah spoke. "Yes, he knows about those two. He knows the canyon where the slave-raiders were showered with boulders, and also the cliff where the slave-raiders were forced to jump."

David Drake's eyes opened wide. "He know these places?"

"Yes," Nasbah said. "A lot of the older people have that information. He said that in the canyon these raiders spoke to the Navajos in Spanish, calling up to them on the mesa, saying 'Come out, Diné!' That happened just before the slave-raiders were showered with boulders. He also said that some of these raiders survived, though they ran away. Later, they came back and dug out some of their dead. Does it say that in the records?"

David Drake shook his head no. "These were two separate incidents. Does he know that?"

Nasbah asked her grandfather, and he spoke a long time before she translated his answer. She said, "Of course he knows that. The second incident you described of slave-raiders being forced to jump off the cliffs is older. It happened perhaps seven generations ago, and there were no women among those Navajos who forced the slave-raiders to kill themselves because the men had hidden their women and children in preparation for events to come. The other incident happened perhaps twenty years after that. The people were in poor condition, living on berries and game. The Navajos involved in showering the slave-raiders with boulders were men, women, and children."

"That's amazing," Drake said. "Just amazing! How is it that there are no accounts from the Navajo side regarding this?"

Again, Nasbah translated. The old man looked at Drake and spoke directly to him. Nasbah said, "None of the white people have asked."

Drake's wife carried platters of food to the table, and quickly set it. As the entire family and Nasbah and her grandfather ate, Drake described the ad he had placed in the papers and journals that dealt with southwestern history. "It's pretty far-fetched that we'll get anything back as a result of it. But nevertheless, we don't have that many other choices."

Finally, an hour or so later, the old man began to dress himself for his new experience, his first flight, to Washington, D.C. He traded his old jeans for western-cut slacks, and the shirt he put on was red velveteen. It had real dimes sewn in two rows on the center of the sleeves and around the cuffs. Silver buttons were at his throat, and stamped silver pieces were sprinkled around the collar. He wore a wide belt with silver concha rings. He was brushing off his large black hat, which had a silver hat band and silver spider, when Nasbah entered the child's bedroom where he had slept. She was dressed simply, with long turquoise nuggets dangling from each ear. When she had combed the old man's long, white hair and retied it in the *chonga* knot, the old man put the hat on his head, and the two were ready to go.

David Drake peeked in the room just then and said, "I thought we'd take the long way, through Old Town. Your grandfather might enjoy it."

Old Town was packed with tourists, even on this fall day. Drake parked the car and said, "He can walk around if he likes. There's plenty of time."

Under the portal sat a row of Pueblo people selling their wares, bright turquoise and clay pots. Jonnie Navajo headed in that direction. The Pueblo vendors saw him right away. As the old man studied the strings of turquoise spread out on black velvet cloth, a Pueblo man spoke to him. "*Ya'tééh*," he said. Jonnie Navajo answered, "Yes, *ya'tééh*." The two men began to gesture to one another, and the Pueblo man indicated he would trade for the old man's hat band.

Nasbah turned to Drake and said, "I'm a little nervous about going to Washington. I think that it will be very different from Albuquerque, from Old Town."

Drake laughed. "You'll be all right. But you're right about one thing—

it's a zoo. People from all over the world are there, every place you can think of. If you don't mind my asking, why are you making this trip? How about your grandfather? Is he nervous about it?"

Nasbah watched her grandfather now. The old man had moved down the row of vendors and was laughing with another Pueblo vendor, taking little notice of how the tourists responded to him, snapping his photograph in subtle and not so subtle ways. "My grandfather is looking forward to it. We're going there because Willie has called for us to come. There's probably no other reason that would make my grandfather go. He plans to visit the ocean and bring some ocean water back here. It seems that his uncle had some of that water and now Grandfather wants some, too."

Nasbah and Drake crossed the street to sit on a bench in the middle of the plaza. "I'd like to thank you for letting us stay at your home last night, and for breakfast this morning," Nasbah said. Drake's eyes were following the old man in the crowd of tourists. A blond woman tourist was speaking to him now. Drake wondered what the old man would say to this tourist.

"I enjoyed it," he said. "Your visit has helped me redirect my energy to this project."

"It must be important to you," Nasbah said.

"Yes," he said. "I've always had this interest in Indian history. I just zeroed in on Navajo history in the last few years, though, and was going gung-ho on it until. . . ." Drake stopped speaking.

"Yes?" Nasbah asked.

"Well, until my sister's death a few months ago. As a matter of fact, she lived in Washington, D.C."

Nasbah remembered what Willie had said.

"I think Willie mentioned that to us. I'm sorry," Nasbah said.

"Yes, I am, too," Drake frowned. "Perhaps if she had died in a more natural way, I could accept it. As it is, even today, I'm not certain exactly what happened to her. She'd been acting strangely before her death. I think she was overworked and under severe stress." Drake bit his tongue. He'd said too much.

Nasbah's grandfather was coming toward them. He was ready to leave. Nothing else interested him in this place for the moment. He spoke to Nasbah, who translated for Drake, "He said that most of those people are from the Pueblo of Santo Domingo. He wants to go now."

At the airport, Drake walked Nasbah and the old man to one terminal and told Nasbah how to get to the gate where their plane would leave. He left Nasbah and the old man on the second floor and got on an escalator going down to the first level. The old man watched him ride down, then turned to Nasbah and said, "Only the white people would think of that."

People stared at the old man. They made no effort to hide it, but the old man was calm about it. A woman seated on a hand-carved bench was telling a teenager, "*Indio. Apache.*" Someone else was pointing at him from a telephone booth.

Nasbah said, "Come on, Grandfather, let's go."

The old man started to follow Nasbah and then turned around and went back to the woman seated on the bench. He pointed to himself and said "*Indio. Nabéjo!*" The woman said, "Navajo?" He nodded and smiled, "*Nabéjo!*" and then followed Nasbah down the terminal.

They came to a line and stood at the end of it. Nasbah watched the women place their purses on a long table. The purses moved by themselves and disappeared behind a curtain. While the purses moved along, the people in the line stepped through a metal gate or doorway. Just then a sound came from the doorway as one of the passengers ducked through it. Lights flashed on the machine. The passenger was pulled aside by two or three people in uniforms who were supervising the purse check.

Nasbah put her purse on the table and it moved toward the curtain. Then she stepped through the gate, asking one of the people in uniform, "What is the purpose of this?"

"Security," the officer replied. "It prevents bomb threats and plane hijackings."

Another officer, a woman, whistled at Nasbah's grandfather. "Would you look at that silver he's wearing! Is it real?"

The officers looked Jonnie Navajo up and down. "Where are you heading, sir?" one of them asked.

"He doesn't speak English," Nasbah said.

"Well, tell him that he has to take off all that silver before he goes through the gate. Any metal will set off the alarm," an officer said to Nasbah.

The woman officer spoke. "I don't think that will be necessary. Just take him in and check him. It's not likely he's going to be carrying any weapons onto the plane."

The younger man took Jonnie Navajo's arm and led him to an office. In a few minutes, he brought the old man out and let him go to Nasbah on the other side of the security station.

Jonnie Navajo was chuckling to himself. "What did they do?" Nasbah asked.

"He felt inside my clothes," the old man answered.

When Nasbah and the old man reached the stairs that led to the gate, Nasbah took an escalator. The old man refused, climbing each step carefully. Again, their appearance in the waiting area caused a stir. The old man ignored it, and went to look out the window at the incoming planes.

At one door, passengers filed into the waiting area. A loudspeaker was announcing that the plane from Los Angeles had just arrived and that passengers could pick up their baggage on another level.

Anita Mondragon stepped inside to the waiting area, relieved to be back in New Mexico and to leave Mary Lou on the plane for the last stretch to Oklahoma City. She was on her way to the ladies room to wash her face and comb her hair when she noticed Jonnie Navajo standing alone at the window gazing up into space. Dressed like that, he was the last thing she expected to see here in the airport. It woke her up. She had been anxious to be in her car and on the freeway, but now her steps hesitated. She sat down on one of the chairs nearest her and picked up a newspaper that someone had left behind. She held it up in front of her as if she might be reading, but she wasn't. She was watching the old man. It was strange that he interested her. He looked out of place here, out of his element. *That* interested her.

Oh, she knew that he was a Navajo. She couldn't live this close to them and not know a Navajo. She knew a few Pueblo Indians by sight, too, but that was all. And, of course, the stories about them. . . .

Jonnie Navajo took a seat too. Nasbah was right beside him. He asked her, "Why did they do that back there? Feel my clothes?"

Nasbah explained, "Some people steal planes, Grandfather. They take guns on the plane and steal the plane."

Jonnie Navajo looked at her. "What? These people are very strange."

The woman across from him, holding a newspaper in her hand, was watching him. He looked at her and then away.

Nasbah was at the window again, saying, "Here's our plane, Grandfather."

He rose and went to the window. After a few minutes, he said, "It is possible to steal one of those? Just drive it away?"

They watched the airline personnel outside open the plane door and move steps up to it. Finally, the passengers started to climb the steps and go inside. When the stewardess took the old man's ticket, she asked if he could climb the steps. Nasbah assured her that it would be no problem, and then the two of them went outside to board the plane.

Anita Mondragon went to the window and watched the old man carefully climb the steps to the plane. Again, she asked herself what would make an old man like that leave his home to go up into the sky. She glanced at the desk to read the flight's destination—Washington, D.C.

She stood at the window for several minutes after the plane could no longer be seen. She felt as if she had been asleep for several days and had dreamed so many dreams. But now she was awake. The old man woke her up, brought her back home. Somehow it felt good. Yes, she could "feel" again. She wasn't numb anymore.

In the air, Nasbah and her grandfather looked down at the earth. The old man said, "I think that it must be possible to see the sacred mountain of the east from here. I think it is possible that the twins, Monster Slayer and Born-for-Water, saw the earth from up here when they traveled on the rainbow to visit their father, the Sun. Yes, Nasbah, there are some songs where one of the twins is saying to the other, 'there is the sacred mountain of the east' as the twins returned home." The old man began to hum in the sing-song voice of men who realized the need and purpose of these endless songs. It made Nasbah relax. She felt glad that she was not alone.

23

WASHINGTON, D.C.

RUSSELL entered Willie Begay's room. Russell was in good spirits, anticipating seeing Junior and Wilbur. In contrast, Willie was in a lousy mood. He had just argued with a nurse and he'd been uncooperative with the hospital staff most of the day. At the sight of Russell, however, Willie smiled and asked, "What's it like outside?"

"Awful," Russell lied. "You ought to be glad you're in here."

Russell was at the hospital to get instructions on Willie's family, who was to arrive later in the day. He had promised to meet them at the airport and wanted to tell Willie about his own guests, who would be in D.C. either today or tomorrow. Russell described Wilbur in detail.

"That old man sounds interesting," Willie said. "Sounds as if he knows a lot."

Russell nodded. "You could say that. He knows about the outdoors, the wind, the sky, the earth, and he knows people, but not in the way we think of when we say that we know people. Yep, our folks have always kind of thought that there is something special about Wilbur."

"I'd like to meet him if I can. My grandfather would probably want to talk to him too. Old men understand each other better than young men do. They speak in the same way and understand the whole picture, no matter what language they know. At least most of them do. I guess there's always exceptions. I myself like to talk to old people. I enjoy them, I really do," Willie said. "If I had the knowledge of my grandfather, I probably wouldn't be in here now wasting time and money."

His comment brought both Russell and Willie back to the hospital room.

"I guess I'd better go now," Russell said. "I'll be back in the morning. Don't worry. I'll take care of everything this afternoon." He waved and left.

After Russell left, Willie slept for a couple of hours. When he heard people talking, he opened his eyes and stared at the partition that separated him from the patient in the next bed. His sleep had been restless, and he had dreamed an odd dream.

In his dream he walked alone through a narrow canyon. Sheer cliffs, thousands of feet high, reached up to touch clouds, which moved swiftly from one wall of the canyon to the other. A few trees grew up the cliff sides, piñon at the bottom and spruce and fir at a higher level. Between the canyon walls ran a cold, clear stream that was shallow in some places, but had threatening, dark, deep swirls at other locations. Willie saw himself walking leisurely through the canyon. It seemed as if he had all the time in the world. In several places along his walk he noted traces of ancient civilizations, that although silent for several generations, still managed to scream out at him. High up in the golden cliffs hung little houses set within the canyon walls. "Enemy ancestors" were what the Navajos called the ancient people who had once lived there. Willie squinted up at the square, little black windows, which were the only evidence that the silent, empty, abandoned houses were actually there. At Willie's feet were broken sherds of pottery in orange, brown, red, gray, and black-and-white variations. Willie had a fleeting impression of the pots tumbling out of the houses and crashing into so many pieces at his feet.

He saw himself stoop to reach out for a pottery sherd, when suddenly the cliffs around him turned into angular concrete buildings, and the fast-flowing iridescent stream became a dull gray highway, running and winding between the rows of dark buildings. This change in scenery took Willie by surprise, and he stood to investigate the top of the buildings. The golden cliff-houses had vanished, and the turquoise sky with rolling clouds was replaced by a dull, opaque city skyline.

Willie still held the piece of pottery in his hand. It was gray with black painted lines. At his feet, he saw more pieces of pottery lying on the asphalt, and he reached down to pick them up. He slipped each broken piece into his pants pockets until his pockets bulged, and then he began to put the remaining sherds inside his shirt. The sherds rested heavily against his belly. Then he charged frantically down the street. Just why he ran he didn't know. After running awhile, he was out of breath and sweaty. The sherds stuck to his belly. He stopped at the only piece of ground he could find that was not covered by asphalt or concrete. There he got down on his knees and began to dig. He pulled out the dirt desperately with his bare hands, and soon his fingers felt trickles of blood. Finally, he succeeded in digging a deep hole into which he deposited the pottery sherds. But he pulled other, unexpected things out of his pockets along with the pottery fragments: there was yucca twine, one or two turquoise beads, and strands of white hair. He rubbed his hands on his clothes, but the hair still clung to his fingers. He pulled the hair off and put it into the ground. He dreaded putting his hands inside his shirt, but when he finally managed it, pottery sherds were the only things to drop out of it. He pulled his shirt out of his pants.

Willie then covered the hole he had dug. He did this carefully with dirt and trash, trying to hide it. Next, he attempted to figure out where he was. What direction should he take to escape this place? Suddenly, as quickly as before, he found himself standing in the narrow canyon with the sheer cliff walls. The golden houses, a thousand feet up, hung there again. The swirling stream sparkled iridescently in the sunlit distance. The clouds rolled swiftly overhead. A cold breeze slapped him awake.

And he was surprised to find himself here. In the hospital. His hands were cold. He was angry, too—angry at his own helplessness.

A nurse entered the room and went past Willie. He heard her speak to the patient in the next bed. He didn't listen. At that moment, a visitor entered the room and peeked around the curtain to Willie.

"Mr. Begay?" the man asked.

Willie nodded, annoyed by the continual intrusions. The man came over to the bed and extended a hand. "I'm Ray Worth. I'm a psychologist. Your doctor asked me to look in on you."

Willie set his mouth in a straight line. When Willie didn't respond, the psychologist looked out the window and made some comment about the blustery weather. Then he asked, "Mr. Begay, have you been under stress lately, or any situation of duress?"

Willie shook his head no.

Worth continued, "Well, your doctor is exploring all the possibilities, that is, all the possible sources of your illness."

"Are you saying that my illness is all in my mind?" Willie asked sarcastically.

The psychologist smiled and answered no. He said more, but Willie refused to listen. In a few minutes, the psychologist excused himself and left. Willie couldn't recall one thing Worth had said to him.

The fact that he couldn't remember a conversation that had taken place less than ten minutes before intensified Willie's depression. The events of the last few days didn't hold together either. They were random incidents without sequence or order. Maybe he *was* losing his mind.

Willie got out of bed and walked to the narrow window. His hospital gown hung limply on him. The window overlooked the Potomac River. Willie could see the fishermen, black and white people, sitting at the river's edge. The river was dark and choppy. The sky was much the same. He wanted to be out there, in the open air, and to be able to hear the water and the wind.

He had walked along the river in that same place one Sunday, he couldn't say how long ago, and he had watched a black man fish. But the rats in the nearby park drew more attention from Willie than the fish. The rats, the size of cats and small dogs, darted back and forth through the park where bikers followed a skinny path along the river's edge. The rats in the park came as no surprise to Willie, although he admitted that they did at first, when he learned that large colonies of rats infested the area around the Smithsonian Institution. He himself saw a couple of them, shaggy gray scavengers that ran boldly out in front of horrified tourists.

Willed was tired of the rats, tired of chronic exhaustion, and tired of sleeping and staying in bed all the time. Yet, he knew better than anyone else that he had no strength.

He tried to sing something, one of his grandfather's songs, but he couldn't concentrate. He climbed back into bed to wait for the old man. He was anxious to see him, he had so much to tell him. Would his grandfather ever find him?

Willie smiled, remembering that long ago his grandmother had asked the same question when she had taken her first off-reservation trip, at the age of sixty-five, to a hospital in Albuquerque. She'd made the trip alone, without an interpreter. When the old man, Jonnie Navajo, followed later and entered the hospital room where Willie's grandmother was confined, the old lady was overwhelmed that he had fought all the traffic and found his way through the perplexing maze of concrete buildings. When he spoke to her in Navajo, it was the first time she had heard her own language in three days. She'd longed for it. This recollection made Willie's spirits soar. Now he wondered—just what would the old man think of D.C.?

24

FALLS CHURCH, VIRGINIA

RUSSELL and Junior Snake sat on the floor in the middle of Russell's apartment, which was a large, one-room affair. A wooden room divider separated the kitchen area from the rest of the room. The kitchen was a narrow space that barely permitted Russell to turn around or to open the refrigerator door fully. Only the bathroom was really separate and private. Nevertheless, the large windows in the apartment and the sliding glass doors gave the place an airy, outdoor feeling and allowed a spacious view of trees and sky, which was the reason Russell had taken the apartment—that and the beautiful wooden floors. He found that he could almost forget he was in the city when he retreated to his apartment.

Junior spoke. "Black Bear, I sure appreciate you letting us stay with you a couple of days while we're here. Won't stay longer than two nights."

"Honestly," Russell answered, "I've been looking forward to it. Grandma and Wilbur can sleep on the bed. The rest of us will have to sleep on the floor, though."

Anna stood at the window. "I wish me and this old man could sleep outside, Sonny," she said. "We all brought folding cots."

"Naw, Grandma, that's not done around here. There's crazy people outside who won't let you sleep," Russell answered.

Anna nodded and went to the kitchen. "Erleen, honey, you want to help me fix some sandwiches to eat? We can have a large meal tonight." Erleen started to unpack the food they'd brought, which still sat in three grocery sacks.

While Erleen and Anna prepared an afternoon snack, Junior and Russell visited. Russell was enjoying his guests immensely. He was seldom with family anymore. Junior was animated as he brought Russell up to date on the gossip back home. Wilbur was quiet, smiling occasionally at Junior's jokes, but he appeared tired from the long ride to Virginia.

Several miles away, in Washington, Donald Evans found himself withdrawn and uncommunicative. His girlfriend, Elaine Mintor, sat across from him at the table. She was a pretty woman with an oval face and clear brown eyes. Always cheerful and outgoing, she pleaded with Donald. "It's Sunday, Donald. Let's do something! Let's go somewhere!"

He ignored her enthusiasm and kept chewing distractedly on the sandwich she had prepared for him.

"Hello," she said, waving a finger to catch his attention. "Hello, hello!" She was a tall woman who came to Donald's chin. She stood now, totally annoyed with him, and cleared the table.

"I'm sorry," Donald said. He grabbed her hands to pull her to his side of the table and pushed her onto the chair beside him.

"Listen, Elaine," he continued. "I want to tell you something. I must talk to someone!" Elaine's annoyance changed to curiosity immediately. That was one of her qualities that Donald liked best.

"What is it, Don?" she asked gently.

He hated to be called Don, but let it go for the moment.

"I had a very bizarre experience recently, Elaine. It really shook me." He proceeded to describe his entire experience with the apparition in the attic to Elaine. She gave him her full attention. He described the menacing figure in detail and how the figure had lifted Donald with ease and thrown him to the floor. Donald recounted his own terror at the time. When he had told his story, he watched Elaine to see what her response was going to be.

She considered cracking a joke about Donald's situation, but judged from Donald's sincere and straightforward description of the incident that her timing would be bad.

"What do you think?" Donald asked. "Am I cracking up or what?" He tried to smile.

Elaine answered, "I'm not sure, but what's more important is what *you* think. I recall that several weeks ago you told me you didn't believe in 'ghosts.' Remember that conversation you told me about, your conversation with George Daylight? You were so sure then! You thought that his suggestion of 'spirits'— that's what he called them—was a ploy to manipulate you. Why he would need to manipulate you I'm not sure. But you had no doubts then! Where is that certainty now?"

Donald slumped lower on the chair and held his face in his hands. "I wish to hell I knew!" he said.

"Honey, why don't you go speak to George Daylight about this? He seems to have an inkling of understanding as to what's happening around here," Elaine said, hoping that she didn't sound as if she were betraying Donald.

"No!" he shouted angrily. "Absolutely not!"

"Alright, then," she said, putting her hands on Donald's shoulders. "It was just a suggestion."

"Besides, I heard that Daylight has left D.C.," Donald added.

Elaine could plainly see him shrink away from her even more then. She decided to leave him alone and began to wash the dishes and clean the stove. He took no notice of her activities and moved from the table to the couch in the next room. Elaine kept an eye on him from the kitchen, all the while reviewing everything he had told her.

She tried to decide what to think about Donald's frightening experience in the attic. She knew that her decision weighed on her knowledge of Donald. Was he lying? Did he imagine the incident?

Nearly an hour later, she came to a decision. If Donald said the incident had occurred, it must have happened just the way he described it. Once she accepted that, other questions popped up. The most important of them was whether or not Donald could be in danger now.

She sat down beside Donald and asked, "Just exactly how many people who have worked in that building have committed suicide recently?"

Donald frowned and replied, "I can't say how many because I don't really know."

She was immediately suspicious of his vagueness and asked, "Well, has there been more than one person then?"

Donald avoided her steady gaze. She prodded. "More than two?"

"Four this year, possibly five, if Jean Wurly's death was suicide," he said, deciding to level with her. He ran his fingers through his hair nervously.

Elaine was astonished. "Donald! It that possible?"

Again, he nodded. "Very possible. The grapevine is certain of it. The consensus is that Jean Wurly was as nutty as a fruitcake!"

Elaine was a little shocked at his bluntness. He could see that on her face. He restated the information. "Pardon me. Her sanity was in question. She had seen things in the building, she said, and her fright at being in the building alone had bordered on lunacy just before she died."

Elaine frowned at him. Her questions did not end. "Last year? Were there suicides last year?"

Donald didn't answer.

"The year before that?" Elaine's voice rose a pitch higher, and nearly whined.

Donald threw an arm around her. "That's exactly what's been eating at me, Elaine. When Daylight first mentioned the possibility of a connection between what's in the attic and the suicides, I rejected the idea completely. But, I've done some research since then." He held Elaine's face cupped in his hands. "There have been other suicides through the years and," he hesitated, "other deaths. Freak accidents, similar to Jean's death."

Elaine was now definitely alarmed. "How many people are you suggesting?" she asked.

"I don't know," he answered. "I only went back a couple of years."

"My God!" Elaine said. "The implications! You must speak to someone about this! You must do what you can to stop this!"

"How?" Donald asked sarcastically. "Are people there going to believe that we have ghosts—Indian ghosts—in the attic? Would *you* believe it? They'd rather believe that I've lost my sanity. And at this moment, I'm close to it, Elaine!" He let go of her and sighed deeply.

"Why did George Daylight leave?" Elaine asked. "Is there anyone else here who can help you?"

Donald answered, "I'm not exactly sure why he left. The point is that he's gone."

Elaine repeated her question. "Is there someone else here who he confided in? Someone who can help you?"

"Maybe. Only Indians. But they stick close together. I'm sure they have all discussed his concerns. Perhaps Daylight was actually their spokesman. Who knows?" Donald asked tiredly.

"Who are they, Donald?" Elaine wouldn't stop. "Who are they? Daylight's associates? His friends?"

"Well, there's a Navajo Indian man—Behay, Beyale, or something like that. I've met him three or four times. We've actually only spoken once or twice, though."

"Where does he live? Let's go visit him," Elaine suggested. "He might be able to help you."

Donald looked at her and couldn't help but grin at her impetuousness.

"We just can't go visit him. Why, I don't even know him! I've explained that. Really, I've only talked with him on two occasions, for a minute or two. Besides, I don't know where he lives, but I'm sure he's not in D.C."

Elaine's disappointment showed on her face. "Anyone else?" she asked.

Donald thought for a second. "Russell Tallman," he conceded. "He lives in Falls Church and he's a very close friend of Daylight's."

Elaine smiled. "That's promising. Should we call him? He does have a phone, doesn't he?"

While she checked the telephone book, Donald admitted to himself that he might be able to deal with Tallman. His few conversations with him had been congenial and cooperative, although Geoffrey hadn't gotten along very well with him.

"He's not in the book," Elaine said. "I'll call directory assistance."

Donald allowed her to dial the operator and wondered if he would actually call Tallman.

Elaine hung up the phone and said excitedly, "I have his number! Shall we call him?"

In the meantime, back in Russell's apartment, Russell finished a sandwich with the Snakes. Then he left to meet Willie's family. He invited Junior to accompany him because he was using Junior's car.

On the ride to the airport, Russell filled Junior in on Willie Begay. He gave a brief history of his acquaintance with Willie and the reason for Willie's grandfather's visit to Washington.

Junior was interested. "Ain't it something, Black Bear, that what we see and touch can actually make us ill—sick to our stomachs or sick in our minds? Daddy says it's damn near a chain reaction. Maybe other people could argue about it and see it differently, but I'll have to side with Daddy on this. Something happened to me once a long time ago, and it made me stop in my tracks and really think hard about what illness is.

"When I was just barely a teenager, I seen a man killed. Before that, I saw death, yeah, but the kind of death that I knew up to then had been of a natural and peaceful nature. I didn't know killing, the violence and anger of it. That man died an awful death. He was whipped to death, and I happened to stumble onto him. I didn't even know him. He wasn't even Indian. But I came by, and with no advance warning of it, I was his last contact with another human being in this life. He reached out with his

175

eyes and touched me. I tell you, I was sicker than a dog from that killing, and from touching that man's eyes. I wasn't the victim, but at the same time I was, too.

"I didn't realize that the incident had hurt me deep, until the old folks pointed it out to me. There were signs of my sickness, that deadly contact, and they showed these to me.

"What I'm getting at, Black Bear, is that today our people see and touch all kinds of things that ain't good. It's bound to affect us in some negative way. Maybe we're all a little numb from stumbling onto these things so often. Maybe we're all a little sick from this violent contact, and there ain't no one to tell us how sick we really are. Know what I mean?" They were approaching the airport.

Russell and Junior were late. They went quickly to the terminal where Jonnie Navajo and his granddaughter would arrive. Russell was not prepared for the old man's appearance, but knew the old man and girl at first sight. The old man was vaguely familiar, someone George had pointed out in a magazine a few months earlier. The old man was walking slowly toward Russell and Junior, as much interested in all the people surrounding him as they were in him. The crowd examined the old man openly, but he didn't seem to object.

"Well, I'll be damned!" Junior whispered and nudged Russell with an elbow. "Ain't he something? Look at that silver."

Nasbah came toward Russell and Junior. "Russell Tallman?" she asked. "Which one of you is Russell Tallman?" Russell shook her hand and said, "This is Junior Snake."

"How did you recognize us?" Junior asked.

"You're the only Indians here," Nasbah smiled.

Junior looked around the crowded area and found that Nasbah was right.

Jonnie Navajo now extended a hand. Nasbah introduced Russell to him in Navajo. Both Junior and Russell looked him over quickly and thoroughly, noting his long, tied hair, the wide-brimmed felt hat with the silver band, the turquoise chunks at his earlobes, and the red, earth-colored moccasins.

Nasbah said to Junior, "He says you're very tall." The old man had examined Russell and Junior just as carefully as they had done to him. With that introduction, Russell and Junior collected luggage and led the way to the parking lot.

The old man followed slowly, observing everything and everyone minutely. Outside, he put a hand in the air and his fingers felt it. The air was heavy and slightly damp. It was late afternoon and would be twilight in about an hour.

Jonnie Navajo seemed to be enjoying this particular experience, the attention he received as he made his way to the car. He was in no hurry to get to it and took his time walking through the parking lot. Russell and Junior were slightly amused by the awed passers-by, who stopped beside the old man momentarily to have a good look at him before going on their way.

A few minutes later, when everyone was settled in the car, Nasbah asked about Willie.

"He expects you in the morning, but if you like and if we have the time, we can go over there later this evening. It's quite a distance from here and he can't have visitors after eight. Willie thought his grandfather might be tired. I'll take you over to Willie's apartment now, but Junior's folks are visiting here from Oklahoma, too. They just arrived today. They're old people, too, like your grandfather there. They thought you might want to have a nice big meal with us this evening. After the meal, I'll take you home," Russell said.

Nasbah translated what Russell had said. The old man watched motels and restaurants go by his window. He listened to Nasbah, and with a pleased gleam in his eyes, nodded his head.

Nasbah laughed and said, "Thank you. We would like to eat with you. My grandfather tried to eat on the plane, but the food was too strange. He doesn't eat much, and he said the coffee was too strong and bitter. He is careful with himself, as you can see."

She had barely finished talking when the old man spoke again.

Nasbah said, "He wants to know to what people you belong? He also asked how far it is to the ocean?"

On the way to Willie's apartment, Russell and Junior gave separate accounts of their personal and tribal histories for Jonnie Navajo's benefit. Junior also told the old man about Wilbur and Anna. In turn, the old man, through Nasbah, identified himself with four sacred mountains and many extended kin who for the most part were scattered throughout Navajoland, all except for Willie. Nasbah also explained that this was her grandfather's first flight, causing Russell and Junior to share the old man's laughter and thoughts regarding such a means of travel. Nasbah summed up his thoughts by saying, "These white people weren't the first people to travel through the sky. The holy people accomplished that, but they traveled on the rainbow."

At Willie's apartment, Russell waited while Nasbah and her grandfather freshened up and inspected and familiarized themselves with the apartment before whisking them away to his place. By now it was twilight, and on the way out of the apartment, Nasbah said to Russell, "Grandfather says we'll wait until morning to see Willie. He understands that it is some distance to the hospital and that visiting hours are set at certain times. Willie is okay, though?" She wanted reassurance from Russell.

He answered with a grin. "Willie's going to feel great tomorrow with you folks here. And yes, he's definitely better now." He avoided Nasbah's searching eyes.

"Well, that's what I wanted to know. I called him at the hospital yesterday evening. He sounded better than the earlier times when I spoke to him," she said.

When the group finally arrived at Russell's place, it was nearly 7:00. The apartment smelled of cooking. Russell made hurried introductions to everyone from across the room and then showed Nasbah the phone. "Why don't you and your grandfather call Willie and say hello? He'll sleep better knowing you arrived in Washington safe and sound. And then you two can relax for the rest of the evening, too," he suggested. Russell wrote a number down and handed it to Nasbah.

"Sonny," Anna said, "someone called you today. Erleen wrote it down." Erleen's scribble was on one of the grocery sacks. Russell read the message and put the sack aside.

The largest table in the room, which Russell seldom used to eat on, was set with dishes, cups, and silverware. Junior and Russell washed up for the meal, while Nasbah and her grandfather took turns speaking into the phone. Both of them beamed at each other as they talked to Willie, speaking only in Navajo.

When they had finished, they took their seats at the table. Jonnie Navajo was seated beside Wilbur. Anna was next to Wilbur and Erleen, then Junior sat beside Russell, with Nasbah on the other side of Russell.

Jonnie Navajo now extended a hand to Wilbur, Anna, and Erleen as in the custom of his people. He did not shake their hands, but merely touched them. Nasbah elaborated on her grandfather. "My grandfather is known as Jonnie Navajo. I am Nasbah, and we are from Red Point, Arizona. We have come to this place to see my cousin-brother, Willie Begay, who, we understand, works with Russell. Willie is now in the hospital over here. We have traveled many miles to be with him."

Wilbur interrupted her. "He don't talk nothing but his own language?"

Nasbah said, "That's right. There are many of our people who still speak only one language."

Anna said, "Oh, my, honey, it's all right. Don't worry. Me and Wilbur don't mind old peoples like that. Wilbur talks to lots of old peoples anyway, even if he don't know their tongue."

As Anna told this to Nasbah, Wilbur touched Jonnie Navajo's shoulder and pointed to himself and Anna, then wiggled his hand in a wavy line over the floor. Once more he pointed at himself and wiggled his hand in a wavy line over the floor. Jonnie Navajo smiled broadly. He understood perfectly what Wilbur said, that Wilbur and Anna were Snakes.

Erleen told Nasbah about the Snakes' arrival in Washington and of their long drive from Oklahoma. She concluded by saying, "We are lucky to be able to stay with Russell for a night or two. Do you know anyone else here in this town?"

Nasbah explained that this was their first trip to Washington and that no other acquaintances of theirs lived here either. She added, however, that they did know someone who came here often. She looked at Russell. "Did Willie tell you that Grandfather, Willie, and I are working with David Drake on his Navajo history?"

"No," answered Russell. "But to be truthful, I don't know David Drake either."

"You don't?" asked Nasbah in surprise. "I thought you knew him. He comes here often. A bad thing happened to him the last time he was here. That is what he told us."

"What was that?" Russell asked.

"He said his sister died here in an accident that he didn't know too much about. Willie told us that this woman had seen people before she died—Indian people who were already dead."

Russell pushed his food away. "Is that so?" he exclaimed. "That wouldn't be Wurly, would it? Jean Wurly?"

"I don't know her name, but David was very saddened by his sister's illness and death. From what we understand, she had seen these awful things for several months, and then she died."

Russell shook his head. "Yes, that is what I have heard, if she is the same woman."

Anna was aware that Wilbur had lifted his head to hear this new information. Wilbur was also trying to recall in detail what Russell had told him a few weeks back, in Oklahoma, about some Navajo Indian man who was in trouble over here in D.C.—he had some "mind trouble," Wilbur surmised. That man's name was what? Willie Begay? Did Sonny say the name? Did he say *that* name? Wilbur turned to the old man on his right and now completely understood why the old Navajo man had traveled this far. Wilbur nodded to himself as all the bits and pieces fell into place.

"What kind of thing are you working on with this Drake fellow? Is he any good? Does he know much about what he's doing?" Russell asked.

Nasbah phrased the question into Navajo for her grandfather and replied, "Grandfather says Drake knows as much as the next white man."

Wilbur grinned and then nudged the old man. They smiled broadly at one another.

"Actually, Russell, Grandfather has Drake working for him, too. It's interesting that this arrangement has worked out. Because this white man is a researcher and a historian, Grandfather has given him a special research project." Everyone at the table listened. What would an old man like Jonnie Navajo want from this white man?

"Many years ago, about one hundred and fifty years ago, one of my grandfather's ancestors was stolen from its family. It was a baby girl who was stolen by slave-raiders, and she happened to be a twin. My grandfather has asked this white man to track down this little girl. Grandfather is interested in what happened to her and is a historian himself. He knows that Navajo captives were stolen and sold in Colorado, New Mexico, and Utah for several generations. Drake is looking through the records for us in New Mexico and later he will even look here in Washington. Grandfather understands that there are many records about the Navajos here, and other things that originated with our people and other tribes. This is what Willie said. Is it true?" Nasbah asked. She stared at Russell.

Wilbur did, too.

Russell responded, "Well, yes, in a way it's true. Of course, there are many documents about almost all the tribes, but in order to sort these things out, much preparation and knowledge is needed before the records can begin to be examined. I hope Drake can find the information for you or at least help you out a little. Willie hasn't talked with me about this. It does sound interesting, I'll admit. I know a little something about the history myself. Navajos, Apaches, and Pueblos weren't the only ones stolen. This happened to several tribes. The slave-raiders were several groups of people. Some tribes even dealt in slavery themselves."

Nasbah's grandfather now spoke briefly to Nasbah. She said, "Grandfather has discussed some of Willie's work and training here in D.C. with him. In a way, Grandfather has come here for two reasons. First of all, to help Willie, and second, to see for himself what is here that came from the People. Grandfather is not concerned with getting these things returned to the People, for that is quite a major undertaking and involves many things. No, as I said before, he is a historian, one of our people's historians. He does not read or write, but he has knowledge that covers many generations of our people. He is also a *haataalii*. You know what that is, don't you?" she asked, staring at each face around the table.

Russell nodded. Junior wasn't sure. Wilbur and the others were interested.

"He is a singer, a medicine man, and a practitioner of half a dozen ceremonies. Again, this is one of the reasons Willie has asked him over here."

Junior spoke up, "Well, Nasbah, my daddy sitting over there is one of those people, too. Maybe he don't do exactly the same things as your grandfather, not being from the same people, but Daddy is one—we don't call them that, though—and my mama sitting across from you is also a medicine woman."

Nasbah gave her grandfather this information. Jonnie Navajo looked at Wilbur and Anna thoughtfully and nodded his head up and down.

Junior continued. "We're out here on a sightseeing visit like Erleen said. Daddy and Mama have both been here to D.C. before. Daddy has helped out these white researchers several times, trying to give some advice and guidance on the Indian artifacts that the white people keep here in the different institutions."

Nasbah translated and then asked, "My grandfather wonders what your father thinks about this situation."

Everyone looked at Wilbur. Jonnie Navajo kept eating. He was hungry.

Wilbur answered, "Ahm. Well, little girl, ain't easy to say. They's a whole lotta pieces here. I been out here lotta times. Can't figure everything out yet—probably can't be done. Some things is pretty plain to see. Maybe you and this old man right here is going to see that, too. Then, other things ain't so easy to see—they hide from us peoples."

The group finished the meal and Erleen poured coffee for everyone.

"Well, what do you say we all go do some sightseeing tomorrow, after you've had a chance to take care of your business with Willie?" Junior asked Nasbah. "We'd be glad to have you and your grandfather tag along. We'll do it in the afternoon sometime."

Nasbah talked with her grandfather and he agreed to the sightseeing in the afternoon. Wilbur wanted to talk more seriously with the old man. Again, he touched the old man's shoulder, and indicated that they should move from the table to the couch. Jonnie Navajo stood and stretched and told Nasbah that he had enjoyed the meal very much. Nasbah followed Wilbur and her grandfather.

At the table, Junior watched Wilbur and Jonnie Navajo and asked, "What'd I tell you about old folks like that? Daddy can talk up a blue streak with man, wind, or stone, you name it!"

The doorbell rang. "Kind of an odd time for company," Russell said, looking at his watch. It was 7:45.

Erleen answered the door, and stepped back to call, "Russell, you have some company." In the doorway stood two people, a man and a woman. It took Russell a minute to recognize Donald Evans. It had been months since he'd last seen him, and Donald's appearance here was totally unexpected. Both Wilbur and Jonnie Navajo turned to momentarily look at the visitors curiously. Donald looked at the elder men and nodded in greeting. The two elders then lost interest in Donald and turned away.

"Well, this is a surprise," Russell said. "Are you lost, or have you come to pay me a visit on purpose?" He grinned, and Donald felt less guilty about intruding here this evening. Elaine liked Russell immediately.

"Good evening, Russell," Donald said. "Please forgive us for this intrusion. I called earlier. I wouldn't have the audacity to show up on your doorstep if it weren't important. May we please have a couple of minutes of your time?"

Russell invited the two visitors inside. "So that was you who called?

Well, relax, Evans," he said. "I don't know you very well, but well enough to know that you mean exactly what you say. Come on in. If you don't mind that fact that I have other company this evening, then I'll be glad to talk to you."

"Well, we could come back later this evening if necessary," Donald said.

"That's no good either. I'll have company for a few days."

"I see," Donald said, and gently pushed Elaine into the apartment. "This is Elaine Mintor, Russell," he said.

Russell guided Donald and Elaine into the apartment and said to his other guests, "Don't mind us, folks, I'll be with you in a minute." Then he gave his attention to Donald and Elaine. There was no place to sit. "Do you mind sitting on the floor?" he asked. "It looks as if all the chairs are taken."

The three of them sank down on the wooden floor, side by side, and leaned against the wall. Russell was on one side of Elaine. "What's on your mind, Evans?" he asked.

Erleen brought two cups of coffee and handed them to Donald and Elaine.

Very quickly, and with some embarrassment, Donald quietly explained the nature of his visit. He stated that he had already been visited by George Daylight, and George had mentioned his concern that perhaps suicides and apparitions were mysteriously linked together in the building where Donald worked. Further, Donald admitted, George's concern had made little sense and had little meaning for him at the time George had presented his case. But in the interim, Donald, on his own, had proceeded to do some investigation into this possibility and had found, to his amazement, that George might be on the right track. Donald stopped just short of telling Russell anything more and waited for Russell's response.

"So?" was Russell's only response. "So?"

Elaine squeezed Donald's arm. He had no choice but to continue. "George warned me specifically of one of these 'ghosts'—a man, a tall, violent man. He said that others had seen this man. I didn't believe him, of course. How could I? It all sounded too preposterous!" Donald sighed.

"So?" Russell commented again.

"Damn it, Russell," Donald said. "I saw him. I can't believe it myself, but I did see him!"

"Where was this?" Russell asked with interest. "What happened?"

Donald told the whole story to Russell. He ended by saying, "Now, what do I do? How do I handle this? I'm at a complete loss." He downed the remainder of his cold coffee and threw up his hands.

Russell quietly stroked his chin. Finally he said, "Are you asking for my help?"

Donald was exasperated. "Of course I'm asking for your help! Why else would I be here? Can you help?"

Russell looked from Donald and Elaine to the others around the room. Wilbur was still conversing with the old man and Nasbah, and Anna had joined them. Erleen and Junior kept bumping into each other in the tiny kitchen area.

"You know, Evans, you may have come at the only time that I can offer some help—the only time. But it won't be me who will help you or advise you. It will be that old man over there." Russell pointed at Wilbur.

"What?" Donald asked. "That old man? What can he do?"

It was Russell's turn to sigh. "The thing is, though," he said, "*you* must ask him." He fixed Donald with a burning glare.

"Can't you do it, Russell?" Donald pleaded. "He doesn't even know me. Why should he do it for me?"

"How bad do you want help?" Russell asked.

Donald thought briefly of Geoffrey. Even Jean Wurly's face flashed before him for an instant. "Okay, Tallman," he said. "Okay."

25

ALEXANDRIA, VIRGINIA

OCTOBER 1969

NASBAH and her grandfather woke early in the morning. Actually, the old man had made a lifetime habit of rising before dawn. Now he waited patiently for the morning light, watching it spread through Willie's apartment from the slats of the venetian blinds. Last night Russell had given Nasbah a schedule of buses, with directions to his office. Shortly after sunrise, Nasbah and the old man would set out to meet him. Because Russell understood how easily the two might become lost, he'd also given her a telephone number for just such an emergency. Now, after fixing her grandfather a cup of weak coffee and a bowl of sweet cereal, Nasbah helped him put on a jacket, and they ventured out to learn all about the transit system.

There were several people at the bus stop when Nasbah and her grandfather arrived, but this group all rose at once and boarded two buses that stopped for a second and then left. When the next bus pulled over, Nasbah asked the driver if this bus went to Washington. He answered no, but pointed to another bus, cruising toward the stop. Nasbah's grandfather by then had claimed a place on the bench next to an odd assortment of people who had gathered while Nasbah had questioned the bus driver. When the appropriate bus pulled over, Nasbah grabbed her grandfather's hand and pushed him up the steps.

The bus was nearly full. All the passengers stared at Nasbah and her grandfather. Nasbah smiled at one or two people, but they didn't return her smile, just a cold, fish-eyed stare that stayed on her and the old man. Nasbah pushed her grandfather to the only seat available, while she grabbed a strap that hung from the bus ceiling above the center aisle. There were several passengers standing in the aisle, several of whom now released the overhead straps to get off the bus, Nasbah presumed, as the bus neared the curb.

Nasbah wasn't exactly sure where or when to change buses. Russell had said to change twice. She leaned over the seat in front of her grandfather to ask an elderly woman where they should change. The woman looked at Nasbah coldly and turned away, refusing to answer. She totally ignored Nasbah.

Then Nasbah felt her grandfather tug at her. An oriental man with thick blue-black hair stood beside her grandfather. "Need some help?" he asked with a smile. Nasbah smiled gratefully. She handed him the bus number she needed. The bus stopped again. The passenger next to her grandfather left. In fact, the whole bus emptied. Nasbah sat down beside her grandfather, and the oriental man sat across the aisle. He wrote something down on the paper.

"You'll have to get off in about ten minutes—here." He tapped the paper. "It's downtown. Then switch to a D.C. bus." He wrote again.

Nasbah thanked him. "We're new here."

"You don't say," he said and laughed. He was very friendly and open. In the next ten minutes, he gave his entire history. He was from Japan, but had arrived in the United States many years ago. He had no wife at present, but had three children. One of them lived in Washington with him. When he tired of talking about himself, he began to question Nasbah about her grandfather.

Jonnie Navajo was intrigued by this stranger. The oriental man pointed to the old man's bracelets and rings. He even lifted one of the old man's feet to examine a moccasin. Nasbah wasn't one to talk much, but she did return smile for smile. "This is your stop," he finally said as he pulled the cord and the bus slowed.

Nasbah and her grandfather stepped off the bus to find themselves swallowed up by another crowd. One, then two buses, pulled up along the curb, but these weren't what they wanted. Her grandfather stood beside her, trusting her completely to guide and speak for him.

They stood on the corner for another fifteen minutes before the bus arrived. By then, Nasbah had become worried, fearing that they had missed it. Nasbah was the first person on, checking with the driver to be certain that they were on the right bus. As she pushed her grandfather to a seat right behind the driver, she asked the driver to please let them know when and where they should get off to meet the next bus.

They rode for another twenty minutes, and when Nasbah and the old man were the last two passengers, the driver parked in a long row of buses and pointed to a single bus parked about a half a block away.

"That's the one you want. It'll leave in about ten minutes," he said, glancing at his watch. "Better git on over there now. It fills up fast. Then you goin' to have to stand. Might be that old man don't want to stand."

Nasbah translated for her grandfather, and the two of them cut across the street. Nasbah ran ahead, claimed a place in line, and pulled her grandfather into it when he reached her. They would have seats.

The bus was packed. Still the passengers kept climbing aboard. There were businessmen and businesswomen, tourists, hippies, and foreigners. For the first time that morning, both Nasbah and her grandfather could enjoy this new adventure.

Behind them a large woman with a painted face spoke loudly. Her bright pink lips clashed with her orange hair. She was evidently describing the sights to a visitor, a black man with dark glasses and ringed fingers. Across the aisle from Nasbah sat two Indian women in bright saris. Gold bordered their dresses and the bright fabric covering their heads. Nasbah's grandfather tried to turn around to see who else was on the bus, but by now the aisle was filled with passengers who blocked his view.

The bus began to move away from the curb, and the orange-haired lady behind them started to point out and describe landmarks along the way. Nasbah tried to listen, but the constant stop and go of the bus and the flurry of departing and boarding passengers didn't permit her to hear much. Only the mention of the Kennedy Center and the Lincoln Monument made her realize that her and her grandfather's destination must be near. Russell had told her that.

Traffic was heavier too. In fact, the four lanes of traffic came to a complete stop in some places. Long rows of buses honked impatiently, and lines of cars stretched for several blocks in front of them. Nasbah and the old man could see that the bicyclists were the only ones making progress now. They bravely darted in and out of the lines of cars and other vehicles.

Nasbah then heard the orange-haired woman mention "the White House," and she turned to see where she was pointing, off to the left, up ahead. Nasbah could see only an iron fence, but a crowd of tourists along the fence did seem to indicate that there was something behind it. Slowly, the traffic crawled. Pockets of tourists occasionally brought all the traffic to a standstill before the bus reached its final destination. Along the sidewalks, Nasbah and the old man could see vendors on each block with carts or trucks of food or drink. There was a rapid pace to the flow of the crowds, too. The old man pressed against the window to stare at the people outside. Every kind of people on the earth must be represented here!

The bus finally stopped. The driver parked and at the same time said to Nasbah, "This here is the place you all want. Get on off now!" The bus parked behind several others. Nasbah and her grandfather were not quick enough to get up into the aisle before all the other passengers surged toward the nearest door. They were the very last to climb off the bus.

Jonnie Navajo's moccasined feet made their way down the Washington street, which was made of red brick. People sat on the curbs and on the steps of massive buildings that lined the street. Pigeons cooed at the tourists and flew from the street to the steps, picking up the crumbs left behind by the ever-moving crowds.

Nasbah took her grandfather's hand and guided him from the nearby crowd that seemed ready to engulf them. She pointed to a place on the steps of one of the buildings that two people had just vacated, and her grandfather sat down in the crowd of strangers already claiming places there. Everyone around them spoke languages other than English. This wasn't noticeable to Jonnie Navajo, but it troubled Nasbah for a moment. She looked around at the exotic group on the steps, and with a smile, realized that she and her grandfather fit right into this varied group of people.

"Grandfather," she said, "there is every kind of people here."

"Yes," he answered, "it's true. Perhaps there are some Navajos, too, besides us." He smiled, and Nasbah smiled too.

"There aren't any Navajos here, Grandfather," Nasbah said, "but there are other Indians. See?"

Russell and Junior Snake were walking toward them, but they did not see Nasbah and her grandfather. "Russell!" Nasbah yelled and waved.

In a few minutes, Russell and Junior reached them. "I was worried about you two. I thought that maybe you had some problems getting here. Me and Junior came to look for you. We've been walking back and forth on this street for about twenty minutes."

"What time is it?" Nasbah asked.

"Almost 10:00," Russell answered. "Junior is going to drive us down to the hospital, but his car is parked about two blocks from here. Parking spaces are hard to come by. Cost damn near a hundred dollars a month! Hope you don't mind walking a couple of blocks."

Nasbah explained all this to her grandfather, and then Russell and Junior led the way to the parking lot. "Grandfather says that it seems that we have seen every kind of people today," Nasbah said to Russell.

He answered, "That's what Junior was saying. I guess every people in the world are here today. Hey, does your grandfather want a drink?" he asked.

They were standing beside a vendor with a big umbrella. "Orange," answered Nasbah. Russell purchased orange juice for everyone, and they continued walking toward the parking lot. "Hey, Junior," he said after awhile, "what say we wait here for you and you bring the car over. Heck, it's just a block from here."

"Yeah, okay," Junior said, and went on.

In a few minutes, a car appeared beside them, and the group was on the way to the hospital. In the car Nasbah asked, "How far is the ocean? I must get some ocean water for my grandfather before we leave."

"It ain't that far. Maybe we can drive over there, Russell?" Junior volunteered. Russell nodded. "If everything works out, why not?"

Privately, Russell wasn't sure that everything was going to work out. He hadn't talked to Wilbur yet about Donald's request. Donald was going to have to ask for help from Wilbur himself, but Russell could discuss it with the old man beforehand. The only thing was that back in Oklahoma, Wilbur was pretty adamant about leaving things alone. For this reason, Russell was uneasy about how things were going to work out. He tried to pay attention to the conversation he now heard between Nasbah and Junior, but his heart and mind weren't in it. He was going to have to help Evans somehow in convincing Wilbur to step in and help Evans out. But the truth was, a lot of people could benefit from old Wilbur Snake's intervention. It might be hard to convince Wilbur, however. It might not even be possible.

"This it, Russell?" Junior asked. The group had arrived at the hospital. Russell nodded.

"I'll let you off here and go back and park the car. I'll just wait in the lobby for you," Junior said, and opened the back door for Nasbah and her grandfather.

Willie had watched the time all morning. When Nasbah and her grandfather entered his room, Willie positively beamed. "Where's Russell?" he asked.

"He's waiting in the lobby," Nasbah answered. Then she and her grandfather went to hug Willie.

Willie was so thin! Nasbah felt the bones in his fingers before she let his hand go. She allowed her grandfather to take the only chair in the room and she stood by the window.

"I'm so happy to see you," Willie said. "Did you have a good trip? What was it like flying through the sky?" The three visited for about a half an hour before the discussion finally came around to their reason for being there together today.

"Nasbah has informed me that you are not well, my grandson," the old man said.

"Yes, that is true, Grandfather," Willie said. "I don't think that I have been well for some time now. I don't know for certain just when this illness began, but it must have started shortly after I got here. I have never had these problems at home. I was well and my health was never a problem. Grandfather, I have lost some weight." Willie pulled on his hospital gown, and Nasbah winced at his shriveled body. "Sometimes I cannot eat. Whatever I eat does not stay in my stomach."

"What do the doctors here say this is?" asked Nasbah.

"Well, so far they haven't been able to say. But if you like, when the doctors come around again, we can all talk to them," Willie suggested.

"This loss of weight and not being able to eat, are these the main two signs of your illness?" the old man asked.

Willie stared out the window to the river. "I have bad dreams, Grandfather. I can't rest. It seems that my mind is always awake. It seems that my mind is always racing."

Willie was quiet after that. Nasbah and the old man were thoughtful. Russell peeked in the room. "How're you doing today, Willie?"

"Come on in, Russell. Thanks for bringing Nasbah and my grandfather over here. I don't know how I'm going to repay all your help. Maybe when I get out I can help you in some way," Willie said.

"When's that going to be?" Russell asked.

"Two days, possibly. Two days. I think by now they've come to the conclusion that the whole thing is in my mind. What do you think about that? Do you think I've imagined the whole thing, my weight loss, everything?"

"Well, hell," Russell said, "maybe just getting out of this damned place might perk you up. Right now, I just wanted to come in and tell Nasbah and your grandfather that we're going to be chased out of here pretty quick. It's almost noon. I can see to it that your folks come back this afternoon or this evening. I plan on showing them the sights around D.C. for awhile this afternoon. Is that all right with you, Willie?"

"Oh, yeah, I want them to see a little bit of D.C. besides just sitting here with me. Maybe this evening they can come back over here." Willie was tired. Just this visit had drained him.

Willie spoke to his grandfather, encouraging the old man to see the sights before going home. The old man nodded in agreement. With plans now made, Russell went to the lobby. Before the old man followed, he turned to Willie and said, "I do not doubt that you are seriously ill, my grandson. And I do not doubt that a prayer or sing of our people will aid you when you go home. It will, it always helps. When I return tonight, I will do what I can, although we are in this place." Nasbah followed the old man out of the room after he gave some instructions for his evening visit to Willie.

Junior chauffeured everyone back to Russell's apartment. The ride started quietly. Russell was preoccupied with how he was going to get Wilbur over to Donald Evans's office. He and Donald had decided that that was the best way to approach Wilbur. Perhaps going over there would help convince Wilbur of Donald's predicament.

Jonnie Navajo's thoughts were on Willie. The old man needed more information about Willie's behavior in the lat few months. He voiced his thoughts to Nasbah.

"Russell," she said, "my grandfather requests some information. He says that you have been with Willie often these last few months. He suggests that you may have noticed when he became ill, or how he has behaved in this period. Would you please share this with my grandfather?"

Russell didn't object. Pushing thoughts of Evans out of his head, he tried to remember just when Willie's troubles had begun. He said, "Maybe George would be better able to answer your questions, but he ain't here no more. He's gone back to Oklahoma. It was George who noticed that Willie wasn't himself at the beginning. I didn't really pay any attention back then. George and Willie had a couple of classes together and saw each other on a daily basis. At that time, they were both involved in research projects, and they both visited a number of museums, libraries, and archival centers together. George always felt that Willie's illness had something to do with their research. But he never said that in so many words. He just hinted at it."

Nasbah translated this for her grandfather and then asked, "What kind of research were they doing?"

"History," answered Russell. "Indian history. Anyway, by the time I realized that what George had been saying about Willie was true—that something was happening to Willie—everyone else saw it, too."

"What happened?" asked Nasbah.

"At first, Willie lost a lot of weight but gained it back very quickly. But right after that, his weight and health seemed to fluctuate. One day he was fine, the next day he was sick— back and forth, see? Willie didn't seem to worry about himself at that stage. A few weeks later, though, George mentioned to me several times that Willie was acting strangely. Willie had become absent-minded and sometimes incoherent, but these periods would pass, and Willie always returned to normal. But I guess that the situation was actually turning worse, not better. About a few weeks ago, George and I visited Willie at his apartment on a Sunday afternoon. Willie seemed okay when we got there, but while we were there, he literally went out of his mind. We actually lost him for a few hours. He simply was not in touch with reality at that point. He didn't even know that we were there. He might have hurt himself if we hadn't been there. He screamed and carried on, all in Navajo, and held his head like it was going to explode at any minute. George and I ended up tying him to the bed to keep him from hurting himself—or us!"

Junior looked at Russell in surprise. Russell saw the look and defended himself. "What else could we do? Allow him to wreck the apartment, or himself, or us? What if anyone else saw him like that? Believe me, if you'd been there, you would have done the same thing!"

Nasbah translated this for her grandfather. The old man was not shocked or surprised. He asked a question. Nasbah repeated it. "How long did this last, and what did you do to help him? You did try to help him, didn't you?"

Russell answered, "It lasted maybe five hours. George and I burned some cedar for him. That's how our folks handled these problems back home. Maybe it's not what your grandfather would have done, but it's the only thing we knew to do."

Nasbah spoke to her grandfather.

Russell continued. "And do you know that to this day Willie still doesn't remember the incident? That wasn't the only time Willie went out on us, though. There was another time, too. That's when Willie ended up in the hospital. I was back in Oklahoma then. George had been trying to get Willie to visit a doctor because of his consistent loss of weight and his very sensitive stomach. On this occasion, George happened to be with Willie. George said that Willie was fine one minute, and the next he was really out of it. Willie shouted about someone being in the room with them. Actually there were plenty of people in the room all right, because Willie and George were in a research area that's heavily used. But the person Willie was screaming about was someone that only he could see. In other words, Willie was screaming about someone that everyone else in the room knew was not there. They thought he was stark raving crazy. George took Willie to the hospital after that incident. But word about Willie's behavior got back to Willie's supervisor and his advisor at school. Willie was more or less advised to follow through on the tests that his doctor wanted to perform if he wanted to continue working and going to school."

Russell was through. Nasbah began to talk to her grandfather.

"Then George may be right," Junior said. "Maybe Willie did stumble into something, touch something that is kind of reaching back at him. Russell, things like that happen. Sometimes we can't just brush things off." That ended the subject of Willie's illness for the time being.

The afternoon tour of the city went quickly, much to everyone's surprise. Anna and Wilbur inspected each monument carefully, while Erleen remarked on Wilbur's previous disinterest in these things on the long drive to Washington. Anna touched and rubbed the marble and walked around each monument, thoroughly looking everything over. Erleen tried to explain what she could to Anna. "This is the George Washington Monument, Mama. You know who George Washington is, don't you?"

Anna stood looking skyward and asked, "Erleen, how come it comes to the top like that? What's that for? How come this pile of rocks is here anyway. I seen it before. I always ask Wilbur, I say, Old Man, how come these white peoples make a pile of rocks to George Washton, anyway? George Washton wasn't nuthin', Erleen."

There were several tourists around Anna and Erleen, and more than one arched their eyebrows at Anna's unflattering assessment of George Washington. Wilbur was nearby and saw this interest of the tourists in Anna and Erleen. He decided to turn on his hearing aid to hear what was being said.

"That no-good rascal, always lying to us like he did. Wilbur always forgive George Washton, no matter what George Washton did to us. Overlook George Washton, Wilbur told me." Anna would have continued, but Erleen brought a finger to her own lips, indicating to Anna that that would be enough.

"What's she talking about?" Erleen asked Wilbur.

"Well, what'd she say?" Wilbur asked. Erleen repeated everything to Wilbur. He smiled brightly. "Anna's right. Right 'bout George Washington, but she ain't talking about the one that's here. See, Erleen, you know how some of us peoples back home got white people's names? Well, she's talking about that George Washington back there. Ain't Anna's fault, really. These white peoples gave us those names anyhow. Had to live with that. She's just saying what's true."

Erleen firmly led Anna and Wilbur out of the growing crowd.

At the Lincoln Monument, Russell tried to fill in the old folks on written history, black and white history. Anna and Wilbur were polite, and they appeared to be listening. Nasbah herself was quite overwhelmed at being able to stand in front of Lincoln, and she translated Russell's history lesson to her grandfather.

Jonnie Navajo stroked his chin thoughtfully as he listened. He studied the crowd of tourists, noting some black faces and many white faces. He looked at Anna and Wilbur, their diminutive frames beside Russell and Junior. Then he looked back up at Lincoln's sculptured features, the sunken eyes staring out into space.

"Slaves?" he asked Nasbah. "This man is the one who freed the black slaves? What about the Indian slaves? Did he free them, too?"

"There wasn't supposed to be any more slavery after that," Russell answered. "I can take you to some of the places where the black slaves hid when they tried to escape from slavery before Lincoln set them free, if you would like to see these places. There are some sites nearby."

When no one responded, Russell walked back to the car. Behind him, Erleen snapped photographs of Nasbah with her grandfather under the imposing figure of Abraham Lincoln. Russell had decided that their next stop was going to be Donald Evans's office. But first he had to prepare the group for it. He looked back and found Erleen now snapping photographs of Anna and Wilbur. Finally, the group walked toward Russell. Junior spoke for all of them. "Russell, the old folks want to know where the Indian things are."

Russell smiled, looked at his watch and said, "You know, Junior, I was just going to suggest that our next stop be one of those places."

Donald Evans waited for his guests to arrive. After 3:00 one of the security guards called up to his office, asking for the necessary permission to issue visitor's passes to Russell's group. Donald heard them climbing the stairs.

Junior had to bend and duck into the doorway. Erleen, then Russell, followed him. Donald pointed to the chairs he had borrowed a few minutes earlier. Anna and Wilbur sat down to the right of Donald. Nasbah and her grandfather then entered the attic.

Nasbah took a chair beside Russell without hesitation, but Jonnie Navajo stood at the door momentarily and swept the room with a furtive glance. He saw first the tables of reconstructed pottery, then the shelves of prehistoric pots, vases, and ladles. On the other side of the room, he saw the metates and stone knives. He frowned and reluctantly took the empty chair beside Nasbah.

Russell now formally introduced everyone. He opened the conversation by telling Donald that the group was interested in seeing the collection housed in the attic. But before Donald had a chance to respond, Wilbur lifted a hand and held it in the air a minute to get Russell's attention.

Wilbur asked, "Sonny, we at the top of the building?"

Russell nodded.

Donald stood and pointed around the room. He said, "Well, as you obviously can see, we have some artifacts of prehistoric Indian origin. But before I show you the rest of the collection, I would like to briefly explain the nature of the collection. This museum has long been a repository. . . ."

Wilbur turned down his hearing aid. He'd decided not to listen. Jonnie

Navajo wasn't interested either in what the man said, and wouldn't have listened even if he'd known the language. The things in the room spoke louder to Jonnie Navajo than the man ever could. On the other hand, Erleen, Junior, Russell, and Nasbah carefully hung on to Donald's every word. Anna's eyes were on Wilbur.

Anna was getting old, Wilbur thought, seeing her in this light. He was getting old, too. He didn't have to look at himself to know it. He could feel it. Perhaps he had no personal power anymore. Perhaps Anna had no personal power anymore. He recalled her words about George Washington and smiled despite the place in which he now found himself. And what about the others in the room? Had they any power? The old Navajo man certainly had it, but his granddaughter? Junior? He was surely in his thirties by now. And Russell? The only one he could really count on here was Anna. He and Anna were the only two . . . and they were so old.

Evans was still talking. Words were pouring out of his mouth without an end. Wilbur could see them jump out like puffs of smoke. ". . . to preserve specimens of ancient and extinct Indian cultures," Donald ended. Wilbur didn't hear the words, but tried to clear the smoke from his eyes.

Jonnie Navajo was becoming impatient, or nervous, the longer he sat here. His moccasined foot tapped the floor twice. His fingers also tapped his thigh. Once more he looked around the room and into the corners of it. He feared the worst.

Finally, Donald stood and led the group to one of the cabinets and pulled open the bottom drawer. Wilbur knelt down to look inside. Donald began to talk about the items in the drawer. The puffs of smoke from his mouth dropped into the drawer. Wilbur saw them land on the dull, white skulls. Jonnie Navajo was leaning over Wilbur, peeking into the drawer, and when he saw the contents of the drawer, the old man raised a hand over his eyes involuntarily, as if to shield himself. Then he took several steps backward and stood for a moment. Wilbur's eyes followed him. The old man spoke to his granddaughter and then surveyed the room again.

Nasbah asked Russell in a low voice, "Has Willie been up here? My grandfather wishes to know." Russell said yes, but was distracted by Donald's comments about the items in the drawer.

Jonnie Navajo nodded his head vigorously when Nasbah gave him the answer. Now the old man understood everything. He understood Willie's illness. Wilbur watched him. Wilbur knew that the old man knew. Their eyes locked for a minute, and in this locking, they understood each other. Jonnie Navajo motioned at Wilbur Snake, and Wilbur Snake understood that the old man would not permit himself to stay in the room. Wilbur nodded.

"Nasbah," the old Navajo said. He pointed toward the door, and she went out with her grandfather. No one noticed that Nasbah and her grandfather had left the room except Wilbur and Anna. Nasbah closed the door to Evans's office and she and her grandfather sat together on the stairway. Her grandfather was quiet and thoughtful, and she left him alone.

Wilbur viewed the contents of the cabinets in the attic with the others in the room, and in this time, hundreds of thoughts raced through his mind. He didn't shut any of those thoughts out, but gave them free rein, and finally came up with an idea or two about this place that he hadn't had before.

Now, without advancing to the boxes and trunks in the back of the room, Donald retreated to his chair. When everyone else had also settled back down, Donald leaned toward Wilbur and said very tiredly, "I'm worried, Mr. Snake. That is why I visited Russell last night. Russell has advised me to discuss my troubled state of mind with you." Wilbur adjusted his hearing aid. He looked at Russell with a slight frown. Russell looked down at the floor.

Donald continued. "I've recently been advised by certain Indian people that it is this collection up here that has so powerfully affected my well being. At first I rejected this idea as preposterous, but I have since learned that in this building there have been many deaths of people who have worked with this collection. I think that I'm past the point of wanting to debate whether or not ghosts exist at all, or whether they exist here in the attic. Nor do I wish to discuss this collection, at least just yet. I'm simply not up to it. I know only one thing. I do not wish to become suicidal, or for my death to become the next. . . ." Donald looked at Russell, but Russell wouldn't say anything for him. Donald had to make the request himself.

"Mr. Snake, I understand that you might help me, if you would agree to it. Will you help me?"

Wilbur said, "Old mans don't know everything. But once in awhile, they can help if everyone's willing. Tell this old man something. A young man like you believe in anything yet?"

Donald hadn't expected this question. He nodded. "I believe in God, if that's what you mean."

Wilbur answered, "Old mans and womans likes to believe in lotta things. Guess beliefs wouldn't 'mount to much if what we believe didn't have to do so much with power, our power. . . . Overlook this old man who asks something like that. Had to be asked, 'cause you and me is different. Not in our skins, but in our minds."

26

WASHINGTON, D.C.

DONALD sat alone in the attic after his visitors left. Wilbur Snake had led them away. Snake had said that he had to think. That was all. He had to think. . . .

At this point, Donald wasn't sure whether Wilbur had agreed to help him or not. Donald had finally repeated his whole story, such as it was, to Wilbur. After Donald had told the story, Wilbur only shook his head and grunted. The other members of Wilbur's party had listened without comment or expression. Wooden Indians. It was strange. Strange that Donald found himself in this situation. Strange that he had no one to go to but *them*. In fact, *they* were strange—strange to take his word, his story, as fact like that, so readily and without question.

Now what? Russell had followed the others out of the attic, saying only "I'll get back to you, Evans." Donald found his jacket and wearily made his way to Elaine's place.

Much later that day, at Russell's apartment, Wilbur sat with his feet on the coffee table. Junior and Russell sat with him. Russell didn't want to press Wilbur for a decision regarding Donald, and so kept silent.

"When do you want to head back home, Daddy?" Junior asked. "We don't want to use up Russell's welcome."

Russell waited for an answer, too, but added sincerely, "You're always welcome here, Junior."

Wilbur answered, "That's what I've been thinking 'bout, Junior. I'd say day after tomorrow. Russell, Sonny, that all right with you?"

Russell nodded. Wilbur still hadn't said anything about Evans.

Junior continued. "I'd kind of like to drive to the nearest beach, Russell, to take that old Navajo man out there. He wants some ocean water. He's going to take it back to Arizona. I'd like to help him out with that if I can. He's on foot, no transportation. That be okay, Daddy?"

Wilbur agreed, then turned to Russell and asked, "Sonny, how 'bout that white man today? What do you have to say 'bout him?"

"I don't know him too well. I've talked with him only a couple of times. Old Man, I know that you don't have to help if you don't want to. It's up to you," Russell conceded.

"Truth be, I can't help him, Sonny. Fact is, he has to do it hisself. Sonny, that's what peoples don't understand, old peoples and young peoples, too. They don't believe it."

Junior said, "Will anything change because Daddy helps him out? Is he going to change the way he thinks or the way he is? Is he going to do anything about those things he's keeping in the attic up yonder?"

Russell sighed. "Nothing will change, Junior. You know it. I know it. What he is is forty years of thinking that way. It'd be unrealistic to expect too much."

"He's backed into a corner, ain't he? He don't know what's happening up there, and he don't really trust us, either. I'd sympathize with him, except for the fact that he's not even honest with us about what he's got up there. Maybe he thinks he can keep it hid. . . ." Junior said. Wilbur nodded.

"What do you mean?" Russell asked in surprise. "I thought he was pretty straight with us, showing us the collection so openly the way he did."

"Huh-uh," Wilbur grunted. "He ain't ready to show everything. Maybe that's why these things is showing theirselves. . . ."

"You don't believe what happened to him?" Russell asked in shocked surprise.

Wilbur nodded. "Aw, Sonny, it's one thing I don't question. It happened, all right."

"Well, then, I don't understand," Russell argued. "Junior said that Evans didn't tell the truth."

"He didn't," Junior said. "But he didn't actually lie, either. He just didn't say or show everything."

Russell thought about this and finally had to agree. There were the boxes in the back of the room, the trunk. . . .

"Don't matter to us, Sonny," Wilbur said. "Don't matter to us, 'cause me and Junior ain't the ones who's asking for help. 'Sides, me and Junior already heard 'bout what's at the back of the room."

"What *is* there?" Russell asked quietly.

Wilbur answered, "People. People like you and me."

"Spirit people?" Russell asked.

Wilbur nodded. "See, Sonny, some peoples think that it's the body of a man by itself what makes a man alive. But they's more to it. A big part of us peoples is something we can't even see, but it's the part that makes us peoples different from other peoples, the trees, the animals. Then, too, that unseen part is what makes peoples live, and be like other things what live. Old peoples say all living things is related to one another.

"When things die, Sonny, the unseen part of them separates from the side we see. We just see the side that dies.

"Anyway, Sonny, a lotta times—when a man's body rots away, or his heart don't pound no more—us peoples sometimes think that that man— his spirit, his memories—ain't there no more because his body died. The part of him we knew by sight is dead. But we're absent-minded too, and we forget that we ain't never seen all of that man in the first place. Sometimes we doubt it then, that that man's got two sides to him, the seen and the unseen. We doubt that there's anymore to his life than what we seen. You know, Sonny, sometimes too we can't see very good either—poor eyesight. We're pitiful, Sonny. We try to know the whole universe, but we set our minds when we're like pups and learn to see only certain things. Maybe 'cause us peoples is scared sometimes—scared to look for something more, but even more scared to find it and accept it.

"Now those peoples up in that building—the ones in the attic—can be looked at a lotta ways. We can say they's dead. We can say they's just bones or pieces of a man's hide. We can say they ain't no room for questions 'bout anything up there.

"Sonny, I can say it, but it ain't in me to think that way. A lotta old peoples thinks that nothing ever dies. Not the trees, not the grass, not the animals, not the people.

"These things is wondrous things, Sonny. When you and me talk 'bout how one thing lives in a certain way and dies in a certain way, and that's all they is to it, we make the mystery of that life into a tiny thing. It don't mean nothing then.

"Human animals, Sonny, is very strange. We're known to stalk and kill each other like our animal relations, yet we hold ourselves apart and over them. We don't claim kinship.

"A man's body is wondrous, too. Old peoples likes to think that it's holy, too. Any part of it stands for the whole . . . a hand, fingers, a breast, the hair. And the body itself—the blood, flesh, and bones—stands for the unseen part of the man. . .his memory, his mind, and his spirit. A man ain't fully a man without them.

"As pitiful as we human animals is, Sonny, we got power. In this way, we're just like our animal relations, because they got power, too, like the sun, the trees, and the wind. This power we got is to live. Our bodies is connected to that power just like the unseen part of ourselves is tied to it too.

"Sonny, say a man is killed or dies. We see his body killed or dying over there, Sonny. But we can't see the man's mind and spirit. We say, 'look here, here's a dead man'! All we can see is that the man don't move no more and we don't feel his heart pound, either.

"Aw, Sonny, when a man's heart don't pound no more, that man's dead. He ain't going to get up and talk to us no more. But his dead body lying there ain't all they is to it. The man lived! He drew breath from the wind! He stored memories! And his mind, spirit, body, and power to live belonged to hisself alone. Us peoples have to face ourselves sometimes. This is what we are. It's the truth, Sonny."

Russell was quiet when Wilbur finished. After a few minutes, he asked, "What did you mean about Evans hiding the truth?"

"That man has to know ever thing that's stashed in the attic. He can't lie to hisself. The pieces of flesh, hair, and bone, . . ." Wilbur said. He looked at Russell.

"Yes," Russell said, "but he doesn't think of these things the way we do. To him, they are no more than pieces of flesh, hair, and bone. They might as well be of animals because it's doubtful that he can tell the difference between animal flesh, hair, and bone and that of human beings. There's no differences, or likenesses, to him." Russell realized regretfully what this admission really meant.

Wilbur frowned and said, "Then I can't help, Sonny. Can't help someone like that. Truth is facing ourselves, and seeing what we is, and swallowing the taste of it. We have to know this to live and to keep on living. That man needs to taste this more than we do right now."

"Why?" Russell asked. He felt like a little boy in school who was failing a very critical test.

Wilbur let out a whole chest full of air in a very tired sigh. "Tell him, Junior," Wilbur said and left the two of them alone for a minute. Across the room, Anna poured a soft drink for Wilbur.

Junior said, "Black Bear, all this is Evans's show, so to speak. What happened, happened to him. It's in his mind, his experience. He's the one who was opened up to it."

Russell was more deeply puzzled than before. "But you said that you believed him, that his story really happened."

"Damn, Back Bear," Junior said, "*everything* is in our minds. The possibilities and the impossibilities. . . . Our minds are the boundaries of our physical selves. Don't you get it?"

Russell shook his head. "Not really."

Junior could see the frustration on Russell's face. He said, "Growing up and watching Daddy live the way he does, I had a chance to see him do many things. In every case, the people who came to Daddy for help had to help themselves as much or more than the old man helped them. They had to participate, Black Bear. What Daddy's getting at is this— can he count on Evans to help himself if the time comes?"

Russell didn't know how to answer. He was silent.

"Daddy says that certain things can be overcome, Black Bear, but there's two things that can't be. The first is our own death, or passing away of life from our bodies, and the second is anything that is more powerful than we are. Because of this, Daddy says that the passing of life from our bodies must be faced truthfully. By this he means that we need to look inside our own minds and face the vastness of our minds, if even for a second, to get a real perspective on the mystery of the universe and the meaning of our lives. Daddy also thinks that each man's power wanes and grows according to the nature of the man. And because of this, each of us is responsible for our own personal power. I'm not talking about dollar power, or power in the electrical outlets, Black Bear, . . ." Junior smiled.

"Yeah, I know," Russell sighed.

"What Daddy is probably wondering about your man Evans is whether or not he has power of something he can draw strength from."

"Damn, Junior, why does it all have to be so complicated? Why can't life be simple?" Russell asked.

"You don't mean that, Russell, and if you do, it's time to go home. Touch the earth and taste it again. We live in a mysterious world. You and me ain't going to change it—it ain't within our power." Junior chuckled. "But we're going to survive until our time is up, and in the end, we'll be grateful for the time we were given to truly appreciate the mystery of our minds and the universe. That's old age, Russell. Daddy says that's old age."

Russell nodded but frowned. He said, "Many people would object to everything you've just said. I guess it's the old man's philosophy, huh? They would find that way of thinking too frightening and threatening, Junior. There are people who work diligently toward a very structured world. Forget the universe—the idea of a 'mysterious' universe would be too out of control. A lot of people *want* everything to be comprehensible and digestible, no mystery to being born, living, and dying."

"Yeah, I know," Junior agreed, unruffled, "but we ain't a lot of people. We ain't never been a lot of people. Our people have always been just a few."

"The other side of the coin, Junior," Russell said, "is that the old man's philosophy ain't viewed as an open-minded one or as a mind-expanding one, either. It's viewed as one bordering on simple-mindedness because it won't conform to anything that is comprehensible to anyone outside of people like ours."

Again Junior agreed. "I'd be a fool not to know that, Russell. Daddy knows too well, too. But our experiences—the experiences of our people and the experiences of other people— have been different. That's why we are what we are."

Wilbur sat beside Russell again. Russell didn't notice him until Wilbur handed glasses filled with a soft drink to him and Junior.

Wilbur wore a broad smile. "Junior," he said, "Erleen told me what Anna had to say 'bout George Washington downtown today."

Junior smiled too. "Did you enjoy yourself today, Daddy?" he asked.

Wilbur nodded. "I seen all these things before, but it was fun to carry that old Navajo man 'round with us. I feel like I knowed him a whole lifetime."

Junior had left Nasbah and her grandfather at a bus stop, with Nasbah insisting that the two could find their way back to Alexandria. Russell had reluctantly agreed to let them try and felt better about it after talking to the bus driver and learning that they would only make one bus change. The driver had promised Russell that he would personally watch out for them.

"I think that old man is going to decide what to do about Willie tonight," Russell said. "They'll probably go back to Arizona within a couple of days, too. I don't know if Willie will go with them. He didn't take any classes this term, but he still has his job to think about. I hope he gets better soon."

Wilbur remembered how the old Navajo had lifted his arm against the things in the attic and how he had backed slowly away. Wilbur had not as yet met Willie.

"So what do you want to do, Daddy?" Junior asked. "About Evans?"

Wilbur's eyes were on Russell, but his thoughts were elsewhere. "We'll go up there, Sonny," Wilbur finally said. "Tomorrow night. To the attic. I doubt Evans can be helped. It's up to him. But we'll see. . . . Call him and tell him that we have to be in the building purty late tomorrow night."

Russell nodded, simultaneously relieved and disturbed that old Wilbur Snake was going to look into this situation after all.

"Now how 'bout that old Navajo man?" Wilbur asked Junior. "Why didn't you take him to the hospital tonight?"

"They went over there in a taxi. I think they wanted to be alone with Willie."

At the moment, Nasbah sat with her grandfather in Willie's room. It was dark outside the window. Willie lay on the bed and listened to his grandfather.

In Navajo, the old man said, "Grandson, we have seen *Washingdoon* today. We saw many things."

Nasbah nodded and told him of their visit to the Washington and Lincoln monuments.

"We also saw some things from Indian people, though nothing from our people. Much was made by the Anasazi, however," Nasbah added.

"Where was this?" Willie asked, and Nasbah explained everything to him. When she was done, Willie asked his grandfather, "What did you see?"

"Enough," answered the old man. "Enough."

The three were quiet for a minute or two before the old man asked Willie, "Did you make the arrangements I requested?"

Willie nodded. "The man who was in the next bed was released earlier this evening, so we are alone. And I explained to the nurse that we must not be interrupted for a few minutes, and she was agreeable. She is the nurse who was in here when you arrived tonight. I'll call her now if you're ready."

The old man nodded.

The nurse came in and looked questioningly at Willie, and then suspiciously at the old man. After a second she asked, "Do you want the door closed now?"

"Yes, please," Willie said. The nurse shut the door.

When she was gone, Willie sat up on the bed, and the old man pulled out a small bundle from under his jacket. He spread the contents of the bundle before him on the adjustable table beside the bed. Then he sat back down, advising Nasbah to turn out the light. The room was dark except for the soft light filtering up from the street lamps two stories below.

Jonnie Navajo began to speak in a sing-song voice. Eventually he became silent and lifted one or two of the items on the table. Finally, he asked Nasbah to turn on the light. The sudden brightness in the room made all of them squint.

The old man carefully rewrapped his belongings on the table and put them under his jacket. He leaned back in his chair and said, "Your illness has to do with something in the place where we were today. You had something that belongs there. It is part of a man. What is this thing?" The old man's eyes met his grandson's directly.

Willie shuddered involuntarily. "Yes, Grandfather," he admitted, "there is something that I came across by accident a few weeks back. Remember I told you that I was going to do all the research I could manage on our people? Well, I was looking at some of the Navajo jewelry and pottery that is kept here in this city. With this pottery and jewelry were pipes and other things. But for some reason, I was brought a scalp, Grandfather! I didn't ask for it and didn't even know they had one here. I didn't know what it was when it was brought to me. It was all wrapped up and when I opened it and it fell into my hands, then I saw what it was, and it was too late then. It was an entire scalp, with white hair, and the ears attached to it!" Willie rubbed his hands on his gown.

The old man nodded, not doubting after his experience today that this was possible. "Well, I suppose that is it, then," he said.

"Grandfather, I have thought about that scalp several times since then. Grandfather, you have often talked about past leaders of our people. Well, in my research, I learned that one of them, one of our most respected leaders, Narbona, was scalped by representatives of the American government near Sanostee, a little over one hundred years ago. That group of Americans had come to make a peace treaty with the Navajos. It is written that Narbona's scalp was carried back to *Washingdoon*. I do not know if the scalp that was brought to me could possibly be Narbona's or any one of a thousand other Navajo men whose ears were cut off and sold, as was the custom back then when slavery was being practiced and when a Navajo's ears meant a bounty. It could have even been White Sheep's if things had turned out differently. Whoever's scalp it is, the damage has already been done," Willie said. "George Daylight also told me before he left that there are dozens of pairs of ears in one of the buildings here. I haven't seen them, but he did."

Willie's grandfather sighed. Maybe he had seen them himself. The coils beside the desk? What were those things? The old man asked, "Where did these things come from? How did they get here?"

Willie answered, "Most of them were gifts to the government. Before the government received them, they were traded or bought and sold."

The old man looked at Nasbah and said, "You told me that that man we visited today, the one with the hollow eyes, put an end to slavery, huh? But I'm afraid that our people are still being bought and sold, even though they are dead—and have been dead for hundreds of years! Even worse, some of the people are not whole. They remain in bits and pieces, and yet these pieces are also being traded, bought, and sold, like so many sheep! When does it stop?"

Willie and Nasbah couldn't answer. The nurse opened the door then and peeked in at Willie. "Just a few more minutes," Willie said, and she disappeared.

The old Navajo said, "I will say a protection prayer now, and we will see whether or not it works outside the four sacred mountains. It won't hurt to say it." He began to pray an ancient prayer, in the custom of his people. It was a prayer for any one of the people who understood its age, its meaning, and the existence of such prayers and people.

When it was done, the old man said, "Grandson, you should have a ceremony for yourself on your return home. Then you can go forward with your life."

27

WASHINGTON, D.C.

THE group left Russell's apartment about 9:00. Junior drove them through the district, stopping a moment at the iron fence behind the White House and at the Capitol lit up by floodlights.

There were beggars in the street, which was otherwise fairly empty of traffic. One of the beggars came to the car holding out an open, shaky hand to Junior. The beggar was a white man wrapped in rags, and he had sores on his hands and face. Reaching through the window, Erleen put a couple of dollars in his hand. The man sniffled at her and walked out of the headlights of the car into the darkness.

Junior parked the car in the lot beside the building. It was the only time Russell had ever seen the lot so empty. Only three other cars were there.

The building was dark inside and out. Only the sidewalks around the buildings were lit in spots. Donald waited at the door with Elaine and a night security guard.

The security guard held a long flashlight, which he shined on Russell, Junior, Erleen, Anna, and Wilbur. Next he shined the light on the bundle that Wilbur carried. Russell thought he was going to ask them to open it, as was required with all articles taken into and out of the building in normal hours. Russell looked at Donald, and Donald shrugged. Next, the guard snapped the light off and led the way into the darkened building. He proceeded first to his security station, wrote the names of everyone in the group, and the time, and then unlocked one of the hallway doors leading to the elevator. The guard took the group to the top floor, where everyone followed him to another set of doors that eventually led to the attic. After unlocking the last set of doors, the security guard left the group to return to his station on the first floor. Donald thanked him, and the guard answered, "No problem. You'd be surprised at how many people here have odd working hours."

Donald climbed the steps to the attic first and used his own key to unlock the last door. He turned on the light and waited for the group.

Wilbur was slow, deliberately slow, and was the last to enter the room. Donald sat at his desk with Elaine beside him. Anna spoke to Elaine. "Honey, us peoples got to sit on the floor." Anna took off her coat and Wilbur handed her his jacket, which Anna put on Donald's desk. Wilbur went to the back of the room. "Come on back here," he said. "Pull these things outta here." He wanted the stack of boxes and the trunk moved.

Junior took off his jacket and picked up the trunk without too much effort and carried it to the front of the room. Russell followed him with the boxes. He made three trips.

Wilbur settled down on the floor, his back resting against the wall. Anna slipped off her old lady shoes and sank to the floor, at Wilbur's side. She pulled off her stockings, too. The others followed suit, except Elaine and Donald.

"Sit down," Wilbur said. "Over there." He wanted Donald to sit directly across from him. Donald sat with Elaine beside him. She pulled off her coat, trying to make herself comfortable.

By now it was well after 10:00. Junior glanced at his watch. Wilbur began to unwrap the bundle he had carried into the building. The outer wrapping he spread out neatly before him, and on top of this he set the second wrapping. Then he placed the items in a row. Donald studied the things in front of Wilbur. He had seen other things, similar to these, here in the collection. He had no idea what each was or the purpose of each. Wilbur asked for a glass of water.

"We'll have to go downstairs," Donald said. "I'll show you."

"Do you have a glass?" asked Junior.

"There's a plastic cup on the desk," answered Donald.

"Won't do. We need a glass," Junior said.

Donald stood up and led Junior down the stairs. "We can borrow one downstairs."

While they were gone, everyone sat quietly. Elaine felt out of place, although none of the group objected to her presence. To Russell she whispered, "I hope you don't mind that Donald asked me to come with him this evening. I wouldn't have missed it for the world," she said sincerely, with a look of eager anticipation.

Russell had never seen the woman before her appearance at his door. He was careful now. "It's not a party. . . ." he answered softly.

She grinned at him despite his words, and he frowned in return.

Junior carried a partly filled glass of water to Wilbur. Donald sat down again, but Junior stood. He asked Wilbur, "Do you want all the lights out?"

"Ain't no more lights in here 'cept those in the ceiling?" Wilbur asked Donald.

"There's a lamp on the desk. I think it's working."

"Turn that on," Wilbur said to Junior, "and turn ever thing else out."

Junior did as he was told and returned to the group after he closed the door to the room. The group sat in semi-darkness. The fluorescent beam of the desk lamp was vague behind the cabinets.

Donald could hardly see. Elaine nudged him with an elbow and grinned broadly at him. For some reason, that annoyed Donald and he pushed an elbow into her side, harder than he'd intended. She felt the jab and sobered.

In her heart, Elaine couldn't take this gathering very seriously, although her mind tried to rationalize her presence here. It was for Donald's sake. . . .

Donald himself couldn't help but be skeptical. There was no doubt in his mind that if such an extraordinary thing hadn't happened to him, and frightened him so damn bad, he wouldn't be here! Now, he had to see this evening through.

Anna noted Elaine's odd behavior, her light attitude about being involved in this. It was too early to make a judgment about this white woman, but Anna made a mental note to be cautious with Elaine. This white woman would not strengthen the group tonight, although she did complement the white man very well.

In Anna's eyes, the white man was frightened. Frightened of the group? Frightened of being here tonight? Frightened of that which he had already experienced? Frightened of the unknown? Anna didn't know. But he *was* here. That meant something.

In the dim lighting of the desk lamp at the far end of the room, everyone was a shadow. Across from Donald, Wilbur's frame was small and two-dimensional. Anna's was even smaller.

Wilbur was doing something with the items in front of him. Donald couldn't see clearly. Wilbur gave something to Anna, which she held in her lap. Wilbur held something up in front of him, at nearly eye level. It looked like the glass that Junior had borrowed from downstairs. Something covered the glass.

A few minutes passed while Wilbur continued to work with the things in front of him. Then he asked Junior, "Did you bring your own light?" Wilbur could see Junior nod.

"Now, us people's going to sit in the dark for a little bit. It's alright, though. Don't be scared," Wilbur said.

Anna could see Elaine grin from ear to ear. Erleen had been through this many times. She sat beside Anna, between Anna and Elaine. Erleen leaned her head back against the wall with her eyes closed. She was relaxed and prepared.

Russell had his legs crossed in front of him. He had taken off his boots and sat between Donald and Junior.

Junior was now standing, in stocking feet. He walked back to the lamp on the table. The room went black. Junior returned carrying a small flashlight in his hand. It emitted a soft, flickering, yellow circle of light barely four inches across on the floor in front of him. When he reached the group, he took his place beside Wilbur, swung the light around once on everyone, and then turned the flashlight off.

None of the group was able to see anyone else. Darkness was everywhere. Wilbur waited a minute for his eyes to adjust to it. He could feel Anna at his side, but couldn't see her at all. After a few seconds, he was able to identify where Junior was in relationship to himself. The darkness rustled loudly in front of him. He adjusted his hearing aid to be able to hear more.

"Now," Wilbur said, "don't be afraid."

Elaine and Donald had no idea what was happening. Elaine couldn't help but giggle and reach out to Donald. Her hand groped for him in the dark.

"Sit still," Wilbur said. "Don't move."

Elaine covered her mouth with her hand to keep from laughing out loud. Then a brush of air swooped past her. This surprised her and she stopped smiling. The door must have come open.

"I think the door is open, Donald," she said.

"Quiet," Wilbur said. "No matter what you see or hear, be quiet." Wilbur's voice was angry.

Now there was a loud rustling again in front of Wilbur, the same rustling that had been there earlier, but it was several feet away. He strained to listen.

Russell was tense. After the lights had gone out, he was sure that something was behind him, but he knew that everyone in the room sat in a circle facing each other.

Anna felt it before anyone, even Wilbur. She felt the motion of mass around them, and the presence of it. She was not surprised in the slightest. The mass was not visible, but was a stir in the darkness, and Anna said, "Old Man, Wilbur Snake, I'm thinking that something is here with me. I can see it now, Old Man," she said. "It's behind you. Poor thing. I feel sorry for it."

"What is it, Anna?" Wilbur asked. "Tell us what you see."

"It's a . . . a . . . I can't see, Old Man," Anna said. "Wait, it's a boy, just a little bitty boy."

"Let him go, Anna. Don't hang onto him," Wilbur said. "Anything else?"

Anna answered, "A man. I see him, he's with other peoples. You see them, Wilbur?"

Wilbur grunted.

"What do they want, Wilbur?" Anna asked.

"Nothing," Wilbur said. "They don't want nothing."

Donald didn't see anything. Neither did Elaine.

But Erleen could see the people Wilbur and Anna described. The lead man wore a hat of otter skin. That was something that Erleen recognized quickly. These people were of old—entirely of another time. They really were spirit people, wisps of their former selves. Erleen wondered if Junior could see them, too.

The temperature in the room changed. The mood, too, changed abruptly. Russell was now more sure than ever that something was behind him.

There was a shuffling sound and a swish, then a fumbling at the cabinets.

"Light," Wilbur said. "Hand it to me."

Junior put the flashlight in Wilbur's hand. Wilbur listened to the sounds, aimed the flashlight toward the sounds, and snapped the light on.

The light was on the figure's mid-section. He was naked. Wilbur moved the light up, over the broad and hard shoulders of the man, up to his face, which was turned at an angle away from them. His black hair was long with streaks of gray, and hung below the man's buttocks. His legs were slightly muscular with a thong of hide wrapped securely around one of his ankles. Wilbur held the light on the thong and the hide that trailed after the moccasined foot.

The figure took no notice of the light skimming over him, or of the group. He was very tall, about the same height as Junior, and he appeared to be very real, flesh and blood.

Donald was petrified by the man's appearance again. Elaine, for the first time in the evening, was speechless and startled, forgetting about Donald and everyone else there.

Russell recalled Wilbur's description of the man, that the man before him was very dangerous, and his heart was "black." Still, Russell was fascinated by what he saw.

The figure ruffled through the cabinet drawers, becoming more frantic and angry as he searched each drawer. He hit the cabinet with one hand and the cabinet wobbled. Then he turned to face the group.

Elaine's heart skipped. The man was very handsome, although his eyes were painted in a black horizontal stripe across his face. It appeared that he did not see the group before him. He was searching for something else. His face registered panic and then anger. He turned and dashed away, his hair whirling after him. Wilbur turned the flashlight off again.

"White man," Wilbur said in the dark. "What was here?"

Donald realized that Wilbur was speaking to him, but he was still too stunned from seeing the man again and didn't understand the question.

"What do you mean?" he asked.

"What was in this place?" Wilbur asked again.

"Boxes," answered Donald.

"Old Man," Anna said, "that white man has to get them boxes."

"Aw," Wilbur said. "White man, go and carry those boxes back over here."

Donald was shivering. He hadn't realized it before, but he could feel his teeth clicking together now. He was cold.

Russell could hear Donald's teeth chattering. "It's all right," he said, "I'll get them."

"The white man ought to do it, Old Man," Anna said. "Sonny shouldn't get in the way."

Wilbur said, "Anna's right, but the white man's afraid. Junior, you go, you know what to do. . . ."

"I'll do it, Daddy," Junior said, standing and groping his way in the dark.

"Now don't be scared, you two," Wilbur said to Elaine and Donald.

"It'll be all right." His words, however, had no effect on Donald, whose teeth continued to chatter louder than ever.

"Git ahold of yourself!" Wilbur said to Donald harshly. "You going to hurt ever body here if you don't get ahold of yourself!"

Elaine took Donald's hand and held it in her own shaky hands.

"What's in those boxes?" Wilbur asked after Donald had calmed down somewhat.

"I don't know," Donald whispered.

Wilbur and Anna frowned at Donald's voice in the dark.

"I really don't," Donald said a little louder, defending himself. "I opened only the big box. I haven't always worked up here. I moved up here just recently."

"What's in the big one, then?" Wilbur repeated.

"A boy," answered Donald. "A mummified boy."

In the dark, Wilbur's and Anna's faces couldn't be seen. The looks that registered on their faces couldn't be seen. But Erleen winced, and Russell shook his head in disbelief.

Junior could be heard pushing three boxes, stacked on top of one another, toward them. Wilbur snapped the light on for him. Junior was breathing hard and said, "Daddy, they's something on the other side of the cabinet. I don't know what it is. It moved, though."

When Junior had unstacked the boxes, Wilbur instructed him to open the tops. Junior asked whether Wilbur wanted him to unpack the boxes.

"Leave them alone, Junior, we don't know what's in them. Might hurt ourselves," Wilbur said and turned the flashlight off again. "Now, you all don't move. Quiet!"

They waited. Wilbur and Anna were patient—these things took their own time. Junior was finally able to be comfortable in these situations, after all these years. And Erleen, she'd come to terms with this kind of experience long before she'd met Junior. She shared Wilbur's and Anna's view of the world completely. That was what had set her apart from the other women Junior had known as a very young man. Wilbur and Anna had seen this quality in Erleen long before Junior understood that she possessed it, too.

Russell had never participated in anything like this before tonight. He knew that such gatherings did take place for similar purposes, but he had always chosen to stand on the sidelines of his people and frequently crossed over to the other side—the Anglo side—which demanded other things of him. Sometimes, the other side demanded that Russell deny this part of himself. Always, Russell had yielded to the demand made of him, but now that he was getting older, he found that he lacked something undefinable but critical to his own vision of himself. He found that what he had always thought was a strength in himself was actually a weakness—a defect, so to speak—in his own unique maturity or immaturity. He also admitted to himself now—to this drifting darkness—that he hadn't really believed his elders, believed their stories or their philosophies of life. He had doubted and even feared them and the ideas that had shaped the elders. The road Russell had chosen was easier. He'd deliberately chosen it for that reason alone. He didn't have to confront any mysteries. Everything was decided for him: this is right, this is wrong; this is true, this is false; this is good, this is bad; this is the "real" world, this isn't. . . .

Again, there was a sound behind him. Russell glanced over his shoulder, but darkness covered everything.

In another part of the room, a swooshing could be heard, followed by a flapping of air. It felt like wings to Erleen. She remembered how Wilbur had once fanned her with an eagle wing to bring her out of an illness. She had opened her eyes to consciousness and the swish of the eagle wing fluttering at her ear.

A moaning began, and the beginnings of a vague, mournful song. It was unlike anything ever heard to anyone in the room, except Wilbur and Junior. Wilbur had sung that song for Junior years back, and for Anna, too. The melancholy song came from the other side of the room, but drew steadily closer to them.

"When the man comes 'round here, don't look right on him. Watch him only out of the corners of your eyes," Wilbur whispered, for Donald's and Elaine's benefit more than anyone else's.

The figure moved toward them, singing mournfully. Wilbur snapped the little light on, in the direction of the figure, while he looked toward Donald. All of the group looked away from the figure, although the figure could be seen beside the cabinet, facing the group. The singing stopped. The figure saw the boxes.

The figure moved toward them in three giant steps. He was real. His body had substance and weight. The floor creaked under him.

He knelt down on the other side of the boxes. The man was more youthful than old. His hands were large and graceful, even as they opened the flaps on one of the boxes. He pulled a full-length bearskin, with the head attached, out of the box. He ran a hand over the fur and stuck his hand back into the box. When he dropped the bearskin, there were painted figures on the other side of the fur. The man felt the other contents of the box, and then threw that box aside. He leaned toward the next one. His hair fell forward into the box. He put a hand in this box, and then after a few seconds, pushed the box away. It tipped over.

He pulled the remaining box to him. It slid over the wooden floor. He repeated his search of the box and shook in anger as he stepped over the box.

Next he turned on the group. He saw them, and they saw that he saw them. The nearest person to him was Russell, sitting at the figure's feet. Russell concentrated on a spot on the floor in front of him. The man's gaze lingered on Russell, then went to Junior, Wilbur, Anna, and on to Erleen and Elaine, and then to Donald. All of them behaved as if they weren't aware of the man's presence.

The man knelt where he was, beside Russell, an arm's reach away. He had singled out Donald. He stared at Donald. Donald began to shake. Without warning, the man threw a rolled fist into Donald's shoulder. It came as a genuine surprise to Wilbur and Anna, and as real pain to Donald, whose other hand went up to his stricken shoulder.

Donald turned to the figure beside him and looked into its face, the hate-filled eyes. Donald's teeth started to chatter again.

"White man," Wilbur said softly, "look at me."

The man's eyes flashed at Donald, and he yelled . . . or did he? Perhaps Donald imagined it. The man slapped Donald's face with the back of his hand. Donald's face stung.

"White man," Wilbur said, "don't look at this thing. Look at me!"

Elaine began to scream.

Donald refused to listen to Wilbur. He tried to get to his feet but couldn't. Anna rose, putting a hand on Wilbur's shoulder for support as she pulled herself up. Her bare feet stepped over the things in front of Wilbur, and she put herself between Donald and the threatening figure. Her long, calf-length skirt touched Donald's face as she stood over him, blocking his view of the figure that had struck him.

"Look at Old Man," Anna said. Donald ignored her, and pushed away her skirt. The angry figure was gone.

Anna sat down beside Donald, who was shaking violently. "You're scaring yourself, white man," she said firmly. Then she put a small hand on Donald's face and pushed it toward Wilbur, who held the light just under his chin. It illuminated his face in a warm, red glow.

"Look at Wilbur, now. Ever thing's okay. See Old Man over there?" Anna coaxed.

Wilbur was a shadow against the wall. His eyes were smooth and glossy in the dim lighting.

Elaine sniffled beside Donald and hunched over her knees. Wilbur flicked the light over her and Donald's faces.

Donald didn't look well. There was a pained and fearful expression on his face.

"Ought to stop here," Wilbur said, looking at Anna. She leaned around Donald and saw Elaine weeping into her hands. Donald leaned on Anna. She tried to hold him up. She could feel him jerk involuntarily at her side.

She nodded in agreement with Wilbur at the sight of Donald and Elaine.

"I'm okay," Donald said in a stutter. "Really. I'll be all right."

Wilbur looked at Junior, and Junior's mouth formed the silent word no. Russell was in complete agreement with Junior. Donald looked like hell.

Suddenly there was a loud knocking at one corner of the room behind Erleen. Erleen didn't move. Her eyes locked on Junior's.

The knocking became more violent, and the flashlight Wilbur held stopped shining. The room was pitch black.

"Turn the light on," Elaine said in a tiny, whimpering voice.

"Can't," Wilbur said. "It went out on its own."

"You're lying," Elaine said. She crawled forward to where she thought Wilbur was, scattering the things in front of him. She felt water on the floor. She found the small flashlight, and tried to snap it on. It wouldn't work. She threw the flashlight on the floor, and it made a rolling, thudding sound. Another knock came from behind Junior.

Anna stroked Donald like a baby. His head was on her legs, and his whole body shuddered. He sobbed into her skirt.

"Then turn on the light in the room!" Elaine cried hysterically.

"All right," Wilbur agreed. "All right, Junior. Go ahead. These peoples is scaring theirselves. They going to hurt theirselves."

Junior stood, stepped in a spot of water, and made his way toward the door and the light switch.

The knocking behind Erleen stopped then, and a brilliant light flashed quickly and was gone. Small spots of light moved in other parts of the room.

Anna stopped listening to Donald's sniffles and concentrated on the explosion of delicate lights. To her they were quite spectacular and very beautiful.

A burst of light came from behind Wilbur, illuminating his frame in a gray silhouette for a second.

Another explosion of light flashed between Erleen and Elaine. Elaine screamed. Erleen tried to calm her, but the afterglow of bursting lights caught the illusion of a figure, an Indian woman, naked to the waist, huddled against the wall. The movement of the woman was electric in the stillness of the bursting, floating lights. In the next second, the woman was gone.

Junior was at the door. He flicked the light switch on. Nothing happened.

Leaving the switch on, he moved toward the desk, to the desk lamp. Like the wall switch, the desk lamp refused to work. He began to work his way back to Wilbur.

The lights in the room continued to float and pop through the air. Junior ignored them, although they landed on him and seemed to bounce on him. When he realized that he could feel the charge of them on his face and hands, he closed his eyes, shutting them out, until he was near Wilbur.

"Lights won't come on, Daddy," he said, sitting down beside Wilbur. Wilbur had already come to that conclusion.

"How's he?" Wilbur asked, meaning Donald. He could see Anna by the glow of hundreds of pinpoint floating lights.

"Out," Anna said. "He passed out. Poor thing, nearly scared hisself to death." Donald slumped to the floor.

Wilbur could barely make out Elaine. Her body was poised too stiffly, but otherwise she appeared calm.

"All right," Wilbur said. "Anna, this old man is going to need some help. Have to set things back to what they was again."

Anna nodded. She patted Donald and stood up. Wilbur stood up, too.

"Wait, Mama," Erleen said, pulling herself up to join them.

Junior stood opposite Erleen. "Hey, Black Bear," Junior said. "Give us a hand. Get up."

Russell stood. The lights bounced and popped around the standing figures. Wilbur, Anna, Erleen, Junior, and Russell were faceless, two-dimensional silhouettes in the electrical shower of lights still floating through the room.

"Now take ahold of my hand," Junior said. Russell took Junior's hand. Russell felt a gust of air at his back.

"Now take Mama's hand," Junior said, and Russell took Anna's hand. The air was cooler on Russell's face. It swept the lights around and upward.

As each hand linked with another, the lights in the room were swept out and dispersed by the cool air circulating around the figures.

Elaine's sniffles could be heard again. The fluorescent desk lamp then flickered, and the light bulbs in the ceiling came on. The room was familiar again.

Wilbur began to gather his things together. He was tired. These things always made him tired, and tonight he was more tired than usual. Anna went to him and helped him up off the floor. "Old Man," she said, "let's go home. This place ain't no good. We old peoples. Some old peoples ain't got their right minds. After tonight, Old Man, maybe we ain't got our right minds no more. We got to hold on as long as we can, Wilbur. These kids don't even know what's happening. . . ."

Russell looked at Donald still lying on the floor, and at Elaine with her swollen eyes. He admitted to himself, uncomfortably, that Anna's words often made him smile in their simpleness—but he knew now that what she said was true.

28

WASHINGTON, D.C.

NASBAH and her grandfather were returning home this afternoon. Junior had taken both of them to a Delaware beach the day before, where the old man had taken off his moccasins and waded into the cool ocean water to catch some of it in a jar. Wilbur, Anna, Erleen, and Russell had gone along for the ride. They had made a day of it, even though the air was chilly and the ocean waves rolled at them in choppy curves. Besides themselves, there were not too many people on the beach: an artist with a canvas on an easel, and a few people sitting in chairs or on blankets in the sand.

The old man had enjoyed it thoroughly, as he had enjoyed his quick trip around Washington. But today he was anxious to return home, to his sheep and livestock, and to the four sacred mountains. He had seen and heard enough here to last him for the rest of his life. Nasbah felt much the same.

Willie planned to follow in a couple of weeks. It had been Willie's choice entirely. The hospital had let him out yesterday, and he'd spent the day at his apartment alone, planning and putting his thoughts together about his life and his health. He felt better already, and his grandfather assured him that he would *be* better. He would become well again. Willie believed it. The hospital staff, as hard as they'd tried, could not accomplish this. They were at a loss to explain the nature of Willie's illness and had finally admitted it on his last day there.

Willie's grandfather gave no definite instructions on how Willie should recover, aside from repeating Navajo stories to him, and Navajo philosophy. In the end, all he told Willie was that Willie was a Navajo, a member of the People who were given a particular pattern of life to follow. It was as simple or as complex as that.

In a couple of hours, Willie would call a taxi and take Nasbah and his grandfather to the airport and see them off. Junior had left last night with his wife and the older Snakes for Oklahoma. Willie had met them just before they'd left.

Russell was still in Washington, of course. Last evening, Russell had described to Willie what had taken place in the attic a couple of nights earlier with Donald and Elaine. Willie hardly knew Donald, but he was not surprised at Donald's behavior. He didn't know Elaine. In Russell's words, nothing was going to change here, although Russell had told Willie that the experience had definitely changed him. Willie, even though he didn't say it, felt exactly the same way about Washington through his own experience, illness, and healing.

"Are you going to stop at Drake's in Albuquerque?" Willie asked Nasbah.

"Only because the pickup truck is there," she replied.

"How is his project going?" Willie asked. Nasbah filled him in on their small start.

"And what about your project, Grandfather? Has Drake been able to find anything about our long lost grandmother?" Willie asked.

"Nothing," the old man said. "I don't expect too much now, after coming here. At first I thought it might be possible to discover what happened to her. But it seems to me that not many people in *Washingdoon* even knew of the slavery in our part of the country. The truth is that we may not be too well known here. But it doesn't matter, Grandson, because we know who we are."

29

LAS VEGAS, NEW MEXICO

NOVEMBER 1969

THE Las Vegas sky was clear as only New Mexico skies could be at this time of year. Anita stood at the door of her house sweeping off the slab of cement and the steps in front of the door. She wore an apron and a print dress. Her white hair hung in loose strands at the sides of her face. She pushed these back into the bun that held the rest of her hair. She had cleaned her large home most of the day, with the help of two young women who had scrubbed the floors and walls. Anita couldn't bend down to the floor as easily as before, so these young women did it for her. The house cleaning was now finished, and one of the girls was fixing an afternoon snack of posole and tortillas.

Anita planned to entertain this evening. Her guest was a fine old gentleman from Tecolote, the area south of Las Vegas. Sooner or later she expected him to propose marriage to her. A year ago, she wouldn't have considered marriage at this late date, but this was today, and already she had decided that she would say yes when he asked.

Anita and the two young women sat down to eat, and after that, Anita paid them for their help and they left. Anita now had plenty of time for a nap and would still be able to do all the things she wanted to do before her guest arrived.

On the table beside her was a stack of magazines and papers. She selected a handful of these and went to her bedroom, where she lay down and began to skim the publications. She wasn't a very fast reader, but it was the articles on New Mexico that caught her attention. In one of the tabloid papers that summarized the week's art activities in New Mexico and new books on New Mexico, she came across a strange advertisement. Normally, she wasn't interested in history or book reviews, but her own life had been so upset recently by family history that she now found herself seeking more information on New Mexico and Indian history.

The ad wanted descendants of Indian slaves in the area to contact the writer. How strange this request was! Anita found it disconcerting to her new-found identity. The ad seemed to request her acknowledgement of this identity when she had just barely accepted what she had learned! To ask this of her right now was entirely objectionable! She pushed the paper aside and fell asleep while thinking about the disturbing advertisement.

That evening, as she waited for her suitor, she reread the ad. It stirred her thoughts again. After all these years, she had learned without a doubt that *she* was part Indian! Someone knocked at the door. Anita met her guest graciously at the door and then led him into the room. He was white-haired, with very brown skin and a quick smile. He was perhaps two or three years older than Anita and almost her same height. All in all he was not a bad catch, Anita confessed to herself as she watched him during the evening.

They made small talk at first, and then Anita excused herself to go to the kitchen. While she was gone, the man picked up the paper and ran across the same ad that Anita had discovered. When she returned, he still had the paper.

In Spanish, she asked whether or not he had seen the strange advertisement. He nodded his head and answered, "Maybe I should talk with this one. Perhaps it is with me he wishes to speak," he smiled brightly.

"Oh?" asked Anita.

"Ah, yes," he said. "Don't you know that is what I am called at home?" Anita smiled hesitantly and said no.

"It's all because my grandparents were part Indian. I don't know what kind of Indian they were, but I think Apache. Yes, it's true, Anita. I am one of them, I confess," he said. "I can't deny it." He laughed heartily.

Anita then led him into the kitchen and seated him at the table. Before she sat down with him, she crossed back into the other room, took the newspaper he had left there, and tossed it firmly into the trash can beside the kitchen stove. It would not trouble or embarrass her any longer. Now she would enjoy the rest of the evening. She joined her suitor at the table and tried to imitate his light-hearted manner.

30

ALBUQUERQUE, NEW MEXICO

DAVID Drake sat at his typewriter, slowly typing out the first draft of his work. It was nearly finished. Perhaps it would be done by the end of January if he was lucky. He would certainly need Willie's help in the spring. Actually, the way things turned out—with Willie not being available in the winter—could end up causing Donald Evans's work to progress more efficiently. When they finally got together then, they would be working from a finished draft instead of a fragmented one. David stopped typing to stare out the window that framed the mountains. He wondered how Willie's grandfather had fared in Washington. An old man like that in D.C.? He smiled to himself, remembering how the old man had looked when Nasbah led him into the airport.

David had not been at the house when Nasbah had claimed her vehicle as she and her grandfather returned to Navajoland. Nasbah had simply said they expected to work with David in the spring. She had also said that Willie would be home for good in a few days, but David hadn't seen him yet. He was probably back by now.

David's first draft of the Navajo history was over four hundred pages so far. Of course, he would have to revise and rewrite it after he received his readers' comments on the manuscript. All three readers were historians and friends. Looking at the manuscript, stacked neatly in a box before him, he had to admit that he hadn't written all too much that was new, and the perspective from which he'd written wasn't so radical either. But his research was impressive, even if he had added nothing new to what other histories had already said many times over. And even lacking a unique Navajo perspective, the work would stand on its own merits in the eyes of his colleagues.

Perhaps he had hoped for too much to begin with. One or two of his colleagues had raised eyebrows at him when in the excitement over his own project, he had shared his plan to incorporate a unique aspect, a Navajo aspect, to his study. He claimed it would be both critical and timely to this "new" history. The responses he received from the two people were not what he'd expected.

One of them said, "The writing of history is based on substantiated fact, Dave, of which we have too few for the Navajos. It's sad to say, but nevertheless true, that without records, there is no history. Also, you must take care to remain objective in your work. A history of the scope you suggest would be weakened by any sentimental hogwash that could be construed as romanticism of these people. As a friend, I would advise against taking a Navajo perspective. You're a better historian than that— you don't need it, for Christsake! What you're suggesting has potential problems for your average reader. Need I mention the stuffy historians? Dave, they'll hang you. Don't rock the boat."

David winced at the recollection of this conversation and thought about his ad regarding Navajo/Spanish slaves. . . . "That ought to do it," David said aloud.

The other colleague was just as clear about David's plan. He'd said, "Those people are uneducated, Drake! Let them write their own history when they become literate. Writing a history from the time of dragons is what you'll be doing if you get their input. Listen, I've lived here in the Southwest all my life and I *know* these people. They believe in myths of monsters and a half a dozen worlds. People with that background will not have any credibility when it comes to a written history. You'd be jeopardizing your future."

David had considered and finally taken the advice to heart. His professional reputation would be at stake. He had put years of research into this project, and much time and money. He sighed now and walked to the window. The mountains were a picture, a lovely, still picture. The thought that he could go outside and touch them hadn't occurred to him in many years.

A long time ago, it was the mountains that had brought him to the Southwest. A long time ago, it was his interest in the Pueblo Indians, the Apaches, and the Navajos that had brought him here. But at this moment, he was just as far away from them as he ever was, no closer to them than the mountains.

He turned back to his typewriter and history. The doorbell rang. David glanced at the door and then at his watch. It would be the mailman at this time of day.

David gathered the mail and poured himself a cup of lukewarm coffee. At his desk he sorted the mail and separated two letters. The first letter bore a Taos postmark. It contained only a couple of paragraphs, stating that the correspondence was in response to his ad in the local paper. The letter said that the correspondent was a man in his sixties who was Spanish and part Indian. Would David be interested in helping him find out to which group of Indians he belonged? David threw down the letter and opened the next one. This letter was made up of several pages. It was from a teen-age girl who lived in Clayton, New Mexico. She had proof that she was of such ancestry. What did he want? Why was he interested? The girl had a Spanish surname and had even included a photograph of herself. She was dark and small. The details of her letter were interesting, but it was not what he needed.

These letters today brought the total response from his ad to a grand total of three. What was he going to do?

When he'd begun this project years ago, he'd had such high hopes for it. He really intended to add an Indian point of view to the history of this great country. He had set this lofty goal as a child, fascinated by Indian people. Even as a kid, he realized that American history had never been written from an Indian point of view. He would take the next step toward this reality years later.

However, there was an inherent problem in his plan, as he discovered in his adult years. When opportunities to write a history from an Indian perspective came his way, he was unprepared. He wasn't Indian and had absolutely no one-to-one relationships with Indian people. Consequently, there were no resources to draw on that would give him insight into their present existence or their past. The solution was obvious. He would have to find an Indian historian, if there were such a thing.

Along came Willie Begay. . . . Cultivating a relationship with Willie was as easy as taking candy from a baby. First of all, David was no slouch as a historian or researcher. Secondly, David did identify with Indian people in some respects. He tended to view Indian people as "underdogs" in today's world. This was a notion that David kept deeply hidden inside himself. Anyway, David had hoped Willie would take note of these two strong points.

Actually, the reason Willie encouraged the friendship was not because of David's professional background or because David fancied himself a "do-gooder" for the Indian cause, but because Willie wanted to be in-volved in the workings of the outside world. To Willie, the real world was the Navajo world. To David, the real world was the Anglo world. Willie crossed back and forth, and the outside world reaffirmed for Willie the reality of the Navajo world, and he protected it. But in order to do this, he had to be involved in the outside world.

In any case, Willie was amiable to David's suggestion for a Navajo history. This led David to the old man, Jonnie Navajo, and the elusive search for Navajo slaves.

Sitting here now, David realized that at this minute he really did think it would have been much easier to do without the old man's input. He wouldn't have had to listen to the old man's long tale, and he wouldn't have had to rethink his own history of the Navajos. So far, the use of the old man had only caused him a great deal of inconvenience.

David was at an age where he was no longer young, and he tolerated inconveniences less and less. He was slowly relinquishing the ideas he held as a child. He was becoming more practical and realistic about the world in which he lived. As a result of these concessions through the years, he had already decided what choices he would make if necessary.

He had already decided. Maybe the choices were made years ago. But at this moment, he knew with certainty what he would do if necessary. He would really try to carry out the wishes of Jonnie Navajo and, to appease him, try to latch onto some little bit of information about the missing twin baby. Failing that, and if no more leads came to him, David decided that the old man would have to accept this and deal with it.

On the mantel above the fireplace was a photograph of Jean. This caught David's attention briefly. The woman in that photograph was well-composed and confident. She looked nothing like the woman who had died over a year ago. David still felt wounded when he looked at that photograph. He would never be able to understand what had happened to her. If there were some way he could turn back the clock and change things. . . . She might have lived. . . . He would never be over her. They were family, she and David, of the same blood, of the same mother and father. . . .

His waiting manuscript reclaimed his attention again. Yes, David had decided, he would do what was right—for him. He would do only so much for the old Navajo man, and that was all. He would do only that which was required of him in exchange for what he wanted from the old man—his history, to interpret at his leisure and discretion.

In the long run, David had decided, his professional reputation was a life-and-death matter. This project was not worth the risks after all. When he had a "real Navajo history" in his possession, he could reject it in its entirety or in part, and he could even alter it to suit his needs. He would take care to be objective, fair, and thorough. He couldn't think of anyone who could do a better job.

David felt better now after acknowledging his decision. His peers could be merciless. Survival was the thing, after all.

It was true that a long time ago David had been fascinated by cowboys and Indians. It was also true that a long time ago he'd wanted to write a real Indian history, but that had been a momentary fancy. Great God in heaven, at one time David had even actually wanted to be one of the Indians, as Jean did! Now, he was grown up. Today, things were as clear to him as the mountains in the lovely picture before him. He wasn't a cowboy, or an Indian. He was a historian, and a damn good one, too.

31

PAWNEE, OKLAHOMA

DECEMBER 1969

ALTHOUGH the sun shone brightly, a dusting of snow lay on the hills and in the valleys. The snow was hard, and burning cold to the touch. It had crusted the hills for nearly a week. Wilbur stood inside the chicken wire fence, under ice-covered trees, feeding a couple of dozen chickens. When he was done, he walked back to the house and sat down in one of the chairs still outside. The metal was dry but cold, and it cut through his clothes to his bones. He wanted to feel the coldness of the snow, and the sun. The sun was directly in front of him, but it gave no warmth today, only flat light. Wilbur squinted under its glare and against the bright snow. A strong wind blew at him, and he pulled his jacket a little tighter around him. The woolen cap made his forehead itch, and he wrinkled his forehead as he gazed at the frozen earth around him.

He had spent many years here, had seen and felt dozens of winters from the doorstep of this house. There had been two or three winters when the snow fell in buckets instead of single flakes, and he had trudged through three or four feet of it to get to where he was going. This winter was an easy one.

No matter what season of the year, Wilbur was an outdoor man. He had to come face-to-face with the outdoors on a daily basis or he didn't feel alive. He needed to feel alive. As the wind slapped his face now, Wilbur needed it. When his hearing was better, he'd loved to hear the wind moan and whisper to him. At times he could still hear it, and he hugged it to him as often as he could, as much as the wind embraced him.

All his life he'd made a study of viewing the four directions from this place. He felt the knee-high grass ripple around his legs the rest of the year and welcomed the crunch of it under his boots or in his hands. He knew the water around here by its many colors, the dirt at his feet by touch, taste, and smell. All of these things spoke to Wilbur in a language that only he could decipher and understand.

And there was much to be said on this clear, blustery-cold, winter day. Wilbur listened to the silent screaming sun, the burning-cold crusty snow, and the ice-filled creeks running as slow as suspended time. The wind was snakelike this morning, whipping one way and then another, and curling itself around Wilbur. He could see it move over the land in spiral dips by the movement of the trees and the flurry of dry-ice sifting through the air in little crystals.

He gave himself over to the winter, as he had given himself over to countless, endless scorching summers. He saw himself as a real part of each season. Like the bent tree near the house, he had come through the seasons with it, with the tall grass and the other life here. They had shared the same space and time in a way that two human beings could not share the same things. In essence, the out-of-doors brought much comfort and knowledge to Wilbur, and an awareness of the delicate relationship of all things to one another out there. It met him on different terms than those set by his fellow man. In the bitterest cold and the hottest days, he still found that out here, facing the wind, he was the most alive, the most exhilarated. And out here, there was nothing to block his connection with other life surrounding him. He became an extension of the wind, of the trees, of the land, and of the sun. He could sit here forever. He might sit here forever.

Not even Anna, or his children, Junior and the other child that had died long ago, took the place of what he found out here. They could not. His relationship to the universe, to the world, was for infinity. His relationship to human beings was more temporal.

Anna moved one of the curtains inside the house and saw Wilbur staring off toward the pale horizon. Nearly everything outside the window was white. The wind blew over Wilbur, stirring his clothes, but Wilbur sat frozen, like one of the ice-covered trees.

"Oh, my," Anna said. "This world is purty today. It's like someone just stopped time and froze ever thing in its place, even the sun." She spoke to herself. She was alone in the house. She went back to folding blankets and stacked some paper sacks with them beside the door. She hummed as she worked.

Finally, she sat down at the large kitchen table with a red oilcloth. Her long gray hair, usually worn in two braids, was loose and hung over her shoulders. She wore an old house dress, faded in spots, and an apron. Her feet were in blue house shoes.

Now that Anna had the room to herself, she decided that it was a good time to pray. At first she said a word or two in a language that she seldom used anymore, except in prayers, and then she prayed in English. "It's an old lady again who's calling your name. I guess old peoples calls your name a lot. It seems like old peoples really know you. Sometimes, us peoples has lots to say. . . ." As Anna prayed, she could see Wilbur outside. She continued, "Us peoples, me and Wilbur, is lived a long time. Ain't all our doing alone. We had some help. I been thinking that any day now, my time might come to leave this place. . . It's all right. That's what life comes to at the end. But if Wilbur stays here, I'd ask that some-one watch out for this old man."

Outside, Wilbur was getting numb from the cold. His hearing aid was a cold mass in his ear. He got up from the chair and climbed the steps to the house. Inside, he could barely hear Anna talking in the next room. He walked past her and went into the back bedroom. Anna continued to pray, although Wilbur didn't hear too much of her prayer. Wilbur changed his old clothes for new ones and pulled on a pair of stiff cowboy boots. In the corner of the room was a closet that held just his personal posses-sions. There were a half a dozen bundles wrapped in old blankets or pieces of cloth. Beside these, under several blankets, there were several drums, long drumsticks, and boxes of other items. On the top shelf were three pairs of moccasins.

Wilbur selected one of the bundles, two or three blankets, and one pair of moccasins. He carried all of these into the next room where Anna was, and put them on the table in front of her.

Now he could hear her clearly. She was saying, "This place we been living is good to us. It knows us now."

Wilbur sat down beside her, looked at her, and then spoke. "This is true. Old peoples ain't no good at making lies. Today the world is stand-ing still. The hills is froze, with the grass and the trees and the sun. Old peoples knows this is a powerful thing. This power is beyond us, it's above anyone here, and we have to face it. To this old man, it seems that power to freeze the world, or to melt it in the summertime, is a holy thing. Besides that, it seems that being able to live this long is one more holy thing.

"So, you who can cause the world to stand still, look kindly at us old peoples. These are our thoughts and words, and it has been said to us by our old folks that when we send our thoughts and our words to you, the Creator will see and hear us peoples."

Anna watched the window, and could see the glare of a vehicle hit the side of the house. She motioned to Wilbur that someone had arrived.

"Now, today, me and Anna is going down south, to help some people out down there. It's a long way and we old peoples. Sometimes, we kinda tire out too fast. It's the way we s'pose to be now, but we don't want to be trouble to anyone either. Life is hard on us even when it's easy, and it ain't never easy. It's a hard path to take. But yet, some of us is grateful for it. Its taste is sweet, and we want the sweetness for ourselves and our childrens. We're gonna quit right now and save our words and thoughts that we ain't said yet for the next time 'round." As Anna had begun the prayer, Wilbur ended it, with a few words in his first language.

There was a rapping at the door. Wilbur answered it, letting in two people, a man and a woman. They were bundled in coats, boots, hats, and scarves. They shook Wilbur's hand and he led them to Anna.

"Oh, my goodness," the woman said. "It's so cold here."

While Anna heated hot chocolate, the two people unwrapped themselves. The man was on the heavy side and was perhaps sixty. The woman was just the opposite, thin to the point of looking ill, and was perhaps twenty years younger than the man.

When Anna had served them the hot chocolate, the visiting man began to talk business. "We're very grateful that you people would go all the way south to help us out. As you can see, my daughter is not well."

Wilbur glanced at the woman, as did Anna. For a fleeting second, Anna had the impression of something at the side of the woman. It resembled a shadow, but there was an opaque quality about it. Anna glanced at Wilbur, and he too had seen it, because he returned the glance and nodded to Anna.

"Are you ready to go?" the man asked. "The people at home expect you."

Anna disappeared into the back room. Wilbur answered, "I ain't sure how come you decided to come over here, but it's all right. When peoples ask for help, Anna and me try to help out if we can. Sometimes we don't do no good, though, and we have to give up on it."

The man now dug into his jacket pocket and handed Wilbur a bracelet with a twenty dollar bill. People seldom gave him money. He took the bill and put it into his shirt pocket. He studied the bracelet.

"This bracelet and money is to show our thanks," the man said.

Wilbur nodded. Anna came back into the room dressed and ready to go. She was tying her braids together. Wilbur handed her the bracelet set with blue stones.

"Wilbur, is these *turqwas*?" Anna asked.

"I guess so," Wilbur said.

The visiting man added, "Yes, it's turquoise all right. I bought it in New Mexico a few months back."

Wilbur was thinking of the old Navajo man he had met in Washington. He hadn't thought of him for awhile.

"Oh, my, it's purty," Anna said. "It's just like those things that old man wore back in Washton."

"Yeah, well, we better go, Anna," Wilbur said. He went to the door where the blankets and paper sacks were stacked. He and the other man carried those out the door, and the thin woman followed them. In a few minutes Wilbur returned to pick up his bundle and other things that sat on the table. Anna put on her coat and waited while Wilbur locked up the house. "Junior can check on things tonight, Wilbur," Anna said, following him out to the car.

In the car Wilbur slept awhile, as he was prone to do when he knew that he would be up and about most of the night. He did this to conserve and renew what strength he had before beginning such a night. But he also did this for another reason.

Wilbur was a dreamer. It was through sleep that he first managed to slip away from the stationary points of life. Later he could do it without sleep. It had taken him several years to accomplish this. What had held him back from this accomplishment earlier was his own ignorance. When the realization struck that he should attempt this, he'd already been on the earth for several years.

Actually LeClair Williams had had a lot to do with this change in Wilbur. LeClair had asked Wilbur once what kind of things Wilbur dreamed about in his sleep, as opposed to what kind of dreams Wilbur had while he was awake. Wilbur made the mistake everyone else did and misunderstood what LeClair was really asking him. Then LeClair confused Wilbur even more by asking Wilbur what his body knew, as opposed to what his mind knew. For a couple of years, LeClair had really shaken Wilbur up with his questions. And LeClair never phrased what he had to say in a question. To Wilbur's way of thinking, LeClair's remarks required a response, either in behavior or in conversation.

So Wilbur had turned to Anna and asked the same questions. Anna had answered, "I dream things, Wilbur. I dream about my mamma, my poppa. I dream about Junior and the other one who's gone. I dream things I can understand, and sometimes my dreams is crazy. Sometimes I do crazy things in my dreams. Sometimes peoples die in my dreams. I cry. It's all right if I cry, though. It's just me, and these is only my dreams. Sometimes when I ain't doing nothing and just sit here, something comes to me like a dream, except I'm awake and I feel the dream without no sleep. Ain't nothing wrong with that. Poppa said ain't nothing wrong with that." Wilbur came no closer to understanding where LeClair was leading by asking Anna these questions.

And then during this time, LeClair came to see Wilbur one day. He had a tired look on his face, and was wearing rumpled clothing. LeClair said, "My brother Wilbur, I came to tell you 'bout a bad dream that I dreamt a few times now." LeClair always called Wilbur "brother." LeClair continued, "I must stop dreaming this, or I must change the dream. This bad dream is 'bout you."

Anna had been present when LeClair brought this news. "In this dream, you are alone, and there is deep snow and ice around you," LeClair had said. "Your tracks is deep in the snow and it is bright in places with drops of blood. You are walking away from the sun. Still the sun is blinding. The sun is low in the west, but the snow ain't stopped and it blows against you. Then the sun is blown away, and the snow gets heavy. You fall. You lift yourself up and you try to go on. You look back in your tracks, which are filling with snow. The snow hides them. Then darkness, too, begins. Once more you fall. Your eyes close. Your body is cold but begins to feel warm. And after awhile your body is stiff and froze. You lie there." LeClair had sighed then and said, "Brother, I feel bad. This thing ain't so good."

LeClair had then turned away from Wilbur and left him and Anna alone. No mention was ever made of the dream again.

About three years after LeClair had told Wilbur of this dream, what LeClair had told Wilbur actually happened, except that Wilbur did not freeze. This was because LeClair had changed the dream by telling Wilbur of it. What happened was that Wilbur had stepped into a trap that had been hidden by the snow. In those days, traps were still heavily used, though not too often by Wilbur or LeClair. The accident had caused severe pain and a loss of some blood. What was more threatening to Wilbur was the deep snow and a continuing snowfall.

Wilbur had left the house early that morning with a rifle to shoot rabbits along the creek. He had been at home alone the previous night, and thinking that he would return early, he had simply left the house without word of his whereabouts. By midmorning he had shot himself a dozen rabbits. His accident happened about noon. He was not far from the house, only about six miles. But his throbbing ankle was swollen and looked very bad. Wilbur cut away some of the thin boot he wore and wrapped his leg in a woolen scarf. As long as he stayed off his foot, the bleeding stopped, but when he tried to walk, the bleeding began once more. Climbing up the creek bank covered with snow, he slipped backward and fell. Not only did this increase the pain in his ankle, it bled more. He was also sure that his leg was broken. It was now early afternoon.

Wilbur lay in the snow. He brushed at it for a few minutes, and finally found what he needed—a soggy, wet branch that was sturdy enough to support him. He put this under his arm and started to pull himself along. Progress was slow, far too slow. The blurry sun was hidden behind clouds and showed itself for a few minutes at a time and then was gone. Snow swirled around him. A very strange thing happened to Wilbur then. He lost his sense of direction. The deep snow covered everything around him. Only when the sun became visible for a few seconds did Wilbur correctly gauge where he was. It was still a long way to the house. It would be dark soon. His rifle was heavy. His leg was stiff and sore. The sun was gone again, and without it, everything looked the same. He looked back at his tracks to see from which way he had come. His tracks were quickly disappearing in the snow, and the bright red drops of blood had faded to pink. He was determined to go on, but darkness was right behind him. He looked back at his tracks again. And that was when he remembered.

LeClair had dreamed all of this. Wilbur looked around for a few minutes, and although he didn't recognize the place, he decided he would stay in the vicinity, in a grove of trees. He pulled himself over to the trees and cleared away what snow he could from under the trees and brush. He had two matches in his cap and everything was wet. But Wilbur started a small fire just before it got dark. Then he raised his rifle and fired into the air.

LeClair heard the shot from his house. He was alone, as usual, eating his supper out of a can. He put down the can and opened the door. The snow was thick and quiet. There was no moon or stars.

At home, Anna was worried because Wilbur hadn't returned yet. She'd come home to an empty house, with no word from Wilbur on where he might be. She built a fire and waited. After a few minutes, she went into the bedroom and checked to see which clothes Wilbur might have worn. She didn't learn anything from that, and returned to the kitchen to prepare supper. Over an hour passed while she waited. Then someone knocked at the door.

LeClair carried a lantern and was so bundled up that only his eyes showed, but Anna knew them. "Where's Wilbur?" she asked as soon as she let LeClair inside.

LeClair shook his head. "Don't know," he said. "Is anything wrong?"

"Ain't sure," Anna said. "Wilbur's gone. Didn't leave word. It ain't like him at all."

LeClair had walked over in the deep snow. His house was within viewing distance of the Snakes' homestead.

"I don't like it, Anna," he said. "I don't like this one bit. Something *is* wrong."

He went to the door and opened it. Nothing could be heard. He said, "Awhile ago, I heard a gun, a shot somewhere in the woods."

Anna hurriedly left the room and then came running back in. "LeClair," she said, "his rifle's gone. He went hunting. He's hurt somewhere, I just know it."

"Where would he go?" LeClair asked. Anna shook her head and said she didn't know.

"You got another gun?" LeClair asked. Anna nodded. "Get it," LeClair said.

Anna got the gun and some shells and gave them to LeClair. He went outside and Anna watched from the light of the door. He shot into the air. Snow fell off the tree beside him with a thud. It seemed forever before an answering shot could be heard in the distance. "He's at the creek," Anna said. "I'm going with you, LeClair."

Anna and LeClair walked about three miles in deep snow that night, with two yellow lantern lights and the pack of things LeClair carried on his back. They followed the creek, and when LeClair was sure he'd lost the way, he fired into the air again. They could hear Wilbur call out in the distance. The fire he had started had died, and they could not see where he was at all. He led them to him simply by calling to them.

After that experience Wilbur knew what LeClair really meant. He learned that dreams were a storehouse of possibilities. Later, he discovered too that this was the source of all healing. So that was how Wilbur became a dreamer and a healer. And LeClair had shown this to him.

As Wilbur sat beside Anna now, he snored softly, and then very abruptly he stopped snoring and opened his eyes. "Anna," he said. "I dreamed 'bout that old Navajo man we saw in Washington. He was somewhere far away, some place I ain't never seen. It's a purty place, though, a lotta rocks and sand. In my dreams, that old man was older than he is now. And you know what he was doing?"

Anna shook her head.

"Well, he set in a crowd of people, and he told them something. I don't know what he said. But the people around him first laughed and then looked a little sad. I wonder what the old man said." Wilbur sat up straight and looked out the window at the frozen scene outside. The world looked delicate somehow.

"How come it's so purty outside, Wilbur? Is it because we old peoples?" Anna asked.

Wilbur nodded. "That might be it, Anna. Sometime now, we gonna have to go on . . . have to leave this place."

Anna took Wilbur's hand. "I guess it's all right, Wilbur. Peoples ain't like us no more. You ever think so, Wilbur? Peoples ain't like us no more?"

Wilbur nodded.

"Is that a bad thing, Wilbur? Is we wrong? Us old peoples? Us Indian peoples?" she asked.

Wilbur looked deeply into her eyes and shrugged.

"When you and me leaves this place, Wilbur, I'm going to stay here. LeClair's here, Mama, Poppa, the baby, . . ." Anna said thoughtfully.

Wilbur smiled and said affectionately, "Anna, you a crazy old woman. You know that?"

Anna smiled broadly and answered, "Us old peoples kind of lose our right minds sometimes. Some of us go crazy. It's from this long path we come on. It makes us like that. . . ."

32

WASHINGTON, D.C.

DECEMBER 1969

THE article in the Washington paper gave about three inches of space to the suicide of a prominent anthropologist. The suicide had happened in the early morning hours the day before. The news, the second suicide in two weeks, had shocked Donald's colleagues.

The paper lay on Donald's desk, along with airline tickets and Donald's briefcase. By the door were two suitcases.

Donald was going to "get away," to take a three-week vacation in Hawaii with Elaine. She was going to meet him here and they would travel to the airport together. He wished that he could look forward to Hawaii, but he couldn't. He wasn't even excited about the trip or anything. He was just going through the motions of living.

He had applied for another position, someplace far from here. Actually, he had two serious possibilities, one in New York and one in the South. If Elaine would go with him, he would take her along, but if she stayed in D.C., well, he would still go. His life was at stake here—his sanity was at stake.

As Donald sat at the desk thumbing through the newspaper to pass the time, he heard someone climb the stairway. Nowadays, he couldn't help but tense his body when he heard the stairway creak. He relaxed when he heard someone call, "Yo, Evans. Are you there?"

The visitor was Russell Tallman. Donald hadn't seen Russell for a few weeks. He also didn't know how he felt about him. The experiment in the attic had been a disaster for Donald. He remembered all of it. The day after, when Russell had stopped by to see if Donald had recovered from the previous night, Donald had the impression that Russell was disappointed in him. At that time, Russell had tried to talk seriously with Donald about what had happened the night before, and about what the experience meant. But Donald wasn't up to it. He had been too badly frightened. Stranger still was that Donald and Elaine had not talked about that night since then. It was as if they'd ripped the experience of that night right out of their minds.

Russell entered the room and extended a hand to Donald. Then he sat down. "I hear you're off to Hawaii," he said with a smile.

"Did you also hear about this?" Donald asked and handed Russell the paper.

Russell skimmed the article and put the paper down. He said nothing for a minute and then asked, "How are *you?*"

Donald was angry at the question at first and then realized that Russell was sincerely interested. He put his chin in his hands and his elbows on the desk and said, "I'm looking around for a new job. I can't work here anymore. To tell you the truth, I haven't worked in a couple of weeks. I show up here and that's all."

Russell nodded as if he understood.

"Look, Russell," Donald continued, "I've been wanting to say something to you. I'm sorry about what happened that night. You know what I mean? I went to pieces. . . . I should never have asked Elaine to be here that night."

Again Russell was quiet.

"You know what's odd about everything that happened that night? Elaine and I have never spoken one word about it. We've swept it under the rug," Donald said reluctantly. "We're going away to Hawaii and pretend it never happened."

"Look," said Russell, "don't be too hard on yourself. Maybe this vacation will do you good, and when you get back, everything will be all right."

Donald shook his head no. "It won't be all right. I see things now, Russell. Like that Wurly woman. This thing wants me! It won't be satisfied until it gets me!" Donald's face was red.

Russell raised his eyebrows at Donald's words. He tried to reason with him. "Donald," he said cautiously. "Don't give yourself over to what's happening here." He watched Donald's reaction. "Man, save yourself. Think about that."

Donald appeared to be near tears.

Russell went on. "Wilbur asked you once what you believed about life. You answered that you believed in God. That's why Wilbur agreed to help you out, because you said that you believed in God. He believed that you believed, because that's what you said."

A tear rolled down Donald's face as he said, "I didn't know you were so damn religious!" He tried to smile.

"Actually, I'm not," Russell admitted. "I just know the old man, Wilbur, and not as well as I thought. Wilbur don't talk about God either. He talks about the earth, dreams, power, and people, the dimensions of people, time, and space. In order to believe in something, Wilbur says that we have to have experienced these things on a very personal level. That's the way I understand it. I might be wrong, but it does seem that believing in some higher power than ourselves is going to strengthen us, too. I mean that we become stronger by way of this belief."

Donald spoke. "It all sound like so much shit," he said, surprised at his own vulgarity. "You were here the other night. You saw what was here. Now you're telling me that God is going to take care of me if I believe in him?" Donald was practically shouting.

"No, that is not what I'm saying to you. I'm saying that you have a fantastic opportunity here to learn something, something about yourself and the world around you. At this moment it is possible to save yourself and to learn some secrets of the universe. *You are alive.* Doesn't that mean anything? You're responsible for your life at this moment! Act responsibly! Don't give up and whine now because you've given up. Fix it! And if you can't fix it, if there's absolutely no way, then open up your mind and prepare to learn something from the next experience."

"Are you saying that I'm just feeling sorry for myself? That's very easy for you to say. . . ." Donald spoke belligerently.

"Damn it, Evans," Russell said. "You're mean today. Anyway, I'm not saying that either. I'll try to explain it again. Wilbur says a man has the power to live or to die. Every day we have this power. We're responsible for maintaining this power. It would not be good to give this power over to someone or something else. That's what I'm saying.

"Now, I'd better be on my way. I just came over to say good-bye. I'm leaving D.C., Evans. I'm going to work in Kansas. It ain't home, but it's close enough to it. I'll be back, though. I'm not through with D.C. yet. . . ."

"Why?" asked Donald.

"You know why," Russell said. "I have a lot of things to do. I want to live," he smiled.

"No, really. Why are you leaving?" Donald asked. "Don't tell me you're frightened, too?"

"Really," answered Russell, "I want to live. One of the first things I was taught when I was younger was to know when to be afraid."

"When's that?" asked Donald.

"When there's danger of giving in to fear alone."

"So, you feel it too!" Donald said. "After all that talk of God, and lecturing me about being responsible. You're leaving, too. You're just walking away from me, and this!"

Russell stood and said, "Hey, man, living is hard. You act like a man who hasn't ever been told or ever learned that living is hard, and that it must be done by ourselves, alone. It's true that I came over here today to say good-bye to you, but I also came to say good-bye to this place. It's here, as much as you and I are here. I have an attachment to this place now. I also have an attachment to the big man who lives here. I have feelings and thoughts about him. Do you know how he died?" Russell asked. Donald's eyes widened and his mouth dropped open.

"He died in battle, Evans. I don't know where. . . . But the thong around his ankle was something that men wore in battle, when they fought to their deaths. You see, Evans, they staked themselves to the ground and made a stand there. That's also why he's naked. In those days, the men stripped completely before going to war. . . . In a sense, he's still on that path. And the others who are here, believe it or not, Evans, they each have a story, too. I came here today to say good-bye to them, strange as that might be to you." Russell walked to the door, glanced around the room, and went down the stairs.

Donald sat motionless for several minutes after Russell left. He imagined he heard things in the corners of the room. He thought he saw the giant man at the door. Donald began to think how one would kill such a man. . . .

Outside, in the parking lot, Russell met Elaine. He nodded to her and went on to the car. Just after he opened the car door, he felt her hand on his arm. "Mr. Tallman," she said, "I'm embarrassed about my behavior, the things I did the last time. . . ." Russell cut her off and got in the car. "Forget it," he said. He started the car.

"I'm worried about Donald," she said. "He talks about killing that man we saw the other night. Can you imagine?" She hung on Russell's door. He began to back out of the parking space.

"Sorry, I can't help you. . . ." he said. She let go of the door and he drove away.

33

NAVAJO RESERVATION

NASBAH held a child with black eyes and curly black hair. The child was barely a year old, and toddled around the house when she could. But she was always being snatched up to be cuddled by anyone older than she was. Nasbah spoke to the baby girl in Navajo and the baby smiled.

The house was full with members of the immediate family and extended family. On weekends, the household invariably swelled like this. There was barely enough room to sit down. Outside, children played in the late afternoon sun although the weather was cold.

Nasbah put the curly-haired baby down and went into the kitchen where most of the women were. They were cooking and visiting. Like the other room, the kitchen overflowed with people.

Some of the men had gone to haul water to the house, in one of the pickup trucks, for everyday needs—cooking, drinking, and bathing. They were returning now. Two other men had left earlier in the day, on horseback, to check on the cattle grazing below the mountains.

Outside, under a brush shelter, another man built a fire to roast some meat on a grill. Several women took chairs and went outside to sit beside the fire. Nasbah put on a jacket and went out with them.

The sky began to turn a burning gold in the west as the smoke lifted. Nasbah could see the two men coming in on horseback below the golden evening sky. Her grandfather was also walking toward the corral, his sheep bleating as they came. Outside, the grandchildren began to fuss and whimper.

"Where's Willie?" asked one of the women.

"In town," Nasbah answered. "He'll be back tonight."

"We're going to stay overnight," the same woman said to Nasbah. "It's been so long since we've had a good, long visit here."

Nasbah nodded. "Willie wanted to play a shoe game tonight. If everyone stays, they'll be plenty of players."

The old man, Jonnie Navajo, separated himself from his sheep and walked toward the house. He stopped beside the fire.

"Father," one of the women said, "we'll play a shoe game tonight?"
He nodded and went on toward the house.

Nasbah's grandmother came outside carrying a large pan of meat
to be roasted on the grill. Nasbah took the pan and the old woman
went back inside.

Nasbah stayed with the women, turning the meat on the grill and watching night fall on this place. She had a deep sense of belonging to the
purple mesas and the blue mountains. This was the first time in her life
that she really acknowledged a difference between this place and other
places in the world. In a way, it had to do with touching a part of herself
that she hadn't reached before.

Her grandfather came out of the house again and went toward the
hogan. In a few seconds lamplight shone from the window, and Nasbah
knew that he was building a fire to warm the hogan for the shoe game.

As the family members ate together later, there was much discussion
about family members and matters. Then some of the people left to return to their homes, but a good many stayed for the shoe game. Willie
returned then to inform everyone that he had asked the neighbors to
participate in the game, too.

When another car drove up outside, the family assumed that this would
be one of the neighbors, but it wasn't. The visitor was David Drake.
Willie asked him to sit down at the kitchen table.

"I'll just be here for a minute or two," he said. "I'm attending a
conference in town tomorrow. I'll be presenting a paper on Navajo
history. . . . I hoped to catch you here." Willie had been working with
Drake for the last six weeks. Drake had also been here at the house a
couple of times.

Other cars were arriving at the hogan, and Willie's grandfather walked
past Willie and David on his way to the hogan. The kitchen simultaneously emptied of people. David and Willie were left alone.

"There appears to be a lot of activity here tonight," David said.

Willie nodded. "Yes, they're going to play a shoe game."

"What's that?" asked David.

Willie answered, "What brings you here at this time of night?"

"Well," David said, "several things, actually. We should start on the
next part of the manuscript as soon as possible."

Willie then said, "David, my grandfather has decided that he isn't the person for you. He has suggested a couple of other people, if they are willing. . . ."

"What?" David asked, in complete surprise. "I thought we had an agreement. The money. . . . Your grandfather is a reputable historian."

"We did have an agreement," Willie said. "The agreement was that my grandfather would suggest another person if he wasn't suited to the job. The money doesn't mean that much to him. He's never had a lot of money. And he is unquestionably a historian."

"Well, what made him change his mind?" David asked.

"I can't say for certain," Willie answered honestly.

"Can't you ask?" David insisted.

"I could," answered Willie, "but I'd rather not. He's an old man. He has good reasons, I'm sure. And since he's not going to continue on the project, it might be better if you find another interpreter, too."

"What?" David asked. "You're quitting too?"

"I'm not quitting," Willie said. "I just won't be available to work with *you*."

David sat with Willie in the house for a good forty-five minutes, trying to get Willie to change his mind. Willie didn't budge on his position, but he gave David a list of people to be considered as translators and informants.

Finally accepting what Willie told him, David wrote a check to Willie in payment for Willie's and his grandfather's services thus far. David was a little angry, but he tried not to show his feelings. Outside, singing came from the hogan. Willie walked David to his car. "What are those songs they're singing? Are they having a ceremony or something?"

Willie answered, "They're shoe game songs, David. At one time, the people played this game to decide whether it should be day all the time, or night all the time. . . . They sang those songs."

David grunted, further annoyed by such meaningless information. He didn't want to hear any more. "What if I get lost?" he asked. "I've never been here at night."

"Just stay on the road and look at the stars," Willie said with a grin that David couldn't see.

Willie walked toward the hogan, somehow relieved to have David Drake's history taken off his back. Willie had thought the experience would be different. But in the second week of working with David, Willie realized that he didn't have David's full attention, or commitment, to the Navajo input. The longer Willie worked with him, the more obvious this became. It was with a great deal of regret that Willie had reached this realization.

Several days ago, he had discussed this observation with his grandfather, who had listened thoughtfully and nodded. He had said nothing at the time, but a day or two later, the old man told him, "I think that you are right, Grandson, about this situation. These papers the white man writes are for himself. It's all right, though, because this is how things are today.

"He has not brought any information on the little girl, either. I think he is hoping that I won't remember it. It would be the easiest thing to simply forget about the incident, I suppose. But as long as we don't know what happened to the lost child, we are missing something of our history. Looking back at things, I probably expected too much from this man.

"Grandson, it appears that we must continue to relate the stories and our history in the way we always have. It is appropriate, though. I think, also, that in time, it will be our own people who will write everything down. This thing is coming. It is the only way."

In the long run, Jonnie Navajo now didn't expect too much from the white man. He explained to Willie that he would like to withdraw from the project, having had earlier misgivings about consenting to work with Drake after visiting *Washingdoon*. If he had been asked then, he would have said no at once. He had learned things in *Washingdoon* that had influenced him. He now knew for certain how much of himself, how much of *the People* and other tribes, had been hauled away. He was going to devote his time to more productive things, his livestock and his ceremonies, until someone else came along, someone who really did care about the continuity of *the People*. He realized that it might be a long wait, and in his heart he hoped that such a person might be of his own, one of *the People*. For now, he would continue as he always had, with a centuries-old philosophy and livelihood.

Willie entered the hogan, which was filled to capacity. His grandfather sat on the other side of the hogan with three other old men. Willie made his way toward them.

"It's settled," Willie said to him, waving the check at his grandfather.

"That white man will find someone else to help him." His grandfather nodded. On the other side of the hogan, the people began to sing. Nasbah was among them.

They played until late into the night, and when they came out of the hogan, the December sky was sprinkled heavily with stars.

Some of the family slept in the hogan and others slept in the house. Willie stayed in the hogan with his grandfather and several other people. Before crawling into the sheepskins and blankets on the packed dirt floor, Willie added some wood to the fire. A small boy in a sheepskin by the door said, "Grandfather, tell us a story. . . ." Jonnie Navajo responded in his own leisurely way. At first he told the boy of a coyote who played dead. Then to the others in the hogan he talked about Holy People and stories of long ago. Willie watched the stars through the opening in the roof. He wondered to himself how many times he had heard these stories from the old man. He never tired of them. Each time he heard one, it was like meeting a person he'd known before. When everyone finally slept, Willie still lay awake watching the fire. He sat up, poked the charcoal, added another log, and was surprised to find his grandfather's eyes on him.

"Drake didn't want to find our lost grandmother for us, did he, Grandfather? Were we foolish to ask?" Willie asked quietly.

His grandfather didn't respond for a long time. Finally, the old man said, "I think that we care for ourselves. As a young boy, I was told to care for myself, because of the Holy People. They created us."

"In *Washingdoon*, Grandfather, I questioned many times if we were foolish in our past. Have Indian people been foolish? Most everything in *Washingdoon* seems to make us appear foolish to other men. The papers housed there, the books there, the histories there, Drake's history. . . ." Willie said, feeling very bad about admitting this to the old man.

"I can't speak for other Indian people, only for the Navajo. We have a path laid down for us. I myself have tried to follow it, because I think that it is a beautiful way. These papers, Grandson, they are written by men. That we exist, that *we are here*, this is the one thing that cannot be refuted. Don't confuse yourself with thoughts that lead you off the path. Live! Despite all the odds against it, let us live the best way we can! Take care of yourself, and then these other things will straighten themselves out," the old man said.

"Yes, you're right, Grandfather," Willie said. "But you know, you got me interested in our stolen grandmother, really interested. Like the other things that have been hauled away from us—the pottery, the mummies, the medicine bundles—she was taken too. In a sense, even our history has been taken away. I guess we'll never know what happened to her. Maybe she has descendants somewhere, close by or far away. They may not know that they are Navajo."

The old man answered, "They may come home yet. I have seen such things in my lifetime."

"I've learned a lot these past few months, Grandfather," Willie said. He lay back down. "*Washingdoon* is very far away. I feel good, better than I have felt in a long time. And I think I know why I became ill.

"In *Washingdoon*, I discovered through the papers and other things there that Navajos and other Indians weren't supposed to have survived this long, Grandfather. Did you know that? Everything was against it. I think that that discovery hurt me very much, more than I dared to admit, but I am recovering from it. I took this discovery very personally, and didn't know how to react to it."

Willie listened to his grandfather's reply. "Such things can happen. There is much out there that can be harmful to us. But we can continue to live, in beauty, in spite of everything, with our prayers and our songs.

"Tonight, I looked around this place and saw all my children and relatives. This is all we can ask for, Grandson, along with a sound mind and body. These things are beautiful. Now, I am going to sleep. I must rise at dawn."

Willie could hear him breathing deeply a few minutes later. Then, before Willie realized it, he joined the old man in a deep sleep. A breeze from Beautiful Mountain to the south of the hogan eventually woke Willie a couple of hours later. He rose to stir the fire and went outside to carry in more wood. He couldn't resist standing under the stars for a few minutes. "Beautiful," he said, and went back inside.

EPILOGUE

IT happened that on one fall morning in 1975, the old man Jonnie Navajo died. His death had been expected for some time. He was buried in a red sandstone valley near his winter home.

One year later, Nasbah and Willie and Willie's wife of three years walked up to the old man's grave. It was such a pleasant day that Nasbah suggested they walk farther back into the red valley where there were a couple of golden cliff dwellings. The wind blew through the dwellings as the three people studied them from afar.

"It's a good thing not too many people know these are here," Nasbah said.

"They've already been looted," Willie said, "probably several times by now. People are looking for diamonds and jewels."

"There's no diamonds here," Nasbah laughed.

Willie's wife was kicking up sand with the heels of her shoes. "Look!" she said. Black and white pottery sherds were sprinkled on the ground.

"Leave them alone!" Willie said, more harshly than he'd intended.

He gave one last look at the houses in the cliffs. With the sun shining directly on them, they turned pure gold.

"Let's turn around," Nasbah said.

Willie took his wife's hand and followed Nasbah. As they walked along, he couldn't help but notice pottery sherds lying everywhere, along with human bones. The rains were carrying everything down the wash.

"Let's hope not too many people come out here, Willie," Nasbah said. "They're sure to haul everything away, bones and all! It wouldn't matter whose bones they are."

At Jonnie Navajo's grave, a pottery sherd lay beside the old man's mound. By the time Willie left there, Nasbah's comments about stolen bones had made him very uneasy. If only he could be sure his grandfather's grave would be safe there. . . .